THE ESTUARY

A novel set in East Anglia

THE ESTUARY

TESSA WEST

FOX BOOKS

Tessa West
The Estuary

Published by Fox Books, 16 Broad Street, Harleston, Norfolk, IP20 9AZ

British Library Cataloguing in Publication Data
A catalogue record for this book is available from the British Library.

ISBN 0-9543627-0-5

Cover design by Roland West

Printed in Great Britain by
Biddles Ltd, Guildford and King's Lynn

Tessa West has lived in East Anglia all her adult life. After training to teach she taught in London and Suffolk before starting a family. After a career break she began working in prison education. She completed an MA and was awarded two fellowships prior to her appointment as an assistant governor in the UK's first private prison. She is now a freelance criminal justice consultant. Most of her publications are connected to her professional work and her interest in cycling. Over the last five years she has become increasingly interested in creative writing. This is her first novel.

ACKNOWLEDGEMENTS

Writing *The Estuary* meant that I needed to find individuals who had specific local experience and knowledge and I was fortunate enough not only to find two, but to have them both stick with me for the three years it's taken to write the book. So, my particular thanks go to the two Johns who have become friends: John Moss for so enthusiastically sharing the valuable memories and photographs from his time as a national service-man at RAF Bawdsey; and John White for telling me about Felixstowe Ferry and enriching my knowledge of the Deben, especially by taking me out on his ferry.

The third person I must give particular thanks to is Sara Maitland. Her constructive criticism and support prompted me to get on with it and to make it better – which was just what I hoped she'd do.

In addition, I received information, help and support from a wide variety of sources and I should like to thank all of the following: Dick Booth, Frank Fear, Eric Gilson, Sally Greenhill, John Gorton, the late Sue Gorton, Graham Henderson, Phyllis Hilditch, Naomi Jaffa, John and Pat Jeffries, Sandra Nicholls, Carol Perry, John Saunders, Stephen du Sautoy, Pete Tolhurst, Mary Wain, the East Suffolk Poetry Group, the East Anglian Film Archive, the Suffolk Records Office, the Suffolk Library Service, The Literary Consultancy and the Open College of the Arts.

I should also like to thank my brothers, my children and their partners, and many friends for their constant interest and encouragement. In particular, I'm especially grateful to Roland who understood just what sort of cover I wanted and then worked into the small hours to create it. William deserves to be mentioned too, for his dramatic arrival caused me to re-think things.

For my first family
Phyllis, David, Gordon, Roger

THE ESTUARY

The estuary is coming alight
with the morning. Above the water
an invisible, level block of air
supports a layer of pale haze.
Boats wait. Gulls are silent.
Low orange-yellow banks of shingle
line the shore where the river ends,
the sea begins. There is no edge.
Freshwater flows into saltwater.
Saltwater flows into freshwater.
A cormorant flies out.
Fish, crabs and a seal swim in.
Currents carry mud from Waldringfield
and Woodbridge. Tides suck soil
from Belgium, sand from Dutch dunes.
Down the stretch of the East Anglian coast
winds and waves sweep pebbles south.

From the air a pilot would see how the thin Deben makes its way towards the southwest and then suddenly turns to the southeast before opening itself wide before it runs out of land and into the sea. On a triangular piece of land to the north of the estuary he would notice a manor house and eight tall masts; to the south an untidy collection of low buildings near the shore, a boatyard and two squat Martello towers; he would see a huge bar of shingle across the mouth of the Deben. If he waited for a winter to pass he would notice how the shape of the bar and the colours of the water changed.

From higher up it would look different. If he flew at sunset or sunrise he would see the tapering waterlines of the Stour, Orwell, Deben, Ore and Alde reaching into the land from the polished sea like liquid flickering flames.

*

Robert is sleeping late.

When Maisie's cold nose nudges him he rolls over and looks at the clock. Five and twenty past seven. No need to get up immediately. He pushes Maisie away from his face but strokes her long, smooth ears until his outstretched arm becomes cold. He curls up again into the warmth of the bunk, rocked by the slight movement of the incoming tide. It feels good. He frees his face from the rasp of the heavy winter cover, pulls the bedclothes close.

It was late when he finished work last night, and he has to work this afternoon and again this evening. But the morning is his. He's going to spend it walking upstream along the river wall. He hasn't been far along there before. It won't be hard to find the old jetty where they say good-sized logs get caught, and then he can scout around where people go duck shooting. A gun. If only he had a gun. A month ago someone gave him a duck when it was still warm and glowing with colour and he can remember how soft it was when he held it against his cheek before he plucked it. Only last night one of its tiniest feathers rose up from a corner when he opened the cabin door.

Ten more minutes in bed won't hurt. He sticks his head out of the covers and breathes out. His breath doesn't condense so it can't be that cold. When he and his brother were boys they watched a man hold a burning stick to petrol fumes he blew out of his mouth. It looked as if he was exhaling flames. After that he and Tom used to pretend they were fire eaters by breathing out big Os and trying to create billows of visible air.

Today, as usual, moisture from the cabin's small windows is running down onto the folded newspapers he's wedged under them. The fire usually keeps alight overnight but two days ago he ran out of coal and now the cabin is starting to smell of old seaweed and damp again. This box full of sticks by the stove is the last of a good find of driftwood that turned up on the mud about fifty yards from *Music Maker*. It was sodden and had taken weeks to dry, but it caught light eventually. He had liked watching the lines of white crystals appear along the grain and splutter green before they gave up the ghost.

Unless it's rough he can't tell what the weather's like until he goes on deck. Today, after shoving the damp door hard to free it from the frame, he's out there, in the wind, in the keen air with the whole sky around him. He's almost in the sky. What a day. Strong light rebounds off the river, makes him blink. The sun seems warm but it can't be, it's only half past eight and it's January. Maisie comes running onto the tiny deck and straight across the gangplank that joins the boat to the shore like a stalk. She runs along sniffing the wet grass, squats for a few moments and then she's off again.

These first moments on deck are almost always good. Robert likes to duck through the doorway and suddenly change the interior world for the exterior one. It's light. And there's the river.

He rolls his first sweet Woodbine of the day. *Music Maker* is well afloat and bumping gently against the black and barnacled stumps of old posts that someone must have sunk years ago. The soft river stretches out to the left and the tide is swelling in from the right, from beyond the shingle bar that will soon be covered, from the sea which today is a smooth, shining green. Little is going on. Gulls dive and flap and squawk as they chase bits of fish being thrown over the side of a boat at anchor upstream. Someone is rowing a dinghy out to their moorings.

Robert leaves *Music Maker* and goes to the far side of the river wall. His urine steams. As he returns the dog runs back on board, overtaking him as he stoops to collect an armful of wood from the hatch by the defunct engine. Soon the kettle is on the stove.

Half an hour later they set off. Looking back it's satisfying to see the creamy smoke emerging from the rusted chimney. *Music Maker* will be warm before they return. He must not forget to go and get more coal. Maisie is running on ahead past the flimsy looking gangplanks of neighbouring boats, past two ancient black hulls half pulled out of the glossy mud and on along the familiar path. Her brown and white coat and floppy ears go in and out of Robert's view. She runs backwards and forwards exploring and re-exploring ten yards of the path ahead and a yard on either side of it.

They're going to follow the wall past the mudflats – still covered now by the high tide – past the pastures, and as far as Kingsfleet, the stretch of water just inland from the river. It's a perfect place for wildfowling. But he can't shoot if he hasn't got a gun. Will he ever get one? There's no chance at present. But if he had one he could sell most of what he shot.

Living on *Music Maker* is free, thank God, for he doesn't earn much as a relief ferryman. And he thanks the fishermen too, for the odd few fish, and he's grateful to the Corbys for the carrots and cabbages they give him in exchange for gardening jobs. But even so, how will he ever afford another jacket, new boots? If only someone would take him on as crew in the spring, or use him more often at the boatyard now that there are more leisure boats around. There are still several cold months to get through before then, but it would be good to have something lined up for next year. He pushes away the thought that he has brought this situation about, has knowingly made things hard for himself.

Maisie comes racing back with her ears and tail stretched out behind her. Robert takes the stick from her mouth. As he turns to throw it, he sees the ferryboat with a half load of passengers on its way to the Bawdsey side. He can see the tops of several of the eight radar transmitter masts above the Manor on the far side of the Deben, but not the Manor itself. At night the mast's lights appear as a neat row of red dots hanging in mid-air, and in certain weathers they throw up sparks.

Straight across the river lie flat fields with clumps of trees beyond. Some of the fields have furrows made alternately dark and pale brown because of how the light falls. Looking inland he can see long thin puddles between the ridges at the lower edge of the fields, and sheep sheltering in the dip by the river wall. Further off is the isolated marshman's house on the far side of the pastureland. It's almost symmetrical, the sort of house that one of his younger sisters might have drawn.

Robert walks on, calling Maisie as he goes. She comes bounding up and then stands still for a moment, letting the wind blow her ears the wrong way.

He comes upon a few planks fixed to black posts slimy with seaweed. This must be the jetty. A tangle of branches and a few broken crates are caught against it and he can see how one tide might lodge things there, and how they'd stay trapped until the next one. Not much here today, but it'll be worth coming again.

The river is close because it's almost high tide. Little waves are rippling over the mud banks, oozing their way upstream, dribbling into tiny channels of mud. Two motor boats pass upstream on their way to Woodbridge and Robert waves to the small figure at the tiller of the second. It's a man whom he's thinking of asking for work. He can see he's trying to decide who he is. Robert cannot imagine a situation when someone knows him but he doesn't know them. To his surprise the man waves back after a moment or two.

Robert ties a rope onto Maisie's collar so she won't frighten any wildfowl, but as they turn left and downwards a flock of grey, white and black geese fly up from the Kingsfleet into the sunshine honking hoarsely. Even though this stretch of water is well below the level of the wall its surface is being pushed by the wind so that flat ledges spread across it, like shallow shining steps. They hold their shape for ten yards and then collapse.

He makes his way down to the water. He notes the different angles of the slope, the reeds and grasses, the exposure to wind. He squats down and lights a cigarette but Maisie tries to tug him along the water's edge. He lets her lead him to where she picks up a dead and soggy duck.

"Drop it, Maisie."

He pulls her away and after five or six yards she drops it. They climb back up to the river wall as if going straight into the sky. Clouds are approaching from the east. There will be rain that afternoon and the sun will be covered within an hour. Already the river has become darker. The tide is about to turn and they wait for a minute or two before heading back towards Felixstowe Ferry and the sea. He loves that moment when the water moves but the whole weight of it is suspended. It amazes him how the moon shifts water, draws oceans.

Within half an hour they are back inside the warm cabin on *Music Maker*. Robert takes the bucket of dirty water from the cabin and tips it into the retreating tide. He puts out a sack to remind himself to collect coal the next time he goes out at low tide.

*

It was raining at Liverpool Street Station and now, two hours later, it was pouring as Susan got off the train at Felixstowe. The man who had twice failed to engage her in conversation on the train offered to carry her bags out onto the street, and she accepted. They walked out to the station entrance where she hesitated.

The man raised his hat, "Well, I'll leave these here then, shall I? Goodnight."

"Thank you. Goodnight," said Susan.

She had thought of taking a taxi but instead walked up to a porter and asked how far it was to RAF Bawdsey.

"You'd best take Aldis' bus," he said.

"Aldis bus?"

"Yes, miss. It'll take you to Felixstowe Ferry. It stops down there." The man pointed. "See? That's it."

"Please could you carry my bags? It's pouring."

The man picked them up and strode through the rain with Susan following and trying to avoid the worst puddles. He accepted the tip without thanking her.

She asked the bus driver if he was going to RAF Bawdsey.

"I'm going to the Ferry," said the driver, "that's the best I can do."

Susan looked at him, confused.

"Felixstowe Ferry. Then you'll have to cross the river."

She moved the suitcases along the inside of the empty bus and sat down heavily. Within a couple of minutes the driver started the engine and drove off slowly.

This was a surprise. She had looked up Felixstowe on a small scale map and found it right on the eastern edge of England near Ipswich. She knew this new posting was going to be near the sea, but she hadn't realised there was a river, let alone a river that needed to be crossed by ferry. It made RAF

Bawdsey sound remote and somehow rather insecure. This was odd, seeing as the first thing Daddy had said when she told him about her posting was, "That's marvellous. Bawdsey's famous."

She peered out of the window through the runnels of water but there were few lights.

The sound of the engine changed as they went up a slope. After her journey from Bristol she was keen to arrive but her determination to present herself in the best light possible was flagging. Why hadn't she travelled earlier in the day? Why hadn't she worn uniform? Her new coat was damp and might not recover its thick, green pile she had stroked with pleasure when she tried it on in the Ladies' Wear department at Swan and Edgars and considered it well worth all those coupons.

She looked round at the seats of the empty bus. Her stomach was uncomfortable and she wished she could undo her waistband. Thank goodness she was nearly there. RAF Bawdsey. She'd been thinking about it for weeks and only a few days ago Daddy and Aunt Rose were teasing her by saying that she spoke of little else. She had protested that that was her father's fault – it was he who had told her so much about it and sung its praises. He had said, "You'll be able to make a difference. That's what's important: making a difference. It's a wonderful opportunity – you couldn't have a better posting. It'll give you an invaluable grounding for future promotion."

She had remonstrated that she had only just been made Flying Officer and then phoned Bridget who had been posted there a couple of months ago, but Bridget did not even mention Bawdsey's prestigious reputation or history.

"It's amazing," she had said, "It's such a special place. It's quite glamorous."

"Glamorous? What on earth do you mean?"

"You'll see when you get here, you'll be so happy here. And I've met a very, very nice man."

"Already? Bridget!"

It would be such fun to see her, after all these months.

Susan was woken by a grating sound as the road surface changed.

"We're here."

The driver lifted her cases off the bus and announced, "This is the Ferry."

This wasn't anything. This was a dark and windy place. It was nowhere.

"That's the name of this place, miss: Felixstowe Ferry. And the ferryboat is over there. Look." He pointed behind her.

She turned round. There was one bright light and some small moving lights ahead. She couldn't see a boat.

She was standing on shingle. There was no more road. The driver got into his bus again and drove round in a crunching circle and back towards where they'd come from.

She was left in the dark. There were a few houses behind her but she felt abandoned. This was not like the RAF at all.

She picked up both cases and walked slowly in the direction the driver had indicated. Perhaps that light was on a boat. No. It was on the beach. But something was moving. Yes. There was a river right in front of her. Wavy white reflections shone on its thick black water. And there was a boat.

A voice came from it. "Leave your bags there, miss. You get in first and I'll fetch them on for you. Mind your feet, it's slippy."

A couple of narrow boards lay across the stones and a step had been let down on ropes against the side of the boat. Susan made her way along the boards warily and climbed in. A dog was in the prow, watching her, wagging its tail. She fretted again about her coat as the ferryman climbed out and picked up her suitcases. He lifted them up over the gunwale and let them drop the last few inches so they landed on the floorboards with a thud, splashing water on to her ankles and new shoes. Without looking at her he climbed back in, started the motor and reversed away from the shore. As he turned the boat and headed out into the river Susan looked back. They were moving away from a small group of buildings and their few lights. Ahead was blackness.

The rain had stopped but a sharp wind smacked her face with

cold and pulled strands of hair loose from under her smart little green hat. There was a seat but it was soaking wet. She stood with her arms folded across her stomach. Which way was upstream, which downstream? When had she last been in a boat?

The ferryman was almost still. In his black oilskins, with the tiny red glow of his cigarette waxing and waning he was leaning in a relaxed posture over the tiller, staring ahead for most of the time, steering a straight course and occasionally looking from side to side.

There was a single, pale light ahead. They were nearly there. The ferryman stood up as he decreased speed and nosed the boat up to the rubber tyres hung against a small jetty. His dog jumped down from the prow and into the boat. Susan stepped up and over the side and waited for the man to hand up her cases.

When he'd done that he said goodnight but the word was half lost as he went back to the tiller.

The boat reversed and swung out into the river and towards the other side again.

Now she was wide awake. The noise of the boat's motor lessened as it moved further away, and she had the sense of being out of place. At least she was off the train and off the boat. It must be near here.

Where now?

She saw a gateway. Was that the entrance? Yes. There was the sign: RAF Bawdsey. What a relief. She walked over to the barrier and was greeted by an RAF Policeman.

He saluted. "Good evening, ma'am. I hope you've had a good journey. The Commanding Officer asked me to see you to your room tonight." He pointed back to where Susan had left the cases, "I'll carry those up the drive for you. It's quite a walk when you're tired."

He went over and picked them up. "It's this way, ma'am. We'll be there in five minutes."

They walked side by side up a wide driveway making their way along a loose curve. As Susan's eyes became accustomed to the darkness she could see there was open space to the right and big trees to the left. The wind was no longer so wet or cold and she was feeling better. Perhaps the man expected her to start a conversation? It was up to her, really, because she was an officer. But she didn't want to and they continued at the brisk pace she set and he fell in with. Each of them altered the length of their steps as they went up a gentle slope and she was conscious of their double sets of footsteps overlapping.

The shape of a big building loomed ahead. They were making for a doorway in an arch with high towers on either side. The man pushed at the heavy door and held it open. The light in the porch was bright and as Susan entered from the dark she stepped sideways to avoid something on the floor. It was a mosaic of a huge prancing hound with chains flying out from its collar.

"I'm sorry, I should have warned you. It makes you jump, doesn't it? People often think they'll trip over it." The man stood to the side as he spoke.

They both looked down at the hound until Susan walked across it, treading on its legs and haunches.

"Would you like to come along here? Your room's upstairs."

They went in single file through the entrance hall and up a staircase. There were paintings, wooden panelling, a slight smell of cooking and of leather. Then the man stopped.

"I'm not supposed to go any further. This is just for WAAFs and officers." He smiled and put the suitcases down. "I'm going to have to leave these here. Is that all right?"

"Thank you very much. That's fine."

"Your room is number seven. It's at the end of the corridor on the right. And there's a bathroom somewhere along there too. Is there anything else you need?"

"No thank you."

"The Officers' Mess is downstairs. You can't miss it. Breakfast's at eight."

Susan moved one suitcase at a time to the outside of room seven. She wasn't used to the friendly yet polite way in which she had been addressed. She opened the door and humped the cases inside. She hung up her damp coat and hat before going down the corridor to the lavatory.

Returning to her room she slipped off her shoes, pulled up her skirt and petticoat, undid her suspenders, took off her stockings and eased herself out of her roll-on. That was better. Finally she undid the waistband of her skirt and stepped out of it. She looked round the room. There was a bed covered in a blue bedspread, a washbasin, a bedside table, a dressing table and a chair with two white towels folded over its back. The curtains were drawn. It reminded her of the sort of hotel she had occasionally stayed in with her father and aunt. It had been fun sharing a room with Aunt Rose, except when she was much younger and had to go to bed early. It wasn't fair she had to be in bed when it was still light and Daddy and Rose were having dinner downstairs.

She might be able to see where she was if she opened the curtains. She pulled one back but the window behind wouldn't budge and appeared to be painted shut. The second one opened easily. She leaned out, immediately soaking her left sleeve on the ledge.

It was an astonishing sight – shining wet roofs and a turret that seemed to be tiled in white. Above and beyond these was a wide expanse of sky mostly covered in dark clouds. The moon was just emerging from below them and it looked as if their edges were outlined with thick charcoal. Further off were acres and acres of moonlit sea.

That first night she dreamed about the mosaic hound. It was barking fiercely and as it snapped and snarled the chains flailed out from its neck. She knew she ought to approach it and grasp the chains, but its teeth nicked the side of her hand, drawing blood.

In the morning there was blood on her nightdress and sheets. When she drew back the curtains sunlight flooded across the room.

*

Two weeks later Robert is asked to run the ferry for the whole of Monday and Tuesday because the regular ferryman has to go to Kent for a funeral. Good. Not only will he earn a few extra shillings but this is proof he's trusted. However, there's no point in dwelling on this, no use him getting his hopes up just because the skipper happens to be away for a couple of days.

It's still dark when he unties the boat from its mooring on Monday but by the time he's taken the boat through the choppy water there's a small group of people waiting quietly on the shore. These are the RAF people who rent cottages at Felixstowe Ferry and need to go to the Bawdsey side. As he approaches the beach he can see the smoke from their cigarettes rising into the lamplight. The first bus is coming across the golf course, its lights trundling along unevenly. It stops outside the café and unloads its passengers. Most of them are servicemen wearing grey greatcoats and they walk alone or in pairs towards the boat. It's strange how at this time of day they do not seem quite so sure of themselves as they do later on.

They come on board quietly. There are no fares to collect. Everyone is employed by the RAF and so entitled to a free journey. They just climb on and lean against the side or sit on one of the benches. This first crossing is always quiet. Robert thinks he's the only one who's really awake.

And the estuary is wide awake too. By the time they're out in midstream the sky is brighter and dark clouds are moving fast across the horizon. This is what Robert thinks the expression "the cold light of day" really means. Cold, light and day all present in equal measures.

He has to steer in a sharp curve to overcome the combined effect of the wind coming off the far shore and the incoming tide that's rushing past the moored boats. The boats are being dragged so their buoys tilt and show the different colours of their undersides. He judges it accurately, turning downstream at the precise place and speed needed to come alongside the jetty smoothly and accurately. As usual, everyone hurries to get off, and one or two nod thankyou as they step over the side and onto the land.

Three young men wearing forage caps are sitting on their kitbags waiting for the ferry. They laugh and chat as the others walk past them, then climb in, carrying on their conversation as Robert reverses and heads out into the estuary again. A line of geese fly low and powerfully against the wind, making for the sea. The noises of the wind, engine and water drown the words of the three airmen and the pushy, breathy sounds the wings of the geese must be making.

Even before the boat is secured on the other side the three men jump onto the beach. One, pulled sideways by the weight of his bag, slips and splashes mud up his trouser leg. He groans noisily while the others laugh and the next queue of passengers files along the planks and on to the ferry. A few minutes later Robert turns the boat round and is on his way back to Bawdsey.

Looking out to the east, he sees the clouds continuing to make their way from north to south. Maisie stands in the prow with her tail stretched out like the Red Ensign which flaps stiffly from the stern.

*

By the end of her first week Susan had learned a large part of what she was supposed to be doing. She was disappointed. The work was neither as varied nor as demanding as she had hoped. But she was not going to accept things as they were. It was clear that things could be done better. As a start, she made a point of learning the names of all the officers and a good number of the airmen and airwomen. She had discovered that if she addressed people by name they usually showed her greater respect.

But Bawdsey Manor was an extraordinary place. It was quite unlike any other RAF station she'd been to or heard of. The main building was a unique stately home on a spectacular green and wooded estate with an amazing view across the North Sea. It demanded admiration. Daddy had told her it was only about sixty or seventy years old and had been built by the Quilter family. Now the Air Ministry used not only the Manor, but also other buildings around the grounds, some of which had had a different function originally. There were modern additions too. Four of the eight radar masts were three hundred and fifty feet high and made of steel. Each of these grew upwards out of a base like a gigantic, shining splayed foot that grasped the ground. The original four were made of wood and seemed like poor relations. The radar transmitting and receiving equipment was in half buried concrete buildings or wooden huts. Daddy was right. It was a privilege to be working here.

But it was curious. Things seemed slack. At morning parade only half of the men and women were detailed to go to their real places of work. The others seemed to be given some minor errand or task such as working in the cookhouse or moving furniture in and out of rooms in the Manor. Some just seemed to walk off to wherever they chose. In the afternoon the shift not at work was apparently allowed to leave the camp. On her second day Susan saw groups of airmen and women walking down towards the gatehouse and the jetty, and discovered they were free to take the ferry and then the bus to Felixstowe. It was as if they were on holiday. Surely this couldn't be right? But no other officer seemed to mind the place running at half speed. Why on earth didn't they feel as she did?

At the first formal dinner, after grace had been said, she sat down at the table and watched one of her fellow officers speak to a red-haired waitress who was serving the soup. He had obviously made a joke and was now tipping his chair back on two legs so he could lean behind his neighbour to say something else to the woman.

Susan looked along the table at the people opposite. Most people were talking but Mark Rivens, who was exactly opposite, was facing directly towards her. He smiled.

"How are you finding it here? What do you think of this place? "

"It's not like any other RAF station I've been to."

He laughed. "It certainly isn't. But do you like it?"

Susan hesitated, looked down at her plate.

"You're frowning. What's the matter?"

"Nothing. I was just, just thinking." She picked up her serviette and unfolded it. "Yes, it's ok here. I think I'll like it."

Mark leant to his left as the red-headed waitress served him. When she moved on he turned to Susan again. Susan was well aware he had noticed her at breakfast on her first day and on several occasions since. She knew from Bridget that he had been keen to be introduced to her without delay and she was pretty certain he had engineered a seat near her for this dinner.

As she accepted a piece of bread from him she was spoken to by the girl on her left whom she had met before. Good. They talked about people they both knew at Cranwell until the soup plates were cleared.

While that was being done Susan faced across the table again and found Mark still looking at her. She met his eyes briefly but looked away along the length of the table. This was definitely more than politeness. Well, she could deal with that. She had come here to work, to seek promotion, to get on with things. She was not going to be side-tracked.

While she was served with vegetables Susan studied her plate, the chandelier above the table and the paintings on the wall beyond. A clatter of cutlery told her everyone had been served and was starting to eat. She picked up her knife and fork.

Mark offered her the mint sauce. She thanked him and took it before turning to answer a question from her neighbour on the other side. Without making it obvious, she glanced round when reaching up to push her hair off her collar and neck. He was still watching.

*

Susan accompanied Alex Croft round the camp at the first opportunity. She wanted to be well prepared for when it was her turn to be Duty Officer but their tour seemed casual compared to the way it was done in other camps. It wasn't like an inspection at all.

"Is it because the whole place is so informal, or because people really are doing what they're supposed to be doing?"

"Both, I think. And it's a good thing, isn't it? It makes being Duty Officer easy."

"But doesn't anything ever go wrong? Surely there are times when things aren't done properly, or aren't done at all?"

"Well, I suppose that happens, sometimes. But I shouldn't lose any sleep over it. The war's been over for years now. There's nothing that matters desperately."

But that wasn't the point. It was about doing things properly.

The fact that the war was over was immaterial. Things would just slide if they were allowed to. Susan stepped out smartly as they walked on past the Radio School and turned right into the MT yard. There were two trucks with their bonnets up and two men working on each of them. As soon as Alex and Susan entered the yard several other men in overalls came out of the workshop.

"Good Morning sir, ma'am. We're having trouble with the brake cables on these vehicles, but we should have them fixed in an hour or so. Then we're going to start on a major overhaul." The man led them inside to where an engine stood on a bench.

"It's from a winch. The cable was replaced a few months ago but it must have been stronger than the housing, so it's been pulled out of shape here .. and here.. It's going to be useful for training, though, because we've had to dismantle the whole thing and now these two.., " he nodded across the bench to two young men covered in grease, "will learn how to reassemble it." One of them pulled a face and everyone laughed.

How did this place work? It seemed everywhere they went there was good humour and an absence of real authority. Where was the carelessness or lack of discipline? It must be there somewhere. Still, once she was Duty Officer in her own right, she would tighten things up. Those mechanics had not even stood to attention and Alex hadn't seemed to mind at all. Daddy would be appalled if he could see this sloppiness. She'd make sure things improved.

Then Alex took her to one of the Chain Home Low receiver blocks. It was a wooden building under one of the towers and she felt as if she was walking into a big garden shed, but it was a relief to get out of the wind. Once inside the camouflaged entry it was dark, but warm and snug, almost cosy. A group of men and women wearing headphones were concentrating on the lighted screens in front of them. Alex looked over the shoulder of one of the radar operators and beckoned Susan. The operator noticed their arrival and nodded a greeting, but kept talking to his absent listener.

Susan watched. This was fascinating. What did all this mean? The screen was covered with a grid. That must be to do with location. And running from top to bottom was an undulating line. What could that be? Then there were flickering lights and pulses which were presumably echoes of objects somewhere right out above the North Sea, perhaps a hundred miles away. At training school they had learned basic facts about how micro sound waves are sent out and how they bounce back when they meet something, indicating the size and location of whatever they hit. Even though she did not understand all of what the airman was calling out – especially as he had a very strong Welsh accent – she knew he was giving information to enable the plotters to gauge the speed and direction of an object's travel.

For a minute or two she watched a regular blip appearing to the left of the screen. Obviously it could be a plane, but perhaps it was a ship.

She pointed to it. "What's that?"

"The laundry, ma'am," said the operator.

"The laundry?"

"It's at Walton. There's a laundry at Walton and it's got a tall chimney and on clear days like today we often pick it up. There's not much else we pick up on land."

Thank goodness she hadn't said anything. Of course radar could detect stationary items too, if they were big enough. But how did the operators distinguish what each blip meant? Oh, of course, the continuous line across the screen was the coast. Why hadn't she realised that? And if that was the case, that blip couldn't be a ship because it was on land.

She wandered round the block, noting charts, notices, pieces of equipment, a forage cap, two greatcoats, several cups, a tin opener, empty Heinz baked bean tins. It was pretty messy. She noticed how the operators reacted to her slightly differently than they did to Alex. Was this just because she was new? Probably not. It was just that female officers were treated and judged differently from male ones. That's how life was.

Alex nodded to her that it was time to go and they left the block, suddenly emerging into the strong light and wind again. The cold brought tears to Susan's eyes as she screwed them up against the dazzle. A volley of barking hit them as they walked back past the dog compound.

Susan was thinking about Alex. He hadn't impressed her. All he had done was to walk round and talk to a few people. What good would that do? Of course he needed to talk, but surely he should have done something too? Nothing would get better by itself. He hadn't even written anything down. It was only when officers did things that anything would improve. Alex was pleasant enough, but that wasn't the issue. And even if people here – even officers – didn't seem to know or care about Bawdsey's importance in the Battle of Britain she could still do what Daddy wanted her to do: she could make a difference.

*

RAF Bawdsey
February 16th 1952

Dear Daddy,
Thank you for your letter which arrived on Monday. I was so pleased to hear you've found a man to look after the garden while Mr Jenkins is in hospital. Please give Mr and Mrs J my best wishes and tell them I hope he'll soon be home again. And remember your promise to me about not doing any heavy work yourself – I don't want you flat on your back again.

Yesterday we had a service for the King. Quite a few people went to London for the funeral, and our service was very simple – just a few prayers and hymns. I felt sad about it and everyone's feeling it. It's so hard to imagine Princess Elizabeth being Queen, isn't it? She's only two years older than I am.

Last Sunday Kathleen and I and Daphne borrowed bikes and went for a ride on our side of the estuary. We rode along the only road that goes anywhere and it took us to Bawdsey (which is a village as well as our station) and on to Alderton. We stopped to look at a Martello tower (like the one on the opposite side of the Deben). Up close it was HUGE. It was amazing to think about men building it and even more amazing to think about them blowing up the one which used to be here, which was what the Quilter family did when they built this Manor. It left a whopping hole in the ground which is now a sunken garden.

Then we rode on to a place called Ramsholt which is nothing but a pub (unfortunately closed) and a tiny quay, and it must be really pretty when the tide's in – today there was masses of mud between us and the water. At low tide it's very flat and boring. But then we had to ride back the way we had come, because this little corner of land has only got a few lanes. I was STARVING by the time we got back.

Did I tell you I have an Admirer? His name is Mark, and he is a Flying Officer who is ex- Aircrew, but he injured the muscles in one of his arms and so he can't fly again which is a great shame. He's very nice, and he's smashing looking, and he's keen on me but I am NOT going to fall in love with him. (Too much to do).

Some of the work here is boring. There is not enough work for the airmen and women, so it's difficult to supervise them. But although in my last letter I told you it feels quite slack and that annoys me (and you'd hate it) I like not having that silly shouting anymore. By the way, few people seem to realise that this was THE place for radar. They're amazed when I tell them what you told me about Watson-Watt etc.

And it's a gorgeous place. Now spring's coming the trees are getting greener and when I took a short cut through the gardens the other day there were masses of bulbs shooting up, just like along the drive at home. But it doesn't feel like home yet, and although you've always said that the RAF is like a family, it still doesn't feel like one to me.

I'm going to a concert this evening. Someone has brought their collection of gramophone records, so I'll be listening to Beethoven and Bach. Last time Kathleen and Jenny took their knitting but were told they weren't allowed to do it unless they made sure their needles didn't click!

A big hug, Daddy, and lots of love,
Susan

And my love to Aunt Rose too!

*

Robert has been given a parcel to bring across the river and deliver to a man in Harbour Villas.

When he's done this he extends his walk along the path as far as the Martello Tower and then goes down onto the beach with Maisie. It's strange how this beach is made of stones while less than a mile away the shoreline is just mud. But out there are even more stones. The wide, flat bar across the mouth of the estuary alters its shape slightly with the sea's every coming and going. It's made entirely of shingle, shingle that started off as rock and is gradually being worn down to become sand. And this is the bar, invisible at high tide, that he's heard people get stranded on for hours.

He throws a stone towards it and Maisie chases out, barking and splashing, and then races back hoping for another. He searches for a stick and flings it as hard as he can but the wind brings it back further along the beach. Maisie fails to follow it and is just running round in circles. Robert turns towards the fallen stick and the houses and huts that make up the Ferry. He doesn't often see it from here. The place looks very small, very close to the water.

He looks across the estuary and sees something different about the Manor. It looks softer, smaller. The trees are getting their leaves and beginning to hide the buildings. Open areas are being filled in with colour and movement. It will look beautiful in summer. Mother would like this view.

He picks up the stick and holds it out so Maisie will follow him up off the beach but then shushes her down and holds on to her collar when he sees two boys having a slow bicycle race. In silence, they're concentrating on remaining upright and covering as little ground as possible. He watches them, interested to see who will last the longest.

After a minute the younger one, standing on the pedals of a bike that's too big, topples off.

The other one says, "You need blocks. Let's go back to mine, we've got some you can use. My sister used to have them and I can fix them on."

The boy who has fallen is picking gravel off his knee. Robert watches him get up, mount again and then ride off with his friend towards The Victoria pub.

It was only last year when he helped his sister Lizzie learn to ride. He had run along behind her trying to keep her upright and reassuring her that he was there, that she wouldn't fall and that yes, she was riding all by herself. He tried to picture her as she must be now, ten months later. He missed her and he missed Sally, and he missed his mother. He didn't miss his step-father, but he thought about him often. He had been glad to see the back of him, relieved to be free of his constant criticism. He'd show him that he could manage on his own, was quite capable of looking after himself. He'd thought before of leaving home, and when his stepfather had said he was returning to Scotland, and that Robert would never be as hardy as a Scot, would never succeed, he would not have gone with them for the world.

He continues as far as the beach and stands against a hut in the boatyard while the ferry unloads. He knows many of the passengers by sight. How different they are from the people he met when he did his National Service two years ago. Most of his time in the Suffolk Light Infantry was horrible. These RAF people always seem happy. The officers seem to be reasonable human beings and there are so many women. They're more like a group of civilians than a group of service personnel. He has seen several couples, in uniform and in broad daylight in public, kissing each other passionately.

He and his friends went for weeks without seeing girls, and then when they did, there seemed to be all sorts of obstacles to stop them getting together. Juliet. Fair-haired, thin, tall. Quite delicate, somehow. She was the daughter of a coal merchant who used to heave black sacks off the lorry and dump them outside the camp boiler house each week. One day Robert turned up at her house to take her to the pictures. Her father came to the door and shouted at him that Juliet was not going out with any squaddie, and if he saw Robert near their house again he would thump him. He had never understood why the man had been so fierce.

Four men, all younger than him, are walking to the bus stop together, smiling and chatting. How can life be so easy for them?

"Come on, Maisie, let's go."

As they return Robert notices something odd about the way

Music Maker is lying. She's floating but she's not completely level. And is she further downstream than usual? Something's wrong. What's preventing her from floating freely? Has something heavy inside her shifted and made her tip?

There's no reason not to step onto the gangplank, even if it's wonky, but he's saying to himself, Please don't let her sink, don't let there be anything seriously wrong.

"Robert, wait a sec."

Jack's calling and waving from the next boat, *Pretty Girl*. He gestures to show he's coming round.

Robert waits for him on *Music Maker*'s gangplank.

"I noticed she wasn't lying right half an hour ago. And I know why."

"I do too." Robert has just seen that one of the ropes that holds her is gone.

There should be two ropes attaching her to posts in the water, and two attaching her to metal posts driven into the ground. At low tide these are slack, but they hold *Music Maker* to her mooring. Now there's only one rope, and as the tide ebbs she's being pulled sideways.

"You should have checked those ropes," says Jack, "They must've been rotten. I bet they've been there for years. Just leave her until it's low tide – she can't hurt herself or anything else like this. There's nothing you can do now, but you'll need to fix her soon. I'll give you a hand if you like."

This exchange of words is the longest they've had. Feeling grateful, Robert goes onto the sloping deck and into the cabin. He eats a chunk of cheese and a couple of raw carrots and wonders about the ropes. It's true he hasn't checked them. He's just assumed they will last. Surely rope lasts for years and years? But now he's regretting he didn't check them.

Where can he find rope? He can't ask *Music Maker*'s owner. He's been generous enough in letting him use the boat at no cost. What about the ferryman? He'll have rope and would certainly give it to him. But no. He considers three fishermen in turn. One of them has coil upon coil of rope in his shed, but Robert doesn't want to ask him.

He'll go up to the boatyard and look for rope that's just lying around. There must be some somewhere. He walks across the gangplank feeling annoyed at his own lack of nerve. It's silly to feel like this. He'd be pleased to help anyone in a similar situation, and others would be pleased to help him. Why is it he's so timid, so weak?

But there, under a hut, along with old lobster pots and broken oars and beneath a pile of empty varnish cans and netting is a heap of stiff rope of the right thickness. Paint has been spilt on it and one part is frayed, but it'll do.

Should he try to find out whose it is? He starts to pull the coil free from the netting, and finds there are several pieces. One's about six fathoms long – that's good. He tugs another length from the lobster pots. These two together will certainly do the job. Feeling guilty he loops one of the pieces round his shoulder and walks off with it. But none of the few people around seem to notice him and he walks straight to *Music Maker*, dumps it on her deck, and returns for the second length. He kicks the netting he has pulled out back under the hut and makes off once again, still feeling guilty. Well, he can always give it back if someone claims it. He can tell them the truth: it was just lying around so he thought he could take it.

He sits on deck to splice the ropes together. First he sets about unwinding the strands of sisal. The paint has glued them together but he uses his knife. It's his only decent knife and he broke the tip off it last year. He pushes in the bit that's now the point, levers and opens the end of the first rope out into three loose twisting strands. The second one is easier because it's newer. Then he begins to marry the ropes, interweaving the three ends of the first one over and under the still layed up strands of the second. He needs the knife again, wishes he had a proper spike of his own. He hauls it taut, turns himself round because it's easier to do that than to turn both coils round, and does the same with the other three. Then he examines the rope from side to side, tugs at it. Not bad. He sits up straight again, stretches his back and spreads his hands open just as the one holding the knife is beginning to cramp up.

Several hours later, at low tide, Jack comes over to *Music*

Maker with wide planks to set across the mud to reach the posts.

"I've even got an old door if we need it."

He approves of the new rope. He doesn't ask where it came from.

Robert's feeling better. It isn't going to be as hard to sort this out as he thought. It's good to have Jack with him.

Jack inspects the end of the original rope. "It's been cut."

They both examine the neat, straight end of the almost black, ancient rope. There's no doubt about it. It's been cut. It's not frayed at all.

Robert is silent. What does this mean? Who would have cut it? Why? But the evidence is there – no accident or untying or abrasion could have created this sharp edge of even fibres.

Jack begins to untie the remaining length of the rope on *Music Maker*'s rusty cleat. It was wound ages ago. He has a marlinspike which Robert uses to penetrate the knot and ease it apart, but in the end they have to cut it. Jack's knife slices easily through each of the bands of fibres.

Robert winces. How easy it is to destroy things. It's taken him at least an hour to splice the ropes.

They attach the new rope in near silence, each focusing on their task. It'll soon be dusk. Then they lay the planks across the mud to the post so they can retrieve the other end of the old rope. Jack pulls it in hand over muddy hand and the other end appears from out of the river. It's cut. Double proof.

They attach a thin rope from *Music Maker* to the post, ready for when she floats on the incoming tide.

"We'll pull her round to her proper place with this. It'll hold if we do it gently, and then we can attach the new rope so she's as firm as before. That's all we can do now. Tell you what, I'm ready for a cup of tea."

Robert invites Jack into the cabin. He's never asked anyone in before. He offers him a cigarette while the kettle boils.

"No. I just like my pipe, thanks, but it would smoke you out in here."

Maisie settles down. They stir the last of Robert's sugar ration into their tea.

"Strange business," said Jack. "But don't you bother about it. Try to forget it happened. Just get on with what you do. It'll be all right."

"Thanks for your help."

"That's all right. I may need you sometime."

But Robert doesn't forget the incident even though he wants to. It grows, and that evening he can't get it out of his mind. He keeps worrying about it. How, exactly, could anyone have done it? They must have either got to the post – impossible except by boat at high tide – or they must have been on *Music Maker*. And who? And why?

That night he falls asleep at once, as usual, but when he wakes he's anxious again, listening for noises on deck, fearing he's unwanted at the Ferry, fearing he's unwanted. It's Maisie's warm and lumpy weight in the crook of his knees that reassures him, urges him to get up and get on with things.

*

It was Wednesday. Mark and Susan were having tea with other officers in the lounge. The windows overlooked the grounds and they could see the unused swimming pool and the sports field where a game of football was in progress. Two men in white were walking away from the tennis courts.

Ian was saying "Have you heard, another couple who met here have just got engaged? That's the second this month."

"Well," said Alex, "Bawdsey isn't called the Honeymoon Station for nothing, you know. This place has a reputation to live up to. If you weren't here, Ian, we'd be talking about you and Bridget."

"That would only be because you were jealous."

There was a pause and then Mark spoke.

"It'll soon be the cricket season again, and then there'll be athletics. Susan, you know we have a Sports Day, don't you?"

"No, when is it?"

"June or July? – I can't remember exactly."

"July," chipped in another voice, "And last year was good fun.

Harry Adams nearly threw the javelin at the CO's wife. It had been raining and he slipped."

Susan used to like Sports Days at school. Even at her very first school she remembered winning races and rushing up to Aunt Rose and asking her to hold the little red ribbons she won. At RAF Cranwell she had won trophies for running and the high jump and she had captained the hockey team. But now things were different. She wanted to get on with more important things. Work. Promotion, if she was lucky. The thought of being able to tell Daddy that she had been made a Flight Lieutenant made her chuckle. She was determined that, one day, she would be one.

She asked Mark, "Who arranges Sports Day?"

"You, I expect," he said with a smile.

Oh no! How could arranging Sports Day help her with promotion?

Alex said, "It's a big responsibility, Susan. One year we had a competition which involved taking a tennis ball out of a bowl of flour with your teeth. You shouldn't underestimate what's involved."

Susan didn't laugh.

"Come on, let's go out before it gets chilly." Mark stood up and took the teacups back to the trolley, and they left the room.

He led her out of a back door and onto the lawn. He chuckled, "They'll never tire of teasing people. And they'll be talking about us, you know."

Susan did not reply. She could see two airmen without their caps on. It was only this morning that she'd told some bods off for not wearing their caps. She knew they were only going over to breakfast as they usually did, but that did not make it right. An hour later she'd seen them with their caps on. Did they know she was the daughter of a Wing Commander? Probably. Everyone else did, even though she had not told anyone. Still, it was possible that Bridget had told them. But did people think about her differently because of it? Since joining the RAF, having a well-known father was a mixed blessing.

Just as Mark was leading her right out towards the cliff she suddenly stopped walking. Where was the key of the bureau in

40

the office where she had been working that afternoon? She checked the pocket where she usually put it. It wasn't there, so she must have put it back. Thank goodness.

"You're over efficient, you know," commented Mark.

"No, I'm not. You can't be over efficient. I'm just being efficient, and there's nothing wrong with that."

"Well, no, but even if you hadn't returned the key it wouldn't matter. You could do it when we go back in. You know no one will need it until tomorrow morning. Come on, let's go as close to the edge as we can."

They walked on slowly, enjoying the evening sun but feeling the strong breeze. Mark took his jacket off and put it round Susan's shoulders.

"Have you been here at night? Out on the cliff top when the moon's out?"

"No, I haven't."

"I'll bring you here after the Fancy Dress Ball."

Susan said nothing. Being out here with Mark at night? She turned towards him.

"Would you like that?"

She half turned away, smiling at the view beyond him, "Yes, I would."

Mark took her hand and they stood still watching the sandpipers arrowing into the sea, a sailing boat, the yellowish clouds close to the horizon.

"Look. There's the moon now." Susan pointed to the nearly full moon to the south, white against a pale sky.

"Good. If it's like that today then it'll be perfect for the night of the Ball."

*

Every evening is becoming lighter for longer. The air is warming up in the daytime and across the Deben the fields are becoming greener and greener. Spring is making him feel better and so is the fact that his twice daily search of *Music Maker* has discovered no footprints, no signs of intruders. Nothing is out of place, nothing seems amiss.

He needs a plank of wood to replace a weak board on deck and resolves to look for one when he walks along the beach after the next high tide, after he has run the ferry this afternoon. He's the second man today so he won't have much to do, but the regulations state that if there are more than twelve passengers there has to be a crew of two. So, unless there are things to carry in and out of the boat, he'll have an easy time of it.

He's almost invisible on these crossings. The passengers rarely talk to the main ferryman, let alone to him, so he finds himself watching how they are with each other. He can't always understand what they say because they use words he doesn't know, and some of them speak in accents he's not used to. But there's no difficulty when officers are talking. They speak like the announcers he used to hear on his parents' wireless. It's amazing what they say, and they say so much. They talk about things happening at the RAF camp, about what they're going to do in Felixstowe, about their next leave and where they're going to spend it. All these words. He could never talk as much as that.

Amongst the third lot of passengers this afternoon are a couple of officers Robert's noticed several times recently. The woman is perhaps a little younger than the man. She's good looking, rather serious. He's more relaxed, and although attentive to her and clearly accompanying her today, he's not talking to her but to a couple facing them. He looks honest, trustworthy. Is it something about his eyes? Or because he seems to enjoy people and they seem to enjoy him? Like now, when a loud guffaw goes up from the group and it's this man who's caused it.

"You should be ashamed of yourself, Mark," says someone.

But the man goes on smiling and turns to look at the moored boats they're passing. The woman he's with says nothing, and a wink and a grimace pass between the two men standing behind her. What's going on? Robert doesn't know, but he wishes he knew someone who he could laugh with like that.

Later that day he and Maisie are on the beach, walking slowly along the tide line. He's whistling. It's sunny but cold. They are further from home than usual and have found one stretch with a good haul of coal. He's already filled half a sack with small

lumps. Not bad at all. He decides to return for a pile of fire-
wood he collected and pulled well above the high tide mark, but
hasn't yet found what he's really looking for: a decent sized
plank. He sits down on a tree trunk embedded in the sand while
Maisie sniffs around barking at gulls. She disappears behind
him for a few minutes and comes back with a cloth in her
mouth. Can he use it for anything? No.

"Maisie, drop it."

She doesn't want to let go and runs off when he tries to grab
it, so he crouches low on the sand and calls her, hoping to trick
her. As he does so his attention is caught by some shells. Are
they shells? They're different from the ones he usually finds
here. They're more like stones. Or bones. Tiny triangular, flat
bones. He puts them in his trouser pocket. At that moment
Maisie comes hurtling towards him, still with the cloth in her
teeth. She almost catches him off balance, but he gets up and
swings the sack of coal over his shoulder and walks back to
Music Maker.

There's no need to return to the beach this afternoon; the
pile of wood will wait as other piles have done.

But two days later, when Robert goes back with a cord so he
can tie the wood into a bundle, he sees three boys sitting round
a fire. They're burning his wood.

They don't see him at first and he watches them hit the fire
with sticks, making sparks fly. He starts walking towards them
and soon the one opposite sees him. He tells the others and they
spin round and jump to their feet.

They're burning his wood. Robert begins to run towards
them and they run away from him up the beach, but one trips
and his shoe comes off so he stumbles. Robert catches up with
him and grabs the sleeve of his jacket. He pulls him to the
ground, ripping the jacket, and they fight while Maisie barks
loudly. Robert kneels over the boy, clenches his fist and punches
him on his jaw. The boy grunts, yells, flails out his legs, wriggles
out of his jacket, gets to his feet and shoves Robert off balance
so he falls backwards.

By the time he has sat up the boy is limping away as fast as he
can. Robert picks up a stone and slings it after him. It falls short

and he hears jeers. He picks up another one but thinks better of it. What if all three of them throw stones back at him?

Bastard. Stupid bastard. At least he'll have a bruise. Robert stands up, picks up the shoe and the jacket and goes over to the fire. Maisie follows him. The flames have died down now, but he brings it to life again with some of the remaining wood. He looks up the beach for the three boys. There they are. They've stopped running now they're at a safe distance. He's glad they're watching him. He's furious. He holds up the shoe in one hand and the jacket in the other and then chucks them on the fire.

"Sit, Maisie."

He's trembling. He takes out a cigarette and lights it from an ember. As dusk comes he sits watching the jacket smoulder, the shoe leather curl. If only he'd smashed a stone into that boy's stupid face.

Sods. Over the winter he has seen at least three other men gathering wood and coal. They left it in piles, just as he's done. He learned about beachcombing when he was a boy, knows that anything that's been set aside high up on a beach will be left alone until it's collected. But these boys have chosen to burn his pile for the hell of it.

He walks back without noticing how the mud is so clean, so shiny, that it's almost like glazed earthenware. This morning he heard the calls of godwits and peewits. His heart beat is steady now. He fingers the three small triangular stones in his pocket.

*

When Robert gets back Jack's looking out for him because the postman's given him a letter to pass on. It's from Scotland, one of the letters his mother writes at irregular intervals with her news. He's delighted and he walks across Jack's gangplank to collect it at once. But he can't stop himself from saying, "Some boys burned my wood. I made a pile of wood on the beach and they burned it."

Jack leans back against his wheelhouse doorway. "Do you know who it was?"

"Yes. I saw them doing it," he gestures towards the beach, "But I don't know their names."

"How old were they?"

"Sixteen, seventeen? Something like that. I've seen them before."

Jack pauses. "Well. Are you going to do anything? There's not much you can do, is there?"

"I've done something already. I caught one and I thumped him."

Jack laughed. "That's probably all you need to do. A couple of weeks ago some boys stopped up the chimney of that upside down boat where the old man lives. He came out coughing and swearing, and someone saw them watching him and laughing. It could be the same ones."

"Well, they certainly knew it was my pile. They ran away as soon as I appeared."

"It might well have been them who cut your rope too, but I should think they'll keep their distance now. I'd try and forget about it if I were you."

Forget about it? How could Jack be so calm? Didn't he realise they might do something else?

"What if they do something worse?"

"They won't. There's never been any real trouble at the Ferry, not unless you count smuggling and the Customs men, and that was ages ago. It's not the same now. You didn't grow up in the Ferry, I know, but that's no reason for anyone to want to harm you. You're no threat to anyone – in fact, most people here would hardly know you exist."

That's true. He might as well not exist. He looks down at the letter in his hand: Robert Orves, c/o Boatyard, Felixstowe Ferry, Suffolk. His family seem to be the only people for whom he exists, and he's chosen not to be with them. It still hurts every time he thinks back to that decision, and he's never sure if it was the right one. He makes himself think of when his stepfather made him leave school at fourteen. Why did Robert need an education? he'd asked. He would never be anything other than a labourer.

He feels lousy, has nothing more to say to Jack.

"Come on, now. It's not that bad. We fixed the rope, and even if we hadn't you'd still be alive. There was no real danger. And a pile of wood is a pile of wood. You can't really say you've been robbed. Now, if you'd had a collection of amber or shark's teeth, and they'd been taken from off your boat, that would be different."

"I'd like to find some amber. Have you ever found any?"

"No, but I've never looked. Just keep your eyes open on a day after a storm. That's when people say they see it."

"What are sharks' teeth like? How big are they?"

"I'll show you one." Jack goes into his cabin and comes back out within a few moments. He holds his hand out so Robert can inspect what he's holding.

"Is that a shark's tooth? I've got three of those. I didn't know what they were."

"This is the bit which went into the shark's gum, his jaw, and this is the point of the tooth. They are about a couple of million years old, when there were plenty of sharks swimming around here."

"Are they valuable?"

"No, but they're quite rare. It's amber that's valuable. The bigger the better, but I've not seen a bit bigger than, say, that," Jack indicates the top part of his thumb. "But it's worth collecting. If you have any you should either keep it safe or sell it."

Robert walks back to *Music Maker* with Maisie. He's feeling better but his knee's hurting. It was only boys after all. And he's got three sharks' teeth, and perhaps he can find and sell amber. He lights the oil lamp, makes a cup of tea, sits down on the bunk to open his letter. His mother's neat, slanting handwriting slides straight into him.

Dear Bob,

Well, it's a lovely spring day here today and I hope it is with you too. Dad's been away for two days working on a new dock so the girls and I have been on our own. Sally is liking school now, but she didn't like it at first because she could not understand what the other children said and they could not understand her, but now she's made friends with the girl next door. Lizzie is quick with her spellings and she likes

*learning poetry by heart. She must know six or seven poems already –
it's a treat to hear her recite them.*

*I've managed to find some work in a baker's shop two days a week.
The money helps. You haven't told us where you are lodging so I'll send
this letter to the boatyard again but I wish I had your proper address.*

*Dad's back is still not better. The company still haven't paid any
compensation, and I don't think they ever will. Sometimes he comes
home completely tired out, even after an ordinary day. He says not to
worry but I do.*

*The girls miss you a lot and we all wonder about how you're getting
on. Write soon,*

With much love,

Mum

Squeezed in after his mother's signature is a note from Lizzie in
her round, nine year old's handwriting:

*RoBERT – I can say I wandered Lonely as a cloud all the way through
and part of the Destruction of Sennacarib and Miss May says I have a
good chance of winning the first prize for ressitation. When are you
coming to see us Love from Lizzie.*

He lies back on the bunk and puts out his hand to fondle
Maisie. She jumps up and pushes her nose under his knees,
forcing him to lift them up. She settles into the warm tent they
make. He brings his hands back on to his chest and smooths the
letter out against his jersey.

*

Susan was getting dressed after having a bath. The Fancy Dress
Ball was being held that evening and, after an initial lukewarm
reaction to the idea, she had been swayed into it by the general
excitement. She was going as the Milky Way. On the bed lay
some netting she had dyed dark blue and on to which she had
sewn little white paper stars. This had taken longer than she
had expected, even though it was only necessary to anchor the
centre of each star to the netting with a few stitches. But now

she was pleased with it, and all she had to finish off was her head-dress. She was fixing a silver cardboard five pointed star, not quite securely enough, to the silvery scarf she was going to tie round her head. She had no shoes that suited this outfit, and Kathleen had promised to lend her a pair of silky slippers.

She went next door to where Kathleen was struggling with her geisha girl costume. The authentic Japanese gown, obtained from her uncle who had lived in Tokyo, was going to be spectacular except she couldn't work out how to fasten it properly. Whichever way she fixed it she was left with yards of embroidered fabric trailing on the ground.

"I'm sure it's not meant to be like this. It's just going to drag on the floor and get spoiled, and I won't be able to dance at all. How do you think it's meant to go?"

Susan examined it from front and back, and suggested they started from the beginning again, so she helped Kathleen take it off and spread it out on the bed. After various attempts they worked out a way of linking the loops with corresponding ties, supplemented by a few safety pins, so that it hung properly.

"There, now you look elegant and oriental."

"But I feel like a fat chicken. It's so hot. I'll melt in this."

"You can always take it off later in the evening. Lots of people abandon their costumes – don't worry about it. And I'm sure Geoffrey will admire you whatever you are wearing."

"Well, if Geoff admires me in this, Mark will be even more struck by you in that outfit. You look gorgeous. You do realise he's Totally Smitten, don't you?"

"Yes, I do." In case Kathleen asked about her feelings for Mark she quickly asked, "Where are the slippers, please?"

"Look, they're under the cupboard."

Susan put them on and went back to her room where there was a full length mirror. Everything was fine except her head-dress. It kept slipping over to the right.

Damn. The wretched thing was hopeless. She should have tried it out earlier. She ran back to Kathleen's room.

"It still won't stand up properly. Have you got any more Kirbygrips?"

After ten more minutes they were both satisfied with how

they looked and they walked along the corridor and on to the gallery from where they looked down at the dance floor. The band was playing but no one was yet dancing.

Susan and Mark had agreed to keep their costumes a secret from each other. Susan was confident Mark had no idea what she would be dressed as, but she was pretty sure he would choose something to do with flying. He had told her how he used to love wearing his airman's helmet, goggles and leather jacket, but of course a Flying Officer wouldn't go to a ball dressed as one.

So far the group round the bar included a very large fairy with hairy legs, two gypsies holding violins, a man in a dinner jacket and a wig of shoulder length hair (this was the Pay Officer, who was completely bald), a Pearly King (Geoff), an Arab in full robes, two flappers, a pirate with a real knife which he kept holding between his teeth until he started to dribble and had to wipe his mouth, and a small brown bear on her hind legs whose hand had wriggled out of her paw so it could hold a cigarette.

"Come on, let's go down," said Kathleen, "I think Geoff's going to wilt under the weight of those pearls."

Susan accepted a drink and chatted as more people arrived, looking round for Mark. It was impossible not to join in with the laughter and exclamations that greeted the arrival of an onion seller on his bicycle. This was Sam, who rode round the camp every day, but wearing a forage cap rather than the French beret he had on now. Then a trio of flamenco dancers entered waving their fans and clicking castanets. Airmen and women were pouring in. She saw Winston Churchill and a vicar talking to Spike Milligan and the other Goons.

People started to dance. She watched men leading their partners onto the floor. Where was Mark? Just about everyone else was here. Why was he late tonight, of all nights, especially as it was he who was so keen on the Ball? Blast it. If only he'd come. She took her drink over to the side and stood by herself, keeping her eyes on the door through which she expected him to enter.

After a few moments, Ian and Bridget joined her. Ian said "How do you like my handmaiden?"

Bridget had cut a straight fringe and was wearing very little: a thin, sleeveless top, a short skirt with gold braid sewn into it, and no shoes.

"You look very authentic and Egyptian," said Susan. She was feeling a little hurt that she rarely saw Bridget on her own these days. Did she have to spend all her time with Ian? They used to go out window shopping together, have tea at Lyons Corner Houses. Thinking she ought to say something else, she added "You both look wonderful, and the fringe suits you, Bridget."

Ian said, "I think it does, too." He paused and then said, "Susan – you look lovely – very delicate and floaty. Are you a star?"

"No," she smiled.

"The night, perhaps?" he said, taking off the dark glasses and pushing back his gangster's trilby.

"Nearly."

"I know. You're the Milky Way, aren't you?" said Mark's voice. Susan turned round and looked at the Arab standing next to her in his long cream coloured robes and head-dress.

"You didn't recognise me, did you?" he asked, speaking through his own moustache and a false beard.

Susan was taken aback. It was true. She had not recognised him at all, despite the fact that they had been standing fairly close together for the previous four or five minutes. Had he spoken? Surely she would have recognised his voice? How awful. How embarrassing. She couldn't have looked at him properly. He must have been watching her carefully and she was certain he would have discovered her whatever disguise she had been wearing.

"I'm sorry – no – I didn't. You look so foreign. The beard makes you look quite different."

"Well, I think you're the most beautiful Milky Way," said Mark quietly.

"And you're a handsome Arab," said Susan, keen to make him feel better.

"I'm not just any Arab, you know," he replied. "I'm a particular one, but I bet you can't guess who."

"No, I can't. The only one I know is Aladdin, and you'd have a lamp if you were him."

"I'm the Bedouin of Libya who saved Antoine de Saint Exupéry in the desert, in *Wind, Sand and Stars*."

"Ah, your hero," said Ian. "Susan, has he told you about Saint Exupéry?"

"A little."

"Yes, I have told her, although I haven't read her any of my favourite passages yet. But I shall do."

"Please may I have another drink?" said Susan.

The Bedouin and the Milky Way encouraged the gangster to wave his pistol and make a path through the throng of people round the bar. It was going to be a good evening.

Susan watched Bridget and Ian move onto the floor first, as usual. They were perfect dancing partners and they relished being the centre of attention. Ian was so dashing when he did waltzes and foxtrots, and when he did sambas and tangos he looked positively exotic. She hoped he would invite her to dance later on because he held her properly and could lead her through steps that Mark and other partners stumbled over or didn't know. And Mark had said how, although he had been wary of dancing with Bridget at first because he thought she would find him clumsy, he had found that she followed him like a shadow.

Now Alex was saying, "When – if – those two have children, they'll be more famous as dancers than their parents ever will be as RAF officers!"

Later on in the evening, after an energetic Gay Gordons, just as Susan was wondering when Mark would take her out to see the moon, he reminded her she had said she would go out onto the cliff. She smiled at once.

"I hadn't forgotten. I've been looking forward to it. Let's go now."

Mark led her out of the Great Hall, along the corridor and out of the back door by the kitchen. As the door shut behind them they were cut off from the music and within a few minutes they had completely left behind the noise, animation and light. They stood, still a little out of breath, and allowed their eyes to become accustomed to the darkness. The high-pitched hum of the transmitters was audible because the night was so still.

"Where's the moon you promised me?" asked Susan, "and where are all the stars?"

"Just wait. Look, there's the moon – behind those clouds on the horizon– you can see they are moving," Mark was gesturing out to sea. "And look above you if you want to see stars."

There was a scattering of stars in a cloudless sky. She leant against his side when he put his arm around her shoulder even though it was slightly uncomfortable to walk like that.

As they walked slowly across the lawn and made for the gardens they found they could see more clearly. They pushed through a small gate and entered the sunken garden, past the familiar white statue of a headless woman. Mark paused and pointed at the ground.

"Look, her head's lying at her feet. Someone will fix it back on one day, I expect."

They walked down into the well of the garden with its scent of foxgloves and stock, and across and up to another gateway. Mark pushed the stiff door with his shoulder. Susan waited until he reached behind him for her hand and led her through to a sheltered cavity in the cliff face looking out to the sea, the now almost perfectly full moon and the low pale clouds it had escaped from. It was gorgeous. There was no sound other than the sea rasping the pebbles. Surely he'd kiss her here?

"Look up," said Mark.

The sky above them was now a sea of stars.

"It's a starbow, like a rainbow. But you can never be under a rainbow. It's gorgeous here."

Mark turned, held her and tried to kiss her. She laughed and said, "I can't kiss you with that beard," so he unhooked it from his ears.

"That's better. My gorgeous Milky Way," he said. "Two Milky Ways – one here and one above me. What more can a man want?"

They kissed. It was so good to hold, to be held. Susan relaxed, snuggled up close and still against him. Her head was against his chest. She could feel his rib cage move as he breathed. She could feel his diaphragm shudder when he spoke.

"I wish you'd let me get as close as this to you more often. You coming here has changed my life no end."

"Has it?"

"Things were boring here until you came."

"But everyone likes it here."

"I know, and so do I, up to a point. But it's in the middle of nowhere. Or rather, it's almost in the sea. Look out there. It's just sea, isn't it? Everything's so far away."

He was right, Bawdsey was right off the beaten track, but she didn't mind this at all. In fact, she liked it. It meant fewer distractions from work, but Mark would probably be appalled if she said that now, so she squeezed his hand.

Mark said, "That's the trouble with the Milky Way too. It's so far away."

They looked up at it again and it was even fuller of stars than before.

"Look, there's Orion's belt."

"Where?"

"It's those three stars close together in a line, a diagonal line."

"But there's masses of them. Which three stars?"

"Well, you see that bright one on the left?"

"Which one?"

"Oh, it's too hard to explain. I'll show you another day, another night I mean."

"Anyway," said Susan, "They're thousands, millions of miles away, and we're here."

"Have I ever told you about The Little Prince?"

"No. Who's he?"

"It's a book by St Exupéry. The Little Prince lives on a planet. He's very special. And he's sad. It's a sad book."

"Why are you thinking about it now?"

"Because the Little Prince likes stars. He says everyone has stars, but that stars have different meanings for people."

They did not speak for a moment, then Mark said, "I want you to want me as much as I want you."

Susan turned to him for another kiss. Didn't she want him as much as he wanted her? She did not know.

She said, "I'd like another kiss."

Slowly, they walked back to the building without speaking. The dance music became louder and the lights made them blink.

Ian caught sight of Mark as they re-entered the Ballroom and smiled but then said, "Are you ok? You look a bit washed out. You're not drunk, are you?"

"No. I'm not at all drunk. I'm just thinking." Mark turned towards Susan who was bending her head while a friend tried to repair the star on her head, but it kept leaning over and would not stay attached.

"I can't do it," she was saying, "The safety pin's torn a hole in the cardboard."

"Never mind," said Susan, "It doesn't matter at all now."

*

*When the tide unpeels the mudflats
the smell of the estuary is moist and sweet,
quite different from the smell of the sea.*

*On a mild day it's full of birdcalls,
pink lavender, green reeds. On a calm night
there's the odour of creeks and slime*

*and when the east wind carries the scent
of saltings inland geese spread their wings,
horses snort and sailors turn to the clouds.*

Robert sits on deck smoking a Woodbine as the water laps against the hull. It's dark but the moon, about to emerge from behind a cloud, is starting to lighten the sky and now he can see everything: the boats on the river banks, the ones moored in the Deben, the irregular wooden sheds, the silky river. It seems he's the only person awake.

This evening he's been trying to put the incident of the fire and the fight behind him, and he knows he could really have hurt that lad. He remembered wishing he'd really smashed his face. The only other person he's ever wanted to hurt is his step-father. He used to wish he'd be injured at work so he would be in pain. And then, four years ago, he *had* been injured, and Robert was sure that he had caused this, but it made him feel worse, not better.

Since reading his mother's letter he's been thinking about his family. Tonight he's missing them all – even his stepfather – and especially Lizzie and Sally. He loved taking the girls out in the rowing boat and he had promised to take them fishing. He feels bad that he hasn't kept his promise.

Why is he always worrying about something? There always seems to be worry flooding into every nook and cranny of his mind. It'll retreat but he knows it'll engulf him again. Sometimes it's to do with money, or getting nowhere, or loneliness. Today it's pure, simple guilt about being a source of disappointment to his family. It's all his fault.

He throws the cigarette end overboard. It fizzes as it hits the water.

Why are things so difficult? Has he made things worse by staying in Suffolk? He thought when the family went things would be better, but they're not.

Earlier that evening he ferried a group of quiet and cheerful servicemen across the river. They were from RAF Felixstowe and he found them waiting for him on the beach with unusual shaped cases. He soon found out these contained musical instruments and they were members of a band who were going to play at Bawdsey Manor. It took some time for them to climb on board safely with their trumpet and trombone, two violins and an accordion. They took great care with the huge cello. He was interested in the contrast between the gentle humour displayed by five of them and the noisy outspokenness of the sixth man. He tried to imagine them playing to a room full of people dancing.

He can't imagine himself dancing or even joining in any group which has more than a few men working together, or a family. He has no firm idea about what he wants from other people or indeed from himself but he knows that what he has now, what he is now, is not enough.

Maisie pushes at his leg, whines to be let into the cabin. Robert pees into the river, then opens the door and lets Maisie go in front. He tips his head back and looks straight above him. The Milky Way stretches across with its millions of tiny suns. There's the dog star.

He follows Maisie into the cabin. Enough light is coming in through the windows for him to see his mother's white letter on the table. He undresses, gets between the covers on the bunk. Maisie is asleep first. Robert listens to her regular breathing and the familiar, quivering little sighs that interrupt it.

*

Mark entered the dining room on the morning after the Ball hoping for confirmation of what had seemed to him the previous evening like a shift in Susan's feelings, but she wasn't there. Where was she? She always had breakfast early.

There was Kathleen. She would know. She told him they had come downstairs together and Susan had gone to collect her post before having breakfast. She added, "She was full of energy as usual this morning – no one would know she'd been up half the night. I could hardly get myself out of bed but she was up first thing!"

Mark planned to go to Felixstowe that morning with Philip, a friend who was to leave Bawdsey the following week and who wanted to buy a car. They had arranged to meet a garage owner who had a Morris that Philip wanted to look at.

It was already time for them to leave so he'd have to go without seeing Susan. Pity.

By ten o'clock they were standing in the lukewarm sunshine waiting for the ferry. They crossed the river, took the bus into town and walked to the garage. The car was almost new, a neat little black Morris Minor, and when Philip saw it he was delighted.

"How much is it?" asked Mark.

"£250."

"A lot of money."

"Yes, but I've got it. Well – nearly got it. My father says he can lend me £50, and I'm going to use the £100 my great uncle just left me. And I'm going to need a car, because my next posting's in the middle of nowhere, in Lincolnshire."

"You poor fellow. Bawdsey's bad enough."

"You can take it out for a spin if you want to," said the garage owner.

"Of course! Come on, Mark, I'll drive you to Landguard Fort."

They took off down the road and Philip became ecstatic. "It's smashing! It's a beauty. She's just what I want. Look at all these gadgets – this is for the windscreen wiper, and this must be for the lights – no, it's the indicator! This is going to be £250 well spent."

They roared along at a cracking 30 mph. until Philip had utterly convinced himself the car was made for him. They filled up with Esso Extra before celebrating with a pint of Tollemache. Although he kept standing up to look out of the pub window and check that the Morris Minor was still handsome and still gleamingly his, his exuberation gradually settled down and he asked Mark if he'd enjoyed the ball.

"Very much. Very much indeed."

"What were you? I can't remember."

"I was a happy man. An Arab, actually. A happy Bedouin Arab."

"This is to do with Susan, I presume?"

"Yes. She was the Milky Way. The beautiful, starry Milky Way."

"And you're really in love with her?"

"I think I am."

"And is she in love with you?"

Mark paused. "I don't know. But yesterday was good, and so today I'm feeling good. In fact today I haven't a care in the world."

"It sounds to me as if you care a lot about Susan – but that's a pretty good care to have. Lucky you. Right, we ought to get going. We've got to drive all the way round through Martlesham and Woodbridge. It's miles!"

"Pity the ferry doesn't take cars. It did once, you know."

Philip stopped fiddling with the car key for a moment. "What do you mean? It can't have done. It's far too small."

"Not this ferry – there was a different ferry. A steam ferry. In fact I think there were two, and they carried cars – I've seen a photo of one of them."

"How amazing. I tell you what, why don't we just drive down to the Ferry first? It'll only take us an extra half hour or so."

Mark laughed. "You want to show off, don't you? I know you know the place will be full of people. It always is on a Saturday, especially on a day like this."

Philip got into the car and leant across to unlock the passenger side. As Mark settled himself he said, "How did you guess? Don't forget that I haven't got your charm and charisma. I'm well aware I need artificial assistance to bag a girlfriend."

They set off on the cliff side road, up the hill from where they could see Bawdsey Manor across the estuary, and on across the golf links. Aldis' bus was ahead and Philip resisted his desire to overtake it. Mark remembered Susan's description of when she first came to Bawdsey, and how she had fallen asleep on that very bus. He didn't tell Philip, and he enjoyed that private thought as they followed it. When they arrived at the Ferry they drove straight down on to the edge of the stony beach and pulled up with an impressive crunch to make the maximum impact on anyone who might be looking. They stayed in the car for a minute or two.

"Heads are turning," said Mark with a chuckle, "they haven't seen this car before and they're interested."

It was true. People were looking at them. As soon as they got out two officers ambled over from where they had been sitting outside the pub. Others followed and there was soon a small group standing around Philip and his new car.

"Philip, I'm a brazen hussy," said one of the girls, "If I buy you a drink, will you take me out for a ride?"

Mark and Philip exchanged a glance.

"Of course – but I'm afraid not today. You don't need to buy me a drink but I'm ravenous. Brazen hussy, you haven't got anything to eat, I suppose?"

They ended up walking back away from the beach with a

couple they knew. They toasted the Morris Minor which sat elegantly and blackly beautiful in the sunshine, shared cheese sandwiches and discussed the ball.

Mark soon lost interest in the conversation and was wondering what Susan had been doing that morning. He was eager to be off but could see that Philip was revelling in his treasure from a distance. He stood up, then squatted to find a stone that fitted his hand. He slung it into the sea.

Philip got up. "Ok, Mark. I know it's time to go."

They walked back to the car and turned to wave.

"You're a lucky beggar, Ian," called out one of the men they had been with, "I'd love one of those."

Mark and Philip walked round the car.

"Bugger. The tide's come in. We need to move it fast." Philip got in and started the engine, but couldn't reverse the car because the wheels had sunk into the stones. He got out, flustered.

"We need help."

Mark turned back to the others.

"The tide's come in," he called, "can you come and help us?"

Everyone ran down to the car which they now saw was only four or five feet away from the water.

Philip said, "When I ran the engine it settled deeper into the shingle. We'll have to push it higher up the beach."

He took the hand brake off and the three men tried to push it backwards, but it only budged six or nine inches at a time. They realised they would only be able to shift it if the car was simultaneously pulled from the back.

As the tide edged nearer Philip became increasingly anxious. He looked round for help. Other RAF men and women were within sight and he was about to shout and beckon them when a man came walking along the beach with his dog.

He's carrying some wood and a sack and they see him stop and look at the scene by the car. He immediately understands what's happening and comes over to them.

He dumps his plank and the sack before walking right round the car. His dog runs about splashing in the shallow water. The others, out of breath from pushing, are looking at him hopefully and in silence.

59

"Right," says the man, picking up the plank. "Put this under your front wheels to stop it sinking further. I'll loop this round your back axle. Out of the way, Maisie." He pulls a rope from his bag, lies on the stones on his back and wriggles under the car to fix the rope round the axle.

He passes one end of it to one of the men, comes out from underneath and picks up the other end himself. He tells the rest of them to push on the bonnet and sides of the car and says he's going to count to three and that when he says three they should shift the car.

And on three they move it out of the depressions it has settled into, up onto stones that don't sink so much and across them with increasing ease and so up the beach to a safer, harder surface. A cheer goes up, there's a round of applause and the brown and white dog starts to bark.

Philip relaxes and holds out his hand to Robert. "Thank you very much indeed. That was a close thing."

Robert shakes hands and then walks back with Maisie to collect his plank which is almost afloat. He comes back up the beach to pick his sack up and leave, but Philip stops him.

"Look, I'd like to thank you properly. I dread to think what would have happened if you hadn't come along. Let me buy you a drink."

Robert hesitates, "No," he says. "It was just lucky I was here and had what you wanted. Thanks though." He turns and walks back past the knot of spectators, past the Morris Minor and onto the road. Maisie runs in front.

*

By the time Mark and Philip got back to Bawdsey by the long route it was six o'clock. Philip was taking no risks and drove slowly and carefully. They were held up by horses and carts and stopped only once to buy some apples. They would be just in time for dinner if they hurried.

Susan, Susan. As Mark bathed and dressed he could hardly wait to see her. She'd been in and out of his thoughts all day. He went to the dining room willing her to be prompt as usual. He wanted to sit with her and was hoping she would be as soft and gentle as she had been at the ball.

But she was not there. This was a surprise. Surely it wasn't that she had somehow regretted the previous evening and was intentionally keeping her distance? Let it not be that. As he stood there looking around and checking that she was not coming in from the far door, Bridget came up to him.

"She's not here, Mark. She's gone home."

"Gone home?"

"Yes, she had a phone call this morning from her aunt saying her father had collapsed and was going into hospital for a couple of days, and then there was a telegram to say that while he was in hospital he had a stroke."

Mark stood still. "So it's serious, then?"

"Yes. Serious enough for the CO to allow her compassionate leave. It sounds as if he had one small stroke at home and then another in hospital."

"How is she? How did she take it?"

"Well, she was very upset by the letter and I found her after breakfast just sitting on her bed and crying. But when the telegram came she just whirred into action: she went to see the CO, packed, and left. She was better once she had decided to go."

Mark wondered if Bridget was going to give him a message from her. If she was going to do so, surely she would do so now. But she was already saying, "Come on, we'll miss the soup if we don't sit down. There's room over there by Philip and I want to hear about this Morris Minor."

Mark's appetite disappeared as he took his place at the table. Philip was now capitalising on the day's adventures and had everyone around him laughing as he embroidered the tale.

"The water was lapping the tyres and I was terrified of the damage the salt would do."

"You didn't think of trying King Canute's idea, did you?"

"No. I know the tide will stop at nothing and that nothing will stop the tide. Or is that the same thing?"

"Go on. What did you do?"

"Well, it was amazing. A man appeared out of the blue with

just what we needed: a plank and a length of rope! A sort of guardian angel disguised as a fisherman."

"Who was he?"

"I don't know. I've seen him somewhere around – he must work in the boatyard, I think. And he had this little dog, some sort of a spaniel, which followed his every move."

"Did you buy him a drink?"

"No. I offered him one and he refused it. That surprised me. Actually, he looked as if he could do with a square meal or two. He was an unusual man, I'd say. Wouldn't you agree, Mark?"

Mark looked up from his plate. What was he was supposed to be agreeing with?

"The man on the beach, the fisherman. Didn't you think he was unusual?"

"Well, only in that he didn't accept a drink. And that he knew what to do and had the things he needed to do it, and we didn't. I suppose that makes him unusual, doesn't it? Or perhaps," he said rather sharply, "it just makes us useless."

The conversation moved on and Mark excused himself as soon as the main course had been served.

He went into the lounge and settled deep into an easy chair for a cigarette, relieved to be on his own. He would ask the CO how long Susan expected to be away. And he'd ask Bridget for her address. Or perhaps he should phone her? But where would she be? With her aunt or at her own home?

He suddenly felt fed up. He acknowledged to himself how much he had read into the way she had been the previous evening, how much he was looking forward to seeing her, how long the day had been and yes, how much she mattered to him.

Bloody hell. What on earth was he going to do with himself until she came back?

Other people came into the lounge but settled down at the far end. Ian came over to him.

"I'm going to have coffee. Can I get a cup for you? And how about a whisky?"

Mark accepted. Within a few minutes Ian came back with a tray and sat down opposite him. He poured out two cups of coffee, lit up a cigarette for himself and leant across to light one for Mark. They sat without speaking as their smoke rose slowly, lifting and replacing their cups and tumblers as they drank. The chinks made by the china and glass were gradually overridden by the noise of conversation increasing around them.

Ten minutes passed. Things fell into a better perspective. There would just be a delay, that was all. However impatient he was, nothing could move on for a while. He would just have to wait. He'd find things to do to keep himself busy. He would be ok.

*

Susan woke up in her aunt's spare bedroom with its dark, heavy furniture. When she drew back the thick curtains she had to lift up the lace ones underneath before she could see out properly to the grey street with its grey buildings. New houses were being built opposite. It had been raining and children were walking and cycling past to the school just round the corner. Some held their mother's or a friend's hand. A group of boys were daring each other to jump across a big puddle, while two others squatted to dam up the gutter with twigs.

As a child her walk to school had been past the church, past Mr Ellis's dairy with its rows of milkchurns and in through the gates of Breandown. She and her friends had worn grey skirts, white blouses, long grey socks and grey cardigans.

Within seconds yesterday's events came back to her. The phone call from Aunt Rose had made her want to curl up and block her ears. Daddy. Daddy couldn't be anything but healthy, strong, dependable and there. But then the telegram arrived. That had been like an electric shock. By the time she had seen the CO she had worked out exactly what she was going to do. She then telephoned Rose, packed, got on the ferry, caught the train, took a cab across London and got on another train. It felt better to get on with things and push away – at least for the time being – what had happened and what might happen.

It was not until the very last leg of the journey that she relaxed. She had been close to tears as she stood in the train corridor and impatient to get off. After slamming the door behind her she saw Aunt Rose looking up and down the platform for her. She dropped her cases where they were and ran up to hug her as hard as she had done when she was a child, and sobbed.

Then they had gone home. As she drove Rose told her there had been no change in her father that day. He was conscious but unable to move his right side. He had tried to speak but his speech was slurred. His right eye could only open partially.

"But will he get better? What will happen?"

"They don't know yet. Most people who have strokes make some sort of recovery, but I'm afraid some don't. We don't know how Henry will be, but he's being looked after and he can eat and drink a bit, and when we see him tomorrow he'll be thrilled to see you. I told him you were coming and he was so pleased."

Aunt Rose always made her feel better. And she was glad that after some supper and a bath, the tabby cat managed – against the rules of the house – to sneak in through her half open door and nestle down under the eiderdown. She'd forgotten how this used to happen when she was a child. She had grown up with dogs, which she loved, but one of the best things about staying with Rose was the secret, forbidden warmth of a purring cat snuggled up close.

Just before she fell asleep she thought back to the ball and to Mark. Today, after being awake for fourteen or fifteen hours – much of it spent sitting on trains with nothing to do – she had drifted in and out of thoughts about Daddy, her work and Mark. But this time last night she had lain awake, excited by their evening, by the fact that they were becoming increasingly attracted to each other. And today at Paddington Station she had seen a man at the ticket office who looked like Mark until he turned round. She was surprised to find how disappointed she had felt.

*

Visiting hours at the hospital were from two to four. Rose had planned the morning carefully so it was filled with activity and there would be no opportunity for Susan to sit around and fret. When she heard her getting up at half past seven she took up a tray of tea, insisted she went back to bed for at least ten minutes and sat and chatted with her.

"I'd like you to come to the nursery with me this morning. I need to ask about grass seed and turf and McAusland's are the best people. But first I'd like you to pop out to the shops – you can take my bike – and get me a few things. I've done you a list. Then we'll take the car to McAusland's. I want to take out the small shrubs in the flowerbed in the front and move them to the side bed, and put the front bed down to lawn. I find it difficult to dig and weed much now, and I'm going to pay the Dobson boy half a crown to cut the grass each week and rake up the leaves in autumn."

Susan had always thought of Rose as having limitless energy. Now, hearing this, she realised that she too was getting older, just as Daddy was. One of them could die. One of them – both of them – *would* die. This was terrible. She put her cup and saucer down on the bedside table as she started to sniff. Aunt Rose put her arms around her and hugged her. They sat holding each other until Susan said she needed a hankie and Rose took the one from her cardigan sleeve and handed it to her. Susan blew her nose noisily on the small flowery hankie and immediately smelled the unique, familiar scent.

She looked up and said, "I don't want either of you to die. Not you or Daddy."

Aunt Rose rocked her. "Come on, Susan love."

They stayed like that for a little longer, until Susan was over it for the time being. It would happen again. But it would be better to get up now. Then she would have to just get on with those practical, basic things.

"Come on, why don't you get dressed now? Let's start the day."

Within an hour Susan was off on the bike with her purse and her aunt's ration book. She went to the grocer's and watched the assistant measuring out sultanas into a brown paper bag. Next she leant the bike against the greengrocer's and chose a cabbage, then she went on to the baker's for a loaf of brown bread. It was strange to stand in a queue again. As a Flying Officer she never had to queue, but here she was, holding a shopping bag along with everyone else. These housewives didn't know she was an officer, or even that she was in the RAF or had a serious career ahead of her. She rode home with her bike basket almost full, happy to be amongst people for whom the RAF must be almost irrelevant – at least in peacetime. Station life was now the norm, and to go shopping like this was rare.

By twelve she and Rose were on the way to the nursery. Mr McAusland told them about the relative costs of grass seed and turf, and they ended up deciding on grass seed.

"You'll have to put in sticks and thread to keep the birds off, but if you sow it soon you'll be fine."

On the way back Rose said, "I'll be sorry to lose the colour from the flowers, but perhaps I could put a bird bath there too, or at least a bird table. That would mean it wasn't so empty. I'm sure the Dobson boy will be glad of some pocket money during his Easter holiday."

The morning had been all right once they were over the first bit: they had satisfactorily got through what needed to be done, and things felt steadier. But Susan was quiet as they drove to the hospital. What would Daddy look like? What would it be like to see him? As they walked along the corridors she held a bunch of daffodils like a yellow talisman. Her heart was beating hard when they walked into his ward but a nurse told them he had been moved and led them through to another one. Susan suddenly found herself at the end of a bed in which her father was snoozing, his mouth slightly open, his skin redder than usual, his hair thinner than she remembered.

Rose drew up a chair and beckoned Susan to sit down in it. She did so, and as she reached out to take her father's hand he woke up. He gave her a warm, lop-sided smile.

"Oh Daddy," said Susan, leaning over to kiss him. "Daddy, Daddy." She stayed bent over his chest, her face wet against his unshaven cheek. Rose gently took the daffodils from her.

"Come on, my Suey. I'll be all ry." He stroked Susan's hair. She wasn't expecting him to sound like that. She'd imagined he might sound like someone who was drunk, but it was different. He was unable to say "Sukie", the name he had used for her since she was a child. She waited for him to speak again.

"I use to stro your mother's hair, you know," he said. He ran his words together and failed to enunciate the final consonants, something he had urged Susan to do throughout her life. "But she was much fairer than you. An her hair was really wavy. You tay after my sy. Come on, Suey, you'll have to move, you're leaning on my bad sy."

Susan sat up. This was strange; he rarely talked about her mother.

"Daddy, have you got a hankie?"

"There's one in tha drawer. Rose is marvellous, she wen home and collec up the things I nee. But of course I won be here for long. I'll be home soo."

"Will you? When? How long will you have to stay?" asked Susan, wiping her runny nose.

"Oh, ten days at mose."

"Henry," said Rose gently, "You can't say that. It all depends on how you recover and what the doctors say. We're not going to take any risks."

"Come on, Sue, tell me your news. I wan to hear abou wha you've been doing. Have you le them know tha you wan promotion? You'll have to ma it clear to them or they'll le things drif."

He shut his eyes for a moment and then asked, "What abou tha man who's in love with you? Has he propose to you ye? "

"Susan, you didn't tell me this!" said Rose, "Who is he?"

Susan said nothing. At that moment Mark, Bawdsey and the RAF seemed to belong to another world.

"Oh it's nothing," she said. "It's just someone I've met who likes me a lot. Daddy, what matters now is you." She squeezed his hand hard.

A nurse brought round a trolley with a pot of tea, cups and saucers and the daffodils in a glass vase.

"Wing Commander Cairncross, here are your flowers. Aren't they lovely? I love daffodils. Would you like a cup of tea? Would your visitors like one too?"

She poured out three cups and Rose placed them on the bedside locker. Susan passed one to her father.

"No, Sue, not ye. It's too ho."

She put it down again and picked up her own.

After a minute or two Rose said, "You'll have to hold the saucer for him, Susan. He hasn't enough strength in his hand to hold it and lift the cup."

Susan moved her chair so that she was directly facing her father, held the tea in front of him and waited while he slowly lifted the cup up, sipped and put it down on the saucer again. She lowered the cup and saucer and rested it on the bedclothes, holding it so it did not tip. He slurped and she remembered how he always criticised people who slurped their tea.

He indicated when he was ready for another sip and she lifted the saucer so he could reach the cup easily.

She removed the teacup and leaned back, looking around her for the first time. One patient had one visitor, the two others were alone.

"I'm going to stretch my legs," said Rose, picking up her gloves. " I'm going into the garden for ten minutes to let you have some time together and see if I can get some more ideas for my new garden."

Susan looked at her father, now lying quietly again with his eyes shut. She was used to him being excited about some opinion or project. She remembered clearly his views about Dunkirk. Up to that point she had never heard him swear, but he was on leave when the news was broadcast and she recalled him shouting out "It's bloody marvellous! It's magnificent! Great Scott – this really is Britannia ruling the waves! Bloody hell, it's a miracle. Susan – you must never forget this day." And she hadn't. Neither Dunkirk nor his swearing.

He opened his eyes. "Sorry, darling. I'm very tire."

"It doesn't matter. It's ok."

Susan sat in silence, holding his good hand.

Rose came back in. She had met one of the gardeners who

had snipped off two cuttings for her, so she was delighted, but Susan watched her approach the bed quietly when she saw her brother was lying back.

Susan said, "I think he's dropping off. Should we go now so he can sleep, do you think?"

Her aunt nodded. "An hour's visit is quite long enough." She leaned over to kiss her brother goodbye. "Henry, we'll be back tomorrow. Susan and I are going now."

Susan squeezed his hand, got up and kissed his cheek. "Goodbye. Have a good sleep."

He opened his eyes and raised his hand a few inches. Another visitor was leaving too and they followed her out. She turned at the door and blew a kiss to her husband who waved back. Susan looked at her father again but his eyes were shut, his balding head lying back on the pillow. He looked old.

*

Robert is walking home after a shift on the ferry. It's a fine day and the last fishing boats are coming back in. They've been having good catches recently. He watches two men rowing back from their boat that's now at anchor. Their dinghy is sitting low in the water because of the weight of the fish. Looking further out he can see the wicker pots on *Isabelle*, and her skipper sitting on deck. Robert knows he's tying up the slowly waving claws of his lobsters.

He walks on past where another dinghy is being unloaded. A man calls out to him, "Hey, you! Robert! Come here a minute."

It's Wilf, one of the men who works in and around the boat-yard. Robert goes over to him.

"Do you want a fish?"

Robert stops. He's pleased but he's not smiling.

"Choose a decent sized one then, we've had a good morning."

"Thanks." Robert picks out a cod and lifts it up by sticking his fingers into its gills. It's heavy. "You've been lucky then."

"Yes. We have. We're doing well just now. Now, tell me, I need someone to crew. Could you crew for me?"

"As long they don't need me on the ferry."

"Well, I need someone for Friday and Saturday. Pete's going to be away. When can you let me know?"

"Later on today."

Wilf nods and turns back to his work. Then he looks up again. "Don't you want to know what I'll pay you?"

Robert blushes slightly. He doesn't know Wilf well. He bends down to stroke Maisie.

"It depends on how we do, but you can count on a share of the catch."

Robert nods.

Maisie senses they're on the move again and runs off sniffing every post. Robert follows, pleased with being asked to crew, with the promise of other fish and with this shining fish he's carrying that he's already decided to cook at once.

Once on *Music Maker* the first job is to light the fire. It's already laid and all he has to do is to squat down and light it. He waits for a moment to make sure it's catching. He then tips water out of his can into a jug. He places a wooden board slant-wise over the sink and puts the fish on it, its head to the left, its tail to the right. It almost reaches from end to end – a real prize. He moves the board a little to one side, picks up the jug of water with his clean hand and pours it over the one that's sticky from carrying the fish. After wiping his hand on a cloth he pulls his knife from the sheath on his belt and moves the board back until it's sitting steady again. He turns the fish over so it's under-side up, pierces the skin of its throat with the broken tip, pushes it in and draws it along the length of its belly. The red guts fall out loosely, and he pulls the last few sinews away with a couple of scrapes, pushes them to the edge of the board.

Maisie is under his feet and when he nudges her away with a soft push of his knee she retires to her scorch-marked rug in front of the fire which is burning well. He reaches into the cupboard for a plate and prepares to fillet the fish. He lays his hand flat on its body and presses on it, inserts the knife and draws it steadily along the length of its backbone. As he lifts off each fillet in turn and lays it on the plate, he thinks about how he is removing the flesh of this big cod so only its head, bones

70

and tail are left. He picks up the head and its backbone still holds it together. Then he carries the board outside and scrapes and chucks the bones and the guts overboard.

Back in the cabin he rinses his hands and reaches into a string bag for two onions. He cuts the ends off them and peels and slices them. His eyes are watering. He looks away, wipes his cuff across them and waits for a few moments. He can hear gulls close by, diving and squawking over the fish bits.

He takes one of his two pans and half fills it with water while he prepares some potatoes. They're old with soft flesh and wrinkled skins out of which white shoots are appearing, but they'll do. He's whistling away as he does this. He puts them in the saucepan, adds a little salt and waits for them to come to the boil. Once they're bubbling quietly he opens the small cupboard above his head and takes out a bowl containing the remains of yesterday's meal – a little minced meat in congealed, pale gravy, and a few cooked carrots. He tips it into the dog's bowl.

"Maisie, you're in luck."

Maisie wolfs it down in seconds and goes back to her rug. But as soon as Robert settles down on the bunk to read the newspaper he found yesterday on a bench outside The Vic she jumps up, nosing into his chest and snuggling against him.

He pushes her away gently. "No. Not now. Down."

The cabin is filling up with warm steam that increases his appetite. It's time to fry the onions, and then the fish. He will soon be eating a decent meal. And someone has promised him work. He relents and allows Maisie onto the bunk beside him.

*

Rose and Susan stayed up late listening to a programme on the Home Service about Princess Elizabeth. There seemed to be more about her every day.

"Did I ever tell you I met her once? It was at the opening of a sports hall and stadium – it was hoped that Britain's young men and women would train there and be better Olympic athletes."

"Why were you there?"

"It was when I was journalist. I was reporting on it for the Evening News, and the Princess walked right past me. My photographer got an excellent picture of her."

"Did you actually meet her?"

"Well no, I wasn't introduced to her, but I count it as meeting her. After all, I had to have something to show off to Henry about. He was always meeting important people then."

And he still is, Susan thought. At least he was only a week or two ago, even though he's retired. He's on so many committees and boards and commissions. But what would happen now?

"I'm going to bed now, Aunt Rose. Do you mind?"

"Of course not, dear. I'm coming too."

They tidied up the teacups, turned out the downstairs lights and locked the front and back doors.

"You use the bathroom first, Susan, and I'll see to the landing light when I've finished. Goodnight."

Susan expected to fall asleep at once but she didn't, so she got out of bed trying not to disturb the cat and went over to the bookshelf. She'd often done this before. Where was it? Good. She pulled out a green book: *The Secret Garden*. Rose had read this to her after her mother had died. And now it was Daddy who might die.

She took the book back to bed with her. When she opened it she found the piece of tissue paper covering the frontispiece. The words *It was the knob of a door* were printed on it in red. She turned this over carefully to see the colour plate underneath. It was of Mary, the girl in the story. She had one hand on the door knob of the secret garden and one holding back branches. She was wearing a pinkish dress and her hair was tied back with a ribbon. It was the picture she liked best in the book.

She began to read odd pages. She found herself remembering Dickon and Colin, and Ben Wetherstaff. She went on reading for another hour.

She was woken by Rose coming into her room carrying a tray of tea and drawing the curtains.

"Good morning, my dear," she said, "It's a beautiful day for

72

gardening. I'm determined to mark out where my new lawn is going. You can help me."

Susan thought back to the secret garden she had been reading about, and she held up the book.

"I'd love to. Look what I've been reading."

Rose smiled, "Your old favourite." She put a cup of tea on the bedside table. "There's a letter for you. Who knows you're here?"

"Only the CO at Bawdsey. I had to tell him." But why would he write? Susan was worried and took the letter and opened it at once.

"Oh, goodness. It's from Mark."

"Ah. Then I'll leave you to read it on your own."

"No, don't go. Stay here. I'll read it later." Susan refolded the single sheet of white paper and replaced it in the envelope. Even the first line had brought Mark rushing back. She suddenly had a strong image of him throwing his head back and laughing.

Rose stood up and took her tea to the window.

"I want to curve the edge of the new lawn. What's the best way to do that?"

Good. Susan didn't want any questions about Mark yet. She said, "We could we put some sticks in the ground and wind string round them. Then the man will see where you want the grass seed to go."

"Yes. But I think he's used to straight lines. I'll have to keep an eye on him. I'm going to get breakfast now. It'll be ready in ten minutes. Pass me that cup, dear."

When Rose went Susan had to decide whether to wash and dress before reading the letter, thus delaying the treat, or whether to read it first. She resolved to wash and dress first. She got out of bed, stood the bright, white envelope against the dressing table mirror and went to the bathroom. As soon as she came back, still in her dressing gown, she picked the letter up and sat down on the bed to read it.

April 4th 1952
RAF Bawdsey

My Dearest Susan,
I'm sorry I didn't see you on Sunday and I know perhaps I shouldn't be writing at all because I don't know what's happening. All I know is what Bridget and the CO told me – that your father is seriously ill. I'm so sorry about this and just wish I could do something. It feels so flat without you here.

So, the best thing I thought I could do is to write and tell you nice things. The Ball was wonderful – you were wonderful – and I want to go to more balls, do more things with you. You looked gorgeous and I'm enclosing an extract from my favourite writer, Antoine de Saint Exupéry, because he is mad about flying and the sky and stars and because I am mad about all of them and you. You could not have chosen a fancy dress that I'd like more than the Milky Way!

We had a hilarious time on Sunday. I went to Felixstowe with Ian to get his new car. He is quite in love with it, but he wanted to show it off at Felixstowe Ferry so he drove it onto the beach and it nearly got caught by the tide!

I don't know when you will be back but I'm longing to see you. It's so boring without you. Do you know you have the most beautiful green eyes? I don't think the CO is expecting you back for a few days, but how can I wait that long?

This isn't a long letter because I want to catch the post, but here's the bit from St Ex. It's about when he sets off flying across the desert at night.

I know nothing, absolutely nothing, to rival this time of day. Those who have experienced the inexpressible love of flying will understand me fully. Little by little, then, I am giving up the sunlight. I give up the broad golden surfaces that would have welcomed me if my engines had failed. I give up the landmarks that would have guided me. I give up the outlines of the mountains against the sky that would have warned me of dangers ahead. I am entering the night. Sailing. Nothing left to me now but the stars.

The death of the world takes place slowly. Little by little, I am abandoned by light. The sky and earth merge gradually. The earth rises and seems to spread like a mist. The first stars tremble as if shimmering in

*green water. It will be a long time before they harden into diamonds.
And still longer before I can witness the silent games of the shooting
stars. Deep in the heart of some nights, I have seen so many racing
sparks that it seemed as if a great wind was blowing amongst the stars.*

There. Isn't it marvellous? Do you like it? I do hope so.

*I can't wait to hear from you but I'm not expecting to. I'm sending you
all my love
– for whatever's happening. Mark.*

Mark's neat handwriting filled both sides of the paper exactly,
forcing him to squeeze his name in at the end of the line.

Susan looked at herself in the mirror. No one had ever
written a letter to her like that before. It was a love letter.

She leaned forward to inspect her green eyes.

*

It's Friday and Robert has to be up at four o'clock. He wakes in
plenty of time, makes himself some porridge and puts on plenty
of clothes. He feeds Maisie some scraps, lets her outside to sniff
along the bank for a few minutes, then calls her back in. She
comes bounding back on deck, slithering on muddy feet and
hitting her wet tail against his legs. He makes sure there's water
for her and then strokes her goodbye, regretting he can't take
her with him. He takes his oilskin down from the peg, puts it on
and picks up his knapsack. He puts a bag of bread and cheese in
it and goes out, leaning his shoulder against the door to shut it
firmly. It's pitch black outside. As he crosses the plank he hears a
soft, complaining whine. There's nothing he can do.

He walks along to the shipyard just as Wilf approaches from
the other direction.

"Good. We're nice and early. First, let's load this lot into the
dinghy." Wilf indicates a pile of boxes, netting, a knapsack, a
pair of oars.

Between them they collect everything up and crunch down
to the black water across the stones. They put everything on
board and tug the boat into the water. Wilf climbs in when it's

afloat, and Robert leans against it to push it free of the beach, jumping in over the transom and just avoiding getting his boots full of water. Wilf rows them out into the Deben in silence, feeling his way between the boats as light appears. Robert realises that although he's often on the river this early, there's always the noise of the ferry's engine. Now all he can hear are Wilf's oars – dipping, pulling, lifting, dripping. Each time the oars rise it's as if Wilf lifts some of the darkness off the water. Dip, pull, lift, drip. As Robert relaxes into the rhythm, he sees other oars rising and falling in other dinghies. He's pleased to be among the men setting out for their fishing boats.

When they reach the *Tom and Mary* Wilf reaches out for the anchor rope and pulls the dinghy close against the hull so Robert can climb on board and tie up. Wilf passes up what they've brought, item by item, and then he too climbs up on to the deck of the fishing boat. Then he unties the dinghy from the *Tom and Mary* and secures it to the anchor rope. The sky is becoming lighter by the minute.

Robert stows the boxes under the benches, puts his knapsack into the wheelhouse.

Within ten minutes Wilf has cast off and the boat noses steadily out to the sea on the full tide in the company of five other boats. Robert is proud to be part of this tiny flotilla heading out from the estuary to the east and into broad daylight.

*

Mark made up his mind to ask the CO when Susan would be returning. The CO was a warm, approachable man who knew everyone on the station and when Mark saw him walking up the drive it seemed easy and the obvious thing to ask him about her.

"Sir, have you got a moment please?"

"Certainly." The CO stood still.

"Sir, do you know when Flying Officer Cairncross will be back?"

The CO looked at Mark. "Is this a purely professional enquiry, I wonder?"

Mark felt himself blush. He smiled, and so did the CO.

"I'm expecting her to phone today or tomorrow. I can't tell you more than that, I'm afraid. But I'll let you know when I hear."

"Thank you, sir."

Mark saluted and walked back towards the main building.

"Oh, Rivens."

Mark turned back to face the CO.

"Do you want to get in touch with her? I've got her address – I'm sure she'd be happy for me to pass it on. Or you could phone her."

"Thank you, sir, but I've written already."

"Ah, have you? That's all right, then." He paused.

"I say, Rivens."

"Sir?"

"You won't let this get in the way of your work, will you? Easy to let things go or get out of hand a bit, you know."

"No, sir, of course not." Was he talking about relationships in general or Susan in particular?

"Good. You're doing very well, you know, and so is that young lady. I'm very pleased. You'd be sorry to see her leave here, I'm sure. Still, we'll wait and see."

See her leave? See what? Mark was confused. Susan had only been here a few months. What did the CO mean?

The CO smiled again and Mark realised he had given away more to the CO than he intended. Still, what did it matter? Bawdsey was a station where it was impossible to keep a secret, and anyway his interest in Susan wasn't a secret and he didn't mind the CO knowing. But what had he meant about Susan leaving? Did he mean she might stay away for a long time because her father was ill? She had already been away for three days and that felt bad enough.

*

The doctor led Susan and her aunt into his office and invited them to sit down.

"Well," he said, "I know you want me to tell you that Wing

Commander Cairncross will recover his health completely and be as he was before his strokes. Unfortunately, I can't guarantee you that. A stroke is, in effect, an injury to the brain, and it has an impact on some of the body's functions, particularly speech and the muscles that govern mobility. Usually, with time and some help through exercises, these do begin to function again – but probably not as well as they did. Your father, Miss Cairncross, has unfortunately had two strokes. Two injuries to the brain. He will need a period of convalescence and although I can give him medicine it is possible he might have a further stroke. I'm sorry to have to tell you that if he does, it could be even more serious."

Susan was taking in what he was saying as clearly as if she was being briefed by a senior officer and she was thinking simultaneously of her father's nearly immobile arm and – suddenly – of Mark's damaged arm. He had shown it to her once. He had rolled up his sleeve after a game of billiards and she had seen the uneven scar curving over his bicep. He had said, "This used to be good muscle, but not any more." Susan remembered him adding, "I thought my life was wrecked at first, but it healed well and it doesn't stop me working or even winning at billiards. It might have been far worse."

Her eyes rested on a bent and dying blue hyacinth. Its scent filled the doctor's office as Rose asked, "How long must he stay in hospital, or will he go somewhere else to convalesce?"

"Could he go home? Perhaps he could live with you for a while?"

"Well, it depends, I'm not really sure." Rose spoke slowly.

"That would be a good idea," said Susan, "You could look after him. He'd be much better off with you."

Rose did not respond and the doctor said, "We don't need to make a decision yet. I want to keep him here for another week. Have a think about it."

On the drive home they talked about how her father could live temporarily with Rose.

"He could have my bedroom, couldn't he? It's right next to the bathroom."

"Yes, he could," said Rose. "But I need to think about this

carefully. Susan, I'm sixty six. Sometimes I find just going up and down stairs several times a day is quite enough, especially if I'm to be cooking and carrying meals and doing extra washing. Henry might not be able to dress himself, and what about when he needs to go to the lavatory?"

"You'd much rather he was there than in a convalescent home, wouldn't you? I'd hate to think of him in a place he didn't know with people he didn't know. That would be awful."

"Well, of course I would rather he was with me. But it's not that easy. Being a nurse can be difficult, and I want him to be well nursed."

"I can't think of a better person to nurse him than you," said Susan, her voice warm and indignant. "Do you remember when I had chicken pox? We did that huge jigsaw of Windsor Castle together."

That evening Susan peeled the potatoes and cut up the cabbage – something she never did at Bawdsey and had not done since the last time she was at home.

After the meal and the washing up they watched Marguerite Patten's cookery programme on Rose's new television. Susan sat in her favourite position on the little red velvet footstool which, when she was twelve years old, she had asked her aunt to leave her in her will. Then there was a programme about world population and one of the scientists being interviewed said that within a decade women would be able to take pills that stopped them becoming pregnant.

"How extraordinary," said Rose, "If that ever happens it could change so much. Imagine someone being able to choose how many children to have!"

"Or when to have them. Do you remember in the church-yard at St Agnes, where there's that row of little headstones? It must have been awful to have babies, and for some of them not to survive, and then to go on having more whether you wanted them or not." Susan reached out to stroke the cat. "When I have children, I think I'd like just two."

Watching television pulled her back into the rest of the world – the world where she belonged and which she was keen to get back to now that they were talking about Daddy coming home.

Later on she turned to Rose to ask if she would like a cup of cocoa, but she was asleep in her chair with the tabby cat curled on her lap, its eyes half closed.

Susan got up quietly, boiled the kettle and made two hot water bottles. She would phone the CO tomorrow. She'd be back in Bawdsey on Saturday and ready to work on Sunday. That would give her two more days here. That should be enough. Daddy would soon be home here with Aunt Rose. She'd look after him and he'd be fine. They'd both be fine. He never gave in. He was amazing, he never ever gave in. And he'd be keen for her to go back to Bawsdey, get cracking with making a difference and perhaps doing more training courses.

She went upstairs to put the bottles in the beds and draw the curtains, then came down again and woke Rose gently. She took the cat from her and urged her up the stairs.

"Come on, Aunt Rose. It's bedtime."

They hugged at the top of the stairs and said goodnight.

Susan sat up in bed and read Mark's letter again in the light from the small bedside lamp whose shade was edged with little cream tassels. She didn't remember that once she had played with those tassels when listening to how the robin had led Mary into the secret garden.

She would write to Mark the next day. She wondered what to say in her letter. And how would she end it?

*

The low shingle bar guards the estuary.

Currents constantly rearrange
the round, rusty stones, piling
some up in the lee of a slope, pulling
others out into a shell shaped fan.

From the shore the bar looks like
a swollen scythe until the high tide
shrinks it to two level hillocks
surrounded by sea. They lie in wait.

80

Robert doesn't often go out fishing. His river journeys are usually confined to his usual back and forth run, and to ferrying men to and from their boats anchored midstream. He's not often far from the jetty or the landing stage. So when he returns with Wilf it's a rare pleasure for him to approach and enter the Deben from the North Sea. As the *Tom and Mary* sails carefully across the bar he knows that beneath them fresh and salt water are mixing in an infinite variety of ratios and densities because of the tides, the rain and the wind. He imagines water in strands which weave and split and rejoin and separate like some huge splice until it's completely impossible to distinguish what's river, what's sea. It's all just water, but it's clearly sea out there behind them and river up there ahead of them.

On their left the Martello towers are squat and solid – unlikely estuary guardians that he's been told have never been put to the test because the guns which once stood on their battlements were never aimed at the French fighting ships they were built to resist. On the right of the estuary stand the four thin, steel radar masts and, at right angles to them, the wooden ones which are older but still hold their ground, still hold their own with the steel ones. He has heard passengers say that these masts helped to win the Battle of Britain but, although he knows that radar can perceive enemy planes as they approach, he doesn't know how it works. He knows bats can avoid things they can't see because of their in-built radar system, but this does not help him understand how the masts work.

Today Bawdsey Manor looks like a castle with its green turret and its towers. He can't see anyone on its lawns. On the other side of the river, between the Ferry's low buildings, he recognises individual huts and there's Aldis' bus driving off across the golf course. The flat Deben stretches ahead, narrowing as it reaches the curve in the distance. Wilf slows down as they approach the moorings and Robert looks down into the water. It's quite clear today. He can see about a fathom of the mooring rope disappearing towards the bottom, its line bent by refraction. Sometimes the river is so full of sand that if he scoops up a balerful he can hardly see through it.

Back on shore, they unload the fish, weigh it and carry it up to a truck. It's a decent sized catch. Wilf hands him two half crowns and a couple of good sized sole.

"Thanks. You did well. I might need you again so stop in at mine sometimes. I always tell them in the pub if I'm short of a deckhand. But I've never seen you in the pub, have I?"

Robert shakes his head as he puts the coins in his pocket. He didn't expect these two half crowns.

"Then you should go, lad. That's where the young ones go. You look as if you could do with a bit of company."

Robert does not know what to reply, so he picks up his knapsack and the fish and sets off for *Music Maker*.

Wilf calls after him, "If you come to the Vic on Friday, I'll buy you a drink."

Robert hesitates before he calls back, "Yes. Ok," and sets off home. It feels very good to have fish in one hand and cash in the other.

Maisie is scratching at the cabin door even when he's still on the gangplank, and she's nearly squashed when Robert tugs hard at the door until it springs free from its damp frame. She fusses round him while he makes a cup of tea and spreads the last of the marmalade Mrs Corby gave him on a slice of bread. Then he unwraps a bone from a piece of newspaper and holds it out to Maisie.

He takes the tea and bread on deck and puts down a sack to sit on. Maisie follows him with the bone. He sits back and leans against the wheelhouse, listening to the soft slurps made by small waves and smelling the marshes as the tide backs off them. He watches a red-sailed dinghy tacking. He's always surprised and impressed by how even novice sailors can use the wind in such a way that they are able to travel against it.

It's rare for him to have money without needing to spend it at once, and he's whistling softly through his teeth. He's not sure about going to the pub. There are times when he wishes he knew someone to go fishing with. He remembers how his mother sometimes referred to his stepfather as a loner, and how she wished he wasn't. She used to say: He needs friends as well as a family, – a man needs the company of other men. Robert stops whistling. Is that what he is then? A loner?

He decides he'll go to the pub.

*

Mark's friends knew he was hoping for a letter from Susan and they all knew when one arrived because he was reading it at breakfast. They waited expectantly and he cheerfully announced to the table, "She'll be back tomorrow! She's arriving at Felixstowe at twenty past seven in the evening."

Within seconds he had considered and rejected the idea of asking Philip to lend him his Morris Minor. He was not quite so badly or madly in love that he needed to drive all the long way round there to collect her and then drive all those miles back again.

Mark had to concede that having a car added a different dimension to escorting a woman – Philip was proof of that. But he reluctantly abandoned the idea of surprising Susan, embracing her, carrying her bag, opening the car door for her and talking with her in comfort all the way back to Bawdsey. He decided he would go across on the ferry, take the bus and reach Felixstowe station by the time the train arrived. He would be there on the platform as she got off the train. He'd still embrace her.

While he was making these plans he was re-reading Susan's letter. It was short and to the point but he brought himself back again to the special sentence: *I'm so looking forward to seeing you.* He relished the underlined *so*, wondering if she had underlined it after writing that particular word *so*, or after the *you* or even after she had finished the letter and was reading it through. He had never seen a whole page of her handwriting before. It was round and rather childish and quite unlike his own elongated scrawl that his sisters and mother complained about. He thought of her hand forming the letters of Dear Mark. The D and the M were upright, solid. He looked at the envelope and saw that the F of Flying, the O of Officer and the R of Rivens were the same. They stood to attention, like sentinels heralding the small, neat letters which followed them. But the S of Suffolk was tilted slightly – not so tidy. He turned back to her signature. Yes, the initial S could be described as at ease. This, he decided, was the letter he liked best, this soft, curving S that Susan had written thousands of times and had now written for him.

"He's not even hearing me, let alone listening."

"Mark! Are you there?"

He looked up and the three men opposite him roared with laughter.

"You were in a complete dream! You're really gone, aren't you? Can't you just forget her and think of me for a minute – one minute only?" pleaded Max.

Mark smiled.

"Go on, what is it? I'm listening."

"It's my birthday tomorrow – Saturday – but I'm Duty Officer then so I can't go out. So we're going tonight instead. To the Ferryboat Inn. Coming?"

"Of course. I'd love to buy you a drink – and," he looked round the table, "probably a few other people too."

He rose from the table contented mainly because Susan would be back tomorrow but also because he was going out with friends. He took the letter back to his room, re-read it and put it inside the book of poems by Federico Garcia Lorca he had bought the previous week and whose magical simplicity had bowled him over and made him resolve to study Spanish and to write poetry.

Good grief. He was supposed to be at the Radio School at nine. It was twenty past already.

*

Robert wakes up needing to piss. His head hurts. He goes out on deck, finds the sun is well up. He hardly sees the dozen or so sailing dinghies ploughing strongly through the white tops of waves until they reach the buoy where they turn, flap their sails, and ride on in a procession.

He stands with his back to the wind and then suddenly bends forward over the low rail at the edge of the deck and vomits. He looks at the murky stream spewing out of his mouth with its bits of unidentifiable and half digested food. It sinks and disappears into the river. The next mouthful he throws up is yellow. There's a strong wind and he's very cold and wants to be inside, but another wave of nausea hits him and he retches over board again. He keeps his head down and spits the last slimy bits out until his stomach relaxes. He wipes his mouth with the back of his hand.

*

As Mark shaved on Saturday morning he had a headache. Susan would be here within ten hours. Last night at the Ferryboat had been excellent and today there would be plenty of time for a golf lesson with Chris. Outside it was fine but windy. Golf, which he used to play well before his accident, might not be easy today, but it would fill up some time.

There was a letter from his mother downstairs, and he enjoyed reading it. It brought London back vividly. He missed going to plays, to restaurants. Unlike this place, there was always something going on there. The main news was that one of his sisters had been abandoned by a long-standing boyfriend. His mother made it clear that this was good news. He began thinking about his parents' health. Touch wood, neither of them had had anything wrong with them for as long as he could remember. It was hard to think of one of them being ill.

He wondered about Max, Ian, Alex, Philip – all of his friends whose parents must be getting older. Some of them spoke about their mothers and fathers often, others never did. Poor Susan. It must be so awful for her. When all this was sorted out he'd take her to London. That would be wonderful. She'd love it. They could go to Kew Gardens, to a show. They'd dress up and go out to dinner.

Ten hours to go. Ages to wait.

But last night had been good fun. Twelve of them had gone over on the ferry at first, and then another four joined them. Max had certainly enjoyed his birthday celebration. Ian had seemed quieter than usual, perhaps because Bridget hadn't been there. It was possible they had had a row, but hadn't Ian said something about her not being well?

When they had walked into the Ferryboat Inn they went down a few steps and into a thick fug. This was what always happened. The smoke lay in a layer until someone opened the door, which moved it around making everyone cough. They had all squashed up together and got served without a long wait, despite the pub being fuller than usual. Some of the older fishermen were there, sitting in their favourite chairs and smoking their pipes. Several couples who must have driven out from Felixstowe for the evening had taken a pair of tables. RAF personnel filled much of the rest of the place.

When they emerged to take the last ferry home it was wonderful to step out into the clear, quiet night. They stood on the beach hearing only the wind, the sound of feet on stones.

A group of young men had passed them running and laughing, led by one wobbling on a pushbike.

"Where on earth do they live?" asked an officer new to Bawdsey. "They seem to be heading for the river, and it looks as if they've had too much."

As they waited on the beach a guffaw went up. Looking back they saw that the rider had fallen sideways and was sitting on the ground tangled up in his bike.

"They're harmless, no worse than us," said Mark, "and it must be boring living here, mustn't it? At least we have a ferry to take us back to some sort of civilisation."

They were back in Bawdsey on time and Mark delayed going to bed. He was anticipating the next day with great pleasure, and decided to join in the late night billiard session. Someone had produced a bottle of whisky.

Now, having finished breakfast, he folded his mother's letter and went back upstairs. His head was clearing. He needed to borrow a couple of golf clubs and see when Chris, the station's acknowledged master of golf, wanted to go out with him.

"Let's go soon," said Chris, "It's blowing a bit and it's not going to get better. And it might rain."

Within an hour they had caught the ferry and were on the

course. After a couple of demonstration drives Chris stood back and watched Mark show him his swing.

"How can I compensate for this arm having less strength?"

It wasn't easy. He did as Chris suggested by slightly altering the position of his feet, the turn of his body, the way he held the club, but neither of them felt they were making much progress.

"Bloody hell. I'm getting worse, not better."

"It's something to do with the way you follow through. I'm sorry, Mark. I'm not being much help."

"Don't worry about it. Thanks for trying. I don't think my arm can do what I want it to do, let alone what *you* want it to do." He didn't want Chris to feel bad. "It's like not being able to serve well in tennis because I can't throw the ball up."

"But your arm hasn't stopped you beating us all at billiards, has it?"

"No, it hasn't." Mark straightened his back.

Being injured had wrecked his chances of playing tennis well, and that had been a real blow. He had liked being a good player, and, once he knew he could not fly again, being good at something physical felt very important. So when he was off work and recovering he'd practised snooker for hours. By the time he came to Bawdsey he could beat most people hands down.

He looked out across the course towards the Deben which lay unseen below them. To his right were the Martello Towers, and in front were about twenty small white triangles moving backwards and forwards, apparently across land, by invisible means. On the far side of the river he could see a horse and cart moving slowly along a lane, coming in and out of his vision in between trees. Taking Susan to London would be a treat, but even walking along that lane with her one evening would be marvellous. Eight hours to go.

*

Susan had finished packing by nine o'clock on Saturday morning. The ward sister had given her and Rose permission to see her father in the morning because her train left before visit-

87

ing hours began. Although he was still much the same he would be coming home soon and that felt so good. He would recover. He always did. Part of Susan's childhood had been spent listening to him and other people recounting his near accidents, his foreign fevers, his extraordinary ability to come through dangers and exploits.

The story of the crash in Italy was one of her favourites. Daddy, flying a plane in freezing fog over Italy, had seen the pilot of his companion plane crash into a forest. He had landed in a field as soon as he could and set off on foot to find the plane. When he reached it his friend was alive but injured. It was obvious he could not be moved without a stretcher and someone else to help carry it. Her father had taken struts and lengths of wood from the wreckage and made a bed and a shelter before setting off to find assistance. He returned six hours later with two men, rope, Italian sausage, hard bread. The rescuers produced a small bottle and offered it to the injured pilot. He took it, drank and spluttered, "What the hell's that? Are you trying to kill me?" The four men ended up finishing off the bottle, singing and sleeping close to each other round a small fire. Two days later Daddy and co-pilot flew off in the plane which was hardly damaged, and were welcomed back as if from the dead.

She held her hero's hand knowing he would come through as usual. Rose had not said much more about him living in her house, and this must mean she was no longer worried about it and could look after him there.

"I'll be back to see you as soon as I can," Susan told him, "You'll be fine. Aunt Rose is going to look after you and there isn't anyone better to do that than her." She stroked his hand tenderly.

Her father replied, "Lovely to see you. Have a goo journey ba to Bawsey. Nex time I wan to hear all abou your young man, and abou your promotion."

Susan laughed and looked up at him and then at Rose. "He's not really my – well, I don't know. He's very nice. But I'll do my best to get promoted!"

"Come on, Susan," said Rose smiling, "We need to get to the

station." She leaned over her brother. "I'll be back this afternoon, Henry. Goodbye for now."

"Goodbye, Daddy," said Susan, taking his hands and holding them to her face. She was suddenly unable to speak. She clung to his hands until the feeling lessened and she could say, through her tears, "Please get better, I do so want you to get better."

Rose took Susan's arm as they walked away down the corridor.

In ten minutes they were on the platform.

"Will Mark be at the station to meet you this evening?"

"Yes. Well, I think so. I expect so." She turned towards Rose and confessed. "Well, I *hope* he's there, anyway!"

Susan found a seat on the train and waved to Rose. How things had changed in a few days. She tried to remember how worried she had felt when she had arrived, how she had been longing to see both Rose and Daddy. Now she was thinking about Mark, her work, herself.

*

As Rose drove home she was thinking less about Henry and Susan and more about David, the man she was to have married in 1923. She and David had been in love for two years before he was killed in a motor bike accident. Even now, thirty years later, she sometimes found herself thinking about him for several days at a time.

She drew into the drive, unlocked her front door, and went straight to the sideboard table. She took out a pile of letters. Then she made some tea, put on her glasses, settled down with her feet up on the small red footstool. She never knew about these letters. Sometimes they made her feel old, at other times young, sometimes sad, sometimes happy. She picked out a favourite photograph of the two of them in a rowing boat. David looked serious as he tugged at the unfamiliar oars. He was more at home on wheels than in a boat. She was in that white and blue spotted dress, wearing a rather floppy sun hat. The person who had taken the photo was also in the boat, leaning back to get them both in. His legs reached into the foreground. They were just about to negotiate a lock on the Thames. That had been a happy day.

She put the letters and photo on one side and poured herself another cup of tea. She thought about Henry again. It was sad about his strokes, sad that Susan had had to go back to Bawdsey. It was difficult dealing with all this on her own although the RAF would help her. She had not yet told Susan she had already found out that the RAF had hospitals and convalescent homes and that it would certainly be possible for Henry to go to one. That would be much the best solution. Having him here wouldn't be easy, especially if he needed looking after for weeks.

It was already 1952. She and Henry were both in their sixties. What would Henry do, what would she do when they were older and unable to look after themselves or each other? She was having to think about this sooner than she expected.

She stood up, needing to do something practical. She went upstairs and took the sheets off Susan's bed and remade it ready for next time. She had promised to come back soon. She would be well on her way by now, looking out of the train window and probably thinking about Mark. Lucky girl. And lucky Mark too. It would be good to meet him. He sounded nice.

Susan had left *The Secret Garden* on the bedside table. Rose opened it randomly at the part where the children and Ben Wetherstaff are out in the garden and Colin asks Dickon to sing. He sings:

> *Praise God from whom all blessings flow,*
> *Praise Him all creatures here below.*
> *Praise Him above ye Heavenly Host*
> *Praise Father, Son and Holy Ghost.*

She hadn't been to church for two weeks. Henry went every Sunday. Perhaps she would go to St Agnes on Sunday. Yes. That was a good idea.

*

Robert drinks a cup of warm sweet tea while sitting on his bunk on a beautiful summer's morning when he had promised he would mend nets. He has never had a hangover before.

He had not been sure what time to go to the Victoria but when walking around the area in front of it and unsure about going in, he saw Wilf enter. So he went back to *Music Maker*, decided he didn't have time to eat, slicked his hair down with water and changed into his other, better, jersey and trousers. He walked back to The Victoria, pushed open the heavy door and stepped inside. He was not familiar with the smoke, the fruity smell, or the people who were grouped round the bar. He froze, not sure what to do, but Wilf saw him at once and called out to him.

"Robert, over here. Come over here."

He walked slowly to the group in the corner of the pub and nodded a greeting to Wilf and a couple of older men he knew. With a start he saw they were sitting at a table with the three boys who had burned his wood. He decided he would not show that he had met them before and was relieved they did not say anything either. They were older than he had thought, must be about to do their National Service. One of them, Billy, was Wilf's son.

"What'll you drink?"

Robert did not reply. He knew pubs sold beer and cider and gin but wasn't sure what to ask for or how to ask for it.

"Black and tan, lad. You'll like that."

Wilf gave Billy some money and he came back a few minutes later carrying three large glasses of black liquid topped with creamy foam which he placed carefully on the wooden table.

"Go on, one of them's for you. Cheers!"

Robert took a cautious sip but failed to find what lay beneath the froth. He wiped a white moustache off with his sleeve, avoided looking at his companions and tried again. This time he reached the drink that looked like black milk. It was good. Not like those sips of beer he had occasionally stolen from his stepfather's tankard on the kitchen table and which he had thought tasted like a stone might taste. Now his mouth was full of a delicious, rich liquid. He drank it slowly before licking the creamy residue from his lips. No one asked him anything so there was no need to speak. He noticed he was a head taller than Billy and his two friends. He remembered he had money in his pocket. By the time his glass was half empty he felt good.

By the time his second glass was half empty he was listening to a story about a dinghy that capsized, and by the time it was empty he was telling everyone about the day he pulled a Morris Minor off the beach as the tide was approaching.

"They didn't offer you a drink? They did, but you didn't take it?"

Everyone roared with laughter.

Tony, the one whom Robert had fought, said, "I don't believe it! You daft bugger!"

"Another black and tan? Good lad."

Someone moved and Billy squeezed up on the settle so there was room for them all to sit down, but as soon as space was made for him he needed to get up and go outside to the lavatories. This meant negotiating his way past shoulders, past bearded faces puffing over their pipes, past the bar. Once he had gone through the back door and relieved himself he felt his cheeks flushed, his spirits high. He pushed his way back inside again, and made his way back to the settle. They were all laughing and he joined in without knowing what they were laughing at.

They started to talk about the speedway behind the Ferryboat Inn. Tony asked if he'd ever done speedway racing.

"I've only ridden a pushbike."

They all laughed again.

"That's what we ride. You should come and have a go some-time. At any rate you should come and support the Ferry Falcons – we're your local team."

Robert had seen and heard the speedway racing but it had never interested him at all. Tonight, however, it sounded good.

"Yes, I'd like to. My boat's very close to the track. Do you know where it's moored?"

Tony and Billy exchanged glances. Robert sensed an awkwardness. He looked down at his nearly empty glass, wondered if he should be offering to buy people drinks now. The thought of going back to the bar past all those people, buying drinks and carrying them across to the table seemed quite impossible. He finished his drink slowly. Black, he had learned was Guinness, and tan was bitter. He was glad he had decided to come to the Vic.

Wilf said, "Your mooring lines were cut, weren't they?"

Robert found himself jolted back to a memory. "Yes."

"It was a joke really. Stupid," said the third youth.

"Yes," said Robert again. "The ropes – well, it doesn't matter now."

Wilf's voice cut harshly through the haze. "Yes, it does matter. It was a wrong thing to do. People shouldn't go around cutting ropes and causing damage."

Despite being in a happy haze Robert realised both that Wilf did not know about the woodpile and that the boys did not want him to know. It all seemed ages ago. A hand was being stretched out towards him.

"Sorry," said Billy.

It was several seconds before he realised he was supposed to shake hands with Billy, then with Tony and then with the third boy. They were apologising.

"We didn't know you then."

The mood had changed and Wilf, who was sitting behind the table, got up to leave, which meant that others had to move too.

"You boys are damn fools sometimes," said Wilf.

Then everyone started to leave. Robert was not at all sure what his legs would do when he stood up, but they worked.

Once outside Tony collected his bike from where it was leaning against the pub wall. As he swung his leg over the cross-bar Billy said, "Careful or you'll ride into those people."

Tony rode off, wobbled, hit the kerb and changed direction abruptly so that he was riding straight towards the telephone box and the men who had just come out of the Ferryboat Inn. As he hit tussocks of grass the front wheel turned sharply and he fell with a yell of pain.

Billy, Robert and the third boy ran over to him laughing.

"I've hurt my leg," complained Tony, sitting half across the crossbar on the ground, "and my elbow."

"Never mind you," said Billy. "Look at the front wheel!"

Robert picked up the bike and tried to spin the wheel. After looking at it for a minute he said, "I can fix that, if someone's got a .. if someone's got ..."

He could not for the life of him remember the name of the tool he wanted. He looked round but he was on his own. The others had gone and the sound of the engine of the last ferry of the evening was receding.

He left the bike where it was and walked back to *Music Maker*. He let Maisie out for a brief run, shut the door, unlaced and pulled off his first boot and then tried to tug off the second. It was all too difficult so he gave up and lay down on his bunk.

Now, as he sits drinking tea, it's all coming back to him. He's still in his best clothes, still has his left boot on. He's not sure how he feels about the previous evening at The Vic. Maisie is looking at him. Was it good? Did he enjoy himself? He pulls the rug across him, turns his eyes away from the bright sunlight that's pouring into the cabin and goes back to sleep.

*

Susan was already imagining herself back at Bawsdey but as the underground train stopped at Edgware Road she realised she wasn't even half way there yet.

"You'll take a taxi, Susan, won't you?" Rose had asked, but as she only had one bag to carry and more than an hour before her train she had taken the Metropolitan Line. It would probably be sensible to stay in the station at Liverpool Street, but she had already decided to go out and have a cup of tea in a Lyons Corner House when she arrived there. It was good to get away from the noise of trains and she settled herself at a table in the Corner House. Not long now.

Suddenly a group of four Negroes appeared directly outside her window. They were looking straight at her and she felt quite embarrassed. How extraordinary. She had only ever seen Negroes once before. How awful it must be to have come from a sunny, hot climate like Jamaica or wherever it was they had come from to London. For a moment it seemed as if they were going to enter the Corner House, but they walked on.

She returned to thinking about Mark. Still three hours to go before she would look out of the train window and – there he'd be, waiting on the platform at Felixstowe. Her mind was going round and round: Mark, Daddy in hospital, Mark, Daddy. And there was work too. She liked her work.

She was becoming more and more interested in radar because since being at Bawdsey she had often stood behind radar operators watching the little marks on their screens and listening to what they said when they read off the bearings. In winter she had liked going into the half-buried concrete buildings and flimsy looking wooden huts which housed the hidden and secret receivers. Now, although it was summer, she liked walking out of brilliant daylight and into their cool gloom.

Mark could not believe this – he was horrified. Surely, he said, watching screens in darkness could not beat being outside on a fine day in July within a hundred yards of a cliff top and a magnificent view across the North Sea? He was critical of Susan's recent habit of reading about radar. She did not need to know, because she would obviously never be an operator. Why waste time doing that when she could be reading poetry, or novels? He had just bought a new anthology of war poetry, but he had Wordsworth and Keats too if she preferred. Susan countered that that was not the point. The point was that radar interested her and it would continue to be vital for the RAF. And no, she wasn't afraid to admit it: it was true that she sometimes preferred working to doing other things. And she hadn't read a poem since leaving school.

Mark had replied "My poor Susan, I don't know whether to admire you or feel sorry for you." She had laughed then, not minding whether she earned his admiration or his sympathy. But she had decided not to tell him that she'd asked the CO about the possibility of doing a course on radar. He'd said he'd make enquiries for her, and she could tell that even asking about this had impressed him. Mark needn't know about it until later.

She had a thirty minute wait at Ipswich when she changed trains. She found a seat in the evening sun. There was only about an hour before she would see him. Were Mark's eyes blue or brown? How could she not know? He had known hers were green from the very first time he met her. But she had a picture in her mind of how he walked, and how he stood with his weight on one leg – his right one, now that she stopped to think about it – with the other turned out slightly, and his left hand in his trouser pocket.

Would he be in uniform or not? Probably not. No, not on a Saturday, of course not. He would probably be wearing his brown sports jacket with an open-necked shirt. He liked to dress comfortably because, he had explained, he had spent years cooped up in a small cabin with the same clothes on for hours at a time. He had not minded then, he said, but he wanted to wear different things now.

Susan had a Ladies compartment to herself. The train drew up at Trimley. Nearly there. The harvest had already started. Tractors were pulling binders, but there were horses too, their bridles held firmly by boys in case they shied at the whirring arms of the machines. Daddy used to take her to watch fields being harvested when she was little. She used to sit on his shoulders for hours as he carried her across acres of yellow. She remembered feeling high and safe, but once there was an accident when a farmer's boy was stabbed with a pitchfork. Daddy had lifted her down and sat her on a tarpaulin next to the lad and then torn a sleeve off the boy's shirt and bandaged his hand. Susan had seen the blood seeping slowly through the cotton and her father, when recounting this piece of family folklore, always ended by putting on a west country accent and saying the exact words the boy had spoken: "Me mum only stitched that shirt yesterday."

Daddy. Daddy in the hospital bed, ill. She suddenly imagined him having another stroke – hadn't the doctor said that might happen? She wanted to be with him again, sitting close to him and to Aunt Rose. And what if Rose became ill? What if they were both ill, or both of them died? And now she was travelling further and further away from them. Her small, close family was at risk.

The fields and woods gave way to houses, and they were in Felixstowe. As they slowed down she checked her hair and touched up her lipstick in the mirror above the middle seat of the compartment. By the time they stopped she had picked up her shoulder bag, pushed down the window and was resting her small suitcase on the seat. As the train drew up she opened the door, took her case and got out. She looked up the platform. No Mark. She looked down the platform. He wasn't there. Perhaps the train was a few minutes early and he was still outside. She walked into the station yard but he wasn't there either. She walked quickly back to the Ladies Waiting Room, dumped her bag down and burst into tears.

*

Mark was thinking about Susan as he stood at the bottom of one of the steel radar towers. A small figure was slowly making its way down, and a small crowd of airmen and WAAFs chatted as they enjoyed the unexpected entertainment. The man, a popular member of the rifle team, had climbed up to the top for a bet and, because his friends had not been able to stop themselves from watching him and talking about it, he had been spotted by an officer.

Mark's afternoon had not gone as planned. After their attempt at golf he and Chris had a sandwich in the clubhouse and then went back on the ferry to Bawdsey, taking a little longer than usual because of the Firefly dinghies jockeying up to the invisible line that marked the start point of the race. The river was covered with little white horses, and there was a continual flapping of sails and a noisy calling out of instructions and rushing of wet hulls through the water. The ferryman nudged his way across slowly and sideways, allowing the boat to be taken well downstream by the tide so he could keep his eye open for the frantic tacks of the two Fireflies which had overshot the mark. One passed them at speed, eager to turn and regain a position of advantage. Its skipper was swearing at his crew, at the mainsheet, at the wind, and when the bell sounded he was still thirty feet behind the line.

"Serve him right," said the old ferryman, "that one always tries to be too clever."

97

Within a few minutes Mark was passing the bag of golf clubs out to Chris on the jetty. As they walked up the drive he was anticipating with pleasure the prospect of walking down it in a few hours on his way to meet Susan, and then – even better – back up it again with her.

Once changed he went downstairs and out into the Jacobean Tea room where tea was served in the summer. It stood next to the Manor terrace, near the lawns that reached almost to the cliff, and it was decorated with tiles that seemed more Mediterranean than East Anglian. Everyone seemed to behave impeccably when they were there, and nobody told the sort of jokes they told in the other lounge – ones that made people snort with laughter and spill their tea. They all agreed it was a place that promoted elegant conduct – at least during daylight hours. After dark it was just as attractive but for different reasons.

Mark was eating a piece of jam sponge when Ian came in. He was pale and unsmiling and hurried over to Mark.

"Can I have a word?" he said urgently and quietly. He turned away and walked off quickly. Mark rose and followed him for over fifty yards, well away from the tea room and from everyone else.

"What on earth is it? What's the matter?"

"It's Bridget."

"What about her? What's happened?"

Ian took out a packet of Du Mauriers and pulled one out and put it in his mouth.

"I think," he paused as he struck a match and drew on the cigarette, "I think she's pregnant." He shook the match to extinguish it and dropped it on the ground.

Mark did not know what to say. Susan came in and out of his mind in a flash.

Ian sighed smoke into the early evening air, "I – she, I mean – might be wrong. But she might be. Pregnant, I mean."

Mark said nothing for half a minute. Then he asked, "What are you going to do? What's *she* going to do?"

"I don't know. She doesn't know."

A foursome of WAAFs were coming up the steps from the sports grounds, carrying their tennis racquets. They waved a greeting to the two men, who half raised their hands.

"When did she tell you?"

"Yesterday. She's been worried for at least two weeks. I knew something was wrong. That's why she didn't come to the pub last night. She's frightened to death. I feel ghastly about it."

"I just don't know what to say, Ian."

"I don't know what I want you to say, but I had to tell someone, and I chose you. Sorry."

"I'm so sorry. For you and Bridget." Mark sat down on the low wall and breathed in the sudden scent of blue lavender. "It's awful. Is there anything I can do to help?"

Ian sat down next to him and pressed his cigarette out with his foot, "No. I don't think so. We've just got to face it."

"Perhaps it will be all right. Perhaps she isn't."

They sat for a full minute in silence, watching gulls circling high on air currents above the cliff. Mark had been told that this was a sign it was going to rain, and he saw clouds approaching from the north.

Then Ian looked up at Mark sharply, "Actually, I've just thought. You *could* help me."

"Good. What?"

"Well, I'm Duty Officer today, or at least I'm supposed to be. I haven't been able to settle to anything. But I need to see Bridget and talk to her. She's refused to see me all day. Kathleen knows something's up and she's told me Bridget keeps on crying but won't say what the matter is. I think she thinks we've had a frightful row."

"Then let her go on believing that."

"I'm going to. But I need to see Bridget. We've got to do something."

Mark wondered what there was to be done, but said, "Go on then. Give me five minutes and I'll get my uniform on. I'll hold the fort for you."

Ian jumped up and shook his hand. "Thanks, Mark. That's grand. Can you be in the Guard Room in ten minutes?"

That had been two hours ago. Seconds after Ian left him Mark remembered he was to meet Susan. How could he have forgotten? How on earth could he have forgotten? He felt sudden anger at himself, at Ian, at Bridget, at everything. Then he thought that if Ian did not take long, or if – and he found himself shamefully half hoping this – Bridget continued to refuse to see Ian – he would still have time to meet the train.

But Ian had not come back by the time Mark walked across the grass at the base of the radar mast where this wretched airman was not yet half way down. This could take ages. He abandoned hope of even getting to the other side of the river before Susan got on the ferry. His mind veered off towards Ian and Bridget and their predicament. He would not wish that on anyone. He had met Ian's mother – a lively and elegant widow whose pride in Ian was boundless. And Bridget. She was so young, so unready for pregnancy or for what could be an even worse solution. And it could happen to anyone.

Trudi. Suddenly he remembered Trudi, an Austrian girl he had met once when he was twenty five and she was eighteen. They had fallen in love for two weeks and had made love in her grandparents' house by the Wolfgangsee. It had been his first summer abroad. He was on a walking tour with a post-war initiative to promote goodwill between young Europeans. He had sprained his ankle on the third day and had to spend the rest of the holiday in the little Austrian village where they were staying. He had met Trudi by chance. She spoke a little English with a delightful accent, wore a dirndl – the national dress of the region – on Sundays, and gave him sweet home-made cider that made him tipsy. How strange that those details should be so vivid now.

There was a burst of laughter. Mark looked up and saw the man had paused and was pretending to shoot an imaginary rifle at two geese flying past. Why couldn't the damned idiot just get on with it and get down?

He had thought a lot about making love with Susan, especially in the few days she had been away. It would be wonderful. It would be so wonderful. He felt excited, impatient and annoyed with himself in quick succession. He knew that if the relationship had progressed differently – or if, if only, it progressed differently from now on, they too might find themselves taking risks. They hadn't come near to talking about this yet.

But Trudi. He had not thought of her for years. He had no idea what had happened to her, but he had thought of her occasionally. There had been times when he had wondered if she had become pregnant. She could have. He could not deny that making love to her had been risky and that the risk had been part of the excitement, the first foreign romance.

The man was getting bigger as hand over hand he descended the rungs. From a distance it seemed as if the geometric patterns of the steel were tilting, but it was the clouds which were moving. The warmth of the afternoon had gone and several of the waiting crowd had already left. This was the third such climb in two weeks and the CO had instructed officers to personally discipline anyone who climbed like this because a man had fallen from a similar mast in Essex and broken his leg. Mark willed him to hurry up. Who cared if he broke his damned leg? Let him fall off from where he was.

He looked at his watch. Seven thirty. What would Susan be thinking?

A cheer went up as the man reached the ground. He was smiling, enjoying his status as hero of the day. Full of sudden anger, disappointment and guilt that had appeared out of the blue, Mark beckoned him with a signal and order so sharp that the audience dispersed hurriedly. He was going to make this fool regret this.

*

Susan did not know anyone on the bus. Not that she had expected to, for at this time of day on a Saturday everyone from Bawdsey who was crossing the river had either crossed already or would be on the bus heading for Felixstowe. It was probably a good thing for she did not want to talk to anyone just now. She'd tidied herself up in the Ladies but still felt dishevelled. At least the journey was almost over. She was looking forward to more than Mark. She wanted to tell Bridget about Daddy, she wanted to be back in her room with its wonderful views of the sea. She

101

was looking forward to the familiar camp routine, and to her work. For the first time she felt as if she was coming home.

She got off the bus and walked straight down to the ferry. If she did not look at the pub there was less chance of being spotted by someone she knew, for on a lovely evening like this there would be groups of RAF people sitting outside. She'd get on to the ferry at once, if it was there.

There it was. The ferryman took her suitcase and lifted it on before she stepped on board. She went up to the prow. A couple of airmen and women stepped into the boat but they stayed in the middle.

The ferryman was in no hurry. He sat in the stern stroking his little brown and white dog and glancing towards the beach every now and then to see if more passengers were coming. Susan was glad when he stood up, thinking he was about to set off, but he only did so to reach into his trouser pocket for his matches. He tapped the end of his cigarette on the gunwale loosely before cupping his hand round it and lighting it. A small wisp of smoke appeared and almost instantly disappeared. He nudged his dog gently off his foot.

Two women came on board with boys who immediately leant over the side. As they did so, pointing at something in the water, their mothers continued their conversation while hanging on to their son's belts. Had her mother ever held on to her like that? Had they ever been in a boat like this together? It was ironic that her mother, a strong swimmer, had drowned. She had been carried off by a current in Cornwall, an incident which she had no memory of at all.

"Mark!"

One of the boys had jumped up and was half balancing on the edge of the boat with his feet scrabbling against the side. His mother pulled him back. A young Mark. Susan looked at him again. She could only see him sideways on, but her Mark would have been quite different when he was eight or nine. He would have been taller and thinner than this one, and his hair would always have been dark and straight, not brown and wavy. And why, why had he not come to meet her?

She gazed across the open river towards Bawdsey. The

surface was cream coloured and choppy in the distance, but close up it was brown and smooth. The engine started and the ferry nosed forwards slowly at first and then faster, making off downstream against the incoming tide. She turned round and saw the ferryman pull the peak of his cap down against the evening sun. He looked comfortable as he leaned back against the side. His dog was standing up with its nose to the wind and its ears blowing up and down like small ragged handkerchiefs.

Susan wished she were at the side of the boat by the boys and their mothers. She was getting blown to bits but she didn't want to move now. Why was it that she sometimes separated herself out? She had chosen to be alone in the prow, deliberately setting herself apart. And she had forgotten how windy this crossing could be. Surely they were almost there? No, they weren't, and they seemed to have gone far too far downstream. This journey was such a nuisance. You couldn't go anywhere without having to cross this blasted river.

But soon the engine's sound changed and they slowed down. Susan scanned the jetty and roadway for Mark. The water slapped against the side when the boat turned broadside on to nudge up against the jetty. He wasn't there.

The ferryman helped Susan out and handed up her suitcase. One of the airmen offered to carry it up the drive, and Susan accepted, remembering the first time she had walked up it at the end of last year. Although they joined the group of people walking towards the Manor, people whom she had seen chatting on the boat, no one was talking now. She was certain it was because she herself was not talking and that made everyone silent. Why did this happen? If this was some power she had, today was the first time she wished she could lose it. Being an officer was not always as straightforward as she had thought it would be.

But there was the fairy tale front entrance of the Manor. She suddenly felt as if she hadn't been away. And there was Mark. She stopped walking when she saw him hurrying out of the doorway. She remained still, smiling at him. She hardly noticed the airman when he put her bag down and only remembered to thank him when he walked away.

*

Robert does not know if or how things might change after his night at the Vic. He tries to remain out of sight over the next few days, worrying that he will either be the target of some other action, or completely ignored. On the Wednesday afternoon, when he's washing out the shirt down which he was sick, he's surprised to hear shouting.

Someone's yelling, "Bobby, are you there? "

He comes out onto the deck with the wet shirt in his hands. Tony and Billy are standing at the end of his gangplank. He nods at them as he wrings the shirt out over the side. Why have they come? What should he say?

"The Ferry Falcons are riding on Sunday so we're practising today. Want to come?"

He concentrates on hanging the shirt on the line he has rigged up across the deck. He takes as long as he can in making sure the sleeves are pulled out straight, the cuffs unrolled. Just as his mother does, he turns it inside out and pegs it by its tails. It immediately catches the wind and billows out like a small, faded blue spinnaker, sending the loose sleeves slapping wetly against his shoulder.

"You can have a go on my bike," says Tony. "It'll be good today because it's dry and you won't skid."

Robert wipes his hands on his trousers while he thinks about what to say. Does he have to give an answer right now? He wants to think about it.

"Come on," says Billy, "You'd like it."

"When? I need to collect some wood."

"Now," say Tony and Billy in unison.

Tony adds, "You can get your wood later. We'll help you, won't we?" He turns to Billy who has squatted down to stroke Maisie.

"We owe you that," says Billy, "When we burned that wood of yours – it was an accident – we didn't mean anything by it. We just started a small fire but then, I don't know, we ended up putting the whole lot on."

Robert thinks about this. It hadn't looked like an accident to him and Billy's not actually saying sorry. But even so, he feels better.

Then Tony grins and says, "Me mum was furious about me jacket. I had to tell her I'd left it on the beach. And I said our dog chewed me shoe to bits."

"What did you say about your face?" asks Billy.

"It wasn't just me face. You knocked one of me teeth out! Look, I'll show you the gap." He opens his mouth and pulls down his lower lip. "Me mum said I'd have to move out if I got into fights. But you were livid, weren't you? I tell you, I thought you wanted to kill me!"

Yes. That was what he had wanted to do.

"And it was only a pile of wood!"

That was true too. He had thought of smashing a stone into Tony's face, just for a pile of wood. What if he'd done so? As it is he's knocked a tooth out without even meaning to. His stomach lurches when he thinks of the damage he could so easily have done.

He looks at Tony again. He's an ordinary, unremarkable lad with a quiff he's taken some trouble over, and now he's joking about it and inviting him to the speedway.

"Ok. I'll be along in five minutes."

As the boys walk back onto the shore Robert turns and goes into the cabin. He bends down to Maisie and ruffles her ears, making her tail wag and her tongue loll out. He could have killed Tony. He could have killed him in that flash of anger.

He puts on his boots and comes back out on deck. Maisie shoots out across the plank and races along the bank. He shoves the door shut and looks out across the Deben. It's shining and dimpled like the brass firescreen his mother stood in front of the rarely used fireplace in the parlour. He remembers the day his sister was christened, and the photograph on the sideboard. It shows him serious in his grey Sunday suit as he carefully held Lizzie in her cream embroidered gown which reached nearly to the ground. He wishes he could see it again.

*

Susan was waiting for Mark to bring her coffee after dinner. It was strange how people had welcomed her and asked about her rather carefully. Usually a big group would assemble after dinner but now they had left space so she and Mark could be on their own.

What would he say? What would she say? While other people were around their conversation had consisted of safe exchanges. How was her father? And Aunt Rose? How long did it take the airman to climb down the mast?

Mark came towards her with a cup of coffee in each hand. Good. Here he was.

He put the cups down.

"I've been counting the days."

"And I was counting the hours. And when you weren't there I just burst into tears."

Mark looked at Susan closely and said, "I feel even more strongly about you now. I've thought about you all the time."

She looked up at him and smiled, then reached out for his hand, leant across and kissed him. Before she went away she might not have done that. It felt wonderful to be close to him now and she kept hold of his hand.

They talked about how she had felt when she saw her father, how Mark had missed her, how thrilled she had been to get his letter, how sorry he was not to have been able to meet her and why he had not met her.

"It was because of something Ian told me. Bad news."

He paused, looked round, checked no one could overhear, "Ian said he and Bridget think Bridget's pregnant. Of course he doesn't want anyone to know but I've told him I'm telling you. He understands that I couldn't not tell you about it."

Susan let go of Mark's hand and put her hands to her face. "How awful. How absolutely awful. How could they have been so stupid? I can't believe it."

As soon as she had said this she realised Mark might not be sure if she thought they should not have made love at all, or that they should have been more careful. She had meant they shouldn't have made love at all, but she wasn't sure whether to say that or not. She decided to say nothing. They sat in silence.

"It's wonderful having you back," he said once more. "Don't go away without me again, will you?"

"I'll try not to. For the time being, at least." What would it have been like if Mark had been with her in the hospital and at Rose's? Well, both Daddy and Aunt Rose would certainly have liked him, but he couldn't have stayed there because the spare bedroom was full of books and boxes.

"There wouldn't have been room for you."

"Wouldn't there?"

"There isn't another bedroom."

Mark lent forward and looked straight into her eyes. He started to say something, but stopped. He squeezed her hand and sat back.

*

Robert has two goes on Tony's bike. It feels quite different from when he last rode because all the Speedway bikes are ladies' bikes which have had heavy gears and racy handlebars added. Even along the straights of the oblong track the one he's been lent seems heavy and cumbersome and he's riding more slowly than he used to on his old bike. After his first go Tony insists he takes part in a race.

He's not sure if this is because Tony is being genuinely friendly or whether he is testing him in some way. He finally accepts. He wants to join in, and at least if he accepts he'll avoid being labelled as either ungrateful or a coward.

He doesn't like it at all. It's fine at the start when everyone sets off in a line, but the bends are as dangerous as they look. As he reaches the part of the track that begins to curve he's so hemmed in by other riders he's sure their pedals will jam into spokes and their chains will tangle. He hears metal scraping behind him, then a shout of *You bugger!* but he rounds the corner unscathed. Within a minute he's already jammed into the noisy whirring and grunting at the next bend. The next straight stretch is a relief and he glimpses across the track and sees that two bikes and their riders have snarled up. He steels himself for the next bend and enters it with more gusto, determined to survive. He ends up sixth.

"Not bad," says Billy, "as it's your first time."

Robert thinks about dinghy sailing and how the worst that ever happens is capsizing. That means getting wet and struggling to right the boat, but there's rarely damage. And water can't wound – on the contrary, it gives way under pressure. As he watches boys limping away leaning on bikes that are no longer rideable, it seems strange that they do this, knowing there's a good chance that will get hurt or their bike will get damaged.

But he's maintained or even gained some honour. Now, safely off the cycle, he's sitting on the grass, stroking Maisie and watching the others ride round. If he shuts his eyes he can tell where they are by the changing sound of their wheels and shouts. Why do they like riding round and round the same circuit? All it has is a few slopes and bends. Still, perhaps that's what they think about him going backwards and forwards on the ferry.

But it isn't the same at all. When he's on the river, the wind, the tide and the weather keep changing so he has to adapt his direction and speed constantly. Every crossing is different except on very still summer days – days like today, in fact. He stands up and turns to face the Deben. The ferry is at the far side, unloading its passengers. It's so simple, so solid, so predictable. He knows exactly where he is with it. He knows the sound and strength of its steady measured engine, and he'll always go on learning about the undertow, the sandbanks and the way the water tugs at the mooring buoys. He watches the next passengers walk down the jetty and into the boat. Soon he sees it making its way across the late afternoon's incoming tide towards the Ferry.

He bends quickly to grab Maisie's collar as Tony draws up in a controlled skid designed to make him step back, each tyre squirting up an arc of fine gravel. He tugs his Ferry Falcons jerkin down as he smiles at Robert.

"Coming to watch us Sunday afternoon?"

He doesn't want to say he will. "Perhaps. I may be running the ferry, but I could probably get to a bit of it first."

"Ok. See you later."

Tony rides off, sending up dust and making Maisie back off.

Robert calls her to him and they walk back to *Music Maker*. He still wants wood, but it's a bad time to go. Billy has said nothing more about helping him collect some. Now that he's alone again he's not sure about Billy and Tony. He stumbles on a stone, stubbing his toe. He has no idea where he stands with them, but it doesn't seem to matter so much now. They're including him. Even if he's not yet sure whether he wants to be included by people who do stupid things, it's better than not being included.

Anyway, there's enough wood for now because in summer he doesn't need a fire as long as he doesn't cook, and he doesn't cook every day. All he needs is a pot full of hot water if he wants to shave. Yesterday he cooked the last of the cabbage and potatoes from the Corbys and tomorrow he'll eat the leftovers cold with the slice of bacon he bought from the grocer's van on Friday. Tomorrow he will buy bread and make do with lettuce sandwiches, and then he's due to go to the Corby's again.

But it would be good to get a fish this evening so he takes his rod and line and chooses two worms from the jar he's placed under a thick plank to keep cool. He carefully stretches each one out before impaling it on the hook in turn, pushing the thin point of metal into its pale, soft body which resists the pressure for only a second. Maisie shows a passing interest in the waving worms but her priority is to settle into her hollow on an old piece of sacking. Robert casts the line out a couple of yards from *Music Maker*'s foredeck. If he happens to catch a fish in the next fifteen minutes, he'll need to go out and gather an armful of timber from the tideline. Although it will be getting dark the light always seems to linger on the river after it leaves the land.

His line leads into the water and he sits looking out at his beloved estuary, waiting for the small tug that will announce a bite or warn him that a fish is interested. Maisie sleeps. Apart from the odd slurp from the bilge, there is hardly a sound.

*

During the week following her return Susan's thoughts were all over the place and she woke up one morning from a vivid dream in which her mother was calling her in from the garden, "Susan, SUsan!" She stayed hidden in her den under the buddleia bush, wanting her mother to come and look for her. But she was watching a bee settle on the yellow insides of a mauve flower and it launched itself off, heavy with pollen, and suddenly lumbered sideways onto her leg. She froze, knowing it might sting her. Just before it did so, she woke up.

One evening Rose left a message, asking her to phone. During the next ten minutes Susan imagined every scenario possible as she looked for an office where she could speak in privacy. Where would they have the funeral?

"Hallo, dear," said Rose in her usual comfy voice, "I wanted you to know that I've fixed up for Henry to go to St Botolph's RAF Convalescent Home. He seems quite pleased about it, he's sure he'll find people there he knows."

Susan breathed out a long sigh. She immediately thought back to the hospital full of patients injured during the war that Daddy had once taken her to visit. She had seen one young man who had lost a hand and another without either leg. This was terrible, but she was still determined to join the RAF. Then, in another ward, there was a black man with a white bandage round his eyes. He was telling a story to a little girl on his lap while his wife sat by the bed. They were holding hands in a loose circle, and the woman was crying silently and the child was chuckling at the story. They were the first Negro people Susan had seen. Did being in the RAF mean she would be part of that world? Was that what she wanted?

"Yes, sorry. Where is it?"

"Just outside Bath, so I can get there by train."

Susan said slowly, "That sounds fine. If he wants to go, that is."

"It's by far the best arrangement. I can't possibly look after him as well as they will, and I can get there at least twice a week – and he's not out of reach for other people from here either."

"But what about me?"

"Well, it'll be just as easy – even easier in fact – than coming here. If you take the train to Bath it's only ten minutes walk away, and I can meet you there and bring you home here."

Susan's heart sank at the thought of making the long journey to the west country again. But Rose was right. It was certainly no worse than going to Bristol.

"Are you still there, Susan?" Her aunt's voice softened. "Are you all right? How are you feeling?"

"Oh, I'm ok. Everything's fine here. Really." She tried to brighten up.

"Well, I hope you are, my dear. There's not much more news from this end. It's nice to see Henry with a bit more energy now. They think they'll move him on Friday, but I'll let you know if that changes, and I'll get the address and phone number for you – I've left it in my bag upstairs."

"You could pop it in the post. I won't need it yet, will I? Give him lots and lots of love from me."

"Of course I will. And how's Mark?"

Susan said he was fine, said goodbye and put the phone down. She felt pleased the arrangements were being sorted out, and sorted out faster than she expected. He wouldn't be at home, but there was no point in fretting over this.

Now, what was it she had been doing before speaking with Aunt Rose? For a moment her mind went quite blank and she had to stand still by the door and try and remember. She had lost track and recognised with a start that this was something she never, ever, did.

Why had Aunt Rose asked about Mark? Although she had told her about him she felt slightly uncomfortable about being asked. It wasn't about Rose knowing. So what was it then?

She had to admit to herself that in the last few days her feelings for Mark were not as strong as on the first evening back, and Aunt Rose was presuming all was as it had been. And so, of course, was Mark. What, exactly, had changed? What was different? It was certainly to do with her, Susan, and not Mark. It was she who had changed. When she was away it had been good to tell Daddy and Aunt Rose about him, and she was well aware how they were wanting and expecting her to meet someone who made her happy. And Mark *did* make her happy, but it seemed he made her happier when they were apart. How could that be? Somehow, back here there was so much else to get on with and he had not remained as important as he had been when she was at home. Like today, when some radar operators had decided to set up a transmitter when it tripped. They should have waited for the Fitter but they hadn't, and a man had been thrown across the room by the force of the voltage. Things couldn't go on like that, for goodness sake. Something had to be done, and it was her job to do it.

She went out into the corridor and came face to face with Bridget. This wasn't what she wanted now. She was feeling embarrassed because of the news about the pregnancy. In fact, she was rather dreading talking to her. And Bridget wouldn't want to hear about Daddy just now. Although they had been friends before Bawdsey, they had not spent much time together recently. Susan didn't know what to say, but she knew Bridget was relying on her.

"Here you are! At last! I've been trying to get hold of you since you've been back but you keep disappearing."

"Sorry – you know I haven't meant to, I want to – oh, Bridget," Susan broke off as she saw her friend's face go blotchy and tearful.

"Can we meet after supper? Let's go for a walk and get away from everyone. There's so much I want to tell you."

It suddenly felt easy to agree. "Ok, that's fine. Straight after dinner, then?"

"Oh, good," Bridget hugged her quickly before turning round and hurrying back the way she had come.

Susan followed her slowly to the front door. As she stepped from the cool interior into the brilliant evening sunshine she did not notice the mosaic hound and its flying chains. Being outside made her feel better and she walked along the roadway, past the CO's house and the entrance to the walled garden. The walled garden, yes. That would be a good, private place to go with Bridget.

She thought about Daddy and wondered how he was feeling about going to the convalescent home. And Mark. What about Mark? She had come back to Bawdsey longing to see him, but things were different here. They were different and difficult. And now there was Bridget to think about too.

And here she was at the Guard Room. She would not be expected here, and everything would not be in order. This felt more like it. She was getting back to normal, getting into the pattern of things again. But as she approached the redbrick stable block people were converging by the archway and making for the cookhouse. She glimpsed up at the clock in its asymmetrical black and white timbered turret. Five to seven already – suppertime. Blast it. The afternoon had gone.

*

Robert is digging up maincrop potatoes for Mr and Mrs Corby who live near The Vic. This year they are relying on him to do the hardest digging, and he's pleased to be of use and to earn a bag full of vegetables by way of reward.

He has worked his way along the three rows, digging carefully under the plants and enjoying the satisfaction of levering up a forkful of pale potatoes. He's thinking about taking fish from the sandy sea, potatoes from the sandy land. He leans down, separates them by shaking the tubers or picking up a few at a time and then lobbing them carefully into small piles on top of the turned earth. Mr Corby follows with a bucket, stooping to collect them and then walking back to the end of the row where he tips them into a wheelbarrow. Maisie is running backwards and forwards.

Robert pauses and stands up straight, holding up a huge potato.

"Look at this one."

Mr Corby smiles. "That one will make a meal by itself. Joyce won't need to roast a joint next Sunday."

When he's finished he goes indoors to wash his hands. At first he can hardly see where he's going because it's dark after the bright summer's day. He walks past the pegs with thick coats and a tweed cap like the one his stepfather wore, past the mangle and the carpet sweeper. The fish he has brought them is lying in a dish on the wooden draining board. He rinses the earth from his hands in cold water at the kitchen sink and shakes the drops off as he goes back outside. Mr and Mrs Corby are sitting on the bench, drinking tea and eating rock buns, and he sits near them on the warm, green grass that already needs mowing again. He never once sat out in the garden with his own parents like this. He stirs his tea, thinks how he prefers digging potatoes to pushing the mower across this uneven patch. He accepts a second rock bun. Maisie sits in the shade, her tongue hanging out.

Mrs Corby says, "That's a good job done. Thank you. Potatoes mean a lot of bending for us." She continues to speak and as she does so he thinks how they, like his mother and step-father, have lost a son in the war. There's a photo of Alistair in a silver frame in the centre of the mantlepiece. He feels today as he's felt before – that in some way he's there in their son's place. This is all right, for at times he feels they are there in his parents' place.

When he's replaced the fork in the shed, he says, "I'll come and do the grass for you on Tuesday if you want."

They thank him again for the fish and he goes home to *Music Maker* with a string bag half full of the potatoes that he's accidentally stabbed with the tines of his fork, a perfect cabbage, a lettuce that's begun to shoot and a jar full of earth and worms. He thinks about his own mother and the patch of garden she struggled to control, and he marches along with Maisie at his heels, whistling.

*

Mark was studying the typewritten proofs of technical manuals. There was a pile of them to read through and check for accuracy against the original handwritten drafts. It was such boring work. Far better to be doing something physical and practical. But someone had to do it and, knowing he had precisely the experience that was needed, he volunteered. It was a succession of jobs like this that occasionally made him think about applying for another posting.

Now, sitting sweatily in his shirt sleeves, he looked out through the window of his office. If he sat back, sank lower in his chair and moved a little to the right his view was composed almost entirely of sweeping green lawn and pale blue sky.

After a minute or two he sat up straight again and placed his left forefinger on the top of the next page of the new script and the point of the pencil in his right hand on the appropriate place of the old text. As well as focusing on the main business of checking calculations and references, he had noticed not only ordinary errors such as missed capital letters but headings that did not match the sections they referred to. This was not something that could be done half heartedly: he had to concentrate on every line, every word.

But he was a Flying Officer, not a technical secretary. Damn, damn, damn. Not being able to fly again was such lousy luck. Taken off guard he sat still, gazing at diagram 2(iii) of Annex B on page 34. As usual, he tried to stop feeling sorry for himself by thinking about something positive. Susan. He would take her out for a walk this evening at sunset. It was marvellous that she had returned from her family less formal, less contained and softer. He looked out of the window again. He wanted to kiss her. Now.

He counted up that there were about five hours between now and sunset, then applied himself to his work again. Aha, the next diagram was incorrectly labelled. This small success provided him with a new impetus. He found himself able to focus better and stuck at it until Ned offered him a cup of tea.

"Already?" he asked.

"It's five and twenty past four," said Ned, "How much longer will that lot take you?"

Mark indicated a pile on the floor and a pile on the desk. "This is the not-yet-touched pile, and this is the finished pile. But although it looks as if I'm over half way through, the ones I'm doing now are the worst – there's more technical data in them. I reckon I'm about a third of the way through. I'll be finished by the weekend I should think."

Suddenly Susan walked in through the open door and both men looked up in surprise. Mark stood up and took a step towards her.

"Susan! How nice!"

"I didn't know you'd be in here," she said, equally surprised, "Why aren't you in your usual office?"

"Because of these," Mark indicated the piles of paperwork. "They all have to stay here so I have to come to them. And what are you doing here?"

"I'm looking for the new Pilot Officer. He's supposed to be on duty but he's disappeared." She picked up one of the papers and looked at it briefly. "So I wouldn't say no to a cup of tea."

"Of course," said Ned, "I'll go and pour you one – we've just made a fresh brew."

Susan sat down at an empty desk and Mark sat down again too. She must have called in because she was looking for him. Trying to find the new Pilot Officer was obviously a pretext. He sat smiling at her in delicious silence, willing her to say something special.

"I'm going to one of the CH Blocks next," said Susan. She looked out of the window.

Mark watched the way her hair fell over her ear, and how she pushed it back. She was so pretty. Thank God she was back at Bawdsey.

"They'll be finishing work soon," said Ned, returning with the tea, "They won't be doing much."

Mark stood up to fetch the sugar.

Susan said, "They've got at least another half hour. I'm going now precisely because it's late. Last time I went at this time they had nothing to do and two of them had their feet on the desks, so I warned them."

Mark chuckled but noted that Ned said nothing and wandered off back to his own side of the room, which Mark guessed meant he thought Susan was over zealous. In the silence that followed Ned started to work again. Mark watched Susan drink her tea.

He wished he had said something when Ned was out of the room. How could he have missed that opportunity, brief though it was?

Her neck was pale and from it she had swept up her hair that he called warm brown but she called mouse, and tucked it under her cap. Once she had sat still and let him take off her cap, take out her hairgrips and allow her hair to fall onto her shoulders in a silky, slow undoing. That was the first time he had pushed both his hands into and under her hair, fingering slowly past her ears and holding the nape of her neck gently before pulling her towards him.

She got up to go. "Thanks for the tea," she said. She half turned at the door to smile at both men before going out.

Mark looked back to Ned who said nothing but immediately turned to his papers again. Mark followed suit, determined not to brood. He focused on page 39.

Susan made her way out on to the path which led to the technical sites. Ahead of her the four steel transmitter towers stretched upwards into the clear June sky. The man who had recently climbed one had certainly been enterprising. Despite receiving a fierce dressing down from Mark and a nominal punishment, he was almost universally regarded with admiration and affection. What a view he must have had. He would have seen the whole station, the cliff, the sea, the river.

She was heading for the furthest of the towers. The wooden hut was situated immediately under the tower. Mark had once likened these huts to the dens of spiders. He said radar operators were like spiders in that they sat in their lairs under the vertical webs they had woven and they could tell when their webs were being touched. She had not taken him seriously but he had insisted this idea was not at all fanciful, because sensing movement was as much the essence of radar as it was of spider webs.

As she walked inside she was conscious of the familiar cool but stale atmosphere. She was pleased to find herself faced by each person's battledressed back. The three national servicemen and the one woman were all engaged and busy. At last, everyone was doing what they were supposed to be doing, but there was a strong smell of toast.

Susan spoke loudly to make sure they all heard, even with their headsets on.

"It seems as if I need to remind you that this is a workplace, not a canteen," she said. "Next time I come here I don't want to smell the remains of your last meal, nor see your collection of empty milk bottles."

She went and stood behind the PPI operator first and

watched the round screen over his shoulder. Like a thin hand on a clock, the movements of the yellow traceline mirrored those of the aerial in the sky above them. It rotated evenly round and round the black screen, bringing to light the constant curve of the coastline and the echo of a plane to the east. A small elongated oval appeared each time the trace approached the plane and disappeared when the trace had passed it. As they watched, it was gradually moving further and further to the east and towards the edge of the screen. The operator drew another arrow with his chinagraph on the screen to show its direction, and erased the last one he had drawn.

She deliberately stayed until five minutes before they stopped work, knowing they must be counting the minutes and hoping she would stop watching them and be gone. She was well aware her presence was both an imposition and restriction, but she didn't mind. She had told herself on numerous occasions that if she was an officer she couldn't expect to be liked all the time. Satisfied, she went out, conscious that behind her the operators would probably be letting out a silent cheer.

It was a glorious evening. As she walked back towards the Orangery in the bright sunshine and eager to change out of uniform, she was thinking about radar and defence, and the folly of not manning the Operations Rooms outside office hours. There was clearly no imminent danger of invasion, but it was undeniable that England was undefended and at risk when no one was dealing with the incoming information. The towers and their rotating aerials provided constant information, but Bawdsey – and presumably all the other radar stations – only registered some of it. How easy it would be for Germany or another enemy to send bombers if they knew. How could the RAF allow the radar system which had virtually won the war to be relegated to a part-time operation?

This was something she had wanted to talk to Daddy about, but not now, oh not now. She remembered Rose's phone call and tried to imagine her father in an RAF dormitory. No, of course he would not be in a dormitory. He was a Wing Commander. He would have a private room, But would he like that? What would he do? How long would he be there for?

She went upstairs to her room in the Manor house. She took off her jacket, undid her laces and kicked off her shoes before flopping down on to the bed. There was more than enough time to wash and change before the evening meal and she was not going to hurry.

There was a knock and Bridget put her head round the door. Oh dear. Bridget, already.

"Good," she said, "I hoped you'd be back early." She came straight in and sat on the bed.

Susan swung her legs off the bed, sat up and put her arm round her. "Are you all right?" she asked. Then she said, "You know I know, don't you? Mark told me."

Bridget shut her eyes and said nothing for a minute, let herself be held. Then she pulled herself up and away from Susan, and opened her eyes.

Susan waited.

"It's – I," she began. Then "I just don't know – I don't know." She put her hands to her face and started to cry. Susan turned and comforted her as the small sobs grew into a crescendo.

She held her until the waves of crying subsided. She'd have to get a hankie for Bridget. She freed herself slowly and fetched the large, white handkerchief that Mark had given her when she scratched her leg on some brambles. She offered it to Bridget who blew her nose noisily and dried her wet face. There were dark, damp patches on both their collars and shirts.

"I'm sorry," said Bridget.

"It doesn't matter. What matters is you."

Susan looked at the clock. It was time to eat. "What about supper? Do you want any?"

"No, but you go and have some. Can I stay here? I don't want to go back to my room looking like this."

Susan hesitated. She ought to stay, but Mark was expecting her, and she was hungry.

"Will you be all right on your own?"

"Of course. I'll wait here. I don't want anything to eat."

Susan said, "I'll have to change first. I'm all hot and sticky." She chose the first skirt and blouse she saw and changed quickly. As she leant towards the mirror to put on her lipstick she saw Bridget shake off her shoes and lie back on the bed, her arms above her head.

"That's better," said Susan, "try and relax a bit. You look exhausted."

She walked to the door and paused before she opened it.

"I'll be back as soon as possible. Don't do anything desperate."

"I won't, but I feel awful."

Susan thought she looked awful too – much paler than usual. She walked back, leant down to her and gave her another hug. Slowly she stood up, went out and closed the door behind her quietly. She felt bad leaving Bridget and worse as she hurried to the dining room.

*

The sea floods in softly.
It encroaches on beaches,
creeps along marsh and mud,
insinuates itself into little channels,
inches its way up barnacled posts.

An almost flat expanse of water
shifts. The creek that was empty
an hour ago is already full.
The wet weed is all but covered.

Redshanks rise from shining banks,
revealing their white rumps,
their trailing white wing tips.

Robert stands in front of the boat with a paint pot in one hand and a brush in another. The planks of the underside rise up to a level considerably higher than his head. He will need a ladder later on. First he scrubbed the planks and now he's beginning to paint them. It will take him all afternoon and the best part of

120

the next day, but it's work, good work, and he likes being in the boatyard where he can see what's going on and where Maisie can sniff around or snooze on the step of a fisherman's hut.

But there's nothing much going on this morning. The ferry-man, who has just bought the boat and intends to sell it, came down first thing to inspect the repairs he made yesterday. Robert watched him cutting out damaged wood, measuring up new pieces and fitting them in to the gaps. It always intrigues him to think how lengths of wood fixed together in a certain way can float and survive being thrown about by slabs of water as heavy as rocks.

Robert puts the pot down on the ground, stirs it with a stick, dips the brush in, loads it with paint, wipes the bristles on the edge of the pot and reaches up to draw it firmly along the top plank. There's too much paint. It comes running down across two or three boards and over his hand. He uses the brush to mop it up and sweep it sideways along the planks. He wipes his hand on his trousers. He has to stuff the corner of the brush in between where the edges of the wood meet to make sure he covers each overlap. He does it again, being more careful. Dip, wipe, reach, pull the brush along, finish off.

It's steady work and after an hour there's an ache along his shoulder from reaching up and stretching. When his pot is empty he walks up to the ferryman's hut to refill it from the big can. Maisie trots after him. Before returning to his work he goes to the tap at the end of the boatyard, bends his head under it, opens his mouth and lets the water run in. Maisie laps up the spilt water. Robert wipes his mouth on his sleeve and walks back down to the boat. As he gets near the sun comes out and it's easy to see the contrast between the painted and the unpainted wood. Clear progress. Working the ferry does not give the same satisfaction; it's never finished, except at the end of a day. The river is always there, people always need to cross it. When one load's been taken across, there's another waiting. Not like paint-ing. When this is painted it will be done, finished, and the boat can be launched again.

As he paints he thinks about his father, his real father, who was a boatbuilder in Felixstowe. He must have painted dozens of boats – or perhaps he had someone like him, Robert, to paint them for him, just as the ferryman has him. He dips and wipes and pulls the paintbrush. His father would be about fifty if he was still alive. What might have happened if he had not died? Would he have taught him and Tom how to build boats? How might life have been different? If his father had not died, if his mother had not remarried, if Tom had not been killed, if if if.

He puts the brush down and reaches out both his arms. It's particularly good to stretch the fingers of his right hand which have spent much of the morning in the same position. He turns away from the boat. The bus is trundling towards them. There is a queue by the beach waiting for the ferry which is approaching from upstream. It must have gone to deliver someone and their shopping to their sailing boat, probably either to *Louisa* or *Maid Betsy*.

"You're making a good job of that."

Robert turns round to see the ferryman.

"Why don't you give yourself a rest? Come back in half an hour or so. Go and get something to eat."

Once Maisie sees Robert's on the move she fusses round him. He takes his time and walks down to the shoreline where the tide laps up at him. He watches its tiny tongues reach out towards his boots and be overtaken by more and more falling over themselves as they urge forward. The tide is only one aspect of the river. He looks upstream, marvels at how the narrow Deben has made its way through Suffolk's soft landscape to widen and spread out here at the Ferry – right in front of his eyes – where it meets the North Sea.

He raises his head and looks up to the brown and shifting surface that seems as solid today as the green fields opposite with their speckling of red poppies. It's easy to see how the river supports boats, birds, the wide sky, huge, white clouds. He suddenly realises how Jesus could have walked on water.

He calls Maisie to him and she comes rushing up from the water's edge.

*

Clean shaven and wearing a new shirt, Mark was waiting for Susan as she came down to dinner. She was late but the impatience he had just started to feel disappeared the moment he saw her. She looked so attractive even in this dark maroon dress which she liked and he didn't.

Before he could speak she said, "Bridget's just been with me. She's been sobbing and sobbing."

They were the last people into the dining room and Mark silently held a chair out for Susan and then squeezed in to the last seat available, in between her and Ian.

He felt for Susan's hand and gave it a squeeze. She didn't return it.

The meal was served almost at once and he turned to speak to Ian. But he too was quiet. The situation between him and Bridget seemed to have knocked his spirit for six.

"Who's coming to the pub later on?" Ned called down the table. "We're going at about eight."

Mark looked at Susan with his eyebrows raised in enquiry.

"No, I can't," she said quietly, "I've got to see Bridget."

"But I thought," Mark dropped his head and then raised it again, "but I thought we were going to spend the evening together."

"I've promised her I'll go back. She's in a dreadful state."

"But you can't rush off at once. I've hardly seen you at all for the last day or two. Please, Susan."

He saw her waver at his disappointment. Then she said, "Well, just a few minutes, then. I've left her in my room. She's so upset."

God. He'd waited all day for her and now it was Bridget who mattered most. And now Philip was droning on about the play they had just begun to rehearse and would be performing in a few weeks.

"You've all got to come. It's *An Inspector Calls*, by J.B. Priestley. It's going to be super."

"Who's got the main parts?"

"The Inspector's an airman called Moss. He's very convincing and he's learned all his lines already, unlike some of the officers in the cast." The speaker nudged her neighbour as she spoke.

"Trust me. I'll learn them in time, it's weeks away. I haven't had a chance because they keep asking me to play cricket."

"What's it about?"

"Can't tell you. Top secret."

At last the sweet was served and within minutes Susan and Mark excused themselves and went out on to the terrace where the stones and walls were giving off the heat that had been pouring into them all day. Mark lit their cigarettes. He had looked forward to this moment, but could see at once that Susan was less accessible again. She said nothing as she drew on her cigarette and he knew he could not reach her. Bloody hell.

"I'm going to have to go," she said, "Sorry."

"Oh damn it." he said, "Why does it have to be like this? We've hardly had a moment together today." He threw his cigarette end on the ground and crushed it with his shoe. "And tomorrow's no good. I've got to go to RAF Felixstowe all day and I've accepted an invitation to a retirement do for someone I used to work with."

"Well, we'll have to wait until Thursday."

"But I want to be with you now! It's important. Can't you see how I feel? I thought you cared about me. I thought ..."

He stopped himself and sighed, put his arms on her shoulders and turned her gently to face him properly. That was better. She didn't say anything but she leant her cheek against his jacket and put her arms round his waist. Was it that she didn't care about him? He was sure it wasn't that. It couldn't be. It mustn't be.

He started to stroke her hair but was still feeling annoyed as well as upset. What could he say? Anything he said would probably make things worse. This had never happened before with girlfriends. He had met them, courted them, enjoyed being with them and then the friendship had just drifted apart. But not like this. Except, he had to admit, with Trudi, with whom things had been passionate and fast and then quickly over when he returned to England. But Susan was so important. He dreaded the thought of this ending.

After what seemed like less than a minute he felt Susan extract herself.

"I've got to go, Mark. Bridget looks suicidal."

He let her go. She went back inside slowly, not turning to look at him. He looked at her narrow waist, watched her full skirt swishing as she walked. He thought it very unlikely that she had ever made love. What would she think if she knew he had done so, and with more than one woman?

Bugger it. He didn't know where he was with her. He checked his watch. Ten to eight. There was just time to catch the others up on their way to the ferry.

*

Rose was tired. She had gone to the hospital early to see Henry before he was moved. She wanted to pack all his belongings herself, to ensure nothing was forgotten. Even then she nearly missed his spectacles which he was wearing when she packed his suitcase, but had placed on the bedside locker while waiting in the wheelchair before being taken to the ambulance.

Henry sat in his Paisley dressing gown with his long legs bunched up uncomfortably. She could see he was both unhappy and worried. He hated not being able to get on with things. She recalled how once, when he was about nine and she was six, they had been out for a walk with their parents. They wanted to run on ahead and had been given permission but told to wait when they reached the farm gate. When they got there it began to pour with rain. Rose had wanted to stay by the gate as they had been told, even if it meant getting wet, but Henry had said that was stupid and he was going to shelter in a barn he could see from the gate. Rose had stayed on her own in the rain, willing her parents to hurry up. When they arrived their mother was upset by the fact that Henry had left her on her own, but their father had praised him and said he was made of sterling stuff, and had laughed at Rose because she looked like a drowned mouse. This was so unfair. She had not known what sterling stuff was, but she understood she wasn't made of it, and she wished she was.

Now Henry sat with his eyes closed as he was pushed along the corridor, his small suitcase on his knees, with Rose following.

She saw him taken backwards into the ambulance and waved goodbye, promising to visit him that afternoon.

She drove home and heated up the tomato soup she had prepared the previous evening. She sat at the kitchen table and opened the newspaper. There were several articles about the first atomic weapon which had been exploded near Australia. She read bits but the news hardly mattered today. She ate slowly, adding a little salt to the soup, and she spread some soft butter very thinly onto the slice of bread she cut from yesterday's Hovis.

Then she cleared the table, took the breadboard outside the back door and brushed the crumbs off. It was wonderful out of doors. She would take her cup of tea out here and make the most of it. While the kettle came to the boil she washed up the few dishes and took down her favourite cup and saucer with the pattern of little blue flowers which looked like speedwell but which she had decided, long ago, were not. She put them on the tin tray with a tiny bowl of sugar and a jug of milk and carried them into the sunshine, leaving the door ajar. After replacing her empty cup on the tray she allowed herself a little snooze. She did not wake until the cat jumped on to her lap.

An hour and a half later she drove slowly up the drive of St Botolph's Convalescent Home for Retired RAF Officers, under an archway of magnificent beech trees. She had wound the window down. She pulled over when a car came towards her and acknowledged the driver's wave before continuing and then, after rounding a curve, saw a large redbrick building in front of her. Its windows reflected the sun in long rows of even rectangles. They reminded her of the small blocks in a paint box, although all of them were white. She parked and went in through the main entrance.

"Good afternoon. Is it Miss Cairncross?" asked a woman who had risen from her seat at a typewriter to meet her.

Rose nodded as she took off her gloves.

"We're expecting you. I'm Miss Brearley, the receptionist. Your brother has settled in well. Please come this way."

She led Rose along a corridor. The floor was of polished

floorboards, the walls were of oak panelling on which hung paintings of aeroplanes. The women walked side by side in silence until Miss Brearley slowed down as she led the way up a staircase. Rose could see into the bedrooms and saw that some were occupied and some were not. No one passed them. They finally turned into a room where Henry was lying on his side, his face turned to the wall. It felt a little gloomy but a gap between the heavy drawn curtains let in one wide shaft of daylight. This fell across the room, the bed and illuminated the floral pattern on a section of wallpaper.

"Wing Commander? Wing Commander?"

There was no response.

"Henry dear, it's me. I've come to see you."

When he stirred Miss Brearley turned to Rose. "Good. He's not fast asleep. I'll leave you with him. You can stay till half past four."

Rose looked round the room, walked over to the window and pulled back one of the curtains. The view was full of the bright green leaves of the beech trees. They almost hid the drive but she could see her car which she had not parked quite squarely.

Henry's trousers and jacket had been hung up in the wardrobe and his suitcase placed on top. His dressing gown was over the end of his bed, his slippers underneath. As he did not attempt to sit up she sat next to him and reached across to pull up the thin blanket which had slipped from his shoulder. He grunted a thankyou and she patted him.

She sat back and shut her eyes. There was no sound at all, little sign of life. She had an immediate sense that this place – however good it was supposed to be – might be too dull, too quiet. She took out her knitting and freed up a length of the soft, cream wool that was going to make a cardigan for the baby son of a neighbour. She moved her chair into the shaft of sunlight in order to check how many rows she needed before she had to work the next buttonhole. Only six. Henry gave a low cough but stayed in the same position. She was just going to sit with him, just be with him. He would not be alone then, and nor would she.

*

Susan had persuaded Bridget to come out of the building and into the garden.

"Come on, let's find somewhere that's private and sunny. It's better than staying inside – you're not looking well. Come and get some fresh air." They took a rug to sit on, and walked into the walled garden.

They found a corner where there was no breeze and where they could easily see anyone coming. There was a soft humming of insects, a scent of mint. They spread out the tartan rug and took their sandals off.

"So," said Susan gently, "tell me."

Bridget plucked at grass, rolled on to her stomach. A long minute passed.

"Well, it's just – you – I think I'm pregnant." She crossed her arms above her head and rested her forehead on them. She said something else in a muffled voice.

"I can't hear you properly. What did you say? "

Bridget lifted her head, paused and said slowly and evenly, "I think I've missed my period."

"You *think* you've missed? Can't you be sure?"

"No. Not really, because I'm not always regular. It could be all right, but I don't think it is. In fact, it can't be."

Susan waited again.

"Last time we made love, we didn't – he didn't – use anything. It must have happened then." Bridget picked the heads off daisies as she spoke. She put her head down into her hands and her voice became a quiet, boxed in wail. "And I don't know what to do."

Susan leant over and rubbed her tensed up back.

"What does Ian think?"

"He says he loves me and he wants to marry me, but he's as worried as I am. He feels so responsible – but it's not all his fault, is it? It's mine too. He thinks my parents will be so angry."

"Do you want to marry him?"

"Yes. No. I don't know. If this hadn't happened I might have wanted to – I'm not sure. And it's my mother's birthday next week, and I wanted to give her something nice – I didn't want to have to tell her this."

"But you don't need to yet. You aren't even sure if you really are pregnant. It may not be true." Susan paused. What could she say? "But what would your mother think? Would it be so terrible for her? When I met her last year I thought she was such a steady, sensible person. I can't see her falling to pieces."

"She wouldn't fall to pieces, but that's not the point. She'd be unhappy, not hysterical. She'd put a brave face on, but it wouldn't be what she'd choose for me." Bridget's voice rose to a sort of squeal, "and it's not what I'd choose for me." She buried her face in her folded arms again.

Susan lay on her side, put her hand on the small of Bridget's back and looked out and up at the sky. A straggle of seagulls was making for the coast. A ladybird zoomed towards her face and veered off again. She breathed in a waft of something which reminded her of the vegetable garden at home. Poor Bridget. But how had they let it happen? She shied away from even trying to answer that question. She shut her eyes until she sensed Bridget was calmer.

Susan asked, "Is there anything I can do? Do you want me to do anything?"

Bridget turned round and looked straight at Susan. "Tell me what to do. I need to be told what to do. I can't trust myself to decide anything at all. Ian thinks we should tell his parents and my parents as soon as possible, so they have time to get used to the idea before – before it's born."

The mention of it – the potential child – silenced them. They heard footsteps on the gravel path and Susan turned round. It was a couple she did not know well. They were walking slowly towards them with loosely held hands. Bridget looked away while Susan smiled at them as they passed.

They sat in silence for a while. Then Bridget smoothed her hair down and off her face. "I'm sorry," she said. "I'm an awful nuisance. It's all my fault."

"You're not. It's not."

"I was going to tell you the day after the ball, but you weren't

129

there. It was strange knowing that Mark was missing you, and I was too."

Susan tried to imagine Mark looking as if he was missing her. Would he be quieter than usual? Might he perhaps sit and smoke on his own? Perhaps he was doing that now? She felt a pang of guilt.

"Well, I'm here now, anyway. And I don't think you should do anything or say anything. Just try and get on with ordinary things for the time being."

"Yes. It's strange – I've found I can do that. Although all this is going on I can still work, still do what I'm supposed to do. I even played tennis on Friday."

They stayed sitting quietly, listening to the long grass swishing behind them, the chirp of an unseen bird.

Bridget was the first to stand up, "Come on, let's go back."

Susan stood up too. They picked up the rug together and she shook and folded it with Bridget as she had shaken and folded sheets with Aunt Rose a week ago. Only a week ago – less even. So much had happened.

"Are you going to see Mark now? Oh – you must have wanted to be with him this evening – I must have spoiled your evening." Bridget put her hands up to her face.

"No you haven't. Don't be silly. You haven't done that at all. It's all right. There's all the time in the world to see him."

*

Mark hurried after the others down to the jetty and saw the ferry was already untied and about to leave. He yelled, waved frantically and kept on running, knowing that Ben at least would try to persuade the ferryman to wait. He charged down on to the jetty and almost jumped into the boat. Everyone hooted with laughter. The ferryman looked up at him briefly as Mark thanked him for waiting, but he was more interested in his task of backing away from the shore.

"We thought you weren't coming!"

"But here I am!"

Mark's spirits had risen with his decision to join the party, the rush to reach them and the welcome he received. He got his breath back and looked out at the river. Downstream the water was as bright as a mirror, reflecting pinkish clouds in smooth mauve coloured undulations. Upstream it was darker, almost purple, and stretching away to the north. Creamy bubbles poured onto the surface of the water behind the stern.

Where had the word *wake* come from? It had such different meanings: the opposite of sleep, funerals, water behind a boat. He must look it up. The motor chugged away evenly, not altering speed at all as they crossed. The only other boat on the move was a dinghy making slow, steady progress to a yacht moored midstream. The person rowing laid down an oar and waved. The ferryman waved back. What a peaceful river it was on an evening like this. How simple life could be.

He jumped out on to the shingle ready for a good evening and determined to forget about Susan for a few hours.

Max commented, "You look full of beans tonight, Mark. I'm surprised, seeing as Susan isn't here. But I don't suppose she feels like going to a pub just now."

"Max, I may look full of beans, but I assure you I intend to be full of beer very soon."

Max laughed and walked up to the Ferryboat Inn with him. They settled outside the pub and took turns to fetch a round of drinks. The talk was mostly about the Royal Family and next year's coronation. Some people thought Princess Elizabeth was far too young to be Queen, others thought she would be good. And anyway there wasn't anyone else, and what about – who was it? The prince who became a king when he was a boy. Was it Edward? Which Edward? One person said Royalty was a thing of the past, and he was rounded on soundly by everyone else who pointed out that if he thought that, then he shouldn't be in the Royal Air Force, should he?

Mark enjoyed a couple of beers as the conversation moved on to the RAF Canberra's extraordinary achievement: a return flight across the Atlantic in a single day. He was pleased and proud to be part of the RAF. Good God, he was as lucky as hell to have these good friends, this good life. And Susan? Well, these things happen. Everyone has their ups and downs.

Everything would be fine tomorrow. He stood and raised his glass.

"To you all, Ned, Chris, Ben, Max, friends, everyone, to the RAF!"

"To the RAF!"

Then he sat down heavily, his energy suddenly gone. Later, as they sat in the cooling evening, he noticed the ends of his companions' cigarettes brightening to red as they drew on them. Then they faded, then they brightened again. They made the individual rates of people's breathing visible, and at times they almost coincided, showing how everyone's breathing was – for a few moments at a time – in unison. As he drank the next pint he felt increasingly proud of his friends.

As he got up to go to the lavatory he remembered Susan. He had hardly thought about her, and his disappointment didn't seem to matter now. And here was Trudi again, appearing in the middle of his evening out. He had a sudden image of the Wolfgangsee, the lake where they swam, her teaching him to say Grüss Gott instead of Guten Morgen.

"Another? Or are we ready to go?" called Chris from the gloom.

It was nearly time for the last ferry and the evening had cooled down. Mark picked up his jacket from the back of his chair, put it on and slowly followed the others down to the shore. The ferry appeared gliding smoothly towards them.

"It looks strange, as if it's floating on the surface," said Mark.

A chorus of laughter went up. "Of course it's floating – it's a boat!"

When they got in Chris stood next to Mark. "You've been quiet tonight."

"Yes. That's true."

Mark tipped his head back and looked up at the stars. How amazing it must have been for sailors, finding their way across oceans by these small lights in the sky. To be out of sight of land but in sight of stars – small suns that were only visible on fine nights. When had St Exupéry first looked at stars? It must have been long before he learned to fly. When he got back he must re-read some of *Wind, Sand and Stars*. No, not tonight.

He had no idea how he was even going to manage to walk up the drive.

He was last off the boat and he stumbled slightly, causing the ferryman to step forward to steady him.

"Goodnight, sir."

The others had gone ahead. After signing in at the entrance he zigzagged slowly up the drive. He stopped when he reached the bridge over the stream known as the Jordan. Ben was waiting for him. They sat down together on the ground and leant back against the brickwork.

The moon was a crescent. What an elegant, delicate shape. Was it female? Surely the moon was female. Mark tried to think of myths but his brain would not do what he wanted. Suddenly the lines of a poem he'd learned years ago came back to him and he recited:

> *We are the music makers*
> *We are the dreamers of dreams*
> *Wandering by lonely sea breakers*
> *And sitting by desolate streams*
> *World losers and world forsakers*
> *On whom the pale moon gleams*

"That sounds very mournful," said Ben.

"Yes, it is. I am mournful."

"Is this about Susan?"

"Yes." But it was about Trudi too.

"Well, my advice is don't let any woman stop you enjoying life."

"But she makes my life enjoyable."

"She's not doing that tonight, is she? Come on. Let's go in."

*

Since the fire and the fight earlier in the year, Robert has taken no chances. Now, each time he walks along the tideline and gathers up an armful he carries it back to his starting point. Then, when he has as much as he can take back in one go, he ties it up with a length of thin green rope, tugs the bundle taut and slings it over his left shoulder. Maisie leads the way up from the shingle, onto the path and onto *Music Maker*.

It's a perfect day for it. A few days ago a strong east wind helped push the tide and its debris well up the beach, and since then it's been hot. There's a lot of accessible, dry wood so it's worth making several trips. Before carrying the third lot he sits down for a minute or two on a tree trunk that's half buried in the beach. Carting wood isn't heavy work, but it's awkward. He rubs his right shoulder where it's sore from the rope. He's tried to protect himself by wedging a piece of folded up sack under the rope, but it keeps coming loose as he walks and it never seems worth stopping, readjusting the load and starting off again when there's only a short distance to go.

He lifts up the next bundle with care. It's mostly planks, and he sees they have rusty nails sticking out of them. This time it'll be better to swing it onto his right shoulder – awkward because he's lefthanded. Out of the corner of his right eye he sees a large, bent nail pointing towards his neck. It's not worth risking it. Although he'll be all right unless he trips, for it's more likely to slip away from him than towards him, he decides to stop and adjust it so it's safe.

Less than ten minutes later he lugs the load across his gang-plank. He leans over and lets it fall onto *Music Maker*'s deck. He unties the rope and pushes the loose wood up against the rest, picking up some of the planks and putting them on the pile. Not bad. One more lot will be plenty.

Once she sees he's going back, Maisie charges past him and heads straight for the beach again. He follows her, wondering whether to bring an axe next time. Probably not. The bigger pieces are usually much wetter and heavier, and anyway, there's so much loose driftwood to be had. It's amazing how the river can be relied on to deliver an almost constant supply. Sometimes it's rather like manna – for even though wood isn't bread, it's something he needs. He walks further along than he's done before and he stoops every now and again to inspect something that catches his eye –a piece of smooth, curved glass, a shell, rope. He has found intact bottles before but never yet a sealed one. Once he came across a brown jacket and apart from being in need of a wash there was nothing wrong with it. He wore it to church last Easter.

This time he finds pieces of torn netting, a broken lobster pot, a wellington boot, more shells than usual. Then about a yard ahead, he sees something shining. He carries on walking towards it, wondering what it could be. A tin, perhaps?

It's a knife. A decent sheathknife. This is a real find. He takes out his own from its leather sheath on his belt and compares them. The river knife is a good inch longer, and the middle of the blade is worn in a way which makes him think it's been used for a particular task, but he doesn't know what. It's been sharpened numerous times and the blade near the handle shows how wide the whole length of it must once have been. It's quite different from his own knife which has worn evenly but has a broken tip. The river knife still has its point. It'll be very useful.

"Look, Maisie. We're in luck."

He's kneeling on the stones. Once the initial excitement of his find has worn off he changes to a more comfortable position and sits facing the water with the sun on his face.

Maisie shows no interest so he chucks a stone into the water and she races out after it, first splashing, then swimming a few strokes. When she turns round and swims back he suddenly remembers Sally learning to swim. She had called out, 'Look at me! I can do swimming!' Her small hands had broken the surface and paddled just as Maisie's paws did now.

He needs to stand and stretch his shoulders. He looks across the river, realises the tide has turned, that clouds are approaching from the west. He sets off for *Music Maker*.

Things are looking up. He came out for wood but is going back with something of more value. In his left hand he holds the river knife firmly by its handle. He's whistling Greensleeves.

*

They were sitting at a table for two. It was Susan's twenty fifth birthday and when Mark invited her out and away from Bawdsey she accepted at once. He had told her he wanted to have her all to himself and spoil her with a special evening "in as close to civilisation as we can get to from Bawdsey". So here they were in The Cavendish, the best hotel in Felixstowe. There was a quiet buzz of conversation. A vase containing five small pink roses stood on the white linen tablecloth of their small round dining table.

Susan hadn't done anything like this for many months and she had enjoyed deciding whether to wear her green dress with the loose, soft collar, or the pale blue one with the little pearl buttons that took ages to do up. Finally she sought Kathleen's help and chose the blue one. It would not have been fair to ask Bridget, although Bridget had the best dress sense. Bridget knew it was her birthday but Susan had not begun to explain what was happening between her and Mark. Goodness, she had enough on her plate already.

She could not deny that her feelings for Mark were less certain than they had been a week ago. It was uncomfortable to think that Mark must be anticipating this evening with apprehension as well as pleasure. Her reason for backing off – there was no other way of saying it – was not that she found him less attractive. She very much liked the way he smiled as she approached, the dark stubble that appeared on his chin late in the evening, his warm voice. So what was it? She recalled her disappointment at not finding him at the station. It seemed extraordinary now to think she had cried when he had not turned up. Why? She hardly ever cried. She had certainly never cried about any other boyfriend. It was something to do with needing him at that precise moment. She made herself think about this. What was special about that precise moment?

It wasn't that she hadn't wanted to come back to Bawdsey. On the contrary, she had been ready to come back as soon as she knew Daddy was on the mend.

But here she was – right this minute – thinking about home again, about Aunt Rose, Daddy, her family. Was this homesickness? It wasn't like the homesickness she had had at boarding school, where she had been physically sick on the first night of every term for two years. But it was something to do with home as well as knowing that her feelings for him were less strong than his for her.

Poor Mark. Because of this they had ended up staying away from each other for three days, in a sort of vacuum. It had almost been a surprise when he invited her out to dinner. She could not have said no, and she didn't want to say no, but now she found herself feeling guilty and therefore determined that he should enjoy the evening.

The waiter removed the soup plates, and the wine waiter refilled their glasses. When he had gone Susan took a sip, looked at Mark and smiled. He put his hand across the table and held it open. She took it in hers and squeezed it. They sat in silence for a minute or two, neither sure what to say. She looked down to where his hand lay with its back on the tablecloth with her smaller hand resting on his open palm. She slowly ran her eyes up past his shirt cuffs joined by one of the silver cufflinks she knew his father had given him, along the creases of the dark fabric of his suit to where the sleeve joined the shoulder, and on to his white collar. Seeing what she was doing, Mark tipped his head sideways to meet her eye. It was impossible not to laugh.

"Chicken? For the lady?"

They both took their hands away.

"Yes, please."

"And your entrée, sir."

Mark nodded at the waiter, who put down the second plate.

Susan picked up her knife and fork but paused when she saw Mark was waiting. He picked up his glass and held it up to toast her.

"Happy birthday, Susan. It's good to have you back." He clinked her glass, tipped it up and drank. As he lowered his glass he looked at her green eyes.

"It's good to be here. I want to tell you – I .." she said. She looked away and then back to him.

"Shush," said Mark softly, "let's enjoy our meal. We've got the whole evening, haven't we?" He leaned forward. "There's things I want to say and ask, Susan. But let's take our time."

Susan nodded, relieved that he was not going to put her under pressure.

137

He picked up his knife and fork.

"Well then," he announced in his usual voice. "Game pie first."

They started to eat, and began to talk about Mark's final abandonment of golf, Rose's garden, the party that was going to be held for the CO and his wife and so on to Ian and Bridget. This was difficult and it was sad. Susan wondered if Mark had ever made love to anyone? Should she ask him? What would he think if she asked?

Mark was her first serious boyfriend. She was certainly not going to make love until she was married. She would *never* find herself in Bridget's position. How on earth could they have been so careless? She resolved there and then not to go to bed with Mark before they were married. It was a shock to find herself thinking this. Did it mean she had been thinking about making love with him? Well, it was true: she *had* been thinking about it.

She was feeling more at ease. Mark was so good to be with. He was interested in everything she said, and even when he disagreed with her he somehow made her feel that his point of view was not opposed to hers and that he valued her opinion. She had not met anyone else who could do this and yet she still held back. As she ate the sweet jam sponge that the hotel had, amazingly, found enough eggs and sugar for, she began to worry about the conversation that she knew Mark wanted.

The waiter invited them to move into the lounge. Mark pulled back Susan's chair and they walked through.

"So," said Mark, sitting back and stirring his coffee. "Let's talk about us now. Perhaps I should start off? Would that be easier?"

She nodded as she leant forward to let him light her cigarette.

Mark took his time. As he tipped up his head to breathe out smoke he saw that the little lightshade behind Susan lit up one half of her head, making her hair look fairer than it was. The other half gleamed like dark, polished wood.

"You are so beautiful. I want to be with you as much as I can." He paused. "But I'm not sure what you want, Susan. What do you want? This week I've not known what's been happening, what you've been thinking."

"I'm sorry," she said slowly. "I'm sorry I've made you feel like that. I didn't mean to. I've been thinking a lot about my family, about Daddy. He could have died."

Mark spoke gently. "But he hasn't died."

"My family threesome is all I've got."

He did not look at her.

"You could have me too." He drew on his cigarette. "Will I always be outside your threesome?"

Susan said nothing for a few moments. Perhaps he would be. She could not say that, though, and not answering the question made her feel mean. And it wasn't quite true that she was thinking just about her family. She was thinking about Mark not mattering to her as much as she mattered to him. This was so difficult. She put out her hand for the handkerchief Mark was pulling out of his pocket. She blew her nose loudly, wetly.

"I don't know. When I was at home I thought about you a lot, but now I'm here I'm thinking about them a lot."

Mark said, "I'm not sure I understand, but perhaps I don't need to. Is it all right for me go on caring about you? I can't stop doing that, you know." He paused. "But if you don't want me to, I'll keep my distance and try not to show it."

What could she say? She did not want to hurt him, and anyway, her feelings didn't stay the same. They'd changed within the last two hours.

"I like you caring about me, I really do. It's just that before Daddy's stroke I was throwing myself into all this – you, the RAF, Bawdsey, but now I seem to be looking backwards."

"That's not surprising."

"But I'm cross with myself because it's not fair for you." Susan wiped her nose and handed back the handkerchief. "You must believe me. Mark, I've never met anyone like you, never thought anyone as important as you before. You're special but I don't .. I can't pretend that you matter to me more than everything else."

"Do you know I love you?" said Mark. "I *love* you. You don't have to stop caring about everything else." He moved his chair slightly so he could reach her hand across the table. "I wish we could spend more evenings together like this."

They both sat back. Something had shifted. Susan felt better. Although she couldn't explain everything yet, she had said the hardest thing, and he had said he loved her. No other man had ever told her that.

He excused himself and left Susan alone on the sofa. Her body almost felt tingly. How could she have been near tears a few moments ago? He had told her he loved her.

Looking round the lounge for the first time she saw that there were about twenty people, mostly in couples. Many of them were older. What would her father and mother have looked like when they dined together? She could imagine her father sitting there as he was now – no, as he had been, she suddenly thought, before his stroke. What would he look like now, really now? He would look – he would look clumsy. He would *be* clumsy. He might spill food. No, don't think about that.

And what would he have looked like as a young man? Like he did on the photo that had stood on the mantlepiece for as long as she could remember? In that loose jacket and slacks, with his arm round her mother who wore a pale dress and had her hair piled elegantly on her head? And had they loved each other? The same amount? Surely they had. But who could tell?

"Happy birthday. Go on, take it, it's for you."

Mark had come back and was holding out a small box towards her.

She reached across and took it from him. "Mark, thank you. I wasn't expecting – well, I wasn't expecting a present because I've been so .. like I've been."

He poured them each another cup of coffee.

"I'm glad you're telling me the truth. It hurts, but it doesn't change how I feel towards you. I'd rather know your feelings than not know them."

"Well, I'm glad I'm here with you now, and that you didn't decide I wasn't worth bothering about."

"Susan! I couldn't ever not bother about you. You know that."

"And now I'm very glad it's my birthday." Susan gazed at the little wooden box, and moved it from one hand to the other. She was itching to open it but was delaying the moment. It must be something very small.

Mark lit a cigarette, relaxed again and smiled as he watched her give in to curiosity.

She undid a little clasp and lifted the lid open. Inside was a piece of blue silk.

"It's the same colour as my dress! How did you know I was going to wear this dress?" She carefully unfolded the silk and drew out a pendant. She held it up. From a thin gold chain hung a polished stone.

"What is it? An orangestone? It's the colour of an orange, a very dark orange. It's beautiful."

"It's amber. They find it on the beaches round here. It's some sort of a fossil."

Susan held it up to the light. She loved the rich colour, the light shining through it. She leaned across to him and said, "I love it. What a gorgeous present. Thank you so much. I've got to put it on now."

She held up the ends of the chain on either side of her neck and turned her back to Mark. When he had taken the ends from her she lifted her hair up and leant her head forward.

"Mm," he said, "nice scent. There. I've done it."

Susan turned to face him. The piece of amber hung just below the neckline of her dress, clear enough for Mark to see her topmost button through it, slightly magnified.

"It looks just right on you," he said. "It's perfect."

Susan took out her powder compact from her bag and looked at herself in the tiny mirror. She smiled at him and leant across to kiss his cheek. "I'm going to call it my orangestone. I like that word better than amber. It's wonderful."

*

After the bumpy, draughty bus ride back to the Ferry, they strolled along towards the boatyard to avoid waiting with the usual group. Some people got off the bus with them, others were coming out of the pubs.

"Careful," said Mark. "There's things all over the ground here. Don't trip."

They picked their way slowly between the dark huts, bits of boats, piles of nets, lobster pots. The night was warm and slightly overcast. No stars were visible. They could hear the quiet lap of the river.

"I don't want stars anyway," said Mark. "I'd rather have you." He turned Susan towards him and kissed her again. "It's so good to have you back. Will you stay as gentle and close as you are now?"

"I hope so," said Susan. She looked out to the estuary. "I want to be your friend, Mark. You're such a good person." She pointed, "Look, there's the ferry."

They made their way back, watched the boat with its small lights nosing across the water and up to the beach. They were the last to climb on. It was full and they had to squeeze in next to the ferryman. When they cast off from the landing stage Susan put one of her hands into Mark's pocket. It felt snug in there. Half way across she reached up with her free hand and felt for her orangestone on its little chain. It was warm against her neck, a treasure from this evening they had spent together, and a good omen for the future. When was Mark's birthday? She ought to know.

"I've forgotten when your birthday is – I'm sorry – I know you've told me."

"July the fifth."

"Then I've missed it!"

"It doesn't matter at all. Birthdays don't matter to me."

"They must do. Mine matters to you, doesn't it?"

Mark put his arm round her and pulled Susan in front of him. She stumbled slightly in her high heels and found herself right in front of the ferryman, and stepped back, glancing up at him.

"Sorry, I'm in your way."

The ferryman did not say anything, but pushed his cap further back on his head in some sort of acknowledgement. He kept his eyes on the dark river ahead, glimpsed to the right and left.

Susan had her face sideways against Mark's jacket. She

watched the ferryman, observed how he continued to look ahead, then from one side to the other, noting the buoy upstream and altering course and increasing his speed just a jot. He was young, younger than she had thought. He only looked about eighteen, but if he was eighteen he'd be doing National Service. Perhaps he was older. He bent down and reached out his hand to his knee, and she saw he was caressing the ears of his brown and white dog that was almost wedged in behind his legs. He straightened up and turned to look right, then left again, not missing a beat. He's sweeping the river, she thought. He's sweeping it like radar sweeps the sky, searching his horizon, looking for potential hazards and risks. This was interesting. She wondered if Mark had noticed.

Mark leant back to look at her.

"Are you ok?" he asked.

"Yes, I'm very ok. In fact. I'm much more than ok."

When they reached the Bawdsey side everyone else got off first before the ferryman turned and stretched out his hand to help Susan.

The two of them walked to the end of the jetty arm in arm. At the end they stopped and turned back. They looked directly at the ferry as the man unwound the rope he had tied loosely to a post on the jetty. They watched as he reversed the boat and they saw his dog jump up on to the empty seat and stand looking out ahead at the estuary.

They walked up the drive and into the Manor. They said goodnight quietly, seriously, meaning their thankyous to each other for the evening. Then Susan went upstairs and slipped quietly along the corridor hoping she would not meet anyone. She undid the buttons of her dress and hung it up carefully before taking the rest of her clothes off. What would Mark be thinking? She hoped he would not change how he was towards her.

Even this evening she had swayed towards him again. Why were her feelings so unpredictable?

She stood in front of the mirror wearing only the orange-stone pendant. The stone hung just above the midpoint between her breasts. It was bigger and darker than her nipples.

She looked at her hair, her face, her neck, her breasts, her shoulders and arms, her chest and stomach. As her eyes went down her body she saw there was blood on the hair and skin between her thighs. It must have just started, for there had been none on her underclothes.

When she lay in bed before sleeping, thinking about Mark, about her father, about home she suddenly remembered Bridget and how she must be longing, absolutely longing for blood.

*

As the sun moved slowly across the room Rose counted the rows on the second sleeve of the little cardigan. She was just finishing off the cuff. If she could complete it by teatime she would be able to sew it up tomorrow morning when she was at home. Sewing up, she found these days, was better done sitting by the south facing French window in daylight than under the standard lamp with its sixty watt bulb that stood near her arm chair. The cardigan's future owner, Christopher, was already two weeks old.

It was a while since she had knitted such a small item, and it was a real pleasure because it could be done so quickly. During the war she had knitted socks and socks and socks for other people's sons, boyfriends, husbands, fathers, nephews, godsons. This had been a labour of care rather than a labour of love but it had felt important to do something practical, and she had been pleased when she received occasional cards and messages of appreciation. Of course there had been times when it was awful to think about the fate of her socks and those who wore them. They must have been on feet as they were blown up or buried in mud or even worse. But one day a year or two ago she was visiting an old friend, Ann, and Ann's son was there, whom she had not met. When he was introduced to her this tall young man had asked, in a voice of incredulous delight, "Are you the Miss Cairncross who supplied me with socks?"

When she nodded he had walked forward, taken her hands in his and fallen to his knees. He had kissed her hands in an extrav-

144

agant gesture and then thrown his head back, so that his fair hair lobbed up in a sudden movement she could recall exactly. He had said, "Miss Cairncross! Your socks saved me! For two years your socks were my most valuable possessions! They were the envy of my platoon!"

She smiled as she reached for the last but one ball of wool and straightened out the tiny sleeve. Of course most of her knitting had been for Henry and Susan. She put her knitting things down and looked closely at Henry. He had slipped slightly to the left but seemed comfortable enough. A trace of thin spittle led from his open mouth onto the pillow, and Rose took her hankie out of her sleeve and wiped it off. He did not respond. His skin colour was better now, it seemed, but perhaps that was just the late afternoon sunshine. September the first already. No one had said anything about him going home yet.

Rose embarked on the main part of the sleeve. Simple, plain stocking stitch. All she had to remember now was to increase and then decrease the number of stitches in each row. As she freed a length of wool the ball rolled under the chair. She got down on her knees and retrieved it from beside the leather slippers that Susan had given Henry last Christmas. She remembered Susan saying, "This isn't a very exciting present, but I don't want you to go and get pneumonia just because Wilbur ruined your last slippers."

Susan. It was for Susan that she had knitted most of all. At least five grey cardigans for school. A brown one for Brownies. And when she was about ten she had asked for a sailor's jersey which she had worn for two whole winters, happy in its big blue and white stripes. Susan was not a knitter. Other than doing French knitting using a cotton reel with nails and a darning needle and creating a yard or two of what she called woolly rope, she had shown more interest in being outside. She enjoyed playing with Wilbur and being in her den deep under the wisteria. She had lined it with rugs and squeezed in a stool, a plank for a table and a box for her teddy bear to sit on. It had been best in there when it was raining because she liked to hear and see the drips while staying almost dry.

Rose counted off the stitches. Twenty seven, twenty eight,

twenty nine. She herself had grown up inside rather than outside. She had had dolls, a doll's pram, a dolls' house. Henry had liked to go fishing but she enjoyed playing the piano with her mother. They had done scales, sung, practised duets together. The metronome had clicked as it sat, squat and angular, on top of the piano. Sometimes she put it on when she wasn't playing. Left, right, left, right, left, right. Sometimes she tried to breathe in time with it. When set at its fastest tempo she imagined it winning a race against other metronomes, and sometimes she slowed it down to try to find the precise point at which it ceased to move at all. The bar did not move when it was hidden, but once opened up it sprang alive and moved with as much energy and constancy as if it were a heart beat waiting to get going again.

"What time is it?"

Rose glanced up as Henry spoke, and patted his hand.

"It's about four o'clock. You've had a good snooze."

He rubbed his eyes, wiped his mouth.

"All I do is snooze."

"That's all right. That's what you're supposed to be doing."

"I'd love a cup of tea."

Rose fetched him a glass of water.

"That'll have to do for now, but someone usually comes round about this time. We won't have to wait long." Rose was longing for a cup herself.

Henry made as if to get out of bed, and Rose let him lean on her. She helped him into his dressing gown, and then he slowly made his way to the door and down the corridor. She watched his slightly bent back. This was certainly progress. He couldn't have taken himself off to the lavatory on his own a week ago. And even the doctor had commented on his clearer speech.

While he was out of the room she straightened out the sheets and pillows and the tea trolley arrived.

When he shuffled back in she asked, "Why don't you sit here on the chair for a change? I bet you're tired of sitting in bed all day."

Henry settled himself down and smiled at her. Rose passed him his tea when she saw he was ready. It was still difficult for him to hold the cup on the saucer securely, so after a few sips he handed it back to her. He reached for it every minute or two.

"We'll have to get you another little table. This one's full already." The bedside cabinet had a jug of water and a glass, two books, two letters and a framed photo of Susan under a laburnum tree. Light grey blossoms hung from dark grey branches.

"I want to go home now. I've been here for long enough."

"Well, you're certainly getting on better. But it's still too soon, you know."

Rose passed him the almost empty cup and he finished off his tea. He gave her the cup back, got to his feet slowly and looked out of the window. One tree in the avenue of beeches was beginning to turn golden.

"I've got to go home sometime, you know. I can't stay here for ever."

*

Mark, Susan, Bridget and Ian were on their way to see the first performance of *An Inspector Calls*. The cast and stage crew had said it was an excellent play and that their production was, of course, superb. They promised their audiences drama and entertainment but refused to tell anyone about the plot.

"I've heard it's a psychological thriller," said Mark. "Culture comes to Bawdsey at last!" They were walking along a soggy path between dripping trees towards the wooden building known as the Theatre in the Woods. "So of course they're not going to tell us the plot."

By the time they arrived at the theatre they were damp. From the gramophone in the corner came Doris Day's *A Guy is a Guy* and then something of Rosemary Clooney's. Despite this they could hear thumps from behind the curtain. The theatre was already smokey.

Mark and Ian made their way into the middle of the rows of seats near the front, and Bridget and Susan followed. Mark was thinking how all of them knew two things about Bridget: that she thought she was pregnant and that she was going home on leave tomorrow and would tell her mother. But they had not talked about any of this except in certain pairs – him and Ian, Bridget and Ian, Susan and Bridget, him and Susan. There were obvious reasons for this but it still felt odd that they weren't talking about it together.

Mark was hoping beyond hope that an interesting detective story would help his friends through this particular evening for it seemed as if at least change, if not difficulty and unhappiness, lay ahead of them.

They were in their places with ten minutes to spare but Ian could not settle down.

"There's time for a smoke. Come on."

Mark stood up again and squeezed after him along the row past other people's knees. He lit both their cigarettes, then leant against the wall and looked back at Susan and Bridget. There was such a contrast between them tonight. Susan's cheeks were brighter than usual from the fresh air. She was pushing back strands of wet hair from her face as she chatted with the row of girls behind her. Bridget had her head down, her arms folded. It was sad to see how all the dance, all the smile had gone out of her. As he watched, Susan turned round to face forward again. She said something to Bridget, then reached out and touched her hand. After a few moments she looked up at Mark but he could not interpret her expression. If only she would come to love him.

At that point the lights flicked off and on.

"Come on, Ian. It's beginning."

"I just wish it were only the play that was beginning."

Mark had never before heard such bitterness in Ian's voice. He put his hand on his shoulder and urged him gently towards his seat.

The curtain went up and revealed a dining room. Round the table, which a maid was clearing, sat a well-heeled family. The play was set in 1912. The pater familias was one of the radar instructors, Desmond, made up to look at least twenty years older than he was in real life. He looked surprisingly distinguished with grey hair. The mother was played by a woman whom Mark did not recognise at all until she spoke. He did not know either of the two airmen who took the parts of the son of

148

the household, or the man who was engaged to the daughter, Sheila. Susan whispered that Sheila was one of the radar operators. He sat back. This could be good. But after a promising beginning Desmond launched into a few long speeches which were far too laboured. That was the trouble with amateur dramatics. They were always too serious.

His left sock was wet and his foot was cold. Damn. He must have stepped in a puddle. Perhaps he was mistaken about the play. Perhaps it was all going to be rather predictable. The father was boring. There was an uncomfortable pause in which Desmond looked fiercely at his son. Then a bell rang and the son said, with relief, "Somebody at the front door." A quiet chuckle from the audience accompanied the arrival of a new character, the police inspector.

That was something new, having the police arrive before the murder had taken place. Mark sensed a shift amongst the audience as the story began to take its course, the characters to develop. Maybe it was going to be all right after all. The girl playing the daughter was a bit dramatic, but it seemed as if she was meant to be like that. She had a long speech and she threw herself into it, giving her account of how she'd made a shopgirl lose her job, and expressing her guilt about it. By the end of Act One the plot had thickened satisfyingly.

The theatre was fuggy. In the first interval someone opened the double doors, which meant those at the back complained of the cold. *I saw Daddy Kissing Santa Claus* was played twice through but was only just audible through the noisy conversation.

Mark was pleased to see that both Ian and Bridget had perked up a bit, and then Susan, completely unexpectedly, gave him a beautiful smile.

Ian was saying to Susan, "I'm surprised by that lanky airwoman, you know the one I mean – the girl? She's really good, she's getting better as it goes on."

"So's the Inspector. I have a suspicion it may be him who's the key to the whole thing."

"You don't think he's to blame, do you? How could he be?"

Mark met Susan's eyes. With a slight nod she indicated

Bridget who was chatting to someone else. She looked fine. Good. This felt better. It had definitely been the right decision to come to the play. Thank God.

*

It was Wilf who said, "Go on, Robert. Get a few more trades under your belt. A man can't have too many trades. Learn as much as you can."

And it's true. When he looks around, there are people who paint houses, mend nets, lift barrels of beer.

He still talks to Wilf and to Mr and Mrs Corby more than to people his own age. Tony and Billy have not come back to *Music Maker* again, and although he has been to the Speedway once he stood there on his own, unmoved by the small crowd's enthusiasm. He much prefers doing to watching. He's been back to the pub only once. He'd like to talk to Jack more, but Jack cycles to Felixstowe every day, even most weekends.

Yesterday Robert helped Mr Corby pull a cloud of old man's beard off a shed it had all but smothered. Then they hauled out a dozen rotten planks and replaced them with smart new corrugated iron. Robert hammered nails through the metal and into two by two battens so they could be joined to the existing walls while Mr Corby dug holes for new posts. Finally, they fixed the new walls onto the upright posts and Robert climbed up the stepladder and fixed the roof back on.

"Now you'll have to creosote it," said Mrs Corby when she came out to admire it.

"It won't take much. I can find some, or even some paint, if you don't mind about the colour. There's often paint left over from jobs in the boatyard."

They piled up bulky armfuls of the loose scratchy stalks of the old man's beard and carried them to an already half-made bonfire. Robert scrunched up some newspaper and pushed it into the centre. It lit at the first go, sending thin smoke into the evening. As the heat increased he loaded on the wood from the shed. It was so rotten it was almost disintegrating like cardboard. The bottom end of each plank had a colony of snails. He put handfuls of them into a bucket and transferred them to the compost heap.

He stood watching the grain of the wood curl in the heat, raking the edges of the fire inwards. A thick pall of smoke began to emerge. He remembered how his stepfather had been injured when a bottle exploded in a bonfire and a piece of glass shot out and hit him as he stood tidying up the edges with a rake. He wondered again about other bottles biding their time and waiting to explode.

"A good bonfire's a real joy," said Mr Corby. "And it's a good thing we've had it today. The wind's getting up."

Robert left at around five with a bag of sweet smelling windfalls from Mrs Corby's sister's apple tree in Felixstowe. It was already beginning to get dark. He whistled to Maisie. The summer was over, but it was still warm.

Today Robert has worked in the boat yard all day, moving timber from where a lorry has unloaded it to where it's needed for one of the boatbuilders. He's offered to help because he's determined to learn as much as he can from this man. He's seen boats being built before, but there are stages he doesn't know about, certain parts of construction he needs to look at more closely. The prow. The keel. Somebody always wants a repair done, and he's sure he'll be able to find occasional work in the yard if people trust his skill.

Now he's back on *Music Maker*, lying on his stomach, on his bunk. His head's leaning over the edge to the right, looking down towards the floor where he's spread out the latest letter from his mother. Maisie is squashed between his legs and the cabin wall. This is his favourite position for reading. He sometimes reads the Felixstowe Times like that, pulling each sheet close to him so they end up all over the cabin floor.

The first line says *My dear Robert*. This is unusual. She doesn't usually put My dear, it's usually just Dear.

My dear Robert,
Thank you for your letter. I hope you'll find somewhere better to stay for the winter. A boat's all right in the summer, but it must be getting

151

damp already now. Let me know where you're going to be. The ferry work sounds good – good to have something regular.

We're all well except the girls were given a kitten and yesterday it disappeared. They are so upset. We've spent hours looking for it, but I think it will come home again I hope.

Dad is back at work full time now, and his back seems all right now, thank goodness. The rent is not a problem when we are both working. Dad painted the kitchen and it looks like new.

I sometimes think you will turn up here one day. That would be a treat.

Sally wants to write something on the other side.

Here is a photo a man at Dad's work took. He takes lots of photos and when dad mentioned to someone that it was his birthday, he said he would take a family picture and give it to him. He gave us two copies and this one is for you. I hope you like it.

With all my love,
Mum

Robert stretches out his right arm to pick up the envelope again. He pulls out the small snapshot he's missed. His stepfather and mother stand shoulder to shoulder, almost the same height. Sally stands in front of his stepfather, Lizzie in front of his mother. They too are both the same height, despite the difference in their ages. Mother has her hair up in a bun, making her face thinner than he remembers. Dad looks serious, but less fierce than he remembers. Sally is smiling at the camera, and Lizzie seems to be about to speak.

The foursome appear square, solid, united. He isn't in it. He isn't in this family photo.

He lays the photo on the floor and picks up the piece of lined writing paper. He turns it over and reads

Dear BOB, Our black and white kitten ran away I am so unhappy. Please pray she will come back to us. Hug from Sally.

He turns back and reads the whole letter through twice more, then studies the photo again. Lizzie is wearing shorts, Sally a sunfrock. They're taller than when he last saw them. Is this door in the corner the door to where they live? The handlebars of a bike poke into the left hand edge of the photo. Whose bike is it? Are the four of them happy? When will he see them again?

He gets up and puts the photo and letter carefully back in the envelope. He fetches from a wooden box the brown paper bag where he keeps all the letters he's ever received. They're all from his mother. He puts the box away in the end of the galley. It's the safest place for them. Then he makes a cup of tea and drinks it slowly. The windows of the cabin are rectangles of blackness.

Later, lying in his bunk, he doesn't fall asleep. He hears Maisie snuffling quietly, and he feels the water pushing on the boat. He knows from its direction that it's not the tide, but wind.

He's thinking about the photograph. He should be in it. So should his brother Tom. There should be six of them. But should his real father be there too? And if he was, then his step-father and Lizzie and Sally would not be. Is that what he wants?

He says the Lord's Prayer. This is easy for he knows it well and sometimes says it when he wants something badly, but he always wonders whether it's all right only to pray when he wants something. Surely it's all right to ask for something for someone else? He says to himself, or to God – he's not sure which – Please may the girls' kitten not be dead. They want it home safely. Please look after my mother. Amen.

*

They settled back into their seats as the lights went down. Susan was sitting between Ian and Bridget. Now the audience was attentive, engrossed and ignoring the minor accidents that occurred on stage, such as a door getting stuck and one of the characters catching her sleeve on a chair and almost tipping it over.

Susan found that the girl in it, Sheila, was becoming more and more confident, challenging her parents. She was the only one who really understood the horror of the situation: a young woman had committed suicide in a terrible, painful way, and perhaps, if people had done things differently, she might not have done. The girl playing Sheila had real presence on stage.

Susan thought she and Sheila had things in common. Sheila was forthright, spoke her mind, had principles. She'd make a good RAF officer if she'd stop blaming herself. But she had a father, a mother and a brother. That made her very different. And she was engaged. In the first scene they were celebrating the engagement. What would happen if she became engaged to Mark – would Daddy and Aunt Rose celebrate? Of course they would. But what would it be like to be engaged? Or to be married?

Suddenly Susan heard Sheila's fiancé admit he had kept a mistress while being engaged to Sheila. Damn. Let there not be too much made of this. It felt close to the bone. Thank goodness, the inspector was turning his attention to the next character. But then he said, "Just remember that this girl was going to have a child." There was little space between her chair and Bridget's and she sensed Bridget tense up. She did not dare look at Ian. Then she heard the words, "It was because she was going to have a child that she went for assistance to your mother's committee." And then, "Go and look for the father of the child. It's his responsibility."

This was dreadful. Ian and Bridget must be feeling awful. There was nothing she could do. They were trapped. Should she hold Bridget's hand? Yes. She reached out and took it. There was nothing she could do for Ian. She shut her eyes and waited for what still might come.

"If he refused to marry her – and in my opinion he ought to be compelled to – then he must at least support her."

At last the curtain closed and the lights went on.

The four of them continued to face forward, in silence, while everyone else got up and stretched their legs. Susan imagined a dozen conversations starting up amongst the audience about affairs and pregnancies and responsibilities.

Mark turned to Ian and asked quietly," Do you want to leave? We don't have to stay."

Ian said, "What I need is a cigarette."

He stood up and made to move along the row to the aisle, away from the others, but then stopped and turned back to Bridget. Mark got up to let him squeeze past him and go back to Bridget. He sat down next to her and Susan looked across the couple's bent heads to Mark. He was looking away from her. That was odd. She decided to join him at the back of the hall.

"Oh my God. That was horrible. Mark, are you alright? You look awful."

"I'm feeling awful. I think we should go. I'm hating every minute."

"Well, it's up to them," said Susan. "We can't leave them here."

Bridget and Ian did not move. They were sitting back in their chairs, not talking. From time to time Ian tipped his head up to blow out a thin curl of smoke.

"What if it gets worse?" asked Susan.

"I don't think it can."

They joined the surge as people moved back to their seats and the lights went down.

As the final act opened Susan regained some sense of perspective. This was a play, only a play. Ian was not like any of the characters who were coming to realise they might have contributed to a woman's death. Ian did not get drunk and steal as one of them did, nor had he had an affair while supposedly being committed to his fiancée. Bridget was not penniless, homeless and she had not committed suicide. And it was 1952 not 1912.

But it was still jarring to hear some of the dialogue: "So you had to go to bed with her?" and: "She told me she thought she was going to have a baby. She wasn't quite sure. And then she was."

Susan thought there was no need to take the play so personally. And yet, the connection between individuals and society was the whole point of it. This family were all tied up with each other but they couldn't untangle themselves. Some of them were trying to protect and some were trying to blame. Is that what happened in families? Had this ever happened in her family? And Mark had looked so preoccupied in the interval. It must have been because he was so worried about Ian. In fact, he seemed more worried about Ian than she was about Bridget. Gosh, that was awful.

Susan heard the words: "Women need someone to love. That's their weakness." Did they? Was it? She would have to think about this, but not now, no, not now. She was willing the play to be over, longing to get away from this family and its problems. To think they had come here to be entertained.

After the applause the four of them made their way through the crowd round the door. Outside it was not cold, but damp and dark. Mid September. A breeze met them as they emerged on to the open path. It was much better to be out of the theatre.

Susan took Bridget's arm, and it felt as if she had to lead her like she would an old person. Bridget was desperate and lonely, and needed a friend and she, Susan, was the closest friend she had. Susan still didn't feel as close to her as when they had been at Cranwell, but she felt she *should* be close. Not like Mark. He had said he didn't want her to feel any obligation towards him. He wanted her to be close only if she really wanted to be close.

She thought about being close to Mark. Must closeness mean sex? Of course it must, although one thing was certain. She must never, never get into Bridget's position. But then, Mark would never let that happen. Ian could be a bit wild at times, but Mark was far too sensible to take risks. If, that was, she should come to love him as he loved her, and they got engaged.

*

The cardigan was finished. Button holes were always tricky but at least there had only been five to do. Rose held the cardigan up. It was pretty. Christopher's mother would be delighted. What a pleasure it was going to be, at some point in the future, to knit clothes for Susan's children. Even though she often looked forward to having a new little person in the Cairncross family she had not really thought about knitting for him or her before. How strange that she hadn't, for it would be such fun. It had taken her years to get over the pain of not having children and at times it had been difficult to be with those who took them for granted. But the thought of Susan's children made her both impatient and happy.

She walked over to the French window, the cardigan still in her hand. The new lawn would be fine next year, although it was bare earth now. The seeds were sown. Yes, it would be an improvement.

The telephone rang and she picked up the receiver.

"Hallo, Westbury 3472".

"Is that Miss Cairncross? It's St Botolph's here."

Rose answered, "Yes." Her stomach lurched.

"Dr Arthur hoped you might be coming in today, as he'd like to discuss your brother's situation."

Rose paused.

"Oh, I'm sorry," said the voice at the other end. " I should have told you there's nothing to worry about – indeed, on the contrary. Dr Arthur thinks he's making good progress."

"Thank goodness. Yes, I was planning to come over this afternoon."

"Good. Can we say three o'clock?"

Rose listened to *Mrs Dale's Diary* as she finished off the tasks she had set herself that morning. After that there was a discussion about why some rationing had been brought back in when people had been told the end of the war would mean everything would return to normal. It hadn't, of course. So many things were different now. Television, for one. She must know at least ten other people with televisions. And attitudes were different, too. Last summer, in Bristol, she had seen a group of women wearing clothes she had thought very showy, and behaving in, well, in a rather vulgar way. Surely this wasn't progress?

Her attention went back to Henry. Could she manage to have him here at home? Would he ever be able to return to his own home? She put up the ironing board and pressed the cardigan under a damp cloth. It really was sweet. Then she ironed the linen serviettes which Susan used to enjoy rolling up and putting in the silver napkin rings. Perhaps things would be all right after all. He was a tough old thing.

By the time she had been ushered into the doctor's room at St Botolph's she was apprehensive again about the meeting.

Someone brought her a tray of tea. She poured a little but it needed to brew. She looked at the bookshelf, the leather chair, a chaffinch on some bright red berries outside the window.

Dr Arthur came in. He had dark hair and a dark moustache. She put him at about thirty five – it seemed so young to be a doctor. He shook her hand, gave her a warm smile. Perhaps it would be someone like this who would make the right sort of husband for Susan.

"No, please don't get up."

Dr Arthur moved the tea tray slightly to put his papers on the table.

"Well. Your brother. He's doing very well, you know. Better than we expected."

"That's good."

"I've talked to the nursing staff and the stroke specialist at the hospital, and we all agree that he's definitely on the mend. However, I must point out that we don't know much about predicting strokes. In your brother's case there was no apparent reason and no warning. It just happened. He's been very lucky. He seems to have recovered his movement and speech almost entirely. But I need to let you know that it may happen again."

"So what will he – will you – do now?"

"Well, as you know he's been having certain medicines to help with the stress a stroke causes, but there is really not much more we can do. And as things stand, it seems as if he'll get along as well at home as he will here."

He paused.

"How does that sound?"

Rose hesitated.

"What, you mean – he'll be all right at home now?" Her voice was full of doubt.

"Yes. He could go home, but we need to think about what that means to you."

Rose heard herself breathe out, almost a sigh. Thank goodness. They cared about what *she* thought. Dr Arthur was waiting, but there was no need to speak at once.

She looked up again and saw that he was looking straight at her.

"Why don't you take your time over this?" he said. "Let me pour you some tea before it gets cold."

He picked up the pot, placed the strainer on her cup and filled it. She thanked him and drank the tea.

She spoke carefully. "I'm not sure how much looking after he needs, and whether I can do it. I don't want to take on more than I can deal with. I'm on my own, you know."

"Is there anyone else who could help you? Does the Wing Commander have any children?"

"Yes. He has a daughter. But she's not here. She's miles away."

"Well, could she come back, for a while at least?"

No, she couldn't. In fact, she probably wouldn't. She had too much else going on. A career, a boyfriend.

"No, she couldn't. Susan's in the RAF, she's an officer. She couldn't just leave it all."

"Well. That's going to be difficult." Dr Arthur sat back. " I'm not sure he should be with you unless you have some help. How about a nurse who came in from time to time?"

"Is that possible?"

"Certainly. Most of the time he would be fine, but there are personal things like bathing and shaving which would be difficult for you. Could you manage if there was a nurse?"

Rose said nothing. How long would this be for? A month? Two months? Six months?

"His local doctor would keep an eye on him and if things were difficult we would have to think again."

"Well, if a nurse came in each day I think I could do it. I'd have to get things ready before he came. It'll take me a day or two to rearrange the spare room and empty some drawers for his clothes." And fetch more things from his house – clothes, sheets, towels. Perhaps she should even buy a refrigerator? She had been putting it off for a year or so. There would be a lot to do.

"There's no hurry at all, Miss Cairncross. He needs to be here for two more weeks at least. Just take things steadily. We won't move him until you are ready."

Dr Arthur stood up and held out his hand. What a nice young man.

She felt better as she walked along the corridor and up the stairs. She was delighted to find Henry sitting up reading the paper.

"Henry, in a fortnight they're going to let you come home to me."

He put the paper down at once and smiled his old smile, "That'll be splendid, Rose. Splendid."

*

Robert thinks that passengers have their own pattern, their own tides. Sometimes the movement is almost all towards Bawdsey Manor, sometimes almost all towards the Ferry. There's always someone travelling against the flow, a sort of small undertow. There's always someone waving goodbye to a friend on the shore, like an eddy trying to swirl backwards while being carried forwards. On the one hand people are crossing north to Bawdsey and south to the Ferry. On the other hand there's the river in its own state of flux.

The ferry is at the floating centre of these flowings. The ferrymen know about the river's comings and goings and about the comings and goings of the people who cross it. Robert is certain he's never carried exactly the same load of passengers back as he ferried out. Not only are there always different people, but each person must be slightly different on their return journey. Just as the river changes its composition but is still the Deben, people change but keep their own identity. And if his passengers change does this mean that he changes too? No. He just stays in the boat. Surely it's getting off the ferry and out into the world that causes change? But it's true he's got taller in the last twelve months. He has to duck now when he goes through his cabin door.

He has seen too that the mood of the passengers alters as the moods of water do. Sometimes a boatload is choppy with bits of conversations and sudden surges of laughter, sometimes it's smooth and reflective. He's often seen a group come on board with some quiet people, some noisy. Then their differences seem to disappear – they settle down together. This used to surprise him until the boatbuilder told him that a captain has to deal at once with anyone who's in a black mood. If it's left to fester, he said, it can contaminate the whole crew.

Now it's ten o'clock on Saturday morning and there's a noisy buzz of conversation on Bawdsey quay. People seem to be in high spirits. The boat is almost full but Robert has been asked if he'll wait for two passengers who are definitely on their way, who will be there in a few minutes. He looks back to the Ferry to confirm that there are only a few people waiting there. No need to rush. He gazes out at the Deben's rivery hillocks, its dips that seem full of silver and brass coins this morning. The mud flats are burnished like smooth gunmetal, but right here, within a few yards on the sandy beach beside the jetty, he can see the spidery tracks of gulls and oystercatchers, and the little coils made by worms.

He looks up and sees the last couple come on board. He recognises them both. They make their way past knees and bags and squeeze in beside him with a suitcase. The man thanks him for waiting.

He releases the rope and lets the tide move the ferry slightly away and upstream from the jetty. There's enough water for him to drive forward, and then he turns upriver and round in an arc to face the Ferry. The engine thuds steadily. A sudden burst of laughter goes up when a gull's grey and white sloppy dropping hits someone's arm. Looking round the boat Robert sees how everyone on his left is smiling, and how those on the right are trying to find out what's funny. Only the couple immediately in front of him, the latecomers, have not noticed. Each of them is looking ahead. They are separate – separate from everyone else and separate from each other. In contradiction to what he usually sees these two remain in their own silence, their own world. The woman looks tired and pale. They wait until everyone else gets off, and then the man moves to pick up the suitcase.

"Here, you get off. I'll pass it over," says Robert, offering to lift the case. As the man climbs out there's a coughing sound. It's the woman. She's hunched over the gunwale, vomiting. The man hurriedly climbs back onto the ferry and puts one arm round her while trying to pull his handkerchief out of his pocket. She takes it and wipes her mouth, then turns back to face inwards again.

Robert looks out towards the bar and the open sea while she recovers. There's nothing to be done. The waiting passengers hold back, uncertain. After a minute or two the man takes the woman's hand and helps her off the boat and onto the landing stage. Robert passes the suitcase over.

When they've gone he rolls a cigarette. He leans against the side and watches the couple slowly make their way over the stones and up off the shore towards the bus. When they reach the road they stop. The woman seems to be looking at the ground. The man puts his arm around her, and then they move on again.

Now they've gone Robert feels the particular buoyancy a turn of the tide often brings. He checks the few boats on the move, checks there's a clear passage in front of him. He reverses away from the beach with seven passengers. That's fine. Sometimes he prefers having only a few. The vomit bobs on the surface, doesn't disperse. They leave it behind.

He throws his cigarette butt overboard and strokes Maisie who he's allowed up by the red ensign.

Behind him, Ian and Bridget get onto the bus.

*

At eleven o'clock Susan was sitting on her bed reading Aunt Rose's letter about her father. He was coming home sooner than she had expected. He was going to be all right. Daddy was going to be all right. It felt as if she had been swimming out of her depth and suddenly found she could touch firm sand. She kicked off her shoes and lay back on the bed. The day had a whole new feel. Turning her head she saw a windowful of pure blue sky. Bliss.

Since returning from Bristol she had filled her time with work, with Mark and with Bridget. Although she and Mark were more settled together, she was still holding back. She knew this, and he knew it and she knew that too. She had still not told him about wanting to go on a course which would mean leaving Bawdsey. He would take it *so* badly, as evidence that she did not care about him. But it wasn't as simple as that. And holding back was partly to do with Daddy and her family. She had not told him of the deepest, worst fear: that she might lose both her father and Rose.

But now, suddenly, this letter had changed things. She went to the window, looked out onto the roofs, a sky full of puffy white clouds, trees whose branches were losing their leaves. It was a gorgeous day. Nothing would stop her from enjoying it. She would spend it with Mark.

They had made vague plans to go to Felixstowe, and she knew he'd wanted to do something more definite. So, she would surprise him. She would go and find him and say, Right, here I am! Where are we going? He hadn't looked himself at the end of yesterday evening. He'd been pale, quiet. He seemed to know a lot about literature and plays, so she'd been expecting him to comment about the play at length, but he said virtually nothing. He was obviously being very sensitive to Ian and Bridget. He really was thoughtful.

Ten minutes later she ran downstairs. Inside her head she was humming:

> *I don't want to let you go so far*
> *I don't want to buh buh bah star*

Where was he? She went into the common room, then through the open door into the sitting room. Ah, there he was, with his back towards her, reading the paper. Good, he was alone.

She said quietly, "Good morning."

He turned round and stood up at once. He put the paper down and moved towards her.

"Susan!"

"I was wondering whether you had anything planned for today?" She could not help smiling a big smile.

"Well. No. I mean – you look wonderful." He kissed her cheek very gently, then her lips.

"Daddy's coming home! I've just had a letter from Aunt

Rose and he'll probably be home in less than two weeks. He's better."

Mark stepped forward and hugged her. "That's tremendous. I'm so pleased." He stood back to admire her again.

"So I want to do something special today. With you. A sort of celebration."

"Of course. I'd love that. I've been sitting here reading the paper and trying to stop thinking about Ian and Bridget. I came down to see them off. I felt so awful about the play. Putting them through that."

"You couldn't have known what it would be about, you can't blame yourself."

"I just felt as if I'd made things worse for them."

Susan took his hand. "How were they this morning?"

"Ok, I suppose. Subdued."

"Well, I wish them both all the luck in the world. I wouldn't want to be in their shoes."

"And when they were just leaving – just walking out of the main entrance, two girls cycled past and one of them called out, 'Bridget, are you going on leave? Enjoy yourself! Be good!' "

"Oh, how awful."

"Well, she'll probably be in London by now. It'll take a while before she reaches Lincoln."

"What's Ian going to do today?"

"He said he wanted to spend the day alone, in Ipswich. I offered to do something with him, but he insisted he just wanted to get away."

They stood silent for a moment. Susan was remembering she had asked Bridget to phone her when she had told her mother she was pregnant.

"So." Mark took a step back. "What are we going to do?"

"Well. If we went soon we could be in Felixstowe for lunch, couldn't we? And then – perhaps you could choose what we do this afternoon – and then we can both choose what we do this evening. How does that sound?"

"Spot on. Should I change? Yes, I must. Give me five minutes, perhaps a bit longer, will you? Let's meet outside the main entrance – I'll be as quick as I can."

Mark hurried out and Susan walked over to the window and looked out at the playing fields. They were dotted with gulls today. If she half closed her eyes it looked as if the grass was growing an uneven crop of white flowers that took off every now and again. Her mind jumped to the lawn at home, to her swing under the horse chestnut tree, to their labrador, to Daddy. He was well again! He was coming home!

*

Mark took the stairs two at a time. Tie or open neck? He put a striped tie on, then took it off and arranged his shirt collar outside his jacket collar. Just before leaving his room he chose a different tie, folded it and put it in his pocket. No knowing where they might end up that evening. He felt in his pockets for cash and cigarettes, then combed his hair for the second time before putting the comb into his inside pocket and checking himself in the mirror.

Last night he had hardly slept. He had been thinking about Ian's determination to go through everything on his own, and how this contrasted with his own retreat from Trudi. He had to admit that what he had done could only be described as running away. Last night's play had brought it all back. He made himself face up to the fact that he had not stayed in Austria but had returned to England with the walking group, not knowing if Trudi was or wasn't pregnant although aware that she might be. That made him as bad as the man in *The Inspector Calls*. Trudi had only been eighteen, and far less au fait with the world than he was. There was no excuse.

He had only ever once told anyone about her. Once, when stranded without fuel all night, he had confessed the story to his co-pilot. He recalled the man: Alan Biddle. In the unexpected and potentially dangerous hours they spent cooped up in a cabin they had disclosed things to each other which they had not disclosed to anyone else. Alan had told Mark about his uncle who was an alcoholic and in prison, and Mark had told him about Trudi.

Alan had listened without comment and had then said, "I

shouldn't worry about it if I were you. Austria. That's where Hitler was born, isn't it?"

Mark had said nothing more. What was the point of saying anything else if Alan took that view. Hitler? For God's sake, what had it got to do with Hitler? How could Alan dismiss it like that? It was to do with him, Mark, and Trudi. Trudi was so young, so excited by his attention. She loved the fact that he was older and more sophisticated than she was. He had said he might come back and see her again, and he had promised to write, but he hadn't done either. And now he understood he might have changed her life terribly. He thought of her parents, her grand-parents, the little village where everyone knew each other, the inn where the walking group had been made so welcome. And to think that he was supposed to be promoting goodwill.

He hurried downstairs. What would Susan say if she knew about Trudi? About how he had just left her? She had no idea about that part of his life, that side of him.

And suddenly, here she was, open and glowing. How amazing life was. She was standing in the sunshine outside the main door. She looked more relaxed now, but less excited than she had been five minutes earlier. He told himself that he must relax too.

"I've never looked at that before," she said, pointing upwards to a coat of arms she had walked under hundreds of times. "You know French. What does it mean?"

"Plutôt mourir que changer. Better to die than change. No, *rather* die than change."

"Rather die than change. That's quite strong, isn't it? Would you rather die than change?"

"I'm not sure," he said. "It depends what's to be changed – or died for. Faith, perhaps. Or identity."

"Your country, I suppose. Rather die than have your country changed?"

"Well – that's what we're here for, really, isn't it? That's what armies and air forces and navies do, don't they? And we're part of that."

"The war seems so far away. All that dying."

They moved slowly towards the drive and its thin covering of leaves shed by the trees beside it.

"Mark, would you rather die than change? Yourself, I mean."

"Of course not. One's instinct is to stay alive. And change can be for the better, can't it?"

Susan smiled and said, "I can't think of anything that could change *you* for the better!" She walked on. "But if that's true, then a country could change for the better too, couldn't it? Like England, for example."

Mark pushed his hands deep in his pockets. "Yes. It could. And we're living at a time when it's trying to."

"What a sombre conversation," said Susan. "Today's supposed to be a celebration of life, not death."

"You started it!" laughed Mark. "Come on, then."

They emerged from the familiar drive and out onto the jetty into the full sunshine and a blast of wind. Susan had to hold her dress down as they waited for the ferry. Mark turned away from the wind and bent his head over his cupped hand to protect the tiny flame while lighting his cigarette. When he looked up he found Susan had retreated to the shelter of the wall and was standing with her eyes closed, her face turned upward to the sun. Her neck stretched up pale from her yellow blouse to her chin. Her hair was blowing all over her face.

He searched for a buttercup growing on the verge but did not find one. He walked quietly over to stand close to Susan.

Without opening her eyes she said, "I know you're there. I can smell your cigarette."

"I wanted to test whether you like butter, but I can't find a buttercup."

She smiled. "It's too late in the year. If you'd grown up in the country you'd have known that. You'll have to imagine you have one. Do I like butter? "

"Yes you do. And you are very beautiful today. Don't move. Just stay like that so I can enjoy you."

"I can hear the ferry."

Mark stood back, turned so his smoke would not blow across Susan, and saw the ferry approaching.

They walked across the quay, along the little jetty past a few boys with their crab lines, and onto the boat. It was a quiet crossing. Susan watched the water and its little starry sparkles.

Mark looked from Susan to where the river became sea, then back to Susan.

"Where shall we go for lunch?"

"Somewhere where we can see the sea?"

"Ok. There's that café on the front. Or we could buy some buns or something and eat them outside. Shrimps, even."

"I'm not sure. We'll get blown to bits."

"Wouldn't you like to go somewhere special?"

"This evening – definitely. But now – no. It doesn't really matter. Let's just wander around until we find somewhere. But not the Alex."

"No, not the Alex. Not on a Saturday. It'll be full of airmen showing off to their girlfriends. And all those Americans."

They climbed off the ferry, walked past the boatyard and up to the place where the bus stopped.

Twenty minutes later they were in the centre of Felixstowe. They walked slowly down to the seafront and sat on a sheltered bench looking out across the North Sea. Mark was holding Susan's hand against his knee. Every now and then he stroked it with his other hand. They watched people going past. Mark noticed families, friends, older couples, children. For the first time he realised that although this Saturday seaside scene was as familiar as one from his own childhood holidays, it was not the same. There was one fundamental difference. There were more women than men. It was not the absence of men that was particularly noticeable, it was rather the presence of women. If he shut his eyes the voices he heard were mostly those of women and children. Women of all ages walked past arm in arm with other women, some in conversation, some silent, stopping to look at the sea or moving on. Friends, mothers and daughters, sisters perhaps. Few were alone. Many children were attached to two women, rather than to a husband and wife.

Mark thought of the other side of the North Sea and its European coastal towns, places like Le Touquet, Dieppe. They must be like this too. There too, women must be re-creating their lives in the imbalance created by war. Making the best of things. Getting on with staying alive and finding a future. A different future no one would have willingly chosen but that was nevertheless the inevitable outcome of the actions knowingly taken by men and supported by women.

The Great War, Napoleon, Nelson, the Wars of the Roses, Culloden, other wars in other places. They had all led to this, had all led to the same outcome: to death upon death, to numerous women having to walk through their lives without men. And Trudi. What about Trudi? If she – if they – had had a child, it would be five, nearly six now, and it would not have the father it should have had.

A group of small boys ran past. What would happen to them? Would they too be killed? Some had already lost their fathers. Would they be survived by their sisters, mothers, future girl-friends and wives? This was a terrible thought.

Susan squeezed Mark's hand, "Isn't it just wonderful to sit in the sun? I think today's going to be perfect."

Mark turned towards her. He hesitated. Now wasn't the time to tell her any of what he had been thinking about. Would he ever be able to tell her about Trudi, even if he married her? Still holding her hand, he stood up. Was it right to keep a secret from your wife? Surely that wouldn't be right.

"Cheer up, Mark. What's the matter?"

"Sorry. Come on, let's get some lunch."

*

Rose unpacked the laundry box and put the towels into the airing cupboard but shook out two of the sheets across the spare bed before tucking them in and putting on the blankets. She turned the top of the top sheet down and tucked everything in at the sides. Henry had not stayed in Rose's spare bedroom for years. As they lived less than five miles away from each other there was rarely need to. But she felt now that all this was going to work out well. She was looking forward to having him. It was important to welcome him home. She arranged the green counterpane evenly and stood up, straightening her back. She was a little out of breath.

What else must she do? He would need a better bedside light. This one would not give out a good enough light for him to read in bed. Since being a boy he had always read for a while before settling to sleep. Over decades he had recommended things to her – Ruskin, Keats, Thomas Hardy, Matthew Arnold, the Psalms.

She remembered how he used to read to Grace, his wife. In the summer he liked to lie on a rug on the ground next to Grace while she lay in the hammock which hung from the walnut tree. There had been one occasion when she had found this intimate scene too much to bear. She had come into the garden unseen by Henry and Grace. They were talking quietly as she approached and it was only when she was very close that she heard what they were saying. It was Henry's birthday and Grace was, at that very moment, telling him that she was pregnant. She had said, "And I think I'm going to have a baby, Henry. Not *a* baby but *our* baby."

Rose had stopped in her tracks while Henry, who had been lying on his back with his eyes shut, got to his feet, leant over Grace and kissed her. Still unseen, Rose had retreated. Now, as she took a towel from the airing cupboard, she recalled how this had felt like a hammer blow. It had knocked her hopes for six. Though nothing had changed in her life, it seemed as if Life was telling her: Rose, not only do you not have a husband, but you have no children. And perhaps you never will.

At the time – because she was determined to express her genuine delight in Henry and Grace's news and not resent it – she had limited her hurt by telling herself that there were thousands of young women like herself. She knew dozens of women whose boyfriends and husbands had been killed. It was no good feeling jealous of what she and all of them could not have – someone who cared, the prospect of children, a life that included being kissed while lying in a hammock in the sunshine. But for years when she felt fragile the memory of this incident made her weep.

She put a towel on the wooden rail, opened the cupboard under the eaves and reached in for the other bedside light she kept in there. Its short flex meant it had to go on the chest of drawers, but it would make reading easier.

And then Grace had died. Who could have thought that

might happen? In her late twenties, when taking part in a Ladies Swimming Club swim at Weston-super-Mare, she had gone further out than usual and was carried out by the current and drowned. It was a blessing that Susan had no memory of this event which completely changed life for Henry, Susan and herself. Henry had employed a housekeeper, Madeleine, who also acted as nanny for Susan, and Rose did as much as she could for Susan while continuing to report for the local newspaper.

Susan hadn't called anyone else Mummy or mother. She had her father, Aunt Madeleine and herself. It had worked. Susan slept in one of two familiar beds and the three of them looked after her lovingly. At her few times of distress – when one of the two new Labrador puppies died, when she broke her leg, when Madeleine left after ten years – she would sometimes turn to her father, sometimes to her. Rose had liked this closeness, this being needed. She had been there when Susan won the high jump, when she was Titania in the fourth form production of *A Midsummer Night's Dream* and when she gave her first speech as headgirl. She was there when Henry was away.

But now it was Susan who was away. Rose held on to the bannister as she went downstairs. This was how things were, wasn't it? Things came full circle. She held the kettle under the tap, then bent to light the gas. And one day Susan would settle down with someone kind. Then there would be a baby, children. That was something to look forward to. As she warmed the teapot she decided to sit outside in the deckchair for an hour or so before making herself scrambled eggs on toast.

On a branch of the horse chestnut a blackbird began to sing. It was glorious for late September. There was a butterfly on the last of the buddleia. Tomorrow Henry would arrive, and perhaps Susan would come and visit him before long. Perhaps she should make a couple of fruit cakes now? If she wrapped them up and stored them in cake tins they would keep for at least several weeks. She would need to check how much sugar she had, and finding dried fruit might be a problem.

*

The Deben descends subtly, slipping away from banks,
sliding under bridges. Its eddies unravel the edges of fields.

Coots upend themselves. A pied wagtail dips and fidgets.
A couple lob pebbles, watch ripples. Cattle stand
hock deep in boggy mud. Two boys fishing on the bank
hold their breath as a snake zigzags towards the reeds.

The river runs out of land hardly higher than sea level,
then loses its name, loses its shape in the estuary.

Robert is sitting on *Music Maker's* deck, his knees drawn up and apart so he can whittle a stick. He's whistling quietly, breathily. Maisie is sprawled at his feet, almost asleep, opening her eyes every now and again when a flake of wood lands on or near her. It's a morning to be lazy, to just be. He hears the river running out, hears its uneven, strong flow round the boat, the posts. He stops whittling and holds the river knife still in one hand, the stick still in the other. The sun beats into the corner he's chosen because it's out of the wind. He's quiet now and shuts his eyes. He hears Maisie sigh.

The sun makes a hot layer of redness over his closed eyes when he raises his head upwards. The red is the light shining through his blood. The centre of the redness lightens and little lines appear like the ones on the mudflats upstream at low tide. He recognises these divisions and connections that seem both random and regular. He's seen before how things like this happen with materials as different as mud and as blood.

He's conscious of his chest rising and falling, the quiet thud of his heart, the warmth of Maisie's body against his bare foot. He puts down the knife and the stick and passes his cupped hands backwards and forwards over his closed eyes. It becomes darker, cooler, then lighter and hotter. A tiny eclipse, he thinks.

He can hear a stonechat, two motors on boats, a shout. Maisie shuffles to scratch herself. But beyond and between these sounds he senses the movement of the Deben. It's only a few feet from him on the other side of the thin pieces of plank that *Music Maker's* made of but further out it's charging at full pelt.

He moves his hands from his face and lets the blood vessels reveal themselves again and the heat return. Maisie shifts herself under his left knee. Still with his eyes closed he places his hand on her hot fur, reaches out to her cool, wet nose, runs his fingers over her silky ears. She's lying with her belly up, and he stretches the palm of his hand over her soft underside that's creamy like the inside of a shell. She shivers with delight, lolls her head back and opens her mouth, revealing the tender, pink secrets of her tongue and the inside of her mouth to the warm air.

He's thinking about the Deben. Where has it come from? From the thread of a stream between green fields in inland Suffolk, from Debenham – a place he's heard of but never been to – and then on through Woodbridge. But the tide brings in vast quantities of water from the North Sea. And, when he looks at it another way, it all comes from rain, from the sky. How old is the river? Months? Hours? Centuries? Or is it always new?

And where does he come from? He can answer that in different ways too: from Lowestoft, from before the war. From an intimate and difficult-to-imagine meeting which took place twenty one, no, nearly twenty two years ago.

A slight change in direction of the wind makes Maisie's hair ruffle against his hand and blows his own hair off his face. What would his mother be doing today? He thinks of her hanging out the washing. She'll reach down to the basket on the ground, pick up a white shirt and shake it out before pinning it onto the washing line with wooden pegs. She'll bend down again: sheets and towels first, then shirts and dresses, then his father's overalls, then underwear and socks.

Sometimes she used to send him and Tom running out to rescue the washing when it rained. They would hurry back in with their arms full of half dry linen and the backs of their shirts half soaked.

The girls. What might they be doing? It's Saturday morning. What do Lizzie and Sally do on Saturdays now? They used to play skipping and clapping games for hours. They would stand opposite each other, signal their readiness to begin with a serious nod, and carry out an elaborate, rhythmic performance of clapping their own and each other's hands while chanting rhymes. If one of them was alone, she would do the same while bouncing a ball against a wall. These girls' rituals amazed him. Boys had nothing like that.

But perhaps they do different things now they're older. Perhaps they have to help at home. They'll be trusted with money now, be sent to run errands. Are they too big for piggy backs now? Too big to have their hands held and be swung round so their feet are off the ground and their hair spreads out and they shriek with delight? Do they miss him?

And what about his stepfather? It's hard to imagine him. What's his face like? Does he have a moustache? He can't remember. It's strange that he can't remember. He must look at the photo Mother sent yet again. Robert recalls the scar under his stepfather's jaw where he was hit by the piece of glass from the bonfire. It was only when he tipped his head back and roared with laughter that it showed, and that wasn't often.

Now he can see more colours through his closed eyelids. Uneven blocks of red and orange merge and shift. Whole skies full, eyes full, of shapes. Is this what blind people see? Do they have views like this? He thinks of the blind man who lives at the far end of Harbour Cottages. He lost his sight in the war. When Robert walks past his house he often sees him sitting at the window. He has always supposed that he was looking at nothing, but perhaps he sees all these colours.

Maisie whines and Robert opens his eyes. The brightness blinds him, causes him to screw up his eyelids again. He faces downwards, tries again, looks at the grainy, worn deckboards with their knots and dents, their traces of spilt paint. As he adjusts to the light he lifts his head to see Maisie wagging her tail.

From where he is most of his view is sky. It's now a very pale blue. It must be late afternoon. The water is quieter now. He gets up and looks out to the river. It's still going out, but it's slowed down, is no longer in such a rush. It's dark here but further out it's pale like the sky.

He goes into the cabin. He's hungry and thirsty. Maisie squeezes in front of him. She knows that when he's going to eat she's likely to eat too.

*

Mark held Susan's hand as they walked into the dance hall. The sound of the band could be heard from outside. It was playing *Blue Tango*. A saxophone tempted them up the steps and to the entrance. Once inside, they saw people they recognised but nobody they knew well.

"Good," said Mark. "We can be on our own."

"Just us. What bliss."

Mark led Susan to a corner table and asked what she would like to drink. He looked round for a waiter.

"I think you have you go to the bar yourself."

Susan watched Mark walk to the bar with his hand in his jacket pocket where he kept his change. While he was waiting to be served he turned round towards her and she gave him a little wave. While he ordered his drinks she surveyed the hall, watched a group of airmen claim some tables close to a table full of airwomen. Mark returned with a drink in each hand, walking carefully.

"Sorry, I've spilt a bit." He placed the glasses on the table. "Here's to us."

They drank together and replaced their glasses on the table together. Mark turned to look Susan straight in the eyes. " I'd like to dance with you right now, please."

Susan smiled, "No, not yet. No one else is dancing."

"Well, I'll just have to sit and look at you, then, if I'm not allowed to dance. Won't you dance with me now, so that everyone looks at us? "

"No, but I will soon."

While Mark sat back and drank Susan felt with her left hand for the small pendant on its thin chain round her neck. She glanced behind her, reached up to push some hair off her neck.

Mark reached out for her other hand. "I think what I'm feeling now is the real thing."

Susan squeezed his hand.

They sat in silence, watching the hall fill up, listening to the band move on to *Delicado*, and then to a tune they didn't know. The conductor kept turning round to see how full the hall was while continuing to lead his players with his waving baton in front.

When they started on the next tune, Mark stood up and presented himself formally in front of Susan. He bowed.

"Please may I have the pleasure?"

Susan smiled and rose and took his hand.

"It's a quickstep. I noticed you decided not to ask me for the tango."

"You know I can't do a tango."

"Nor can I. I'm only teasing you."

He hugged her on a quarter turn.

"How's that for skill?"

"I'm very impressed," said Susan, laughing.

"Ok. Let's see what else we can do tonight." He held her in an upright, steady hold and led her into a chassé.

"Not bad! Let's try it again. You weren't expecting me to do that. One, two, three, four, one!"

Mark counted the beats aloud, "Slow, quick, quick, slow, quick, quick, slow. Excellent! We did it! Bridget and Ian would be proud of us."

Mark heard Susan's tiny sigh as she said, "Yes, they would. I do hope they're all right."

"It's our night tonight, Susan. I just want to think about you and me."

" So do I." But was Bridget all right? Had she tried to phone today?

"Then we agree."

They continued dancing until the end of the tune without speaking. Susan made to return to their table but Mark kept hold of her hand.

"Excuse me, but that was just a warm up. I'm hoping you'll stay here for the next one."

Susan let Mark lead her back into the middle of the dance floor and hold her against him as they set off on a waltz. He was the better dancer and he led well, steering her through the three four rhythm, rising and falling, with his hand in the small of her back, his arm holding hers upright and comfortably, just as Miss Kaye, her dancing teacher, had taught her when she was at school. She and her friends had had to take turns at being gentlemen, and everyone had wanted to dance with her, Susan, because she held them properly, if nothing else, and she didn't giggle.

She could do a waltz easily, but tonight she found she could do more moves in the quickstep than she had ever done before. They even had a go at a foxtrot.

"You're just so relaxed tonight, Susan. You're following so well."

She hugged his shoulder, "It's you who's leading me so clearly."

"It's both of us. We're doing it together."

They continued to dance, talk, have a drink, a cigarette and just sit side by side observing the people around them and listening to the band.

When the musicians took a break and they found themselves sitting in silence, Mark suddenly said, "Right. Time for something different. I'm going to choose someone and you have to state their name, their main ambition in life and their relationship to the person they're with."

"Is this a game? Ok."

"Him. Over there, the one with the sticking up hair, laughing."

Susan hardly hesitated before answering. "That's Andrew McPherson. His main ambition in life is to own a fast car. At present he has a fast bicycle."

"And you must tell me what his relationship is to the person he's with."

"I'm not sure if he's with anyone," said Susan. "Oh yes, he seems to be with that round man who's standing with both his hands in his pockets."

She paused. "I've no idea what Andrew McPherson's relation to Mr Round is."

177

"You've got to say."

"All right. I think Mr Round, who's older, is his godfather. Mr Round gave him a silver tankard when he was born, inscribed, To my Godson Andrew, and now he's wondering whether to leave him half of his estate. Andrew does not know this."

"Very good," said Mark. "Your turn now."

Susan pointed to the pianist.

"The pianist? Ok. Well, he's called Francisco Alberto Jimenez," said Mark, pronouncing the J with a gutteral hiss and the final z with an authentic sounding th, "and his ambition is to play in the best dance band in the world."

"Then why is he playing in Felixstowe?"

"Because he's not achieved his ambition yet. He has a little bit further to go."

"Tell me about his relationship to the violinist."

"No, I don't think he's with the violinist. He's really with the woman in the red dress." Mark indicated a woman sitting alone at a table very close to the stage, "She is Carmina, and you are mistaken if you think they are in love. Actually, she is his sister, and has travelled from Madrid to see him perform. She is married to a banker who has paid for this trip."

"Ah ha," said Susan. "Go on. Choose someone else."

Mark looked round carefully. "That girl with the swept up hair standing by the doorway. What's her name?"

"She's Doris Durbridge. She is determined to be married, have three children called Thomas, Christopher and Anne, and a dog called Rough. She's with that other girl, the one in the blue dress – she's called Felicity – and Doris is very keen to meet Felicity's brother and is hoping Felicity will arrange this."

They were so engrossed in this game that they did not notice the musicians making their way back to the stage and taking their seats again until they launched into a new tune. Men led their partners out on to the dance floor and soon the hall was again full of dancers who shuffled, chattered quietly to each other and sometimes stared over each other's shoulders into the crowd.

The tempo of the dances became slower, the lights lower.

"You're not doing such varied steps now. You're becoming lazy."

"True. I just like moving around the dance floor holding you close, breathing in your hair, your skin, and the remains of your scent."

"Good. I'm not complaining."

"What's this tune? *Being With You*? *Slow Burn*?"

"It doesn't matter." It felt marvellous just to sway a little with him.

"A wonderful evening," he said into her ear.

"Yes," she said into his shoulder.

"I'm loving you."

"Umm. That's nice."

The band came to the end of the piece and went straight into another slow, melodious number.

"Let's just keep going. I could go on dancing with you like this for hours."

"I'd like that."

"Ok, we'll do it. We'll dance all night one day."

"You mean night," said Susan, turning up to look at him with a smile.

"You know what I mean."

The band came to its finale and the lights went up. The dancers stood still as the National Anthem was played and those who were not dancing got to their feet. Then the hall was suddenly full of bustle as people started to talk loudly and move. It was time to go home. The crowd poured out into the street like a river. Some turned left, some right, some went straight over the street and some stayed in a knot by the door and peeled off when their friends appeared.

"I want to stroll back, take our time. I wish we didn't have to hurry."

"Mark, we might miss the last bus and the last ferry."

"Yes, I know. I'm just telling you how I feel."

Susan paused and turned towards him. "I think I do know how you feel. And I very much like how you feel." She pulled him towards her and kissed him gently.

The bus was nearly full and they sat holding hands in silence, looking out of the window at the almost total darkness, not interested in anyone else. When they reached Felixstowe Ferry they let the small group of chatting passengers go ahead and lead the way to the ferry boat.

And there it was, waiting on the dark water.

"The river looks like Lethe," said Mark.

"Isn't Lethe in hell?"

"It's in the underworld, in Hades. It has the power of making people who are about to be reincarnated forget their past lives."

"Would you want to forget your life, do you think? Why would anyone want to forget their life?" asked Susan.

"Because it had been painful. If it had been painful you might want to forget it."

"I hope my life's not going to be painful."

Mark did not reply.

"Don't you hope yours isn't going to be painful?" asked Susan.

"Of course. But who knows what will happen? Anyone's life might become painful. Lots of people have difficult lives. Think of wars."

"Well, we're lucky, aren't we? At least, we're lucky today."

"That's the best way to look at it: enjoy today, enjoy any day, while it's good."

It was a cool crossing. Susan leant close to Mark, "It feels like the end of summer."

"Well, it's nearly October. Here, put your hand in my pocket." He took Susan's hand and placed it in his pocket with his. She felt coins, a ticket, his handkerchief, a button. She liked this warm, enclosed place and linked her fingers in between Mark's, squeezing them. He turned to look at her.

"Is that better?"

She answered him with another squeeze.

The boat thudded through small waves, seemed to hit them head on. It was a rougher ride than usual and kept Susan and Mark wide awake. Susan looked at the ferryman but it was the older one this time. He did not have a dog with him. He stood differently, held the tiller in a different way. The noisy group were in the front of the ferry and every now and again, when spray blew off a wave and onto them, they shrieked with laughter.

Within a few minutes they were at Bawdsey, stepping over the side and on to the jetty. The others ran on ahead, still full of energy. The boat turned and was gone. Mark put his arm round Susan and they made their way slowly up the driveway towards the Manor. They walked in time with one another, in breath with one another. They stopped at the bridge.

"Let's just stand with our eyes closed," Mark said. "We should make the most of every minute tonight."

The trees were being blown about. They could hear branches rustling, dry leaves scuffling along the road and could feel the wind blowing their own hair, each other's hair, pulling at their coats.

"We should come out here when there's a gale," said Mark. After a pause he added, "Even better, we could go to the cliff top."

"Yes – that would almost be like being out at sea. It would be wild in winter."

"We'd have to anchor ourselves down."

Susan reached round Mark and pulled him close. "I'd anchor myself to you."

"Good. I'd like that."

Mark released himself gently from Susan and leant back against the parapet. They opened their eyes simultaneously and looked at one another.

"So. Now I'd like to know about you. I know your name is Mark Rivens. Will you tell me about your ambitions? "

Mark brought Susan's hands up to his mouth and kissed them. He chuckled. "Is that fair? It's supposed to be you talking about me, not me talking about myself."

Susan snuggled against him. "I've changed the rules a bit."

He laughed. "All right then. My ambitions. Well. There's quite a list really. Top of the list is you: to love you and be loved by you. You know that already. Then there's my work. I want to have a decent career, you know that too, you know I care about doing well. And then there are lots of other ambitions."

"Like what?"

"Well. In no particular order, and some long-term, some short-term, there are things like learning Spanish, travelling. Having children. Taking you to concerts, to the theatre, taking you up in a hot air balloon. Becoming a wine connoisseur. Having a cat."

"I didn't know you liked cats!"

"Very much," said Mark seriously, "I love cats. And there's something else too: having peace of mind."

"But you've got that now."

"Well, not quite, actually."

Susan put her hand to his face. "I'm sorry. I know I haven't made things easy for you. In fact, I've made them difficult for you, haven't I?"

Mark paused before saying, "Well, yes. But you've made everything feel much better tonight."

"And now you must tell me about your relationship with the person you're with."

"I'm with Susan Cairncross, She's my girlfriend."

"Uh huh. Go on."

"I've got to think about this carefully. Give me time."

"Ok."

"My feelings for her are very, very deep. I admire her. I think she's beautiful. I want to be with her as much as possible. She's a wonderful person."

A gust of wind blew Susan's hair across his face. He let go of one of her hands for a moment to move her hair from over his eyes.

"And now she's even blinding me."

He kissed her cheek. "It's your turn now."

"All right. I'm Susan Jennifer Cairncross." Susan was speaking more slowly than usual. "My ambitions. My ambitions are. Daddy being well. You. Enjoying life. Getting more done. Being happy."

Mark was resting his chin on the top of Susan's head. He was looking out at the dark scene of trees, an expanse of grass, the Manor.

"Susan, what do you mean when you say You?"

"I mean you – Mark. I mean that you matter to me. I want

you in my life." She stopped as she realised he could think this meant that she loved him, or assumed he wanted to marry her. Did she love him? She had certainly grown more fond of him in the last few days. And might he want to marry her? And would she accept if he did?

"You've gone quiet. What are you thinking about?"

"You. I'm thinking about you."

What a night. It was an amazing night.

She nestled further against him and half whispered, "And I'm so longing for Daddy to be well. I'm longing for it. I'm scared."

He put his hands into her hair, stroked her head. "I know you are, I know. It's going to be all right."

Susan sniffed and reached into Mark's pocket again for his handkerchief. When she had finished blowing her nose, he asked, "Are you going to tell me about any other ambitions? What about your career? I know it's not just a job for you."

"You and Daddy matter most. At least, they do at this minute. You two are all that matter now."

"That's fine. There's no need to say anything more. Don't say a word. We'll just stay here until you're ready to go in."

*

It's a bright, cold day and Robert's setting out for a walk. The day before had been wild and wet and he can't resist a morning like this when the whole place is washed and new. And Maisie can't resist chasing the sticks he throws along the beach. One is caught by a blast of wind and carried into the estuary so she runs to the water's edge, jumps back from the small waves and then decides to plunge in. She swims to the stick, picks it up, turns and swims back to the shore and races up to Robert, dropping it at his feet. She shakes herself into a blur of fur. Drops fly from her coat and sparkle in the sunlight. To keep her from soaking him he flings the stick into the sea and she charges off again.

He wanders up the beach and squats to pick up a handful of small stones. He lets them trickle through his fingers from one hand into the other while he watches Maisie. Something sharp pricks his palm. There's a small green piece of newly broken glass. Just as he's about to throw the whole handful away, he notices something unusual – a pale brown stone, about the size of his thumb and very light in weight. It almost feels as if it might float. He examines it more closely, holds it up to the sun. It's almost translucent.

Maisie arrives again just as he's about to stand up. She shakes herself again and before he can back off some of the water flies up onto his hand and the brown stone. It gleams like golden syrup.

"This is amber, Maisie."

Jack said that if you found one piece you might find more nearby, so he kneels down again and begins a detailed search. After a few minutes he sits on his heels, straightens his back and decides to widen the area he's focusing on. He remembers he doesn't need to dig for it for this piece of amber will have been brought in to shore recently. There must be more lying waiting for him, on or close to the surface. He ignores Maisie pushing against him, wanting more sticks to be thrown. Head down, he searches again.

Within half an hour he's found two more pieces. One's a beauty: an oblong which is rough on one side and smooth on the other, but he's sure it's amber because of how it feels and by its colour. It's not pale at all. The interior is the same brown as the conkers he and Tom used to knock down from trees and prise out of their prickly shells. The other one is tiny, the size of a shirt button, but it's round like a pebble and the sea has begun to polish it. When he spits on it and holds it out on the palm of his hand in the sun it's the shiny sort of yellow he's seen in snail shells.

He puts them carefully in the breast pocket of his shirt. He never uses this pocket so it doesn't have a hole in, but he must take the amber out when he gets home. That's two good finds within a few months. He whistles for Maisie, slings the stick in the direction of *Music Maker*, feels lucky.

*

On Sunday morning Susan slept in. Her creased clothes lay over her chair, one shoe on its side, the other half under the bed. She had put the little pendant safely in a tiny bowl on the dressing table. Also on the dressing table were her tortoise shell hairbrush and comb, two letters from Rose, an invitation to a ball, some hairpins and three photographs in silver frames. In the centre was the one taken at her passing out parade. She was in uniform, smiling at the camera, and her father was at her side, also in uniform but looking more formal and almost at attention. He was considerably taller than her, especially as he was wearing a hat. Susan had taken her cap off because Rose, who had taken the photograph, had said she could not see her face when she wore it. The day of the passing out parade had been tremendous, and she had revelled in the razzmatazz of the day, the sense of shared celebration, her father's praise, Aunt Rose's enjoyment. She had felt both fully adult and about seven years old, wanting to jump up and down once the ceremony was over.

The photos of her and Rose and the ones of all three of them were in the second drawer down of the dressing table. As there was not room to stand more than three photos up at once, she changed them around every month or two. On this particular Sunday morning, the one on the right hand side, nearest the window, was of Rose sitting in a deck chair in a garden. Two croquet mallets leant against a garden table and several croquet balls lay at her feet. She had one hand reaching down to stroke a small dog and she was holding the other towards the camera in a frozen wave. This meant that she looked slightly awkward, was slightly tilted. But she was smiling a clear, open smile at the person taking the photo. Only recently had Susan realised that although she knew from somewhere that Aunt Rose's dress was blue with white flowers and the dog was called Trixie, she had no idea whose garden it was or who had taken the photo.

The third photo, which was on the left hand side and partly hidden by an empty envelope addressed to Miss Rose Cairncross, was of the group of girls she'd met when she first joined the RAF. Susan was third from the left, between Deirdre Stannard and Joan somebody. They were standing in a line, mostly facing forwards, and looking as if a joke had just been told. They were on a day out following a week of exams, and they were full of themselves. Now that she knew about them Susan sometimes inspected each of these faces carefully. Who would have guessed that Deirdre, who was giggling and had her mouth open, was the brainiest? Or that Caroline's entire family had been killed in an air raid? Or that Anthea was to marry an opera singer a year later?

Susan had not set her alarm clock and she slept to eight, nine, to half past nine – much later than usual. As soon as she woke she heard rain. Then she thought of Mark. Today it was Mark that came into her mind, into her consciousness before everything else. And then Daddy. Aunt Rose had said he would be home either today, Sunday, or Monday. She got up and drew the curtains. It did not look as if it was going to stop raining and it sounded windy. She pulled on her dressing gown and went along the corridor to the bathroom. She'd have a treat: a hot morning bath. It would be good to have a long soak before dressing, finding a cup of tea and then beginning the day properly.

She ran the water, hung up her dressing gown and climbed into the white enamel bath. She gradually immersed herself in the almost too hot water and started to recall the previous day in detail: their walk, their meal, dancing, what she had said, what Mark had said, the journey home, saying goodnight. After an initial soak she sank further down and soaped her face, neck, shoulders, breasts, knees and thighs. Then she soaped all the rest of her. She rinsed herself and lay still in the hot water, her hair damp with steam. I want to love you and I want to be loved by you. Those were his words. I want to love you. He did love her. He had said so more than once. I want to be loved by you. He wanted that too. Did she love him? Just possibly. She might do. But what was love? What would she have to feel to be certain that she did love him? Was what she was feeling doubt? Doubt did not seem to be the right word for the way her emotions had swayed away from Mark and now, thank goodness, back towards him again.

Who did she know who was in love? Ian and Bridget had seemed to be in love. (Might Bridget have already phoned, or might she phone today?) They wanted to be together whenever they could, they cared about each other, found each other interesting, and she now knew they made love. She thought of them dancing together, showing off the newest steps.

So, would she make love with Mark if she was sure she loved him?

The rain was hitting the frosted glass in the window and she sank back into the hot water so it swirled round the roots of her hair.

She made herself think about that question again. Would she? No, she wouldn't. It was against all her upbringing. But who had told her that making love before marriage was wrong? Not Daddy. (Daddy would be home today, or tomorrow at the latest, would be looking forward to being with Rose). Not Aunt Rose. There were plenty of things she never talked to Rose about and this was one of them. Not a teacher. Friends, perhaps? No. So where had this strong message come from? Exactly how had she learned it?

She poured shampoo into her hand and onto her hair and massaged it in, piling all her hair up on top of her head. Then she reached for the cup on the cork topped stool next to the bath and rinsed the bubbles off with cupfuls of clean water. She lay back again, heard the rain again. There was something special about lying in a hot bath while it was raining outside.

There was a knock on the door. Someone must be wanting the bathroom.

"It's me, Susan. I'll be out in about five minutes."

Kathleen's voice said, "Thanks. There's no hurry."

Goodness. She had not given work a thought. For the last few days she had been wondering what to do about the working parade, held after breakfast each day. Sometimes it was a shambles. But today she had not given it a thought, and now that she did it seemed unimportant compared to everything else. And what was she going to do about the training course for promotion? Having asked about one, she was sure the CO would be expecting her to go on one. He was clearly expecting her to achieve more. But now, what about Mark?

Susan swirled her hands and created a whirlpool above her

stomach. With cupfuls of water she made a tiny torrent between her breasts across the place where her orangestone pendant had hung, would hang again.

She could hear the wind stronger now, beating the rain against the window. Time to get out.

Back in her room she dressed, rubbed her hair with the towel, recalling for a fragment of a second how Rose used to towel her hair in a rather rough but efficient way. Perhaps Daddy was already up and dressed, ready to go? Or would he be in a dressing gown, even in a wheelchair? She would find out soon.

Bridget wouldn't mind if she borrowed her hairdryer as usual. She went two doors along the corridor to Bridget's room, entered and crossed to where the dressing table stood.

And here was Bridget standing with her little brothers and her parents on Tower Bridge. This was Bridget with her mother on Brighton Pier, both holding on to their hats. This was a very recent photo of Ian, looking very handsome, in slacks and shirt-sleeves, leaning against Philip's car as if it was his own. She felt a sudden tug of affection for them all, even for these brothers and this father she'd never met. She felt for Bridget, for her nice looking family, for Ian, for the unborn baby. It was October now, so the baby might be born next March. March, 1953. How extraordinary. A baby.

She took the hairdryer from its place in the top drawer of the dressing table, plugged it in and switched it on. Should she phone Bridget after breakfast? No. She must wait. It wouldn't help and Bridget had asked her not to phone.

When her hair was dry she returned to her room. It was pouring down outside now and as she stood in front of the mirror she hoped a very different kind of day was going to open up. She wanted to be open to the possibilities that Mark presented, to profit from the near miss of Daddy's stroke.

She took out the two Kirbygrips she was holding in her mouth and leaned forward. Were her eyes green today? What would Mark be thinking this morning? At this very moment, what was he thinking about her?

*

Mark was shaving. Yesterday evening had been one of the best, the most significant evenings they had spent together. He dabbed his cheek with the towel, stretched out his chin and leant towards the mirror again. He pulled the razor across his skin in slow, careful movements, lifting his face and turning his head first to one side and then to the other. Susan had been so soft. No, soft wasn't quite the right word. Gentle, tender. That was it. Tender. He rinsed the razor and wiped condensation off the mirror. And they'd laughed a lot too. It had been fun. He concentrated on his upper lip, made small, familiar scrapes. She had said: My ambitions are you. I want you in my life. She had said those things. She had meant them. She must have meant them.

He dried his face before pulling out the plug and swirling the basin clean. They would enjoy today too. Not like yesterday, of course, it was bound to be different, but they would still enjoy it. They might go for a walk, or even borrow a couple of bikes. He finished dressing and went downstairs for a late breakfast. She might not be up yet. But then, with luck, she might be.

Mark sat down next to Desmond.

"Where's Henry?" asked Desmond. "He never seems to be around when I want him."

"I don't think he's here this weekend. He's on leave."

"Damn. I wanted to get my motorbike fixed today. He promised to help me."

"Couldn't someone else do it? What about Chris?"

"Yes, he might. I'll ask him. I'm impatient because I've got today free. What are you going to do?"

"Not sure. But I'm not going far. Maybe a walk."

Desmond smiled. "With Susan?"

"I hope so."

"Lucky man to have her here. My girlfriend's at Martlesham. That's why I need the motor bike. It's a hell of a journey unless I can get a lift."

"I thought you were going out with Sheila."

"That was months ago! You're so engrossed with Susan you haven't noticed that life moves on! Yes, it was Sheila, but now it's Anthea."

"Are you seeing her today?"

"It depends whether I can get there." Desmond stood up. "I'll try and find Chris, or a lift. If I can get to Woodbridge I'll be ok."

"Good luck."

Mark poured himself more tea and reached for the sugar. He'd have another piece of toast. He could take his time. The day would take its course. Things would present themselves.

He looked out of the window at the rain. A real change from yesterday when they had sat outside, even though it was windy. It was October, proper autumn:

> *Season of mists and mellow fruitfulness*
> *Close bosom friend of the maturing sun.*

She wanted him in her life. He wiped the crumbs from his mouth and fingers with his napkin. That's what she had said, clearly and steadily: I want you in my life.

Some one was saying Susan's name. He turned round and saw Jenny standing at the doorway. She was obviously waiting while another woman walked over to the others she had been sitting with. She was trying to find Susan.

"Has anyone seen her yet? Has she been down for breakfast?"

The girls were shaking their heads and Sheila, Desmond's last girlfriend, looked across at Mark who confirmed with a shake of his head that he had not seen her.

"Then she must be upstairs still. I'll go and tell her."

Tell her what? thought Mark as Jenny went out of the room. He would ask her when she came back. What could that be about?

He helped himself to another piece of toast when a fresh supply arrived, buttered it and then realised there was no marmalade left.

Before he had finished eating Jenny returned and rejoined her friends at the table. Sheila looked at Mark again, stood up and walked over to him. He rose to meet her halfway and she spoke across the empty table between them.

"It's just a phone call for Susan. Someone left a message and she's to phone them back at once. I met her as she was on her way downstairs, and so she's gone straight to the phone."

"Oh, ok. Thanks."

Mark sat down again and finished off his third cup of tea. Bridget. This might be difficult. It might be better not to hear her news in here.

He got up and left the dining room. Susan would be using the phone in the little room at the end of the corridor so he would wait nearby. He hung around wanting to see her and apprehensive about what Bridget would say.

For a second he found himself thinking that Bridget and Ian were getting in the way, were interrupting his relationship with Susan. Immediately he told himself this was a shameful thing to think. Ian and Bridget were his friends, Susan's friends. They mattered. It was awful to have thought that thought.

He stood back to let someone walk past. Why was she taking so long? He must have been here for five or six minutes. Why did Bridget have to take so long? He took out his cigarettes, wondering if Trudi had had to tell her mother the same thing.

The door at the end of the corridor opened and Susan appeared. When she saw Mark she started to run straight towards him. She was crying. She grabbed hold of him, hung on to the sleeves of his jacket, pushed her face into his lapel, hard against his collar bone. She was gasping and he could feel her heart racing

"What is it, Susan? What on earth's the matter?"

She was shaking and she sobbed words into his chest. He freed one of his arms and put it round her, stroking her back.

"I can't hear what you're saying."

She lifted her head up and spoke towards his neck.

"It's Daddy."

She sobbed again, then spoke again.

"He's dead."

*

Robert needs a fire each day now to keep the damp at bay. Unless the sun is shining the muddy side of the boatyard where the house boats are moored has a dank look and feel about it. The mud that seemed silvery or brassy in the summer is now like lead.

Over the last month or two he has gathered a supply of wood that will last for several weeks, and he has worked out a system of storing it so there are always a few dry armfuls. This means he can be sure of starting a fire even when it's wet. When he first moved onto *Music Maker* he used to spend half an hour at a time on his knees blowing and trying to cherish tiny flames, willing them to grab hold of a twig and then a stick. Those early months were ones of dampness and determination. He was not going to give in. He had chosen to live there, chosen to stay behind after his family left, and he was going to make a go of it. There was no point in thinking about anything else, no other course of action open. This was what he had to do.

Today, he has decided, he will write to his mother. He rakes out the fine wood ash through the iron grating with a charred stick, pulls out the battered and overflowing ash tray and carries it out of the cabin. He keeps an eye out for Maisie because he's spilt the tray before when she's tried to beat him to the door. Once outside the wind sweeps the top layer of ash straight off the boat. Robert steps to the gunwale on the side away from the wind and tips the cinders into the river. He watches as the lightest particles settle on the surface for a moment before disappearing.

He goes back inside, shuts the door, replaces the tray, screws up several pages of the East Anglian and wedges them into the black interior of the small stove. He places dry twigs on top of this, and then selects some sticks of the thickness of ordinary rope. Don't be too ambitious, his mother used to say. If you put big pieces on too soon you'll have to start all over again. He strikes a match, lights the paper and closes up the front of the stove. Then he sits back on his heels and reaches out to fondle Maisie's ears, making her beat her tail lazily. He waits, listens to the rustle of the paper catching fire, the small invisible cracklings going on inside. After a minute or two he opens up the front again and pushes more wood onto the flames which are just beginning to establish themselves.

"That's going to be all right," he says to Maisie.

He takes out a sheet of lined paper, an envelope, his mother's last two letters and the biro he found outside the Ferryboat Inn a couple of weeks ago. He fetches the piece of wide plank from under his bunk which he uses as a table and then checks the fire again. It's slowed down so he opens the cabin door to create a draught. Maisie's ears prick up as she hears a rush of air up the chimney. After a minute he has another look inside the stove. That's better. Two of the bigger pieces are burning properly. He puts another one on top of them, shuts the door and goes back to the bunk.

He rereads both letters before placing the plank on his knee and picking up the pen to begin. When was the last time he held a pen? Months ago. He rarely needs to write.

Dear mother.

No, mother should have a capital M. He draws a capital over the small m. Then he writes

Thank you for your letters. I like getting them. I'm glad things are all right. I am all right here too so don't worry about me.

What is it he wants to say? Lying in his bunk last night he was so keen to write, so sure about it, but it feels different now. He tries to think back to how he felt, to what he felt. Being in touch. He wants to show his mother that he cares, that he wants to be in touch. Maisie shifts her warm weight onto his feet. He looks at his mother's last letter again. That had made him feel close. He focuses again on one particular line:

I sometimes think you will turn up here one day. That would be a treat.

Can he say anything to answer that? What? How? He could never turn up there one day. So what can he say? He picks up the biro again and writes

I liked the photo. The girls have grown haven't they? You all look well.

Should he write that he wished he was in the picture? He writes

It's getting colder now that it's October.

Robert remembers the fire. He moves Maisie and the writing things aside so he can get up and tend it. He must keep an eye on it because the wood must have nearly burnt through, but it's fine so he pushes in thicker sticks and a small amount of coal.

Then he settles down again and adds

but I'm snug in my cabin. People say it will be a bad winter.

I've been thinking about you a lot. Did the kitten come home? I hope so.

Mr and Mrs Corby ask about you. I sometimes do jobs for them and they give me things from their garden. Last time they gave me half a huge cabbage.

Please write again

How should he end it today? Love? That's what he usually puts. His mother had put *with all my love*. Love. Probably all mothers put love. And is that what all sons do, too? Probably. But what exactly did she mean when she wrote love? And what does he mean? He writes

With love from Robert and realises that today, for the first time, he really means it.

He writes his mother's name on the envelope, spelling out her surname which he has always wished was the same as his own, and the address. She's hundreds of miles away but the letter will be with her by Wednesday at the latest.

He replaces the plank under the bunk, and puts the biro on a shelf. He props the letter up next to it. He will have to buy a stamp.

When he thinks about it, if a letter could get there in a day or two, so could a person.

*

The CO had invited Susan to use his private sitting room. Someone had produced a pot of tea and Mark had put the milk in the cups, was ready to pour.

"I don't want any tea."

"Susan, you need something. You've had nothing since last

night and it's eleven o'clock already. You'll feel worse if you don't have anything."

"I couldn't feel worse than this."

He filled her cup, put the pot down, sat back and looked at her.

She had cried on and off for an hour and her energy was now ebbing.

Why, why had it happened? What had gone wrong? Daddy was supposed to be getting better. He was coming home. The doctors were sending him home and now, and now he was dead. It had been awful to hear Aunt Rose crying. Susan had never known her to cry before. She was always so comforting, so reliable, so there.

And Daddy. Darling Daddy. He wasn't coming back.

She sniffed again and wiped and blew her nose on Mark's handkerchief again.

"My nose just keeps running."

"It doesn't matter. It doesn't matter at all."

Susan looked at Mark.

This encouraged him. "Go on, Susan, drink some tea. You need it."

She picked up the cup and drank.

"Is there any more?"

"Yes, there's a pot full. Here you are. That's better."

It was another stroke. Out of the blue. No one knew it was coming and no one could have done anything. It was just one of those things.

Susan pushed off her shoes and pulled her legs up under her on the settee.

"I'm cold. I'm freezing."

"I'll go and get you a jacket, or a rug or something. Is that ok? Do you mind being on your own for a sec? "

"I'm ok."

She closed her eyes. When was the last time she saw Daddy? In bed in the hospital. She pictured him lying there talking to her in his changed voice. She tried to remember him before then, before she came to Bawdsey. She thought of the day last year when they had worked together in the garden, him tending one of his big bonfires, her bringing him barrowloads of weeds and leaves. She thought of the photos in his study of him in uniform, in front of an aeroplane, in front of another aeroplane, and yet another. He had a special certificate in a frame on his desk, in pride of place. What was that certificate for? She ought to know. She wanted to know.

"Here you are. A woolly jumper and a tartan rug." Mark held them out to her.

She didn't move. "Thank you."

"I'll put this over you, ok?"

"Umm. I'm trying to remember about a certificate on Daddy's desk, but I can't think what it was."

Mark paused as he spread the rug over her.

"I don't know why I'm thinking about it now. It's been there for years. But how could I not know what it's for?"

There was a knock and the CO's wife put her head round the door. Mark stood up as she came in.

"Is there anything I can do?" she asked.

Mark and Susan looked at each other.

"I don't think so," said Susan.

Mark asked, "Is it all right if we just stay here for a while?"

"Of course it is. Stay as long as you want. Do use the phone in the office next door if you need it, won't you? And there's a cloakroom through here if you want to powder your nose."

She left the room and Mark went to sit on the settee. He took Susan's hand.

Susan sighed.

"I don't know what to do."

"You don't have to do anything. Just be. At this minute there's nothing you can do."

"I need to go home. But it might not be like home anymore. It'll be different. Everything'll be different."

Mark stroked her shoulder as she started crying again.

"Daddy won't be there," she wailed, turning her face into the cushions, away from Mark. "I must go home. Now. I want to be with Rose. I just want to see her."

She sat up properly. "I need to get up. I should freshen up. I'm feeling a complete mess."

"Come on then," said Mark. "Use the cloakroom the CO's wife told you about. It'll save you going upstairs."

"And I'm going to phone up Aunt Rose. But first I need to work out which train to get so I can tell her what time I'll arrive."

"Let me go and find you a train timetable. I'll be back in a few minutes."

Susan was relieved not to meet anyone in the corridor. She rinsed her face with cold water and looked at herself in the mirror. She looked much the same as usual. How could this be? Her life had changed. How could she not look different?

She walked back to the sitting room and found Mark was already there.

He said, "There's another phone call for you."

She hesitated by the door.

"Go on. You ought to take it."

She didn't move.

"Susan, it can't be anything worse, can it? There's nothing worse to come."

"I suppose not."

She frowned as she turned to go out, and Mark went over to the window. He took out his packet of Du Mauriers, pulled out a cigarette and was tapping it on the windowsill when Susan came back again in.

"That was Bridget. She was jumping for joy. She isn't pregnant after all."

He held out the cigarettes in silence, and she took one. As he lit it he asked, "Did you tell her?"

"No. She didn't stop talking for three whole minutes."

"So things are all right, then?"

"Yes. More than all right. They're practically engaged."

Susan suddenly sat down on the nearest chair. "I didn't have the energy to stop her and tell her. She must be wondering why I didn't sound happier for her."

"I'll tell Ian, and he can tell her."

"Thanks. I don't think I could talk to anyone except you just now."

"They'll find out. You don't need to talk about it."

Susan breathed out smoke. "I just don't know what I'm supposed to do."

" I think you're supposed to let people look after you, then have some food, and then we'll find the best train." He held up the timetable.

She stood up and let Mark hold her, fold her under his arm.

"I need to pack. I must do it before I start crying again."

*

Rose had phoned the only undertaker in Westbury. It had not been as difficult as she expected and she had made an appointment for the next day. Perhaps things would be more manageable than she thought.

It was time to make a list of the things she'd thought of since hearing of Henry's death late last night. There would have been no point in phoning Susan then. That wouldn't have achieved anything. Far better to wait until this morning.

She was supposed to have visited Henry yesterday but had decided not to as he was meant to be coming home, coming here, today. He should have been sitting here now, in the brown Parker Knoll chair he always sat in, by the French window. He should have been starting to convalesce.

It had been hard driving to the hospital to see his body this morning, but she'd done it. It was a shock, a sad shock. And at the same time she found herself feeling annoyed that he had died. She had taken trouble to get things ready for him. She had ordered him The Times because he preferred it to The News Chronicle. She had aired sheets, dusted more thoroughly than usual, bought a pair of new towels. She had even splashed out on a chicken as a treat for lunchtime today. It was sitting there in the larder now, already stuffed. She had baked a batch of rock buns and made his favourite onion soup. And Susan. Susan hadn't even phoned to say when she'd arrive. She could be a little unthoughtful at times.

Telling Susan had been difficult. She had not worked out what to say to her on the phone. What had she actually said? She could not remember her exact words. How else could she have done it? She had just held onto the phone, listening to Susan sobbing, and Susan's voice, higher than usual, asking and repeating the same question: "Why? Why did it happen?" Poor, dear Susan. Then she too had started to cry again and they had cried down the phone together.

After that she had felt an urgent need to talk to someone else and had phoned Edith, a neighbour she had been friends with for years. Edith had been marvellous. She just sat with her, drank tea with her, listened, assured Rose that she would manage and that she, Edith, would do anything to help – Rose had only to ask.

Rose knew she would manage. She always did. She took the notebook from by the phone and began to make a list. She wrote Tell. Who must she tell? There were no close relations, apart from Susan of course, but she must not forget the Benthams, or Mr and Mrs Holland, and there were the cousins in Lancaster. Then there were his many friends. Would she have to write to all of them? Most of them were, or had been, in the RAF. What should she do about them? Henry had called the RAF his second family, and it *was* a family for him. In fact, there had been years when it had seemed more like his first family. The RAF needed to know.

She wrote Funeral. She thought of the vicar, refreshments, Henry's body, the coffin, Susan – Susan in tears, in black – notices in announcements columns. And paperwork. That was less daunting because for years Henry had said: Everything important is in the bottom right hand drawer of the desk in my office. It's all shipshape. He was good – had been good – at things like that. Then she wrote House and things. There was so much to do. Susan would have to help her.

The phone went again. It was Marion, the mother of the baby she had knitted the little cardigan for, thanking her and inviting her to coffee tomorrow. Rose explained about Henry and ended up almost consoling Marion because Marion was so embarrassed. She put the phone down. All this was so exhausting. What time was it? Only one o'clock. Still so much day ahead. She looked out of the window. It was a fine afternoon, just the sort of day she'd like to spend outside cutting back seedheads.

She put the kettle on again and stood waiting for it to boil. She was on edge with herself and the world. It wasn't just sadness. Anxiety, fatigue and annoyance seemed to have appeared from somewhere and she did not want them. They were unfamiliar feelings and they were upsetting. Last night she had not slept for hours. She had cried at first but then just lain in bed, thinking about her life as much as Henry's.

She had woken early, worried about phoning Susan, worried about her reaction. And now she found herself worrying about the wretched chicken – should she cook it now and have it cold? – and the fact that the boy who was supposed to rake up the leaves had not turned up as he had promised. The garden was looking really untidy. This was ridiculous. What really mattered was Susan. But why hadn't she phoned?

She took the cup of tea and sat looking out of the French windows, willing Susan to phone. She suddenly had a picture of Henry on the lawn playing one of his surprisingly vicious croquet shots. It made her smile. How amazing the mind was. Less than a day after his death and a minute after feeling annoyed with everything, he was making her smile.

Rose was woken an hour later by someone knocking on the back door. It startled her and she took a few moments to get her bearings. Everything flooded back as she walked the few yards through the sitting room and across the corridor to the kitchen. It was the coalman. He had just delivered the load Rose had ordered a few days ago. She wrote out a cheque and gave it to him. As she stood on the step it seemed warm for October. No need for a fire today. She found these days that as she could not carry a full scuttle of coal she used the electric heater more and more even though it was expensive. Henry had been so sure he would be up to carrying the coal within a week or two. He had said: Why not order a couple of hundredweight? He loved a coal fire.

Then the phone went. This *must* be Susan.

Susan was getting herself organised. She hoped to get the seven o'clock train from Paddington. She would get a taxi from the station and Rose was not to collect her. She couldn't stay and talk, she had to get on the ferry. Rose replaced the receiver and looked out of the window.

This was better than the first phonecall. Susan had been so upset then, but now she sounded more matter of fact, more getting on with things. Could she put Susan in the bed which she had made up for Henry? She would know it was meant for Henry. Would she mind that? Surely it would be all right. She picked up the tea things and took them back into the kitchen. For goodness' sake, she couldn't be expected to keep on changing things round when she'd already done so much and still had so much to do. If Susan was not happy about this she could sort herself out with a sleeping bag here on the settee.

It was three o'clock and lunchtime had passed her by. No wonder she was hungry. She heated up some of the onion soup and put together a cheese and pickle sandwich. It would be important for her and Susan to eat well over these next few days.

How long would Susan stay? Neither of them had said anything about that. How much would a coffin cost? When she'd seen the undertaker she would have to phone the bank. And would that dark suit still be all right? She had not been to a funeral for several years. Did she have a blouse that would go with it? Did it need ironing?

She saw her plate was empty apart from crumbs and a trace of pickle. She had no recollection of having eaten.

*

When he thinks about it, as well as not having a definite end the river doesn't have definite edges. Do these yards of thick, brown mud count as river, or as land? If you can't walk on them, they can't really be land, can they? But they're not really river either, not until they're covered with water at high tide, and then they must be river. So, the river's exact width can't be measured any more than its exact length. And nor does it have an exact depth, for its surface rises or falls by a yard or two each tide.

Do these things matter? Perhaps not – after all there's no need to know exactly what's river and what's not. Except in a war, perhaps. But it's interesting that this whole expanse of water which everyone understands to be the Deben can't be easily defined. This morning the edge of it was over there, just by that post which was nearly submerged then, but now at low tide when the post is sticking high out of the mud, the river ends right over there by the marsh. But it's still the river, still the Deben, whichever way he looks at it. There's just more of it at high tide.

Robert looks at each person coming on board. They're all quite separate – there's no difficulty in deciding where one person begins and ends. Maisie wants to jump up onto the ledge but he shushes her down. She too is completely contained. Just dog, pure dog, separate from everything else. And each of the people on this run – on any run – across the river are uniquely themselves. Is the river uniquely itself? Robert remembers other rivers: the Yare, the Alde, the Orwell. Are they as different from each other as people are different from each other? Yes, they are.

A few people are chatting quietly, a few sit in silence. He recognises several of them, especially one couple – that confident man who gets on well with everyone and his girlfriend. They're not talking today. They're holding hands, and the man is looking back at the Bawdsey jetty they're leaving behind. The woman is staring at the floor and what's on it: her suitcase, her feet in their smart shoes, rope, a tin baler, Maisie curled up on a sack. He can tell that although the woman's eyes are on these things, she's not seeing them. She seems completely unaware of the activity all around – gulls landing and taking off from moored boats; sailing dinghies preparing for the Saturday races; huge grey clouds on the horizon; water slapping up against the hull; buoys being yanked by the outgoing tide. How can she not see these things, not see and feel this wide, alive river?

They reach the Ferry side and everyone walks up towards the café and the bus. The man he likes carries the woman's suitcase. Only three people are waiting for the boat and they tell him not to worry, there's no hurry and he can wait for more passengers. But he has to go, knows he shouldn't delay his journey.

Back they go, across the outgoing flow, past two dinghies that tack and then gybe. In unison their crews duck and their helmsmen tip their heads upwards to check the burgees. Still in unison their booms are pushed out to the same angle and their white mainsails carry the same fullness of wind. Within a minute the one furthest away on the left gradually pulls ahead of the other. They're beautiful to watch as the tide and the wind race them towards the open sea on this dark day, on this deep brown water.

Because his attention has been taken by the dinghies Robert has allowed himself to be carried slightly further downstream than usual. Now he steers so the prow curves round at a sharper angle. The wind hits them from the side, making people grab onto their hats, hold on to the gunwale. He's often noticed how even small changes in the way the boat behaves or in the strength and noise of the wind and water mean that passengers hold on more tightly. Although in bad weather the ferryman occasionally has to announce that the ferry won't run for an hour or two it's rare to have a really rough crossing. And even if people are anxious there's always someone who laughs and seems to enjoy it when the boat feels less safe.

Now, there's a distinct juddering. Maisie's body shakes as she lies asleep on her sack. A sudden thump of water sends a shower over everyone, and one man appears to be delighted by this. He pretends to dive into the river, and his friends laugh.

Robert eases the boat up to the jetty but fails to loop the rope round the post on his first attempt.

"Missed!" shouts the man who's been fooling about.

The boat drifts away and Robert has to steer it close up again and try again. This time he does it.

The same voice calls, "Well done that man!"

They all climb out and several pause on the jetty to light up. It's difficult when it's as windy as this, and Robert sees a few of them in a huddle for some minutes until, one by one, they detach themselves when they've managed to get their cigarette alight. While his next load of passengers come on board he leans back against the side of the boat, his hip against the tiller. He pulls out his pouch and papers and rolls himself a thin twig of a cigarette, sheltering his hands inside his jacket in the lee of the wind. He enjoys each sweet, warm draw.

He glimpses down to Maisie. She's asleep. His passengers are chatting, not yet aware they will be buffeted on this crossing.

*

After Susan's train had gone Mark left the station, went into Felixstowe to collect a book from the bookshop, and then returned to Bawdsey. The day's plans had disintegrated. Once again, just as things were definitely on the up, something happened and Susan disappeared. His feelings swerved between disappointment for himself and sympathy for Susan.

The return crossing was bumpier than usual and he could see several people who could not wait to get off the boat. Even this short crossing had made them feel distinctly under the weather.

He made his way to his room and stood looking out of the window. Dearest Susan. She was on her way home now and given the circumstances that had to count as progress. She was scared and unhappy and he was sure she'd feel better when she was with her aunt. It sounded as if she and Rose were very fond of each other.

She might be away for days. They'd be unlikely to hold the funeral before Tuesday at the earliest and there would be plenty of things to be done. Poor, darling Susan. If only he could be there with her, looking after her, doing things for her. If their relationship was a little further on, he might have been there. If they were engaged he *would* have been there.

Ian and Bridget. That was an unexpected turn of events. Thank God. The possible pregnancy had seemed so important a few days ago, but suddenly it had gone. It would be good to see Ian, good to have him back on his usual lively form. He would have a drink with him tonight.

It was no use staying in his room. He must go and find some food. Although he had insisted that Susan ate scrambled eggs before she left for Bristol he hadn't had anything himself. That's what he needed: fuel.

He went downstairs as tea was being served in the Officers' lounge. Perfect timing. He felt better after two cups of tea and some cheese sandwiches, and better still after a slice of sponge cake and another cup of tea.

Everyone knew about Susan already. A couple came up and commiserated, Alex put his hand on his shoulder for a moment and then two girls approached him carrying cups of tea.

He smiled. "I've had three cups already."

"No, these are ours!" said one of them. "We just thought we'd come and sit with you."

They settled down on the settee opposite him. "Are you ok?"

Was he ok? Yes, he supposed he was. It was Susan who wasn't.

"Susan's really upset. It's completely unexpected. She was told her father was on the mend. She's feeling awful."

"Has she got a big family?"

"No. There's no one except an aunt, but she's very close to her."

"What about her mother?"

"Her mother died years ago."

Both the girls looked embarrassed. "Oh, how awful. How awful for her."

They weren't sure what to say next and Mark wanted to escape, but they had only just sat down. He stretched out his legs and looked at his shoes. He could tell by the clink of each cup on its saucer when each girl was taking a sip of tea. He could not think of any small talk at all. He did not want to be here. Through the window he could see bushes blowing about, a gull racing across the sky.

He stood up. "I'm sorry, but do you mind if I go? Thanks for thinking about Susan and me."

He left the room, went upstairs to get his coat. Outside would be the best place. Even though he felt sorry for Susan he could do without people feeling sorry for him. What a day. It was all stops and starts, all disjointed. He hated it.

As he walked past the sitting room where he had been with Susan that morning the door opened and the CO came out.

"Ah, Rivens. Tell me how things are progressing. I'm sorry to hear about Wing Commander Cairncross's death. A big shock for his daughter."

"Yes sir, it is."

"Did she get off home all right?"

"Yes, I saw her on to the train, sir. She'll be well on her way now."

"Good. Well. She's a sensible young woman. One of our best women officers, I think." The CO's voice expressed more than politeness. "It'll help her, you know. Her training as an officer."

Mark nodded. What was the CO trying to say?

"If it was wartime death would be an everyday occurrence. The war only finished six, seven years ago. It's easy to forget what life was made of then. You just had to get on with it. I'm sure she'll just get on with it too. She's young. She's made of sterling stuff. She'll go far."

"Thank you, sir."

The CO nodded and moved on down the corridor away from Mark who continued towards the door at the far end.

When he opened it, it swung hard outwards with the weight of the wind behind it. He hauled it shut and made his way in the late light to the sunken garden. Within minutes his shoes and turn ups were covered in bits of grass. He found the stone seat he and Susan had sat on in midsummer but it was soaking wet.

He walked round the edge of the garden, making for the entrance onto the cliff side. A blast of wind and noise hit him as he went through. He moved left, into the shelter of jutting rocks. Out of the gale it was quieter and he was able to light a cigarette. He gazed out at the sea and the sky. White horses reached as far as he could see, and behind them the sky was a creamy yellow. He smoked slowly as the brightness faded and was overtaken by a bank of mud coloured cloud coming in from the north. It was becoming darker by the minute.

Did being an officer make death easier? He doubted it. And surely it was different if it was your own family, and unexpected? And was it different for women? Would he feel differently from his sisters if one of their parents died? Probably. But was that because of who they each were, rather than because he was male and they were female?

He could no longer see the white horses, could hardly see the water. He threw away the butt, put his hand in his pocket to warm up.

So this was what loving meant. It meant feeling for someone as if that person were you. If they were happy you were happy, if they were sad you were sad. To love was to be vulnerable. It was about vulnerability, not strength. Why did people talk about love being strong?

He felt freer. What was it?

Susan, Susan. He wanted her so much.

No. It wasn't Susan. It was also a relief to know Bridget was not pregnant. It somehow made it more likely that Trudi had not been pregnant either. There was no logic to this at all, but he felt better. It was time to let Trudi go. What was done was done. Fretting about it now achieved nothing. At last he understood what he had done, and now he must live with it. He was surprised to realise that instead of shying away he was, for the first time, wishing Trudi the true goodwill that should have been hers years ago.

*

The taxi driver put Susan's case in the boot and held the door open for her. She sat back, listening to the hiss of wheels on the wet road. She noticed a new set of traffic lights, the Public Library where her aunt used to take her on Saturday mornings, more and more houses going up. Would they never stop building? They turned into Stephenson Close.

"It's that house, the one with the iron front gate."

They drew up at Bleadon and Aunt Rose was already at the door. She was standing in the porch with the light from the hall behind her, waiting for the driver to drive off, waiting for Susan to carry her case down the short path.

"My dear, at last. Come in out of the wet."

Susan dropped her case in the porch. Then they hugged and hung on to each other, Rose crying quietly into Susan's green collar, Susan sniffing against Rose's woollen cardigan. At last Rose pulled back, still with her arm round Susan.

"Come on in, let's get this door shut. Give me your coat. The front room's nice and warm, go straight through."

She went in and there was the picture of the bluebell wood above the fireplace and copies of The Lady and the Radio Times on the coffee table. Everything was the same. They hugged again.

"Go by the fire. I'm going to make us a drink this minute. I've been waiting for you before having mine. Come on, do sit down."

Susan sat down and held her hands out to the fire. It was good to be here, but was it really the same? It was impossible to identify what was different, but this was where she wanted to be.

Rose came back from the kitchen with a tray.

"Cocoa's good on a night like this. And I've made some rock buns."

Susan took the hot mug and a bun. She was staring into the fire, watching how the orange flames were spiked with occasional blues, greens. The cat came in and made for Susan's lap at once. Stroking her felt good. She purred and purred. She seemed to know. They sat talking quietly, eating and drinking slowly.

"You look washed out, and that's how I'm feeling," said Rose. "I've had such a long day. I'm going to get us both a hot water bottle. "

"I'd like to take puss to bed too."

"Of course you can. She'd like a treat."

After they had hugged again they said goodnight, and Susan shut the door of the little room, got into bed and brought her knees up towards her chest, snuggling the hot water bottle close to her stomach. It was so hot she had to tug her nightdress down so the bottle was not right next to her skin. The cat came in under the bedclothes.

She fell asleep at once but woke up after only an hour. Where was she? Within a second she remembered it all. Daddy was dead. She was at Aunt Rose's and Daddy was dead.

She began to cry, to snuffle into the bedclothes, trying not to make a noise but unable to stop the sobs. She gave up trying to stifle them. The door opened and Rose came in. She switched on the bedside lamp, pulled up a chair, leant over and began to stroke Susan's shoulders.

"I want him back. I want him alive again. I didn't say goodbye." Her words started off as a whisper and then rose to a wail.

Rose stroked and stroked until the shaking settled, the sobbing became soundless.

Susan turned, felt under the pillow for a hankie, pulled back the sheet a little so she could breathe freely. She saw Rose was crying too. Tears were running diagonally across her tilted face until they reached the creases round her mouth, where they altered course and ran down to her chin. She looked so tired, so lined.

They sat for a while, mostly without speaking. The cat was sitting upright, blinking at them, the end of her tail twitching slightly.

Rose was the first to recover. "There's a dry pillow in the airing cupboard. You can't sleep on this damp one."

Susan got up and went to the lavatory. Then she fetched the dry pillow and put the other one on the dressing table while Rose straightened the sheets and took out the lukewarm bottle.

"Do you think you'll sleep now? Are you all right?"

Susan nodded, and got back into bed. The cat snuggled into a dip in the eiderdown.

"Good night, my dear."

Rose left the door half ajar as she had done when Susan was little and returned to her own room.

She was still awake at three am. Less than twenty four hours since Henry's death. He had been such an active man, had always impressed people with his energy. On the day after his retirement, he had announced: They'll have to finish me off, you know. I'm enjoying my life too much. I'm not going to sit around waiting for things to happen.

He had never waited for things to happen, even as a boy. He was far too impatient. But he had mellowed. He had found that waiting for things sometimes worked better than rushing towards them. Recently he had criticised Susan for being impatient, even though he was so proud of her.

But now he was dead. He would not be going to any more of

his committee meetings, not phoning up to tell her about an article he'd read, not walking down the garden to see if the birds were getting through the holes in the ancient netting over the soft fruit. He wouldn't be pruning the forsythia again, or urging her to do something about the leak in the garage roof.

Seeing his body had not been as painful as she feared. When St Botolph's asked if she wished to see him she had said yes immediately, she would come while he was still in his room. He looked younger than he had done over the last months, and somehow neater and smaller. In the past she had often thought that he took up a lot of room. Now that he lay with his arms still at his side and his feet together he was tidy. There seemed to be less of him. She reached out to touch him and noticed for the first time how many brown patches he had on the backs of his hands. She bent over and kissed his forehead – something she had not done when he was alive because he was so tall. She usually lifted her head up to reach his cheek. And now there was a different smell about him too. Not unpleasant, just different. Seeing him had not felt like saying goodbye for ever. Was this because although he was there and clearly dead, she had not yet taken it in fully? Or was it that this was going to be a short separation? If there was life after death, then she would be meeting him again. She was very doubtful about whether there was an afterlife at all, let alone one in which they might meet.

Would Susan want to see him? She was not at all sure. Susan might think she ought to see him. Ought she? When someone died should their child see them? Did it matter whether they did or not? It must do.

Rose had only been about five when she experienced her first death. She had been carried downstairs – how? by whom? – to the front room and her mother had carried her in to see Grandma Loft. Henry was there too and the three of them had said the Lord's Prayer together.

Then, against the natural order of things, it was Grace's funeral next. It was only Henry, herself, their father, two of Henry's closest friends and Madeleine who had been there. It was a time of shock, of total grief. Two year old Susan was not there.

Rose had been away visiting friends when her father died ten years ago and Henry had arranged everything. She always thought he had done that because he had taken no part in their mother's funeral. He had hurried back from somewhere abroad, guilty about not having been at home much for the last few years. It had been held at St Andrew's on a hot day in August, and bees had buzzed around the wreaths.

And now it was time for Henry's funeral. So many deaths. And the war, what about the war? She wanted Henry back, and she wanted her father, her mother, her David to come back. She thought of neighbours and friends, the whole regiments who had been killed in the wars, the millions of men and women and children who had died in the wars in England, in Europe, all over the world.

But they couldn't all come back. This sort of thinking was nonsense. It was pointless. No. Now it was just her and Susan. And then one day, perhaps sooner than she thought, it would be her turn to die. Would Susan be married by then? Yes, surely she would. She must marry. She must have children. The family needed to grow again. It would be wonderful, wonderful, when Susan had a baby.

Rose turned on to her side, exhausted. Today had been very difficult. Tomorrow would be even more difficult. She would have to look after Susan. Wednesday. That's when she wanted the funeral to be held. That gave them four more days including tomorrow, Sunday. Yes, Wednesday would be best.

*

On Monday Susan said she wanted to see her father so Rose drove her to the undertaker's. She chose to go in alone, and Rose was anxious as she watched her walk through the door which the undertaker held open for her and then quietly pulled to behind her. Three or four minutes passed before it opened again and she came out with her face red and unhappy. Rose went to comfort her. She held Susan's cheek against hers, held

211

her taut shoulders and back. She felt her ribs, her thudding heartbeat, smelled an echo of the unfamiliar smell of Henry's body.

On the journey home Susan put her head back, shut her eyes, said nothing. It was hard to know what she was thinking. Perhaps she wasn't thinking at all, just feeling. And after a cup of tea she announced, "Now. What else needs doing? Tell me what needs to be done."

It was a relief to see how well Susan rallied round. Between them they made phone calls, ordered a wreath, shopped, prepared their clothes for the day. Rather than needing to be looked after, Susan offered to meet the vicar, choose the cards to send out to people, talk to the florist.

It was definitely better for Susan to get on with things than mope around. There would be time for grieving. The most important thing was to let people know that Henry had died, that the funeral would be at 11am on Wednesday October 15th at St. Agnes, that people were invited back for refreshments. As Susan found it difficult to talk to family friends she offered to do the letters. Rose didn't find phoning easy either until she discovered it was best not to do any when she felt low. If she left it an hour or two she found she could deal with them in a matter-of-fact way without getting upset. She would have liked Susan to make some of the calls, but told herself that no one is ever ready for these things, no one is ever prepared. So how had she learned to cope with the worst times? Was it through experience? By getting older? Or because she had to? It didn't matter. They were getting things done. Susan was making a big contribution and doing it well. She was a darling. And Edith, bless her, had offered to prepare all the refreshments.

On Wednesday Rose woke at seven o'clock. This was the day. She dressed and went downstairs to the kitchen, drew back the curtains and looked out on her damp, dank garden with its unraked up leaves. She didn't feel as if she had slept. She prepared cereal, tea and toast for herself and Susan. Where had her energy gone? How was she going to get through this particular day feeling like this? She would have to pull herself together. It was a day that had to be dealt with, lived through.

It was cold and drizzling. People arrived on time, made their slow way through the lych-gate, crunched up the gravel path. There was a good crowd, enough to give the hymns some weight, some strength. It didn't sound bad. Henry would have liked to have joined in with:

> *Through the night of doubt and sorrow*
> *Onward goes the pilgrim band*
> *Singing songs of expectation*
> *Marching to the Promised Land.*

Susan appeared calm. She said little throughout the day. It was hard to know what she was feeling but she sang all of the hymns. Rose held her hand while the vicar said uninspiring things which focused on Henry's career. Why wasn't he saying anything about his character, his personal qualities? This upset her. Didn't she and Susan matter? They both struggled with the soft, gentle words they knew had been one of Henry's favourites:

> *Drop Thy still dews of quietness, let all our striving cease,*
> *Take from our souls the strain and stress and let our ordered lives*
>   *confess*
> *The beauty of Thy peace,*
> *The beauty of Thy peace…*

Rose looked around the graveside. The faces made a sort of pallid layer between black bodies and black umbrellas. Over half the mourners were former or current RAF officers, some with their wives. It was true, the RAF was some sort of a family, and today that helped. Then, unexpectedly, a small aeroplane flew over directly above the churchyard. Heads turned upwards and umbrellas tipped for few seconds, and people exchanged glances. It was another reminder to Rose that her brother, now being put into the ground, was a man who used to fly.

Later, when they went back to the house, she noticed how nearly everyone mentioned this aeroplane. They said the incident had cheered them up, and later still, when one of Henry's former colleagues had had several sherries, he announced that it was a positive sign and proof of an afterlife. It wasn't that he was a traditional believer, he explained, but it was the sort of thing that Henry would have arranged for his funeral. Everyone laughed at this, and that helped too.

When everyone had left Susan threw herself into clearing up. Rose sat down and put her feet up on the sofa, shut her eyes and listened to the tap running, the small knocks and clinks made by Susan as she placed the glasses, plates, cups on the wooden draining board, the water gurgling down the sink.

Susan needed to do this. She wouldn't have been able to stay sitting in the drawing room doing nothing, but before they sat down for supper she said she wanted to phone Mark. The phone was in the hall and Rose, just as she had done the previous evening, made her switch on the electric heater for ten minutes first because it was so cold out there.

"I don't want you freezing while you talk to him. Let's warm the hall up first."

Susan didn't spend long on the phone. She came back into the dining room where Rose was putting some macaroni cheese on the table.

"He's missing me a lot."

"And are you missing him?"

"Yes. More than I thought I would."

Rose served the meal on to the plates and passed one to Susan. Susan shook her head, "I don't think I want any supper."

"Are you all right, my dear?"

"No."

Susan put her hands to her face, bent her head so her hair fell forward, but sank back against the chair. Rose put her knife and fork down and got up from the table and went round to Susan. She put her arm around her shoulders, rubbed her back gently.

"I won't see him again. That's what's so hard. Ever."

A log in the fire collapsed into ash and a curl of thick grey smoke.

"And I want to. I want to so much." She paused. "But I can't."

Dear Susan. Rose continued to stroke her. She was looking at

214

Susan's blue cardigan, noticing the way the collar had been joined on, noticing her prominent shoulder blades. Her back began to hurt.

"I'm going to have to move. I'm getting stiff bending over like this. Why don't you come over by the fire?"

Susan moved across to an armchair and made herself comfy, tucking her legs up under her. Rose put their meals on trays and they had them on their laps. They watched the flames lick round the coal, the last logs. They witnessed little explosions sending out tiny sparks and puffs of smoke. They heard the small falls made in the grate as the wood disappeared.

Susan gave a long sigh.

Rose said, "Do you want to go on sitting here? Shall I put some more coal on?" It was good for Susan to sigh. Sighs were healing.

"No. I think I'll go to bed. I want today to be over." She added, "But I wish I could just magic myself into bed without having to get undressed or clean my teeth or anything." She got to her feet and went upstairs slowly.

Rose put up the fireguard, switched off the standard light. Yes, these end of day routines took time, but they were reassuring. She cleared the table, covered up the rest of the still warm macaroni, and boiled the kettle for their hot water bottles.

She knocked on Susan's door and went in. Susan was curled up in bed and her eyes were shut. The cat was curled up at the foot of the bed. Rose bent over her to kiss her cheek.

"Are you asleep already? Sleep well. God bless."

Susan opened her eyes and reached out an arm to hug her.

Rose left both bedroom doors ajar. Once in bed she turned onto her right side, the position she always slept in. She pulled the bedclothes up. She thought back over the day. Dressing in her black clothes. The drive to the church. The coffin. The drizzle. The way Mr and Mrs Andrews and some of Henry's old friends were so warm and compassionate while others, like Dr Watson who had known him for decades, seemed too embarrassed to even say his name. The vicar. The aeroplane. All those people in the house. The cars parked along the road. Clearing up with Edith and Susan.

Was there an afterlife? There must be. This couldn't all be for nothing. There must be meaning. But what was certain was that for her there was less time ahead than behind. Should she go on living in the same way? Was she going to lose every important person in her life? Why? Now, there was only Susan. Susan, who had a whole expanse of time ahead of her, a thousand things to do and a boyfriend who was missing her.

Lucky, lucky Susan. She would be happy. Things would be different for her. It was bewildering how things worked out. Why was life unfair? Perhaps there was no meaning at all. If so, then there was neither fairness nor unfairness. Life was just there.

She began to cry. For herself. For Henry. For David.

Susan did not hear her.

*

Robert is not expecting to work the ferry but after returning home with a small sack of cold, wet coal on Thursday evening he hears someone come on board and call his name. This is unusual. He finishes off filling up the stove with wood before going on deck. It's the ferryman.

"Good. You're here. Could you run the ferry later this evening? My son's ill and my wife wants me to be at home when the doctor comes."

Robert points to the boots and coat he's wearing. "I've only just got in. I can come now if you want."

"No, there's no need. He'll be at least an hour, and Pete's doing it until nine. Can you relieve him?"

"Yes, but what's wrong?"

"The lad's been off school all week. Not like him at all, so when he was sick again after his tea today, my wife said she wasn't waiting till tomorrow."

"I hope he's ok. I'll make sure I'm there by nine."

Robert goes back into the cabin, takes off his boots and coat, puts coal in the stove, lights the gas under the kettle. There's time to eat. He spreads the paper out on the bunk and squats down to read the headlines and bits of articles while the water boils. He stands up to make the tea and while it stews he cuts two slices of bread and opens up the stove front to toast them, but the fire's not picked up yet, doesn't have the right kind of heat. He closes up the stove again, lies the bread on the top.

He slowly pours out a cup of strong, dark tea, adds sugar from the brown packet, milk from the bottle. He stirs it, adds more water to the pot. Then he takes the warm bread, spreads margarine on it, covers it with cheese cut into uneven slices. He sits down and pulls the paper across his knees, reading it as he eats. Crumbs fall onto the newspaper. When he finishes he shakes them onto the floor. Maisie briefly shifts her attention from her bone to sniff out and lick up the morsels.

Then he sits back against the head of the bunk, his feet out in front of him, his hands cupped round the hot cup of tea. Maisie is making slobbering, chewing noises, but the boat is so still and quiet he can hear the fire drawing. This is good. It will be fine and clear tonight, and he'll earn extra money. He need not move for half an hour.

At quarter to eight he puts on his boots again, adds coal and closes up the stove, pulls on his jacket and lets Maisie lead the way along the gangplank and off *Music Maker*. There's a full moon and he can see as well as if it was daylight. He takes his usual route to the beach through the boatyard.

Three men stand with their backs to the sea, talking quietly. A couple hold hands as they watch the progress of the ferry. Their dog runs up to Maisie, sniffs around her until he's called back. There are never many passengers on winter weekday nights like this one and tonight is especially clear and calm.

Robert looks forward to being on the river and he knows Pete will be eager to finish work and get home to his wife and new baby daughter. Two weeks ago, just after her birth, he told Robert, "She's a dear little thing. She just makes us so happy." Robert was surprised. This baby brought out a wholly different side to the man. Did that happen to all new fathers? Is that what his father thought when he was born?

He watches Pete go off towards his house behind the café, turn and walk backwards for a few steps. Then he gets on board and goes to the stern, listens to the still running engine. Maisie follows him up and over the gunwale. The five waiting people crunch down the beach, climb on to the step and inside.

He steers across the incoming swell. It will be exactly high tide when he makes his last trip in a couple of hours. He's warm inside and out, pleased to be on his river, under this amazing moon. Out at sea is the loom of the lightship. By day the lightship itself can't be seen, but on nights like tonight its beam peels past the end of the estuary, sweeping round slowly. In his school library there was a book with a cutaway diagram of a lighthouse and it explained how they were built, how their motors carry the mirrors round, how the lights are magnified. It made him want to be a lighthouseman. It must be exciting to be safe in a stone tower out at sea, alone and responsible, and it would be good to return to the mainland and be greeted by grateful sailors and their families. Lighthousemen must feel proud, but he had had no idea how to become one.

He likes being a part-time ferryman but it can't be like being a lighthouseman. If he uses his common sense there's no danger on the river. There are times when it's stormy or foggy, but it isn't as if the ferry could get lost or founder on rocks, not here at least. Although there have been deaths in the Deben it's much more usual for sailors to be stranded on the bar, and then it's often just a question of waiting for the tide to lift them off. But even so, there is *some* pride in doing the job well. Moving dozens, even hundreds, of passengers from one side of the river to the other has *some* significance. What would they do if there wasn't a ferry?

The loom swings past again, a small, slow flick unnoticed by his passengers. They are admiring the moon's wavy reflection and pointing up to the Pole Star. The journey's over too soon and the last couple, whom he's not seen before, take their time getting off. They dawdle up the jetty while Robert lets the engine idle. Perhaps they're new here.

When it's like this ferrying isn't work. It's pure enjoyment. He earns his money by going backwards and forwards in peace, with no river traffic to bother about and only a few passengers. On a night like this it's a privilege to be on the river. He's not wondering how many more trips he has to make, like he does sometimes when it's raining or it's really crowded, or when people take him for granted.

He's hoping he'll have the final crossing of the night on his own. Just him and Maisie. It rarely happens but when it does it's special and he likes to imagine that the ferry belongs to him. It's his very own, and if he wants, he doesn't just have to go backwards and forwards. He can go upriver to Woodbridge, or round the coast and into Ipswich, even up to Lowestoft. Perhaps he can even go to Scotland.

But the river could never be his, not even if his was the only boat on it. Rivers can't be owned. People can own land, but not water. Perhaps someone could own water enclosed by land like a lake, but not water like this. Not a river, not a sea. But if he's lucky he will at least have the estuary to himself tonight.

As he returns to the Ferry side he sees there's just one person waiting. It's a woman with a suitcase. He signals that he'll get out of the boat to carry it for her.

"Stay there, Maisie."

The woman murmurs her thanks and Robert recognises her at once when he's close to her. She was the woman he'd noticed on the ferry a few days ago, maybe a week ago. It was a crossing in the morning, he remembers. She was the one with the boyfriend who carried her case, and here she is coming back.

But now she's completely different. She takes her time getting on board, walks down the boat to stand near him. She's very near, especially as she's the only passenger.

"What a moon," she says.

They set off.

"Isn't it still tonight? The water's hardly moving."

Robert mutters his agreement. He feels as if he's expected to say something else so he adds, "The tide's just on the turn."

The woman is facing out to sea.

"Oh look, that must be the beam from a lighthouse. I've never seen it before." Then she pauses before saying, "Has it been there long, the lighthouse, do you know?"

"It's a lightship. A good many years, I should think. It marks up where there's danger."

219

"But even if you know where danger is, you can't always avoid it."

Robert slows the engine down. What does she mean? Skippers avoid dangers they know about. It's the ones they don't know about that are dangerous.

"Sometimes things just come from nowhere, don't they? They just happen. And you can't do anything about them."

Is she talking about the sea?

Another minute passes. Maisie stands up, deceived by the slower speed into thinking that they've arrived.

The woman tips her head back and looks at the sky. The moonlight makes her neck pale.

"Do you know the names of the stars?"

"Some of them. That's the Plough , and that's the North Star. And that's – no, wait a minute.."

Robert turns the engine right off, something he's never done before on a crossing. They rock a little, caught on the cusp of the changing tide, the edge that separates the flow from the ebb. The absence of sound surprises him. He watches little waves lick at a buoy. He hears the woman draw in a long breath and let it out in a quiet sigh.

"What's that M? I can see the shape of a big M."

He looks to where she's pointing. "That's not an M, it's a W. It's Cassiopeia."

"It looks like an M to me, but I suppose it depends on how you look at it."

They both laugh.

"And that line is Andromeda."

"Where?"

"Over there, towards the horizon. There's four equal sized stars in a row, and then a square."

She goes on looking up.

"I still can't find it."

She turns round in the boat, continues to search.

"Those three ones close together, over there. What are they?"

"Orion's belt."

"That's it! My boyfriend tried to point it out to me once but I couldn't find it. It's difficult, isn't it? There are so many stars. There's so much light in the sky."

Robert starts up the engine again to bring the ferry in to the jetty.

He secures it, puts her case over onto the jetty beside her and then gets out of the boat and carries it right up on to the hard.

"I may as well take it across to the gate for you."

He leads the way, followed by the woman and by Maisie. He puts the case down, says good night, walks back to the boat and sets off on the final crossing, on his own with Maisie.

This solitary crossing is what he has been looking forward to, but he's thinking about the woman, about what she said. Why was she so different tonight? Was it because they were alone? He doesn't know, but no other passenger has talked to him like that before. He's pleased he switched the engine off and floated free. He'll do it again.

When the boat's secured he walks back to *Music Maker* and pees onto the grass before going across the gangplank. He pauses on deck before going into the cabin. The tide is going out now, pulled by that huge moon. He looks up at the sky. The woman was right. It's full of light. He's rarely seen it so light.

*

Mark searched for the obituary of Susan's father in The Times before he had breakfast. It wasn't there.

Alex guessed what he was doing and said, "You won't find it. He was only a Wing Commander wasn't he?"

"Yes, but.."

"Sorry. I don't mean that he was *only* a Wing Commander. I mean that you won't get an obituary in The Times unless you're at least an Air Marshal. And you probably need a decoration or two as well."

"Ah, yes. I'm sure you're right." Mark put down the paper and walked over to the window. Did Susan's father have a decoration? He rather thought he had. He turned round, and there was Susan. He hurried over, hugged her, felt her hug him back.

"I didn't think you were coming till this afternoon! How did you get here so early?"

"I arrived late last night."

Susan. Here she was, right in front of him. Breathing. Smiling.

"Susan, you're back." She looked tired. She looked lovely. He wanted to propose to her there and then.

"I'm famished. Let's have breakfast."

Mark followed her to the table, noticed her acknowledgement of other people's greetings, aware that most people knew what had happened.

She seemed very composed.

"Are you all right?"

They sat down on either side of a long table.

"I am now – I mean at this minute. But it comes and goes. Sometimes I feel awful again. I'm fine now, I've been fine since getting off the train at Felixstowe, but I was sniffing for most of the journey. There was a lady in the carriage whom I could tell was worried about me. I didn't want to talk to her so I kept going out to the Ladies and washing my face."

Mark passed her a plate and knife.

"Why didn't you let me know you were coming? I'd have come and met you."

She began to spread butter on a piece of toast.

"I don't know, really. It wasn't that I didn't want you to. I nearly did at Ipswich but I managed to jump on a train at the last minute." She took another mouthful, wiped crumbs off with her little finger, and looked up at him. "And I wanted to surprise you."

Mark smiled and poured them each out another cup of tea.

"Does the CO know you're back? "

"Yes. I've just seen him. I told him I'll start work today. Now."

"You don't need to rush into things."

"I need to get on with ordinary daily life again. That's how I deal with all this."

Mark felt doubtful.

She leant forward. "Mark, listen. I want to sit down with you.

I want to tell you about everything. But not now. If I do that now I'll start crying."

He reached across the table and took her hand.

"I have to find my way through this, and my way is to work. I don't want to sit and think about it and be miserable all day long." She squeezed his hand. "But can we meet at lunchtime?"

"I want to see you *all* the time. Of course we can meet at lunchtime."

"Good." She smiled and leaned towards him, looked him straight in the eyes.

"Mark, I missed you. I need you."

A voice called from the end of the dining room: "Susan!"

It was Bridget, calling out as she approached them.

Mark said, "She knows. Ian and I talked for ages the night before last. He and Bridget know about your father."

Susan squeezed his hand before getting up and going over to Bridget. Mark watched them hug each other as they met, and then they left the room together.

This did not feel bad, but things weren't as he thought they might be. He had been expecting Susan to be very upset, to be in tears. And he hadn't expected her at all until much later on. And here she was, apparently ok and in control. Didn't she need him? He wanted so much for her to need him. But that's exactly what she had just said, hadn't she? She had said: I need you, Mark. She could not have spoken more clearly, and she had spoken with conviction. But now she had walked off with Bridget, not with him.

He went upstairs before going to the office. He cleaned his teeth, combed his hair in front of the mirror, looked at himself, saw a serious man in uniform. What was this uneasiness? He went out into the yard and started to walk along the roadway. Was it about her? Or about him? What had he wanted her to be like when she returned? It wasn't as if he had *wanted* her to be upset. But. But what?

He reached the Clock Tower. People were milling around here. Damn. He didn't want to talk to anyone so he looked at the ground as he walked. He reached the office without interruption and sat down at his desk. There wasn't a lot to do. He put his head in his hands. What was the matter?

She seemed so confident, so steady. No one would have guessed that her father, whom had meant so much to her, had just died. So, how would he behave if his father died? He would be sad. But he too would continue to go to work after the funeral. Of course he would. He would probably be rather like Susan was being. So, was he expecting – even wanting – her to behave differently to the way he might? Yes. That could be true. Was this difference because she was a woman, or because she was Susan? This was all so difficult.

There was a knock on the door and it opened.

"Ian!"

Mark held out his hand and shook Ian's warmly. Their talk of a night or two ago had been good. They had laughed a lot, talked mostly about the RAF, but they had become closer. Ian pulled up a chair and they both sat down.

"I hear Susan's back already. Have you seen her yet?"

"Briefly."

"How is she?"

Mark paused. He spoke with caution. "She's ok. She wants to get on with getting back to normal."

He picked up a ruler and balanced it on the back of his finger, watched it sway.

"I only saw her for a few minutes at breakfast." The ruler tipped up and he caught it. "And by now she'll be back at work already."

Ian leant back against the edge of his desk.

"Mark, what can I say? Over these last few weeks I was so frightened Bridget's parents might have forced us apart, or, worst of all, that she would not want me any more. It's been awful. And I can see now things are awful for you for different reasons."

Mark balanced the ruler on the front of his finger.

He had done his best to understand Susan's anxiety about her father. He was her prime concern, and he himself always seemed to come much lower in her affections. There were times when he had not said things or he would have showed how much this hurt, which he did not want to do. It wasn't that she was self-centred at times – or was it? He would do anything for her, but he was still not sure about what she'd do for him. He resented it when it felt like this, like when she went off with Bridget, not him. He couldn't deny it: he was jealous of Bridget, but he couldn't tell Ian that.

Mark put the ruler down, looked at his watch.

There were hours to go until lunchtime. Three whole hours before he could hold her, kiss her.

*

Bridget and Susan sat side by side on Bridget's bed. Susan was leaning back against the wall, her feet curled up under her. Bridget sat hugging her knees. She reached her hand out to touch Susan's arm.

"Mark's been so worried about you. Ian says he was just longing for you to come back."

"I'm glad. I missed him a lot too. There were times when I didn't think about him at all, but at other times – like when we were walking out from the church into the graveyard – I would have given anything to have him there with me. And when I had just seen Daddy. His body, I mean."

She thought of Daddy's thinning hair, his strange sweet smell.

"I was all right in there – in fact I wanted to be on my own with him, and Rose knew that – but when I came out I wanted Mark. I thought I'd talk to Aunt Rose, but somehow I didn't. She knew how upset I was but I didn't say anything and so she didn't either. I felt alone."

"Perhaps she did too. I'm sure you'll talk when a little time has passed. Or perhaps you don't need to. You don't *have* to talk about it."

"I can't explain what got in the way, but I don't want to be alone."

"Well," said Bridget slowly. "You're quite a private person, aren't you?"

"Am I?"

"Yes. You talk easily to other people and let them – or me, at

225

least – tell you about my things, but you don't give much about yourself away."

Susan looked at her. "Don't I?"

"No. It's not a bad thing, don't think I'm saying it's bad, but there are times when I'm not sure what you're thinking. There are other people who tell you their innermost feelings all the time, aren't there? Like Deidre."

"I couldn't be like that."

"I'm not saying you should be. You're you. But it doesn't surprise me that you found it hard to talk."

Susan stretched out her legs and wriggled forward so she was sitting on the edge of the bed.

Bridget asked, "Do you and Mark talk much?"

This was difficult. Did they? How could she measure it?

"Sometimes. Yes. I'm not sure."

"Who usually says most – you or him? I don't mean most words, I mean most most."

Susan thought about this. "Mark, probably. And he asks me questions. He wants to know what I'm thinking."

"Do you tell him?"

"I think so." But did she? Perhaps not. Perhaps she didn't, because he often asked her what she was thinking, and she rarely – now she came to think of it – asked him about what he was thinking in the way that Bridget was meaning. Would he too say she was private, and expressed less rather than more? But was saying more better than saying less? What if she said too much? *Could* anyone say too much?

And what about Aunt Rose? Did she hold things back from her too? Would she say she was private? They talked when they were together, but what about? She'd spent most of her life with Aunt Rose and thought she knew what she was feeling, but did she? Now that she came to think about it, they probably talked more about things and actions than about feelings. And here she was, wishing they'd said more to each other.

"I'm going to write a letter."

Bridget looked surprised. "To Mark?"

"No. To Aunt Rose. You're right."

"What about?"

"Me not saying much about how I feel. I'll write this afternoon. No. I'll wait until tomorrow. I'll think about it. And I'll talk to Mark too."

Bridget stood up. "I'm sorry, I've got to go."

"Thank you, Bridget." Susan stood up and gave her a quick hug. "And I'm very pleased for you and Ian. It was awful to see you both so worried and miserable."

Bridget put her hands on Susan's shoulders and looked straight into her eyes. "The moral of the story is either not to make love, or to take really careful precautions."

"What do you mean?"

"Go and see a doctor. Don't rely on the man, on Mark, doing something. It may be embarrassing, but any amount of embarrassment is better than what we went through. I want you to promise me something."

"What?"

"That you'll come with me when I go to make my appointment. I'm having a cap fitted. You can have one too."

"But we're not.. "

"Yes, but you might."

Susan paused, "Did you tell your parents what happened?"

"Yes. I felt so terribly guilty about the situation, especially towards my mother. As soon as my period came and I was sure I wasn't pregnant, I just had to tell her."

"What did she say?"

"She was shocked but only for a few minutes. She was fine immediately I told her all was well. She was wonderful. Mind you, if I had been pregnant things might have been – would have been – different. She said that now it was easy to think the best thing was for me and Ian to marry, but we shouldn't do that unless we were sure we would have got married anyway."

"So? Are you engaged?"

"No. Or rather, not quite. I think – I hope – we will be, but Ian hasn't proposed to me and I'm not in a hurry. We are just letting a bit of time pass."

She looked in the mirror and brushed her hair. " Susan, I must go now. But will you promise to come with me to the doctor?"

Susan nodded to her in the mirror.

"Good."

As Bridget went out Susan knew that was what she herself should do: let a bit of time pass. Things would sort themselves out.

She rubbed some Nivea cream on her lips. Where was she supposed to be? She had promised to go to see someone in the sick quarters, which meant a ten minute walk right across the station. She put her coat on and set off from the Manor in a cold wind. Only two hours until lunchtime.

*

Rain stabs holes in the swelling surface,
creates tiny craters which heal up instantly.
Each drop adds to the push and pulse
that bulges over banks, slops into bilges.

Down deep eels and crabs make their way
in the halfdark past waterlogged jetsam,
across stones being hidden by sifting silt,
round weed wallowing in the wake of the tide.

The passengers are silent on this trip. It's cold as well as pouring with rain and everyone looks serious and as if they want the journey to be over.

Robert's oilskin has a much repaired tear under the right arm and when he holds his arm close to his side he feels how the damp has reached his jumper and shirt. The oilskin is old and won't see him through the winter. Today's only November 12th, the day after Remembrance Day, and yesterday he went to the service in Felixstowe to mark Tom's death. Now, as they reach Felixstowe Ferry and its flat, wet beach, he decides he'll write to his mother about it.

He's been looking out for the woman with whom he talked about stars. She hasn't re-appeared yet, but she'll be there sometime. Everyone who uses the ferry uses it again. That's what ferries like this one do. They return people to where they came from. He likes knowing he's not the only one who goes backwards and forwards, repeating the same ten minute shred of life again and again.

The star crossing is the best crossing he's had, though. No one else has ever asked him about the lightship and he's never turned the engine off before. That crossing was special. But every crossing is slightly different. There's always a difference in the amount of drag in the tide, the way people climb aboard, the look of the shingle bar, the time of day, the light.

The ferryman is there, waiting to take over from Robert for the rest of the evening. His jacket is already gleaming and dripping.

"Lucky lad," he says. "Get yourself indoors with a decent fire. Don't hang about."

Robert keeps his hand on Maisie's collar until the last passenger is off. When he lets go she leaps off into shallow water and runs across the stones towards the boatyard. Robert follows her into the gloom.

Music Maker, like most of the lived-in boats, looks damp and miserable at this time of year. Lights are on in only a few cabins, and it's still raining hard. Robert walks over his gangplank carefully, knowing how slippery it can be.

Inside the cabin it's just slightly warmer than outside. He takes off his boots and pushes them under the bunk. Then he feels the metal on top of the fire. It's warm. He bends down and opens the front. It's still alight. There's a small pile of glowing coal, a thin stream of smoke – just right for potatoes. He stands up to take his oilskin off and hangs it on the rod he's fixed up at one end of the boat. It looks like a scarecrow. It'll cause a fug as it dries, but he knows a warm damp fug is a price worth paying for a dry jacket.

The ash needs to be emptied but it can be done later. He changes his jersey and trousers but keeps the same shirt on. There isn't anywhere else to hang it and anyway his body warmth will soon dry out the damp parts. Maisie is nosing around under his feet. First she looks for food and then she settles to chew her week-old bone.

"Good girl, Maisie."

Robert takes two potatoes and places them inside the stove. They'll take about an hour – perhaps less. It's not warm enough in the cabin but the fire's just right for cooking. He'll build it up later. He puts on thicker socks, another jacket. He wants to write a letter now but needs to warm up his hands. He pulls his shirt out of his trousers, crosses his arms and sticks his hands up underneath it and into his armpits. He presses his arms down and closes his eyes and stands like that until his hands are almost the same temperature as the rest of him. Then he cuts himself a slice of bread and spreads it with some of the dripping Mrs Corby has given him. He puts salt on the white fat, then dips a crust into the delicious brown meaty liquid that's waiting at the bottom of the little porcelain bowl he must remember to return. He takes another small piece of bread and wipes out the bowl to get every scrap.

Then he takes out a sheet of paper and his pen. He has already decided what he wants to say. He starts off carefully.

Dear Mother,
Don't be surprised at getting another letter from me so soon. There isn't anything wrong.

She might be worried because he doesn't usually write except in response to her letters, and it's her turn to write.

I just wanted to tell you Ive been to a remembrance day service. I thought about all the people who died in the wars, but mostly about Tom. He would have been twenty five now if he had lived.

Is this enough about Tom? If he writes more it might make the letter sad, and that isn't the idea.

I took the bus to Felixstowe and went to the church there. It was packed. There were lots of women and some of them must have lost husbands or sons. I knew three of the hymns from Sunday School even though I don't often go to church now. The service made the war seem quite recent even though it was ages ago.

The church had been packed, but he was disappointed not to

see anyone he knew from the Ferry. Why didn't the Corbys go? Perhaps it was too much to bear.

It's cold here now but I can smell my potatoes cooking. It can be quite cosy in here when there's a fire, but I got very wet today so I'm trying to dry my things. The best place on an evening like this is in my bunk.

I hope you are well.
With love
Your son, Robert

He folds the paper in four and puts it on a shelf. He'll read it again before sending it off.

He opens the stove door and hooks out a potato with a stick. He takes out his river knife and pokes it. Not quite soft enough. He pushes it back, is tempted to add more coal. But this could risk burning it which means less to eat. It's worth waiting another ten minutes.

When he reaches up to the shelf again to get the letter he sees the saucer and jamjar where he keeps special pebbles, the sharks' teeth, the amber. He lifts them down, lies on his stomach on the bunk and looks at them carefully in turn for the first time for months. The teeth are such sharp little things. He'd have thought they were fish hooks if Jack hadn't said, or bones. Well, they are a kind of bone, aren't they? He arranges them in a circle. They'd make a good necklace, they're so delicate.

And the amber. Even in the pale light from the oil lamp he can tell they're jewels. He places them in a line in order of size. One, two three. The middle sized one contains some small dark mark. When he turns it over and holds it to the light it's like a small uneven berry through which he can see the pip. A jewel from the water.

He gets up and tests a potato again. It's done – the knife slides easily in and out. He pulls them all out. They're too hot to hold in his hand so he pokes the knife right in so he can lift them onto a plate. They smell marvellous. He piles on a couple more logs and a shovelful of coal before closing up the stove. Then he chops up small pieces of cheese and butter and mashes them in to the soft insides he's half scooped out of the potatoes. He loads his first forkful, tries it cautiously against his lips, blows on it. It's steaming. It's going to be delicious. He saves the best bits – the dark, chewy skins – until the end.

*

"This place must have been beautiful once."

"I think it's beautiful now," said Mark.

He led Susan through the arched brick gateway and into the walled garden, "Once there were rose trees growing up those walls, and the head gardener probably lived in that cottage. There would have been several gardeners – perhaps seven or eight of them – growing vegetables and flowers for the family. In summer it would have been a hive of activity."

"Look at all those flowerpots! There's hundreds of them." Susan picked one up in her gloved hand. " Goodness, they're full of snails!"

"Sensible creatures."

He took a few steps forward. "This is what I really wanted you to see."

She looked at the building Mark was pointing to. It was built up against the wall, and it seemed to be made entirely of glass. Inside the frosted arched windows were branches, more pots, two wrought iron chairs.

She took his arm. "Let's go in."

Mark turned the door handle and gently put the weight of his shoulder against the door. It opened and he stood back to allow Susan to enter first. He followed her and shut the door behind him.

"The Orangery."

They stood together, their breath billowing out in front of them, looking up to the glass roof, to the glass walls sectioned evenly by their wrought iron frames and unevenly by a few thin brown trunks and branches which snaked upwards and towards the gaps where the panes had broken.

"It's amazing." Susan walked a few steps, crunching the frozen leaves that covered the floor.

"Look, I'm sure this is – was – a lemon tree." Mark pointed to a small, insignificant tree. "And so's this. We've got one at home."

"Now everything's dead."

"Well, it looks dead in November but perhaps it isn't. Here's a stove. These pipes would have kept it warm in winter once. Look at the frost here."

Susan moved to the window, saw how intricate threads of frost mapped themselves across a pane of glass. "They're beautiful."

"Think of the scent here in the summer. Imagine it full of oranges and lemons. It must have been like the Mediterranean."

"It's sad it's been let go."

"Perhaps, but I love it like this. On a December day like today as much as in midsummer." He turned to her. "I'm so glad you like it. I've been wanting to bring you here."

"I'm very glad you did."

Susan linked her arm in Mark's and they walked to the other end, then stopped and turned so they were side by side and facing the sunlight.

Mark kissed Susan gently on the cheek. "Your face is all chequered with shadow."

"So's yours."

"Oh, look." Mark took off his glove and reached his hand out towards a butterfly held behind a film of dust. "It's a red admiral. It's hardly damaged."

"But it's dead," said Susan. "It's very dead."

They fell silent.

After her return from the funeral, at the end of her first day back, she had cried her eyes out with Mark. Since then she had not talked much about her father. Mark wondered whether she would want to say more, especially at a time like this, when they had time and space. Susan turned to face him. Now. Perhaps she was going to say more about it now.

"Mark." She placed her hand on his collar, under his scarf. The sun was behind her and he moved his head slightly so he could look at her without squinting. She paused, and breath came from her mouth and his nose almost in unison.

"I love you. Very much."

Mark looked at her forehead, her hair, her left temple where her pulse was just visible.

"Thank you for everything. I love being with you, I like you loving me. I'm sorry I'm hard to reach. Keep asking me things, won't you? I don't want to be distant any more."

He kissed her, pushed back strands of hair from her face.

"I'm feeling better, and you've helped me to feel better."

He hadn't done anything. There hadn't seemed anything to do, except to be there. Still, he *had* been there. Perhaps that was enough. She had not cried since that first day – at least not with him, and not with Bridget. Perhaps she cried on her own, or did not need to cry any more.

He tipped his head back and looked her straight in the eyes. "That's what I want: you to feel better. In fact, what I really want is you – full stop."

Susan smiled and turned her face up to kiss him.

Mark put his arms around her. He couldn't get near her because of their bulky clothes, but things felt solid and secure. He felt closer to her, closer to becoming part of that threesome which had become a twosome because of a death. He shut his eyes and kissed her again in the cold air, the weak sunlight.

*

Three days later Susan came down to breakfast. She checked her pigeon hole. Since her father's death she had received letters from people who had known him, and only two from Rose but they had spoken more on the phone than they usually did. But here was the letter from Aunt Rose she had been waiting for. She would save it till she had time to read it properly. What would Rose have thought of her last letter? She felt a tightening in her stomach. The only other letter was an official looking one. It could be about Cranwell, and it could wait.

As she drank her tea she looked at the front of Rose's envelope. The twopence ha'penny pale bluey green stamp had been stuck on carefully, evenly, just a little way out from the corner. The Westbury-on-Trym post mark must be one of the longest ones in England. She looked at the address:

Flight Lieutenant Susan Cairncross,
Royal Air Force,
Bawdsey,
Woodbridge,
Suffolk.

Aunt Rose had written to her at several addresses: St
Crispin's School in Bath, at friends' houses during school holidays, in France where she'd spent that miserable month with
the Rouet family, at Cranwell and now here.

Mark was nowhere to be seen. He must have been and gone
already. She got up, the first to leave the table. She made her
way over to Ian with whom she would be working later on.

"I need to go to the Radio School first. Is that ok?"

He nodded, his mouth full of cornflakes.

"I'll be with you at about ten."

She went out of the dining room and straight to her own
room. Before she read anything she made herself clean her
teeth, make the bed and put away the clothes that were over the
chair back. Then she sat down at the dressing table with the
letter.

December 1st 1952

My dear Susan,
Thank you for your letter. It was a special, important letter and I
value it – will always value it.

You are right about what we say and do not say to each other. It's
true that we hold things back. But there are reasons for this – I'm not
saying they are necessarily good reasons, but reasons do exist. I think
all human beings choose how much they disclose to each other, and if
one person discloses more it can either encourage the other person to be
open or send them scurrying off in fear. It's difficult to find the right
level at the right time. Your letter is proof of your desire to find a new
and better level of contact with me. I am thrilled by this. It's what I
want too, but you are the one who has been bold enough to do some-
thing about it. Wonderful Susan!

I wish Henry could know this. Although he never told me (or perhaps you?) much about his feelings, I know he would have been pleased that you've written as you have done. But we were close, and I am feeling a huge hole in my life. Since he retired he'd often phone up and suggest we had lunch together. And we laughed a lot! I laughed more with him than with anyone, and that is such a good thing to do. We were lucky to have each other, especially as we both lost someone we loved early in our lives.

And we – you and I – are lucky to have each other, aren't we? I think you know what my life is like – nothing special, but pleasant enough. That sounds awful, doesn't it? I do mean that it's pleasant – and having no money worries is a blessing – but I'm finding the

Susan turned over the page.

things I like to do most are not so easy now. Like gardening or spending the day in Bristol. I used to go just for an evening, to the theatre or a concert, but now it seems such a haul.

I can only make a guess about your life and I'm sure it's not accurate or complete. I'd love to know more. Please will you tell me more about Mark? Your letter made him sound such a special person, but I want to know why! And how close are you to him? It's so important that you share everything with each other if your relationship is to develop.

I'm wondering how you are feeling about Henry at this minute? Like you, I seem to go up and down like a yo-yo.

How was she feeling? At this minute – not too bad, to be honest. But it was still early, and things were always better in the mornings.

Sometimes I sit here in tears and just have to wait until that feeling goes – I know it will go, and sometimes I remember positive things. Yesterday I was chuckling about the time he tried to fit the door into the greenhouse and had it upside down. He may have been a Wing Commander but he was useless when it came to practical things! I just miss him being there. Each time the phone goes I think it's him.

Susan darling, thank you again for your letter. Do write again. I'm thinking about you – about all of us – a lot.

We haven't even mentioned Christmas. I'm assuming you'll come here as usual. Would Mark like to come? Just a thought.

With very much love,
Rose

Christmas. How could they have Christmas without Daddy? And what about Mark being with them?

She turned back to the beginning and read it again. She had reached out and been met, and this was thanks to Bridget. She was the person who had brought this about.

Susan checked the time. She had to meet Ian. She brushed her hair in front of the mirror. Life was changing. She put the brush down and caught sight of the photo of her with Daddy. She picked it up and studied it for a moment. Daddy. Dear, dear Daddy. No. This wasn't the time for tears or phone calls. It was time to work.

Mark would be thrilled when she asked him. She could just imagine his reaction.

*

Maisie is sniffing along the tideline while Robert collects coal. The sack's half full. It's surprising how often bad weather brings coal to the beach just when he needs it. Today there's plenty of wet wood too, and, for some reason, masses of tangled torn netting. This is worth inspecting. No. Not as good as it seems, except for some rope wound up with it. It smells foul. He puts the sack down to cut off a few decent lengths.

The Corbys have just invited him to Christmas lunch. He'll have to work first, until two o'clock. They usually eat on the dot of one, but because he's working and it's Christmas they're going to have the meal at half past two. That will give him enough time to get home and change out of his working clothes. He's looking forward to the lunch despite what he sometimes feels when he's in their home – that he's somehow standing in for their son.

What can he take for a present? This is difficult. They're

237

going to have roast chicken, because Mrs Corby's sister lives on a farm and gives her one every year. And there'll be a Christmas pudding. So he can't take food, not unless he buys chocolate, and it would have to be a box of chocolates, anyway. It's a possibility. He could promise to help them more in the garden, or with the painting, especially as they've talked about how the outsides of the windows will need to be painted next year. But that isn't a proper present because he's going to help them anyway.

When he has finished sawing it's almost dusk. Never mind. He has something to show for the effort of coming out.

"Come on, Maisie."

But he can't go to the Corbys without anything. Why didn't he think about a present earlier?

Now it's starting to rain, and the wind is getting up. He hurries home and dumps the sack on the deck. He's fed up and tired from having run the ferry until late at night for the last three days. It's never easy when it's wet, cold and dark. He takes off his boots and coat, stows the sack out of the rain. There are still hours of evening. He lies back on his bunk hearing water under, over and around *Music Maker*. Mother will have got the letter by now. What will she be thinking? Perhaps she'll reply before Christmas. He hopes so.

A clump on deck makes him sit up and listen. Someone's up there.

He goes to the door and sees Jack holding an oilskin like a hood round his head.

"Hallo. Would you like to come and have a drink? I'm away to my brother's for Christmas and New Year. I'm going to be there for a month or so, helping him to build a house."

"What, shall I come now?"

Jack smiles. "Not this minute. In an hour or so? If we start drinking now we'd be sloshed by midnight! And I need to wrap some presents for my nieces."

"Thanks. I'd like to."

"I'll see you soon, then."

Robert goes back into the cabin as Jack walks back across the gangplank, still sheltering under the oilskin.

He settles back onto the bunk. That's a nice surprise. He's only been inside Jack's boat once. It'll be a change to go there.

What was it he was thinking about? Mother. Why hadn't he said anything to her about Christmas? He didn't even write the words *Happy Christmas*. He hadn't even sent his love to the girls for Christmas.

Maisie nudges her nose onto the bunk and Robert pats it to encourage her to jump up. He gave up caring about long hairs or wet mud ages ago but he still feels guilty about disregarding his mother's rule that the only furniture dogs should go near is the kitchen table – they are allowed under that. He hugs Maisie in to his chest.

He's feeling bad. He, Robert, has failed to send his family Christmas greetings, and has failed to find a present for the Corbys. What sort of a son, brother, friend does this make him? While he's lying here feeling sorry for himself Jack is wrapping presents and Mrs Corby is probably thinking about making stuffing for the chicken that he, a guest, is going to eat. He could, should, think more about other people. He leans back on the bunk.

He wakes up when Maisie starts whining to go out. He looks at the alarm clock and sees it's eight o'clock. Jack. What time did he say he'd go to Jack's? Is he late? He takes the kettle off the top of the stove and tips warm water from it into the basin. He washes and dries his face, takes off his shirt and puts on the one that's been hanging up to dry. Then he combs his hair and pulls on his jacket. How can he have slept for so long?

Outside it's stopped raining and there's a nearly full moon. He goes ashore, whistling for Maisie. She runs along the grass then follows him onto Jack's gangplank. Jack comes out at once, stands silhouetted in front of the open door and the soft oil light from the cabin.

"Hallo. I was just beginning to wonder about you."

"Sorry. I fell asleep. Is it ok if I bring Maisie?"

"As long as she stays on the floor. Come on in."

Jack steps back so Robert and Maisie can enter the cabin. It's as warm as toast. Robert curses that he didn't stoke up his own fire ready for his return. And there's music.

"Maisie, down. Down."

"Take a seat. Make yourself comfortable," he gestures towards the bunk. He turns the wireless down slightly. "This concert's being broadcast from St Martin's in the Fields."

St Martin's. Where's that? Which fields does Jack mean? He sits down.

"Do you like music?"

"I haven't got a wireless."

"But do you like music?"

"Well," Robert hesitates. "I don't really know. I don't hear music much, except when I go to church, and I don't do that often."

"You should, you know. It's good for the soul." Jack reaches out for the bottle on the table. "Music, I mean – not going to church – though that's good for your soul too, of course. This is cider. Do you like cider?"

"Yes." Robert is glad it's not black and tan.

He looks round at the cabin. It's neater, brighter, more homely than his. There are a few photographs of family groups. On the wall are two framed pictures, one of a windmill, one of a river scene. The bunk he's sitting on has a cover on so it's more like a settee than a bed. A few Christmas cards are pinned to the wall.

"Here you are. Cheers. Happy Christmas."

Robert lifts up his tall tumbler, Jack holds up a pewter tankard. They drink. The cider is cool and sweet and has a slight fizz. It makes Robert sneeze.

"Gesundheit."

"What?"

"It's German for bless you."

"Can you speak German?"

"We had German prisoners of war working on our farm, and I used to spend quite a bit of time with them."

"What were they like?"

"They were good fun, and hard workers. They made a fuss of me and my younger sister and brothers. They must have missed their own children. There was one called Klaus who taught me to fish, and another made a cradle out of off cuts for my sister. It was

240

beautiful. She's kept it. I remember them spending Christmas with us one year and singing Heilige Nacht."

"What's that?"

"Silent Night."

Jack stands up to reach down one of the cards. He passes it to Robert.

"This is from Stephan."

The front of the card is a coloured picture of the Virgin Mary and some angels. Inside there's delicate, slanting type and thin handwriting. He can't make the letters out because they all run into each other. It's very elaborate, very foreign.

"Look on the back."

He turns the card over and there's a pencil sketch of a horse with a cart full of three children. Beside the horse stand a tall boy and three men.

"That's the three little ones in the cart and that tall one's me, I'm the eldest. And that's Stephan, Klaus and Erich. Stephan was always drawing things."

Robert sits looking at the card. It's from Germany, from a German. From the enemy. And Jack's talking about this man as if he was a friend. He clearly *is* a friend. He doesn't know what to say. He looks at the detailed border decoration on the front of the card again before handing it back.

The music stops and a loud noise starts up. It takes him a moment to realise it's the sound of people clapping. Jack gets up to adjust the flue and reach for his pipe.

Robert watches him go through the process of knocking the pipe on the stove, scraping it out, putting tobacco in it and lighting it. That was what his stepfather used to do. It was a sort of ceremony that seemed to require concentration and frowning. He pulls out his own tobacco tin, then takes another slow sip of cider before rolling a cigarette.

An announcement on the wireless makes Jack say, "Good. I love this." He stretches his hand out and turns the volume up.

Music surges through the cabin. Robert has never heard anything like it, has no idea what it's made of. Its tune beats into him, and Maisie pricks up her ears, wags her tail. Jack's tapping his feet and joining in with the chorus:

And we sailed so faaaar and we sailed so freeeee
While my pretty Jenny was waiting for me
I'd said that I'd love her whatever befell
But I didn't know we were sailing to hell
No I didn't know we were sailing to hell.

When it's finished Jack pokes at his pipe again.

"Isn't that marvellous? It's a sea shanty. There's hundreds of them. They sometimes sing them at the pubs here you know. You should go."

Robert slumps comfortably back on to the bunk, reaches down a hand to stroke Maisie. Another tune starts up, and Jack tops up the glasses.

*

"Mark, would you like some more meat? There's some ham, and sausages."

"No thank you, Miss Cairncross."

"Are you sure you won't, Susan?"

"I ate lots on Christmas Day, and on Boxing Day. And since then I've not done badly. There isn't room for any more – except Christmas cake, of course. I can always squeeze in a bit more Christmas cake."

Susan offered to make some tea. "Shall I bring it in here or shall we go through to the other room?"

"Let's have it by the fire. Mark, could you see if it needs building up, please."

Rose started to clear the table. She liked Mark. He was attentive to her as well as to Susan. He hadn't been here for Christmas Day but on Boxing Day he had arrived with a present for her – a book about Venice, a place she loved, as well as a bracelet for Susan. They really were fond of each other. Mark was staying for two nights before their leave ended and they had to return to Bawdsey. Susan had brought down the camp bed from the box room so he could sleep in the sitting room. It would not be a surprise at all if things developed for these two. In fact, it would be marvellous if they did.

There. That would do. They could wash up tomorrow. Rose went through to the other room and found Mark had put on more logs and coal, and it looked as if he had swept up the ashes from the hearth too. He was sitting by the fire reading a newspaper.

Susan came in with the tray. "Oh, Mark, that's Aunt Rose's chair."

He sprang up, apologising.

"My dear, it doesn't matter at all. I'll be perfectly happy over here. Do sit down again."

But he insisted. He checked where Susan wanted to sit and then handed round tea and cake before sitting on the settee. When he looked up at Susan he saw she was laughing. And then he saw Miss Cairncross was smiling too. They were laughing at his good manners in the nicest way. He couldn't help blushing.

Rose was hearing all about Bawdsey. Susan and Mark told her about the place itself (the Manor, the Orangery, the theatre in the woods, the NAAFI), the personalities (the CO, the strange radar instructor, the man who climbed the mast), the magic of radar, bits of their work, Felixstowe, the ferry. It didn't sound like Henry's RAF at all. They told her about Bridget, whom she had once met, and about Ian, but, in an unplanned conspiracy, they censored out Bridget's near pregnancy.

Susan was talking about the children's Christmas party. "Children came from all over the place – it was amazing. When they came into the Manor Ballroom and saw the Christmas tree they were bowled over. They were quite overwhelmed to begin with. One little boy just burst into tears!"

Rose had decided against having a tree this year, and had discussed this with Susan, but she suddenly wished she had bought one as usual from Mr McAusland. Never mind.

"Not that their shyness lasted for long," added Mark. "There were plenty of volunteers and we played oranges and lemons, and musical chairs, and they had a special tea, with jelly, and Tizer."

"And Mark made the fatal mistake of giving one boy a piggy back so he could see the decorations at the top of the tree."

"Why was that a fatal mistake?"

"Because everyone else wanted a piggy back too! He was walking around with a queue following him!"

"I was tired out by the time they went. I even lost at billiards that evening. But it was good fun."

"It sounds a great success. More tea, either of you?"

"No thanks, two cups is plenty for me."

"Susan?"

She shook her head. "But I wouldn't mind another drink. After all, it's the eve of New Year's Eve. You know, another *proper* drink. Have we got anything for now or must we wait until tomorrow?"

"Yes, we have a bottle of whisky. You know it's rare for me to buy a bottle of anything, especially whisky, but recently I bought some."

"Aunt Rose, I'm surprised at you!" Susan spoke in a tone of mock shock, "I've never known you to buy anything except sherry. Whatever came over you?"

"I bought it for Henry."

Rose paused. "I know he likes whisky. Liked whisky. I thought it would help him convalesce." She leant forward and put her arm on the back of Susan's chair. "Let's not be sad about it. He would have wanted us to enjoy it, wouldn't he?"

She bent down to kiss Susan's head. "Go and get it, my dear. It's on the sideboard. Don't forget a jug of water."

Susan went out and Rose looked at Mark. He made as if to speak but Rose stopped him. "It's all right, Mark. We have to go forward. He would want us to get on with our lives."

They both turned towards the fire and sat in silence until Susan returned. Mark moved the tea tray to make room for the tumblers, bottle and jug.

"Would you like me to pour the drinks?"

Rose nodded.

When they each had a glass Rose held hers up in a toast and said in a strong voice, "To Henry."

"To Henry."

How could she make them at ease again? Susan was silent and Mark was uncertain what to say. How easily things could become upset. She was determined not to be miserable when these young people were here. She was not going to have the evening spoiled. Henry would want them to be happy.

"Come on, let's play something. Mark, there's some cards in the top drawer of the little desk behind you."

Mark opened it and took out two packs of playing cards.

"I know," said Susan, "Monopoly! Let's play that. I love Monopoly."

"Mark, I'll have to warn you. She's dreadful when she plays Monopoly! She's greedy and ruthless."

"I'll be banker," said Susan quickly.

"No," said Mark, quickly cottoning on. "You have to draw for banker. You can't just *be* the banker."

Rose chuckled. "See what I mean? Go on, you two, you set everything up. I'm going to get a cardigan. I think we'll be here for some time."

She went upstairs and fetched her green cardigan. It was going to be all right. They were laughing as she entered the room.

Susan was saying, "I know perfectly well it's a game. It's just that I like to win. That's what you're *supposed* to do in games: try to win. There's nothing wrong with that."

Rose caught Mark's eye and he winked.

"Ok, we must each throw the dice to see who's going to be banker. You go first." He handed the dice to Rose.

"Oh dear. A six and a three."

"That's not bad. Now you, Susan."

"Blast." She had thrown a two and a four.

"And now me. Two fives. So I'm banker. Good. Miss Cairncross, shall we let Susan start because she got the lowest?"

He really was good fun, this Mark. Susan, looking slightly flushed, took the top hat. She threw a double six.

"That's more like it! Right, I'm off." She counted twelve spaces round and landed on the Electric Company.

"And I've got another go," she said indignantly as Mark moved to pick up the dice.

He groaned.

"If you'd like another glass of whisky, Mark," said Rose, "please help yourself."

Two hours later most of the money had passed from the neat, separate piles Mark had arranged into untidy heaps of mixed notes on the rug near Susan. A modest amount was on Rose's lap. She had plenty of property and Mark urged her to count up its value, but it was too late, she was ready for bed and anyway, Susan was bound to be the winner. She almost always was.

Rose stood up. The two of them could pack the game away, take things back to the kitchen. They would want to be alone by the fireside for a while. It was clear Mark was quite in love with Susan, but they weren't totally at ease with each other yet.

A few minutes later she put her head round the door, hot water bottle in one hand and *Venice – Crown of Italy* in the other. Mark was putting another log on the fire. Susan had stretched her stockinged feet out along the settee.

"I'm off upstairs now."

They looked up. Susan got up to kiss Rose goodnight, and Mark came forward too. He made to shake hands but saw that her hands were full. She leant forward and offered her cheek to him.

He kissed it and stood back, smiling. "It's been a lovely evening. Thank you."

"Goodnight. God bless." She turned away, shutting the door behind her. The day had been even better than she had hoped.

*

Mid January. The river is smooth, as smooth as it is on windless hot days in July. But now it's freezing cold. There must be a point when the temperature of water drops so low that it freezes over. What would that look like? That could never happen here, of course. The estuary would never freeze over. It's not possible, at least, not unless there's another ice age. And the water's moving here – Robert can see the flow of the tide as usual. But today the surface has fewer waves, fewer rills and runs. It's as if the weight of cold is pressing down and controlling the river, doing its best to reduce its speed, its power.

And it's not just the river that's subdued. Maisie moves less, and so does he. They just do what needs to be done, don't do anything extra. The cold reduces their life. It's the same with the passengers. Apart from occasionally stamping their feet when waiting, once they're on the ferry they talk less. They want to be home and dry.

But the children are different. Near the café some boys have made a patch to slide on. Over the last few days they've created a series of frozen puddles. They've discovered that if they pour on more water in the evening it freezes hard and by morning they have a big, wide stretch to slide on. The outside taps are frozen, but they lug pails of water up from the jetty. Right now two boys are tipping some out while others shout at a smaller one who wants to go on sliding.

"Get off the slide, Davy. *Get off* will you?"

He and Tom used to do exactly the same. They'd choose a place on the street where they could get a good run up before launching themselves onto the ice. They'd slide along while turned slightly sideways, holding their arms out for balance just like these boys are doing.

A cheer and a boo go up. Davy has fallen over and hurt himself. He stays sitting on the ground until his sister comes and takes him home. He walks behind her, his face red from the cold and from crying, holding one of his wrists against his chest. He looks frozen.

Robert trudges past, glad he now has a decent oilskin. The Corbys gave him one for Christmas. It belonged to a friend of theirs who was issued a new one by his employer and, as he didn't need two, he offered it to Mr Corby. Mr Corby at once saw it was too big for him, and said "I know a man who needs this oilskin more than I do. Do you mind if I pass it on to him?"

His friend had answered, "If you know someone who needs it, then that's who should have it."

"It's Robert. You'll have seen him running the ferry, and he works in the boatyard. He's a good lad, and he needs a decent oilskin."

"Then give it to him."

So now he's always dry, even in the worst weather. Underneath he wears layers of jerseys, and it's marvellous that it's only ever his cuffs that get wet now, and that's only on really bad days. This oilskin could save his life.

He enjoyed the Christmas meal. They sat down and he was just about to eat this rare, special dinner when Mrs Corby asked her husband to say grace. Robert sat there with his eyes closed, his hands already holding his knife and fork, his nose already breathing in juicy chicken, steam from the vegetables, scent of hot potatoes, rich gravy.

It was difficult to wait while Mr Corby put down the carving knife, wiped his hands, and said, "Dear Father. We thank you for this food. We thank you for our families and friends. For those who are not here. For peace."

Robert opened his eyes but saw he hadn't finished.

"And for our homes. Our hopes. Our fears. Our future. Amen."

"Amen." Robert looked at the plateful of pale meat, crispy brown skin, orange carrots, green cabbage, white potatoes.

He was pleased with the presents he took. He bought a small box of Black Magic chocolates which he guiltily hoped they would open while he was there. He had not had a chocolate since.. since when? He couldn't recall when he'd last had one. It must have been on someone's birthday, perhaps his mother's.

But the other present he took was better.

He had been going through the small things he had picked up from the shoreline: a spoon, shells, fish hooks, a leather shoelace, a tobacco tin, two glass bottles. He also had some pieces of wood worn into interesting patterns or with unusual markings. There was one flattish piece he particularly liked. It was pale brown, almost cream, and about the size of his hand. It had small, even ridges where the grain had resisted the sea. Spread across parts of the surface were small holes made by woodworm, and some of these had tiny barnacles or pieces of shell wedged in them. It was like a miniature landscape. It reminded him of a photo he'd seen of a desert.

One evening, soon after the evening he had spent at Jack's, he was looking at it carefully, stroking its contours, turning it against the light so the barnacles glinted. They were like jewels.

Getting up from the bunk and treading across Maisie without disturbing her, he reached up to the jar and saucer above the sink where he kept his pebbles. He picked out the three pieces of amber. Two of them were too big for this piece of wood, and they weren't even shiny. He inspected the smallest one. It was only the size of a pea, but there in the wood, just off centre, was a hole of just the right size. He pressed it in. The wood was softer than he expected and it gave a little. Gently, he pushed harder, and it fitted in exactly, as if it belonged there.

It was beautiful: a jewel from the water set in wood from the water. He was sure Mrs Corby would like it.

And she did. "Robert! Thank you so much. I shall treasure it."

As he held out his plate for seconds he glanced up at it sitting on the mantlepiece. There it was, leaning against a little silver jug.

Mrs Corby insisted he had the wishbone. "But don't let Maisie get hold of it. No, it's for you. Take it home. You should let it dry out before you pull it."

She wrapped it in a bit of newspaper for him and he put it in his pocket.

Now, three weeks after Christmas, he walks past the sliding children, the closed café, the boatyard with its covered up hulls. He pushes his hands deep in his pockets and there, in the left one, is the wishbone. He can't think of anyone he can pull it with.

*

From less than half a fathom down
eels and otters look up to the surface,
through the surface, to the light,
to the wavery sun and moon, to the night,
to the sculling feet of gulls, to the keels
and rudders of boats rocking in the tide.

They sense the sea's surge, the shifting
wind, the lie of the water. They swim
in the moon's current, the river's gleam.

Cold days keep on coming but January is nearly over. The wind's been fierce today but it'll be February tomorrow and February will be better, and then it'll soon be spring. It's only a matter of weeks if he looks at it like that. Already it stays light till later. And the year ahead looks promising. Wilf has asked if he wants more work in the boatyard. Of course he does. And the ferryman still needs him at least several times a week. Good. The ferry work is the best work he has.

But he needs more money now because when it's as cold as this he has to have more food. And these boots aren't going to last long. How much are new boots?

At least this evening he and Maisie are holed up in *Music Maker*. Thank God he's not on the river. The stove's roaring and devouring wood and coal fast. He can't ignore the noise of the fire or of the wind and the water smacking on the hull, nor *Music Maker*'s rough rocking. An hour ago he checked his moorings. The water was higher than he expected.

He takes out the newspaper and reaches for an apple. It would be good to have a wireless. Jack had said music was good for the soul. Did he mean it made you a better person? He must have. But how, exactly, could music do that?

A loud thud on the side of the cabin makes Maisie jump up. He puts his hand on her back.

"All right. It's all right."

Something must have blown against it. A piece of wood, perhaps. That box on deck could have come loose. It doesn't matter. He can always find boxes. He thinks that even if he had a wireless, he wouldn't hear much music tonight.

There's another bang, but then the wind drops a little and the fire slows. Could they be in for a real gale? Thank God no one's out fishing tonight.

The kettle boils fast because the fire's so hot, and he makes himself a pot of strong tea. He leaves it for a few minutes before pouring it, then adds milk just as a sudden lurch nearly tips the small bag of sugar over the edge of the shelf. He looks at the clock. Half past eight. High tide isn't until after midnight. It's nowhere near high tide yet. But if the water sounds like this now, it could mean trouble. He ought to look. Maisie watches him pull on thicker socks and another jumper and take his oilskin off the hook.

"Stay."

When he opens the cabin door it blows out of his hand and slams back, catching one of his fingers. Wind races inside, blowing up his bedclothes, plastering the newspaper against the wall. He grabs the doorhandle and pulls it to behind him. On deck the wind whips at him. He holds on to the rail. Under the noise of the wind is the thudding of waves, the creaking and whining of timber. The gangplank's juddering. *Pretty Girl* is bobbing up and down. Pity Jack isn't back yet. Or perhaps he's better off where he is. Everything is only just staying where it should be. It's bad.

He mustn't let himself be overwhelmed. He moves into the lee of the cabin, makes himself stay there. He's still. That's better. Once he steadies himself it's all right. Even now the noise of the wind is subsiding. It's going to be all right.

He goes back inside the cabin. He pulls off his oilskin, opens up the fire and sits close to it. He's cold. His finger is dripping blood on the floor. It's much worse out there than he expected.

Maisie snuggles up to him. Within five minutes he's stirring his cup of now lukewarm tea with a spoon held in his roughly bandaged hand. He stokes the fire again, doesn't care if he uses up every last lump of coal if necessary. He'll stay warm tonight at all costs. Tomorrow things will be back to normal.

He lies on his back. Surely the ferry isn't running tonight? It can't possibly be. And what about the small boats moored in the river? If *Music Maker* is rolling about like this, what about them? Some of the leisure boats might well be torn loose. Everyone knows that even in winter they're not always secured properly.

He tries to gauge if the wind is subsiding or becoming stronger. Sometimes there's a lull but sometimes *Music Maker* is yanked so she tilts and tips. She shudders as something heavy hits her. Whatever that was sounded heavy enough to knock a hole in the hull. He'll have to go out again. He can't just lie here.

He puts on his thick blue shirt, his jacket, a scarf, his oilskin and a sou'wester. Maisie stands up. What about Maisie?

"Stay. I don't want you blown away."

He checks the time. Ten o'clock. It won't be high tide for at least two hours.

This time he manages to hang on to the door and prevent it from slamming. He grabs hold of the rail and stands for a few moments to test the strength of the wind. This isn't just wind. It's ferocious. It's a storm.

He hurries over the gangplank and makes for the main part of the boatyard. Halyards and sheets are slapping violently and two oildrums career past him. Good thing he left Maisie safely on the boat.

Where will the ferryman be? He'll try the pubs first, and then go to his home.

As he reaches the café Aldis' bus is just arriving. What's that spray? Surely the road there isn't under water? But it is. A few passengers emerge at the doorway. They step down hesitantly then lean into the wind, awkwardly. Someone's scarf flies out behind them like a long flag. They look as if they're making for the beach. Why? Anyone can see it's far too wild for the ferry to be running.

Robert sees two men by the landing stage. One's the ferryman and one's Mr White, a man he knows well by sight. He goes straight down to them.

"Good lad," says the ferryman. "Stay here. This may get worse. We might want you around later on."

The people from the bus reach them.

"Blimey, I've never seen the water this high!"

"We've got to get back to Bawdsey."

"Look at those dinghies! They're like bucking broncos!"

The ferryman tells them he's not run the ferry for the past few hours and won't be doing so. This is a real storm. He doesn't want to risk his life or their lives. He's sure they'll be welcomed at the Victoria or the Ferryboat. No, he doesn't know if they can sleep there, and he doesn't know when the storm will be over.

Robert watches the six people run back up the beach. They're shouting and one's holding his arms out as if he's trying to take off. They're excited, like children. Do they think this is a game?

Barrie White is talking with a couple who live next to the Ferryboat.

"But it's so high! Look over there, it's already under water. If it comes any higher it'll reach our house."

"Yes. It's high, and it may go higher. It's been as far as the houses before."

The woman is worried. "It doesn't have to rise much before it'll be a real flood."

"Yes, but even if it does it probably won't get further than your front doorstep. It's been there before, but we haven't had proper floods for twenty, thirty years. And anyway," he added, "there's nothing you can do about it."

Robert looks out to the estuary. It's blacker, wilder, louder than he's ever seen it, and there's more of it than he's ever seen.

The couple go back up the beach. When they reach the top the man turns and shouts something. Robert and the two men look at each other. None of them heard what he said against the wind. The man waves and carries on walking.

They stand facing the estuary. It feels much more like sea than river. The weather is coming in straight off the open sea. Waves crash in further and further, every one of them making progress, every one gaining ground as they watch. The tide and the wind are working together, steadily pushing water and even stones up the beach.

Robert says he'll stay there while Barrie White and the ferryman go round to the boatyard.

It's strange being there alone with the wild river. Is he frightened? He's not sure. He's relieved when the others come back along to where the landing stage is supposed to be but which has disappeared.

"It's bad," says Mr White. He turns to Robert. "We must warn everyone. Everyone who lives down your end will know what's happening, and both the pubs know. But there's others who don't."

He points towards the houses up past the Victoria, in the direction of the Martello Tower.

"There's about an hour to go before high tide. Tell them it could be dangerous. Tell them to go to my house in Harbour

Villas. They'll be safe there. I'm going to phone the police. Go on. Hurry."

Robert tries to run along the road. It's difficult until where the houses break the sweep of the gale. He hammers on doors and shouts until anxious people, some in their night things, come to the door. When he gets to the Corby's home, he goes straight in through the back door which is never locked, and races upstairs two at a time. He puts a light on and catches sight of himself in a mirror. He sees an unwelcome intruder, a wild runaway. The Corbys get up at once, start to find more clothes. They've been lying in bed listening to the wind. They seem more concerned for their next door neighbours than for themselves.

"Make sure you go there next. They've got two young children."

He bounds down the stairs again. Of course it's quicker to go into everyone's house like this. What a fool to have wasted time knocking and calling. He goes next door and to four more houses. Everyone understands the urgency of his message. Every one knows the danger. They all know Harbour Villas is the safest place to be.

He tells himself to calm down, think straight, save his energy. What needs to be done next? The boatyard. The boats, fishing gear could get swept away. That's where the ferryman will be. He hurries back towards the Ferryboat Inn. People are coming out of the houses he's been to. They're carrying torches, children, bundles. Some are shouting, crying. They're like refugees. It's like those wartime photos.

Now he's wading. The water's sloshing into the tops of his boots. He can see into the pub. All the chairs have been placed on the tables so everyone's standing up. They'll be all right. Someone calls out to him to come inside to safety. He yells back but doesn't know if they can hear what he says. He's never heard the waves and wind make this much noise before. Thank God he has this oilskin.

In the boatyard it's wet, dark, grim. Boats have been shifted from where they should be. Canvas tilts are flapping wildly. Loose ends of rope blow out horizontally like poles. Lobster

254

pots, nets, tools, bits of wood, tin cans and cloths are being washed around. Two fishermen stumble sideways as a yacht is washed over.

Barrie White's there and he beckons to Robert to follow him into the boathouse. He wants him to help pull a dinghy free. It's a relief to be out of the full force of the wind but why on earth are they moving this dinghy? As they get it near the doorway it becomes harder because the wind forces them back inside. Mr White tugs at the bow, Robert shoves from the stern. They see Wilf and both turn to ask him to help. Suddenly the front of the dinghy skews round.

There's a rush of roaring, icy water. What happened? Has Barrie White let go? Robert's washed up against the wall. He hits his head, loses his grip on the dinghy. He scrabbles for something to hold on to and pulls himself to his feet.

Barrie White emerges out of the water shouting, "We've got to get this boat out of here."

Robert stumbles to help him grab it again. The water's up to their thighs.

"Where's Wilf?"

"Here. I'm ok. Take these oars."

Robert reaches over, steadied but made clumsy by his full boots and sodden trousers. He braces himself to push again but suddenly the level of the water subsides and the strength goes out of it. They wade to the doorway, push the dinghy out onto a new, unrecognisable expanse of water.

Each of them tries to climb in the boat. At first it's impossible to get up and over the side but Wilf gives Robert and then Barrie a leg up, and then they haul Wilf in.

"We need another boat. We can't fit everyone in here."

"It's ok," said Wilf, "There's enough room."

Barrie says "Not for us, for other people."

"Grab that oar!"

Robert leans out and catches one that's floating past.

Wilf and Barrie each take an oar and row their way out of the boatyard and across where the road should be. All the land between the buildings and the sea has gone. It's all sea now. They're being pulled towards the Ferryboat Inn but even as this is happening it somehow seems as if the spirit has gone out of the torrent, as if they are in its wake and not in the torrent itself.

Once the sea has crossed right over the threshold to the land – the road – it spreads out, pouring itself into the lowest places until it becomes trapped. Now it's bashing up against a group of buildings that hem it in. They watch its level rise and see it smash through the pub door. Robert imagines it pouring down the steps inside, flooding the entire building, tipping over the tables and the chairs that are stood on top of them. Seconds later the door of a neighbouring house collapses inwards under the pressure. All the lights in the buildings go out. Voices yell for help.

"There's a boat!"

Robert and Wilf spin round. An empty boat is coming towards them, sideways, fast. They try to catch hold of it but it whirls past them.

"Come on, row. Row!"

They have little control but manage to reach a huddle of people holding on to each other. Robert holds out his oar for a man to grab on to. They pull close up. He and Wilf get out of the dinghy to help an elderly couple and a family with small children. They half push, half lift them aboard.

Barrie shouts, "We'll take them to Harbour Villas."

Wilf wades behind, sometimes pushing the boat and some-times supporting himself on it. Robert watches them make slow progress up this new, noisy waterway. He wants to help them. Chunks of wood hurtle past as he stands there up to his waist in North Sea. He can't help them. His head feels as if it's been hit with a hammer. He can hardly feel his body. The cold is all over him, in him. He vomits.

When he raises his head he sees the wooden wall of a house float past at speed. He notices the front porch, the letter box, a window with its curtains flowing out behind like seaweed. It bashes up against the phone box. But the phone box looks strange. It's far too low. How could anyone get in it?

He mustn't let himself drown, mustn't fall unconscious. He must get home, get home before he falls. The current drags him and he can't resist it. He lands up at the Ferryboat Inn again, unexpectedly finds he can stand. He grabs hold of a window ledge. He makes his way to the doorway and swims through it. It's dark inside.

A woman is calling "Reg! Reg!"

*

Robert holds on to the end of a settle to steady himself until his feet find the floor, until his eyes get used to the gloom. He can hardly make anything out.

"Reg! Reg!"

The woman's voice sounds higher. She's scared and now she's just screaming and screaming. He'll have to help her. He can't do nothing. He eases his way out of the pub door again. She's out there somewhere. The water is still running fast, but it's lost its fierceness.

He waits for the voice again. Where's it coming from?

She shouts again, and it's somewhere on his right. She must be in one of the cottages to the right. He treads through the waist level water holding his arms out in an attempt to steady himself. It's so slow. It's so cold. He's making for a pair of cottages which sit sideways on to the pub.

He pauses to get his breath back, looks around him. He's the only person there, but there's something big moving across this new open lake in front of The Ferryboat. Bloody hell, what is it? Is it a boat? It's certainly floating. God, it's a car. It's turning round as it's carried along. At first it's facing the way it's going, but now it's facing backwards. Thank God he's not in its way.

"Help! Help me, please!"

The woman sounds desperate and he sets off again. She must be calling from an upstairs window. He looks up at the cottage windows. The water level is half way up the windows on the ground floor and he sees some panes have caved in, but there's no sign of anyone upstairs, and there are no lights anywhere. But the voice is definitely coming from somewhere here. He decides to go round to the back.

Every step is so heavy, so slow. It feels more like thick oil than

257

water. All his limbs are weighed down. He's tempted to stop and take off his boots, his oilskin. They're soaked through and their heaviness is holding him back. But how could he undo laces or buttons? His hands are icy and one of them's hurting like hell.

Suddenly there's a shout of surprise. He looks up and there, leaning out of a window, is the woman. She's crying and she's holding a baby.

"Just stay where you are. It's all right. I'll get you down safely."

She turns back into the room for a moment and then leans out again.

"I've got two other children here but it's the baby. Reg went to get help but he hasn't come back. I'm so worried for the baby. She's only a month old."

Robert makes his way towards her. She's seven or eight feet above him.

"Don't worry. I'll find a way of reaching you."

Her head disappears again. What can he do? How can he reach them and what can he do with them? A boat. He needs a boat. He remembers the empty one which went floating past earlier on. That must have been hours ago. Will he have to go back to the boatyard? He's not sure he can manage that.

He shouts up, "Do you know where there's a boat?"

The woman appears again, "Our neighbours have one. It's in their garden over there." She points to the back of the next house.

"I'll try and get it. I'll come back as soon as I can."

Perhaps that was what Reg had said too. Perhaps the neighbours have already used the boat themselves. Why's it in the garden anyway? Perhaps it needs repairing.

There's about two foot of garden fence showing above the water, and one part seems to have been knocked loose by an uprooted shed that's swept into it. He shoves against the fence at its weakest point, and there, in the small garden which is now a lagoon, is a big egg shaped bulge which he reckons is an upside down dinghy. It's covered with a tarpaulin. Robert tries to get the half submerged tarpaulin off. It's completely unwieldy. It feels like a giant octopus and it takes a huge amount of energy to get it out of the way so he can reach the boat.

And now he finds the boat's tied to something with rope. He needs his knife. He tries to reach under his oilskin to his belt. It's almost impossible. He needs both hands. He has to go back to the fence again and wedge himself securely against it so he can have both hands free. Pulling up the oilskin is so awkward. It feels as if it's glued to him. At last he's able to run his hand round his waist on his belt. There's the sheath knife. He lifts his oilskin up further to pull it out, and he's got it.

He makes his way back to the boat and starts sawing through the rope. It's underwater so he can't see what he's doing. Suddenly the boat moves freely. As he grabs it the knife falls from his frozen hand. It's gone. He's lost it. He knows he hasn't enough strength to right the boat where it is so he half heaves, half pushes it over to the fence and jams it against the fence sideways on and shoves. It rides up the fence but he can't push it far enough. He waits for a moment and gives it a final shove and it falls back right side up.

It's almost half full of water but he works it over the broken part of the fence and at last he's back by the window again. Now there's another head, a little one, looking out at him with the woman and the baby.

What next? It's too far for them to jump. But it wouldn't be so far if he was standing in the boat. He'd almost be able to reach them if he did that. But he can't get into the boat without something to climb on. If only he could see what was under the water. If only he could get this water out of the dinghy.

"Are there any steps, anything I can stand on?"

The woman thinks for a moment. "Yes, the coal bunker. Over to your left there's a coal bunker."

Perfect. He pushes the boat round and it grates against what must be the bunker. He levers himself up onto it and gets into the boat. It sinks lower into the water. Damn, damn, damn. He hasn't any oars. What use is a boat without oars? The woman and her children are better off where they are if he hasn't any oars.

There's a bucket floating near by. He grabs it and bales out water until the boat is floating more freely. Then he uses it to bring himself round to the window. The woman's stopped crying now.

He calls up, "Have you got anything I can use for oars? Even a saucepan would help."

She goes away and comes back with a cricket bat and a big biscuit tin.

"That's all I can find."

He stands up so she can pass it to him. A cricket bat, a bucket and a biscuit tin. Better than nothing.

"Ok. Now I want the children first. I want the oldest, the biggest one first."

"That's Alison."

"Right, Alison first."

Alison leans out.

"Now. You need to put one of your legs over the window ledge. Then I'll be able to reach you. Good. Yes. A bit further. You're doing well. It's all right. I've got you."

The dinghy rocks as she transfers her weight to Robert. He smiles at her. "Well done."

Now there's a boy on the window ledge. He's not so happy.

"I might fall, Mum."

He won't budge.

"Come on," says Robert. "It'll be ok. Look, Alison's done it."

"Go on Davy," says the woman, "the man won't drop you."

After a minute the boy puts his leg over the ledge. He doesn't relax and Robert has to pull him off, but he's ok and he sits down next to Alison.

Then it's the baby. Robert can't quite reach her. Even when the woman leans down with her as far as she can, there's still a good eighteen inches between the little bundle and Robert's upstretched hands.

"I can't reach you, I can't."

"You'll have to let her go, I'm afraid. You'll just have to trust me."

And the woman lets her go and Robert catches her. He holds her against him tightly for a few seconds. He breathes in her sweet baby smell. She's tiny. She's precious.

He glances up at the woman and says, "She hasn't even woken up!"

He passes her carefully to Alison.

Then the woman climbs out and lets herself down face inwards from the window. Robert catches her round her waist as she lets go. The boat rocks again but they're all there, all safe.

He sits down and pokes the boat away from the cottage wall with the cricket bat.

"We'll go to the pub. It's safe in there."

He doesn't know how he'll do it, but it's not far and the wind's lessening all the time. He'll get them there.

*

Robert wakes during the night. He remembers reaching the Ferryboat Inn and helping the family out of the dinghy. He remembers being hauled up the stairs. Someone tipped a strong drink down his throat, and someone took off his oilskin, jersey, trousers and boots. Now he's lying on a rug and covered with a blanket. He must have been there for several hours. He's very cold. His hand's throbbing, his shoulder aching.

He goes to the window. Grey daylight is just appearing. The water has returned to where it's supposed to be. The wind has died down. But everything out there looks different. The space in front of the pub is covered in bits and pieces. A car lies on its side. There are dustbins, half a boat, barrels, tree branches. Where's that small hill come from?

It's very quiet. He turns back from the window and faces into the room. He sees other people asleep on the floor, hears them breathing. It's a bit like being back in army barracks. Who are these people? It's impossible to see in this light. But they're good people, they looked after him.

Home. That's where he wants to be now. The flood has subsided and it's morning. He'll go home. He finds his sodden clothes and carries them downstairs. He wades across the pub through black liquid. It's soft under foot, like mud. It doesn't smell like the sea or the river. It smells like a ship's engine.

He steps up the pub steps and out onto the roadway. If he didn't know the place he'd hardly recognise it. Everything's in the wrong place. That hut, it's Wilf's brother's hut, must be at least two hundred yards from where it belongs. That dinghy jammed up against the telegraph pole looks like the tender to one of the yachts in the boatyard.

He puts on his icy, heavy trousers and boots. It takes ages. They make him even colder. He puts on his jersey and his oilskin. He can't wait to get home.

Music Maker.

For God's sake, *Music Maker*.

He starts to hurry, skidding on thick ridges of loose shingle. He lurches round tyres, a boat trailer tangled up with rope, half a ladder, a sheet of corrugated iron.

And Maisie. What about Maisie?

He runs through the boatyard. May they both be there. Please let them be there.

Music Maker is broken in two. Her bow is half floating on the receding tide, still attached to the post by the rope he and Jack replaced so carefully last year. Her stern is resting on the silky mud. Her insides are like the interior of a slimy, dank cavern. Nearby a blanket, a saucepan and his oil lamp are laid out on the mud and coated with a film of thin brown skin. His brown jacket hangs in the water, its sleeves half under the surface. It hovers there with small ripples nudging at it.

"Maisie! Maisie!"

Nothing moves on *Music Maker* so he looks to his left and right. *Pretty Girl* is still afloat and in one piece though her cabin only has half a roof. Further on are other boats that seem all right, but there are spaces where *My Lady* and *Susan Ella* should be. The water is dotted with floating timbers. On the moorings there are fewer boats than before. An untethered houseboat ambles slowly some yards from her berth.

As the light strengthens he sees more detail. What's that by the shore up there? A body?

He scrambles over cans, netting, bits of wood, a baler, a bike wheel to get to it. It's too small, the wrong shape, the wrong colour for a person. It must be an animal. But it's not a dog, it's a sheep. He bends down to it, sees the fleece is covered in thick silt, the mouth full of mud, the eyes milky.

He stands up straight.

No *Music Maker*. No Maisie.

He walks on. What else is there to do? He'll go and stand on the old dyke.

It's very still. Where has the storm gone? It must have just retreated with the tide. It's over. It's all over.

As he gets close he sees great gaps in the bank. He climbs onto a part which is still solid and surprises a huge heron. It takes off and flies away slowly across the inland lake that stretches out in front of him. Acres and acres of water cover the golf course. It's a new landscape, it's all new. It's the cold light of day, and it's beautiful.

He shivers. It's even colder up here. There's no point in staying. He needs clothes, food, heat. He clambers back down onto the level again.

He'll go back to the Ferryboat Inn. There's nothing else he can do. He'll ask for help.

*

January 31st, Susan had decided, was the day on which she would tell Mark that she had been accepted on a course at Cranwell.

Since receiving the letter informing her of this before Christmas, she had chopped and changed her mind about what she was going to do about it and what she should say to Mark.

Daddy had always encouraged her to strive for worthwhile things. He would have said: Well done! Yes. Do it. Make the most of the opportunity. And he was right. Of course it was important to do worthwhile things. But accepting meant leaving Bawdsey, leaving Mark. Was that what she wanted? He'd be *so* disappointed. And what would she feel? She'd certainly miss him, but it would only be for six months.

She decided to ask Aunt Rose, so she had phoned up and told her about it.

"What shall I do? I don't know what to do."

Rose had listened in silence. She paused before answering.

"I can't make that decision for you, my dear. Only you can make it."

Then she asked, "You say you haven't said anything to Mark about it yet?"

"No. He's no idea at all. And, if I decide to go, I'm worried about telling him."

"Because you're worried about his response?"

"Yes. I'm *dreading* telling him."

"If Henry were here, would you dread telling him that you had decided *not* to go for promotion?"

Would she? "Well, yes. No, I mean. But he wouldn't be angry with me about it."

"Will Mark be angry?"

"No. He won't be *angry*. He's so level and sensible. He'll be upset, though. He'll be unhappy. He'd think I was leaving him."

"Would you be leaving him?"

"Well, no. Not really. I'd still care about him, but I think he'd *think* I was leaving him. I wouldn't be seeing him everyday, would I?"

"No. It would certainly slow down your relationship. I agree that he'd think you were leaving him."

"It's so difficult. I sometimes wish I'd never applied for the wretched course."

"Why not ask Mark? Why not discuss it with him? I'm sure he'd want to be involved in the decision."

Why hadn't she thought of this? What a good idea. She had been so set on sorting it out herself. She thanked Rose. "You're right. That's what I'll do."

Now January 31st had arrived and she and Mark were sitting in the lounge after dinner. It was Saturday but not many people were around.

Mark said, "They're all hibernating." Then he said, "I wouldn't mind hibernating with you."

Susan did not answer, but pulled the brown envelope from Cranwell out of her bag and gave it to him.

"I want you to read this."

He looked at her inquisitively, but she said nothing.

He read it in less than half a minute, then laid it on the coffee table in front of them.

Why didn't he say anything? What on earth was he thinking?

"What do you think?"

"I think.." he stopped. "I don't know what I think."

Susan made herself remain silent.

Then he spoke. "I'm thinking lots of things. I'm thinking about you, about you applying to leave here, about you not telling me about this until now, when you applied, it says here, *months* ago."

He reached into his inside pocket for his cigarettes. "And I'm thinking about me too." He lit the cigarette, drew on it slowly. "But, I don't think I count. This is about you, isn't it? It's about what *you* want."

"It's not just about me, Mark. That's why I'm asking you."

"It doesn't feel as if you're asking me if you should go. It feels as if you're asking me how I feel about you going, as if you've already decided to go."

She took his free hand.

"I haven't."

"Why did you apply if you weren't sure whether you wanted to go or not?"

"I applied soon after I got here, when Daddy was urging me to do well, to be promoted. He was so proud of me even getting Flying Officer. He put pressure on me, I suppose, and I went along with it."

Then she added, "You know I'm ambitious, and I wanted to please him."

"Well, I'm not going to make the decision for you and nor am I going to put any pressure on you. I'm fed up of not knowing where I am with you. It's entirely up to you. It's your life."

He stubbed out his cigarette and stood up.

"Please excuse me. I'm going to the Billiards room. I promised Ben a game. Goodnight."

He strode across the lounge, pushed open the door and walked out without a backward glance.

Susan sat for a moment or two and then hurried out after him. But there was no point in following him. He didn't want to be with her.

*

Susan came down to breakfast after a desperate night during which her head had been going round and round, worrying about everything. It had all been so simple a year ago. Daddy had been well, she had been posted here, life looked good – it was good. How had it all changed?

Nothing could have prevented Daddy from dying, of course. She could not blame herself for that. But should she have stuck to her guns and focused entirely on work and not got involved with Mark? Would that have been better? Or should she, even now, abandon her career and settle for marriage and children? Aunt Rose had never even had that chance, but *she* did, and perhaps she had now wrecked it. Perhaps Mark would just back off from their relationship. He had sounded so hurt, so angry. And the worst of it was that she knew he would never hurt anyone, let alone her. How could she have brought about all these difficulties?

It had been impossible to sleep and as she lay there, still awake at midnight, she realised that there was a tremendous storm going on. The rain was lashing down, and at one point she thought the wind would blow the glass in. This couldn't have just started up, it must have been going on for ages, but she was in such a state she hadn't noticed. She hadn't got to sleep until about five am.

Now, at breakfast, everyone was looking out onto the lake that had been the sports field the day before.

"You didn't hear the storm until midnight? That's just not possible, Susan. It was incredibly loud by about ten yesterday evening. Still, they say love makes you blind!"

"And deaf, it seems," added Alex.

Staff arriving from Alderton talked about how they had driven or cycled through floods and how water was lapping at the West Gate. The road leading down to the Quay, the

Guardroom and the Main Gate was underwater. No one had arrived from Felixstowe yet. The night shift wanted to cross the river and go home but could not do so. The storm must have breached the dykes.

Parties were sent out to investigate exactly what had happened around the camp. They were shocked. Fields were inundated. Bits of boats were floating beside the tops of hedges. One of the radar masts was cut off by the sea from the rest of the station. Everything in the Guardroom had been soaked through. Dead fish were swashing around the drive.

Then came reports from Felixstowe. Things sounded terrible there. As many as twenty people – perhaps more, and a baby, someone said, had died. Houses had been swept away. Boats had ended up in streets. Cars were smashed against buildings. Dead cats, sheep, chickens lay caught against trees and bushes. Whole families had spent the night on their roofs. Some were still marooned. Dozens of homes had been damaged. Furniture, even carpets and beds, had been washed into gardens. Clothes and sheets were spread over the mud. Felixstowe Ferry golf course was underwater.

And it was bitterly cold. It was the first day of February. Even those sent out dressed in great coats and caps were coming back frozen and wet through.

The CO called an emergency meeting. He announced that he'd chosen Susan as one of the officers to head up the repair operation in and around the camp.

Good. This was something she could really get her teeth into, and it was something that would stop her going over and over her thoughts about Mark, replaying what she said, what she should have said, what he said. She had not seen him alone since the previous night. Although they had both been at the meeting and their eyes had met, she could not tell how he was feeling.

She sensed the reaction of other officers to her being given a significant new role. It wasn't entirely positive. But she threw herself into it. They would need sandbags and men to start repairing the breaches in the seawall. Lorries, fuel, food. They'd work all night. Lights, torches. They'd need boats.

They would need more clothing, they must find a fast way of drying things out. Pumps, generators, tractors. Wheelbarrows, ropes, shovels. Each piece of information showed things were far worse than anyone had imagined. There was so much to be done. They had to get men out there and rebuilding fast.

The News came on the wireless. Susan stopped writing. The room went silent. It wasn't just here in the Deben estuary but all the way down the east coast. It was a storm, driven by a hurricane force from the north west. The wind shoved the spring tide, making it much stronger and higher than usual. In Scotland a storm had sunk a ship, drowning over a hundred people. This storm travelled south whipping up the tide in front of it. The swollen North Sea had invaded Lincolnshire, then the Wash, then Norfolk. It punched holes in sea defences, carved chunks in dykes and poured inland onto hundreds of acres of low lying land. A man driving a train found himself facing a wall of water. A lifeboat was snatched from the shore by the sea, ending up miles away. Ships were dumped on land. Dunes were washed away. Huge heaps of sand, shingle and mud appeared.

Then Suffolk. Yes, it was true about Felixstowe. It was the prefabs and their inhabitants that had been hardest hit. No one was sure how many people were affected. And then the storm had gone on to Essex – Canvey Island had been evacuated – and even up the Thames estuary and as far as Kent.

No one spoke when the News ended. Susan stood up.

"This is going to take weeks, months even. Much longer than any of us thought. It's a disaster that's appeared from nowhere. It's not only an emergency but a tragedy. We'll try to make a difference to everyone it's affected, we'll try and help get things back to normal." People sat quietly, taking in what they had heard. They looked at her, and in their expressions she saw both that they wanted to work and that they wanted to work with her.

Ok, what next? For a start, this room was no good. It was hopeless trying to work on desks already covered with papers in a space that was too small and did not have enough phones. Was there anywhere better? She asked for suggestions.

A man asked, "Could we use the church?"

A man asked, "Could we use the church?"

Susan thought about the chapel. Why the chapel? How could that be an improvement? That was where they had held the funeral service for King George. It was far too small.

"No, I mean the church. The real one, the old one that isn't used."

It wasn't a bad idea. Susan sent someone off to find out about it.

They continued to work, pausing only when further information arrived. As soon as the ferry started again the first passengers brought the latest from Felixstowe. Despite numerous evacuations the whole of the previous night, there had been many deaths, a huge amount of damage and real distress. A reception centre had been set up in the Cavendish Hotel. Extra policemen and firemen had been brought in. God, there was so much to do.

At lunchtime Mark turned up. He put his hand on her shoulder and leant towards her. He spoke quietly.

"Aren't you going to eat?"

Susan looked up at him, returned his serious gaze. She reached up her hand to touch his fingers, pressed them against her collar for a moment.

"No. But thanks. I'm trying to work out what we'll need. It's hard to estimate how much petrol we'll use, or how many scaffolding planks, or wellington boots. We've got some stuff for tomorrow, but we'll need an ongoing supply. This could take ages. And we must find more boats. There's places we need to reach that trucks or lorries can't get to. They say the land is either soft mud or it's shingle."

"Can't I get you something? I could bring you a sandwich."

Susan shook her head as she continued dialling a number.

He looked around. Although she wasn't interested in food at least someone had been making sure she was supplied with tea. There were empty cups all over the place. Now she was talking earnestly, making notes of what the other person said. She wasn't taking any notice of him. She had her head down.

*

It was much better having the Flood Co-ordination Centre in the church. There was much more room for plans, papers, maps. They put telephones in, brought in typists. It felt special in there, it felt like what it was: the hub of the operation. There had been danger, there still was danger, but they were making progress.

On Monday February 2nd they were beginning to get to grips with the task of clearing up. It did not take long before airmen were issued with shovels and brushes and sent to the flooded homes of RAF personnel. They hauled out carpets, chairs, pianos, cookers, cupboards, pictures, beds, books, shelves, telephones, clothes, bedlinen. Then they started on the thick layer of murky sludge which covered everything that was left. It was a mixture of sand, mud, oil, sewage, food, river and sea.

At the Ferry the airmen worked alongside others clearing up other homes, the Victoria and the Ferryboat Inn, the café, the fishermen's huts.

Many of those who lived at the Ferry had gone to friends' houses, or to the untouched parts of Felixstowe. Some of them had been exposed to the wind and rain for the entire night of the storm and were in hospital. Others were sloshing through their front rooms and kitchens, trying to find their possessions. They stumbled over plates, dolls, flower pots, shoes, dead crabs. One couple had chairs from the Ferryboat Inn washed into their house through the front door and their own furniture forced out of the back. They were going to row across the golf course and try to retrieve their things.

Susan soon found that this was not a job that could be done in isolation. She was soon in contact with farmers, other RAF stations, the County Council, manufacturers and suppliers of tools, equipment, vehicles. She learned more about Bawdsey and the area around within hours than she had done in the whole of the previous year: the low lying land, the inadequate defences, the previous floods, the risk of more flooding, the nature of spring tides, crops, transport. The need to carry out repairs fast became more and more urgent. It was clear that it had happened before and could happen again.

Help was arriving from everywhere. Farmers were sending their labourers to dig, to carry. Lorry drivers were turning up from Ipswich. Women's Institutes were beginning to brew hundreds of gallons of tea. Pumps and generators were starting to tip the water back into the sea. Thousands of sand bags were delivered. The first supplies of great coats, gloves, boots and leather jackets arrived. Susan was amazed how people were rallying round and joining forces. It must be like this in war time. Daddy must have known this feeling.

Suddenly she needed to go to the lavatory. Damn, her period had started. Why did it always come at the wrong time? She had one sanitary pad in her bag, thank goodness, but she'd have to run back to her room, and there wasn't any time. She hurried out and sat down with her head in her hands. It was all happening at once. Her desk was covered with lists, notes. The phone hardly stopped. Her head was full. Things were only just under control. There was too much going on. She had to keep on top of it. She *had* to be a good example. This pressure could last all week, all month, even longer, and they hadn't even been going for two days yet.

She glanced at her watch. She must get back at once. She must be at her desk in time for the News. Someone was turning on the wireless just as she entered the room. Everyone was expecting The Home Secretary to make an announcement.

Susan sat down, put her elbows on the table and shut her eyes.

To the nation's grief there has been a severe loss of life and hundreds of persons are still missing. We do not yet know the full scale, but as the Prime Minister had stated, the catastrophe must be treated upon a national basis and as a national responsibility. In particular, he assured Parliament that financial support for personal relief and for emergency repairs will be available. In a disaster such as this, sympathy can best be shown by affording unstinting help and work, and the Government feel sure that the nation will, as is its wont, rise to the emergency.

She opened her eyes, sat up straight. It was good to hear that. It reinforced the importance of what they were doing and it encouraged them. Unstinting help and work. That was precisely what they were doing and what they must go on doing. They mustn't waste a minute.

As soon as Susan picked up the phone everyone started working again. Then the CO appeared. At once everyone fell silent and stood up. He motioned to them to be seated but Susan remained standing, facing him.

"Flying Officer Cairncross, how are things going?"

"Sir, at present it's a question of making sure we keep track of what we have. There's a lot going on. We have to sort out what's arriving and where it's going as well as decide on who's going to do what."

"What are the main difficulties?"

"Recording exactly what we're ordering and recording exactly what arrives, and where it is being taken to. But we're receiving so much we can't use it at once, and that's frustrating."

"Yes, I'm sure it is. But it's no good if we get into a muddle. Quite right to keep a check on things."

The CO looked round the room. "Well done, all of you. Keep it up."

The moment the door shut behind him Susan keeled over.

"She's fainted."

"She's hit her nose."

"Undo her collar. Where's some water?"

After a few moments she came round.

"Ma'am, I think you should go and lie down. You need a rest. I'll find someone to escort you back to your room."

What had happened ? Why was there blood on her desk? This was silly.

"I'll be fine in a moment."

"Ma'am, I don't think you will be. You're exhausted. Please let someone take you to your quarters."

"I can't leave all this. There's far too much to do."

"But you've hardly stopped working for thirty six hours. You can't go on like this. That's why you fainted."

Mark. She must see Mark. She dialled his number.
"Can you come over? Now. Please. I need you."

*

Robert is grateful to be warm and dry. And now he's eaten well
too. The day after the storm Mr Corby searched for him and
found him at the Ferryboat Inn. He insisted on taking him
home. Mrs Corby made him undress and gave him blankets,
cigarettes, a hot water bottle. She said his finger was broken and
she bandaged it properly. They sat him in front of the fire and
made him a big pot of tea. The sweet tea itself was wonderful,
but then they cooked bacon and eggs and fried potatoes, and he
had a swig of whisky. They found him underclothes, trousers,
socks, a shirt, a thick green jersey. Robert knows all these once
belonged to their son Alistair.

When had he last eaten? On Saturday evening when he sat in
his cabin with Maisie, listening to the storm getting underway.
That means he's not eaten for a day and a half.

After eating he sleeps on the settee by the fire. He so wishes
that Maisie was curled up against him.

On the following day, Monday, he's told how Barrie White
saved the Ferry. He's a hero. About twenty people stayed in his
house overnight. There would certainly have been casualties if
they had not gone there. Another family remained in their
wooden bungalow when the water was over the window ledges.

"They say they kept it out by leaning against the walls. The
walls were bending with the pressure, but they held."

"So no one died?"

"Not here, thank God. But in Felixstowe, yes. About thirty,
they think. And there are still people missing. It was, still is,
much worse there."

Much worse? It was hard to imagine much worse.

"But let's not forget about you, Robert. Reg and Marion are
singing your praises."

He looks away, stares into the fire. No one's ever sung his
praises before.

He says, "I'm feeling much better now. Thanks for everything. I'm going out now." He wants to see what's going on.

"Don't be late back. You know there's a bed for you here, and food."

He puts on the oilskin Mr Corby gave him and goes straight to the landing stage. He's missing Maisie. The ferry's packed, and some people who want to cross the river are left standing on the beach. The ferryman sees him just as he casts off and he immediately steers round in a loop so he comes close to him again.

"Robert! Stay there till I come back." He waves as he makes off across the river.

Robert looks at the Deben. It's brown, mid-tide, wide, lovely. In the winter midday light it's so lovely.

He looks downstream, out to sea. Not very different from before. The Martello tower is still standing there. It can survive floods, but it can't prevent them. And across the river are those masts. What use were they yesterday?

He looks towards the boatyard. People are starting to shift the shingle that the sea has dumped there. There's activity around almost every house. Everyone's talking. There's so much happening.

"Hallo. Are you all right now?"

Robert turns to the man addressing him. He has no idea who he is.

"Thanks. I'm ok."

"Good. Good to see you." The man holds out his hand.

They shake hands and the man walks on. Why did he do that?

He waits by the landing stage, watches the ferry unload at Bawdsey then take on new people, turn and make its way back across the river. During this time even more passengers have gathered. He looks round for Maisie but she's not there.

The ferryman smiles him a welcome and calls out, "Let this lad in first, will you? Stand back please."

Robert climbs in and goes to the stern.

The ferryman says quietly, "You did well. That's the worst night I've ever known."

Robert doesn't reply. He's facing the café and watching a

couple of men who're starting to unload a lorry. Things are different today. Will they go back to how they've been?

The boat reverses away from the landing stage.

"You did well," repeats the ferryman.

Robert's watching a gull that's following them.

"I hardly did anything. I wish I'd done more."

"You did your best. You helped people stay alive."

"But so did you – so did everyone."

"Not everyone did what you did."

The boat is slapping through small waves.

"Look back to the Ferry."

Robert turns round. The whole shape of the shore has changed. Half of it is the same as it was, but half is not. It's strange.

They pull up to the Bawdsey jetty and exchange their passengers for another load.

As the boat bumps back across the choppy river a small plane appears. It's coming from the north and following the river. It's low in the sky.

"I wish I was in that," says the ferryman. " I'd love to see what all this looks like from up there. You'd see where the sea got in, where the walls and dykes caved in."

Robert hasn't been in a plane but at this moment he's glad he's in this boat on this river, his river. He feels in his pocket for a cigarette, but these are someone else's pockets, someone else's clothes.

"Have you got a cigarette?"

The ferryman nods. "Hold the tiller a moment."

Robert takes it. He's holding the familiar smooth wood again, his arm resisting the known, hard pressure of the water. The red ensign is making its whippy flapping noises. The current is steady. The air is cold and clear.

He should be feeling good but he isn't.

He reaches out for the cigarette, bends towards the cupped match, breathes in a whiff of sulphur. Maisie. She isn't here.

When it gets dark, he goes back to the Corby's. They sit him down for a meal and insist he has the best place in front of the fire. They tell him that horses have been found up to their necks in water, that rats were seen in trees. A house in Langer Road in Felixstowe was blown away and landed up against a tree. The army is being brought in. There are Matador tanks. One man refused to leave his flooded home without his box of sovereigns from under the floorboards. A bowl of goldfish stayed safe even though the table it stood on was afloat. A helicopter landed in front of the pub with milk and bread.

He tries to abandon hoping that Maisie will return. Getting back to normal, that's the most important thing. There's nothing more to be done tonight. It'll be tomorrow, Tuesday, before he can start work. There's so much to do but it can all wait until the morning.

*

Mark accompanied Susan back to the Manor and searched for Bridget to make sure she got upstairs and to her room safely. He hung about downstairs, waiting for Bridget to come back and report. He was relieved when she said Susan had fallen asleep within a few minutes.

"It's pure exhaustion. She just goes at things, doesn't she? Then she gets whacked out."

"She does," said Bridget, "but I envy her that get-up-and-go. That's why she gets so much done."

"It's unlike her to faint. But then – she's had so much to deal with."

Mark walked back to his office. He wanted Susan to sleep for hours and he was longing for her to wake up.

Then he was suddenly struck by what he ought to do. He ought to tell Aunt Rose what was happening. She should know. He wasn't sure if Susan had spoken to her since the flood. He'd phone her now. This minute.

"Hallo. Westbury 3472."

"Hallo, Miss Cairncross. It's Mark."

He heard Rose hesitate before repeating, "Mark?"

"Yes. Susan's Mark."

"Oh hallo, Mark." She sounded surprised.

"Don't worry, nothing's wrong. Or rather, Susan's not very well but it's all right."

"What is it?"

Mark heard a change in her tone. Why hadn't he thought more about what he was going to say? He hadn't meant to worry her.

"Well, she's been working flat out – you know, on the flood, and she's exhausted. In fact, she collapsed, she fainted a couple of hours ago but she's in bed now. Bridget's been looking after her. She'll keep an eye on her."

"Does she need to see a doctor?"

Mark paused. Did she? He hadn't thought of that. Perhaps she did. He had just supposed she needed to sleep and then to eat.

"I don't know."

"Do you think she's ill?"

"No. Not really. Most of all I think she needs to rest. And she's hardly eaten."

"I think it'd be a good idea for her to see someone. I've never known her to faint before."

"She's usually got bags of energy hasn't she? I could try and arrange for a doctor to see her, but I know that all the RAF doctors are working with flood victims just now."

"Well, you'll find one if she needs one, won't you?"

"Of course I will. Did she tell you about the floods?"

"Yes. I've been watching the News, it sounds absolutely terrible. She didn't say much but she said, am I right, that she's been given some particular job?"

"Yes. She's organising a substantial part of the repair work. It's a huge task. It'll take months. She's just throwing herself into it."

"Well, I hope she recovers soon. I'm sure she will. Do phone if something else crops up, and thank you for letting me know. Just give her my love when she wakes up."

"Of course."

"Oh Mark, your thank you letter. It was so nice, so good of you to write. There was no need at all. I really enjoyed you being here. You must come again."

"I'd love to."

"Come again when you and Susan have some leave, in a month or two when it's spring, when the weather's better. But don't wait for Susan to invite you, *I'm* inviting *you*. Come whenever you like."

"Thank you. I'd really like that." But he couldn't accept her invitation unless Susan wanted him to go.

"And I should tell you that there's a practical reason for asking you too. Henry's things. His house. There's going to be a lot to do and.."

"I'd love to give you a hand."

"That would be marvellous. I haven't begun to sort things out yet, but it'll take some doing."

Before saying goodbye he reassured Rose that he was willing to help her and would keep in touch over Susan.

Yes, he'd like to be in her family, in Susan's family. Since the flood he had hardly given a thought to the possibility of Susan going to Cranwell. What mattered most now was making sure she was well.

*

Susan did not wake until Tuesday morning, after a sleep of over ten hours. She got up at once, but Bridget said there was no hurry, people were getting on with things perfectly well, it would be better for her to have a proper breakfast. Susan did not argue but she felt a pang at delaying her return to work. They must be finding it really difficult without her.

At eight thirty she went back to the co-ordination centre. People welcomed her, asked after her, then turned back to their work. Already the atmosphere was less tense, more settled. Already it was beginning to turn from an emergency into an organised operation. Someone had set up a blackboard which showed what was happening where. It was all under control.

Alex, whom she had always had a poor opinion of, was sitting at her desk. He immediately vacated it, but brought her up to date with what had happened over night, and which of their

278

plans were now being acted upon. She couldn't fault him. He was highly organised. This was better. Repairs were beginning to be made. Things were taking shape. He was being extremely helpful, and so was everyone. Is this what Daddy had meant when he said the RAF was a family?

It was worrying to think that this new togetherness might have come about because she hadn't been there. Yesterday, rather than being active and efficient, had she become bogged down? Worse still, could people have people been criticising her?

She must get on with things, stop thinking like this. Boats. That's what the next thing was. They needed boats. She would find fishing boats, she would find someone to take charge of a flotilla.

At lunchtime people staggered their breaks so that phones could remain manned and work could continue. She took a break too. Mark. Where was Mark? He wasn't at lunch. That was a pity. She'd have to go back to work without seeing him.

Today she didn't feel as totally engrossed in the job as she had done yesterday. She found that she was asking herself why she had she been so critical of her colleagues before. She worried about whether thinking about these things meant she wasn't working hard enough.? But she couldn't do more than she was doing. She couldn't phone more than one person at a time, couldn't write with more than one pen. She was getting on with it as well as anyone else.

The afternoon flew by. Only one hour to dinner.

And there he was. Dear Mark, about to start on a plate of mince and potatoes. How could she have thought of going off to Cranwell?

She would have to wait to be on her own with him, but now she couldn't not join in the conversation about the flood, the lasting damage salt water would do to the land, the number of deaths at Canvey Island, how close London had come to being flooded.

But later on that evening they sat together on a settee, smoking and drinking coffee. Susan had tucked her feet up under her and was leaning against him. She was putting off phoning Aunt Rose but aware she would not relax until she had done so. It was so hard to get up from her cosy position against Mark.

"I'm not going away. I'm not going to go to Cranwell."

There was a pause.

"Are you sure?"

She nodded. "The flood has made me think about what matters most."

"Well. Steady on. Lots of things are important. You can't always weigh up what's most important."

"No. Perhaps not. But you're here and you're very important. And right now I can be useful here. And anyway, I think I wanted to be a Flight Lieutenant for Daddy, not for me."

"Susan, you don't have to give promotion up. You'd be a good Flight Lieutenant and you'd love being one."

"But I don't want to be one just now. There are two reasons: one, I want to be with you and I want to be here; two, this afternoon the CO told me he wants me to stay and complete the flood operation, and I agreed with him."

"There's nothing wrong in wanting promotion because of your father. But you've got to do what you want."

"Staying here is what I want. Going for promotion can't be more important than you and what I'm doing now. It can wait can't it?" She sighed. Oh God. It was so much easier for a man. What if it was the other way round? "If you were in my situation, what would you do?"

"Well, if I'd applied for promotion and it was offered me, I'd be tempted."

"What, you'd take it and leave me?"

"I'd find a way to take you with me."

She pulled away from him, looked up at him. Were things becoming clearer or more confused?

He said, "It's an idea, isn't it? Something to think about later on."

Then he said, "It's getting late. You said you were going to phone Rose."

He was right. She ought to phone now.

"Ok. I'll do it now."

She uncurled her legs and stepped into her shoes. Mark regretted losing her warm softness immediately. She stood up and straightened her skirt. He liked that skirt. It showed off her thighs, her small waist.

He lit a cigarette, stayed where he was. The windows were black but through one of them he could see the moon.

Within five minutes she was back.

"Come and sit here again. I want you close to me."

Susan slipped off her shoes and sat down. He put his arm round her.

"I think she was worried. And she asked a lot about you."

"That's nice. I knew she'd want you to ring."

"She was, you were right. You're always right."

"Not always, just often."

Mark stubbed out his cigarette end in the ash tray. He stroked Susan's hair, touched her left collar bone.

"There's been more on the News about the floods. She thinks Daddy would be proud of me, of us all, and of what the RAF's doing."

"I'm sure he would."

"And I told her you rescued me when I fainted."

"It was hardly me. It was that man in your office."

"Yes, but when I phoned you were there at once. Within minutes."

"I'll always be there. You know that."

Susan squeezed his hand.

"I think Aunt Rose thinks .."

Mark turned towards her, interested. "What? What does she think?"

No. She couldn't tell him. Could she? No, not yet. Mark hadn't proposed. But she was sure Rose was right. He would. She put her arm across his chest and hugged him. He was so warm, so solid.

"I do wish you and Daddy had met." She buried her head in his shoulder. "He would have liked you so much. And you would have liked him. I so, so wish you could meet each other. But you can't." She began to cry.

"Ssshh, ssshh. It's all right." He moved his arm so he could stroke her hair. "I wish I'd met him too. I'd have told him what a wonderful daughter he had."

They sat in silence until Mark said, "Come and look at the moon. It's a gorgeous night."

He stood up and switched off the lamp on the table beside them. Then he held out his hands to her and pulled her to her feet. He took her to the window and they put their faces close to the glass. There was an amazing moon. It lit up the playing field. There were stars.

Mark quoted:

> *But the majestic river floated on,*
> *Out of the mist and hum of that low land,*
> *Into the frosty starlight.*

He turned to face her, "Susan, I want you. I want you."

She stroked the back of his hand, ran her little finger over the bumps of his knuckles.

She said, "We could go up to my room. No one's around."

He turned to look at her, put his hand under her chin and pulled it gently so she faced him.

"Are you sure? Are you really sure?"

"Yes. I'm very sure."

*

On Tuesday the Ferry's as busy as when it's Regatta weekend. Robert is shovelling mud. There's a team of people shovelling and a team of people carrying full barrowloads away and bringing empty ones back. The place is noisy with engines, trucks, boats, scraping, talking. They've been at it for hours, and at last the boatyard is getting back to its usual level. The shingle's difficult to shift. It's frozen into big heavy lumps which must be broken up. Even though it's below freezing some of the diggers have taken off their jackets.

All along the east coast thousands of men are filling in tens of thousands of sandbags and carrying them to fill the breaches in the walls. Whole armies of labourers, students, soldiers and airmen are repairing defences and pushing the water back off the land. They're pumping millions of gallons of river and sea back to where they belong.

Robert stands up and stretches his back. He pushes his hands under his jacket and up under his armpits. Despite the rest of him being warm he can't manage to keep his hands warm. He's been given gloves but they get in the way and it's marginally better to put up with the cold. And now it's getting dark, almost time to call it a day.

The airmen working on a house nearby wave a flask at him.

"Help yourself, Bob. There's no point us taking any back."

He pulls his hands out from inside his clothes. He cups one round the tea and accepts a cigarette with the other.

Two children are coming towards them and he suddenly sees it's Alison and Davy. Their parents sought him out this morning to thank him, and they waved to him when they passed a couple of hours ago. And now here are the children. Alison's holding something behind her back.

"Guess what Alison's got for you," says Davy.

Robert shrugs. He hasn't a clue.

Alison shows him something wrapped up in an old piece of towelling. It's long and thin. She passes it over. He still can't guess what it is but Davy can't wait to tell him.

"It's your knife."

He unwraps the cloth and there's the river knife.

"Is it yours?" asks Alison, "Our neighbour found it and Mum thought it must be yours."

"Yes, it's mine."

He takes it and examines it. Yes. It's his. It's the knife he used to cut the rope to free the upside down dinghy, the one he dropped underwater.

He smiles. "Thank you. I'm very pleased to have it back."

Within ten minutes he's back off to the Corby's, carrying his spade over his shoulder and the riverknife in his hand.

It's strange. For the past year he's been worried about money and wondering how he could earn more. And here he is, well-fed, well-clad, well-shod. He still has no money, but it doesn't matter. It's turning out, at least for the time being, that he doesn't need it. And there's a change in the way people are

283

behaving towards him. They're greeting him, smiling, including him.

Tomorrow he'll be working on the ferry again. He's pleased about that. There's a lot going on and things are interesting. All this won't last, of course. Before long he'll have to find somewhere to live and he'll have to earn money. But everything is all right today.

It's hard to stay indoors when he's feeling like this so after supper he walks back down to the landing stage.

It's good to be by the river. He chucks a stone in the water and hears a scrabbling on the shingle. A dog runs towards the splash. A couple stroll out towards the water's edge from in between the huts.

The man says, "He thinks you've thrown that specially for him."

Robert nods.

"Things are settling down again, aren't they?"

"Yes."

The man throws a stick into the river. The dog runs to fetch it and barks when he reaches the river. He runs in a little way, then backs out again, and then bounces in to get the stick. He races up to the couple, drops the stick, shakes himself fiercely just as Maisie used to do. The man, the woman and the dog walk in a line towards the Ferryboat Inn and Robert follows them slowly. He's seen them before but this is the first time they've spoken to him. Or is it that he's never spoken to them?

Maisie. *Music Maker*. What else has gone? What else does he want back? Mother's letters. Is that all? Yes. The amber's gone, but he can find more. After all, the river's given him the same knife twice.

He comes level with the phone box. He stops.

He could phone Mother.

The moon is no longer quite whole now, but there are plenty of stars. He can see Orion well.

He's hardly used a telephone in his life but why hasn't he thought of this before?

The sky is quite clear. The river's as shiny as wet tar. The ferry's on its way back from Bawdsey.

Could he find out her number? He knows her address by heart.

He walks back to the landing stage. He picks up a stone and lobs it in. Waves ripple out, collide gently with the river's own small waves.

He'll find the number. He'll phone her tomorrow.

And the estuary's still there.

Tomorrow the river mouth
will still open into the sea.
And high tides will lick
towards the land again
to reclaim their mudbanks
and swell the river's span.

Gulls will hang in the air
and geese will gather
on the marsh. The ferry
will go to and fro across
the Deben between shingle
and the wide clouded sky.

The estuary will be there tomorrow.